That Magic Night In Hawaii

and Other Stories and Plays

Tom Robb

iUniverse, Inc.
New York   Bloomington

That Magic Night In Hawaii
and Other Stories and Plays

iUniverse books may be ordered through booksellers or by contacting:

iUniverse
1663 Liberty Drive
Bloomington, IN 47403
www.iuniverse.com
1-800-Authors (1-800-288-4677)

ISBN: 978-1-4401-3164-6 (cloth)
ISBN: 978-1-4401-3165-3 (ebook)

Printed in the United States of America

iUniverse rev. date: 03/30/2009

About The Author

Tom Robb began writing these 5 stories and 3 plays in 2003 at the age of 93. As this, his first book, goes to press, Tom is 98. He has always lived an exciting life, with a kind-of "Let's Do It" approach. From a dramatic start in November 1910 - he grew up picking cotton in the hot Texas sun and playing a hot trumpet for the Cooper, Texas Band when the sun went down. His musical proclivity led him into numerous other bands, such as the Honey Grove Band, entertaining at social events throughout Delta County. Tom and a pal were recruited to play in the 144th Infantry Band out of Fort Worth for their encampment at Palacios, Texas in 1927. (The boys received special permission from the War Department to play for the Army at age 17.) He headed a 15 member orchestra that played popular music on WFAA radio in Dallas. For one year he attended East Texas State in Commerce, Texas. Then in 1930 he transferred to Southern Methodist University in Dallas and was a part of the famous SMU Marching Band.

Tom and his brothers worked hard, but lost no opportunity for fun and daring. From tower diving to biplane barnstorming rides, to missing bridges and taking his jalopy for a dip in a river- it just never stopped.

Cast into the world on his own in the midst of the Great Depression, he got a job chasing Special Deliveries for the U.S. Post Office; in 1933 he married his sweetheart that had beaten him for the championship of the county Spelling Bee years before (I think his charm, for her, was not wanting to miss out on "what is this guy gonna do next!"). Things were great in the late 30's: they started a family, bought a house and a Packard, and had the world by the tail.

Then came WWII. He volunteered for the U.S. Navy and served in the Philippine Islands. After Japan surrendered, Tom returned to America aboard the carrier U.S.S. Ticonderoga and zigzagged across the country on troop trains, to knock unexpectedly at his home's door on Christmas Eve.

With G.I. Bill in hand, Tom moved his growing family from Dallas to the "Land of Milk & Honey" (now widely known as California) for a degree in Real Estate at CAL Berkeley. He's been in the area ever since. Always the fun-loving romantic, these period pieces came naturally to him and will amuse all who enjoy surprises, a laugh, and ultimately a happy ending.

Tom is currently polishing up his Memoirs of an exciting journey not yet finished.

Table of Contents

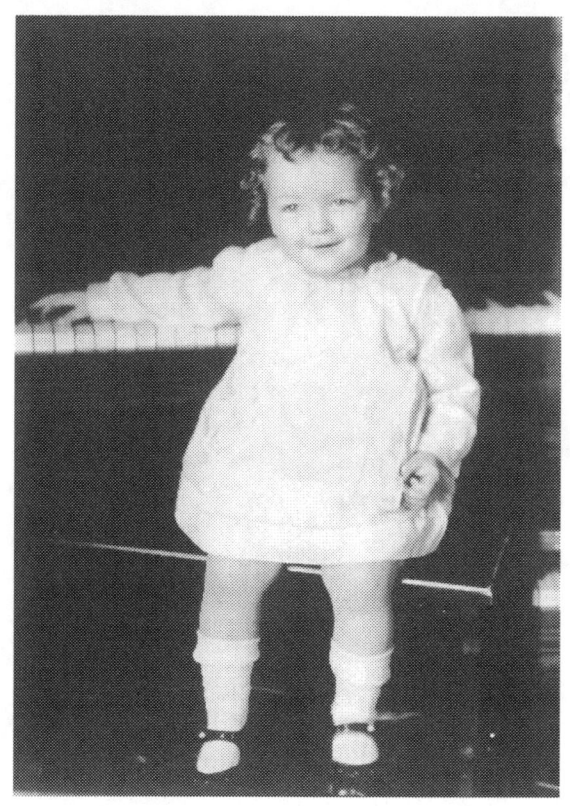

TRY

List Of Characters

LIEUT. HOWARD REED - In the Air Force.

KATHERINE Mill - Girlfriend of Lt. Reed.

M.C. AT DANCE FLOOR

MRS. MIMS - Mother of Katherine Mims.

CAPT. GORDON - Base officer at Wichita Falls Air Force base.

LONNIE - (Capt. Alonzo Fabio) a prisoner of the Vietnamese.

FRANK - (Sergeant Frank Berry) a prisoner. Home Hawaii.

DR. MOORE - The Mims' family doctor.

AL - a truck driver at the Air Base in Wichita Falls.

OLDER LADY - A lady at a farmhouse.

LEU - (HER HUSBAND)

NURSE MARGARET SNELL - A nurse in the Naval Hospital at Oakland.

CHARLIE - Member of Lakewood High School graduating class.
Had band.

ALFIE - A member of Charlie's band. Was also graduating.

CICERO - A member of Charlie's band. Was also graduating.

TED - A member of Charlie's band. Was also graduating.

LUCY - A student of Sunrise Girls College.

GAIL - A student of Sunrise Girls College.

HEADMASTER (KATHERINE MIMS) of Sunrise College.

KELSEY - A student of Sunrise Girls College. A niece of Katherine's.

DEBBIE - President of Student Body at Sunrise College.

LOU - Daughter of the Headmaster of Sunrise College.

GIRL FROM OFFICE - (Headmaster's office)

CHIEF PHILLIPS - Police Chief at Welcome, Texas.

Chapter One

OCT, 1972. It was late afternoon in Lakewood, Texas. A bright sun was being hidden by a huge bank of dark clouds, approaching from the West. Occasional flashes of lightning followed by thunder signaled a storm very soon. In the beautiful white stucco Colonial Hotel in the dark green woods that surrounded the area, a string band played on the terrace. Sitting at a table, drinking a soft drink and drumming his fingers nervously on the table, was a tall young Air Force Lieutenant, about 28 years old; he was waiting for his girlfriend, Katherine Mims. She was late, which was not unusual, because of her job as a typist in a law office. He had just received some bad news that would affect both of them, and was anxious to discuss it with her. Finally, she appeared; an attractive brunette with long lustrous hair and a happy, springy step. She looked about 25 years old. She quickly spied Howard Reed and slipped into a seat opposite him.

"I'm sorry I'm late, Howard. I had to deliver some legal papers to a family who are fighting the foreclosure of their home." "I'm glad you're here, Katherine. I've got some very bad news. I've just received new orders," he said. "Oh, Howard. No! That's awful! I hope it's for not too far away. Where do you have to go?" "It's Sheppard Field in Wichita Falls. That's not very far." "We can still be together. I can come up, or you can come down. It worries me, though. I hope this war is over soon," she said. "I hope so, too, Katherine. Maybe I'll be there for the duration, but I have to be there in 48 hours. It ruins our plans here anyway, for now," said Howard. Just at that moment, the band struck up a waltz, "You Will Always Be My Sweetheart". A few people arose to dance it. "Katherine, isn't that our favorite waltz? Come on. Let's dance it." "Yes. It's our song. I love it!" They stood together after the dance as she gave him a loving kiss. Then they went back to their table and ordered their refreshments. "This is so sudden, Howard. Only 48 hours! We've had so much fun together here. What can we do?" "I've got to start packing. Can you come over tomorrow and help me?" "Yes, I can. I'll call you early in the morning."

Howard —hesitating — "Katherine, I've asked you this before, will you marry me? I love you so. We can do it tomorrow. Harry and Frances are getting married then. He's being called up, too. What do you say, Sweetheart?" "Howard, I love you, too. It sounds exciting! But so soon! I'll think about it and give you an answer in the morning." "Alright, Miss 'HARD-To-Get Girl'. I'll be waiting for a 'Yes' answer this time." Their refreshments came and they started eating. M.C. -at the dance floor mike - "Now Miss Forrest will sing the new ballad, 'My Hero.'" Miss Forrest sang. "'That's such a beautiful song, but so sad," said Katherine, "I'm glad it's just a song." "It happens, unfortunately," said Howard. As the song ended, two of their friends found them and were invited to share the table with them. The four danced several numbers and had a pleasant visit; then Katherine announced that she needed to get home. Howard paid the check and they left. At Katherine's apartment door - "Will you come in, Howard?" "I'd better not this time. It's late and I need to start packing. I'll see you in the morning." "OK. I've got things to do, too. I'll see you then." They kissed and as he started to leave . . . "Don't forget your promised answer to my question." "I won't forget," she promised.

When Howard arrived at his apartment, two Air Force officers were waiting for him. They had new orders for Howard to report to the base at Wichita Falls in time to catch a flight to Fairfield, Calif. There he would be given further orders. Howard tried several times to reach Katherine by phone, but there was no answer. The officers helped him pack, then drove him the 60 miles to Sheppard Field, just in time to catch the flight to Fairfield. Four other airmen also caught the flight. Howard barely slept on the trip, he was so worried about not contacting Katherine.

When he arrived in Fairfield, he was able to reach her on the phone. "Katherine, I've tried to call you. I'm in Fairfield, Calif. Two Air Force officers picked me up as I got home last night, with new orders. I'm on my way overseas, I think." "Oh, Howard. I've been so worried. I spent the night with Mother. I tried to call you this morning, but no answer." "They're paging me now, Katherine. I'm sorry! I've got to go. My flight is waiting. I'll write you as soon as I get to a base somewhere. I love you! Good-bye, Sweetheart!" Katherine - in tears now -," Good-bye, Howard! I love you too!" She collapsed in worry and tears on the sofa.

Howard was flown to Hawaii, where the plane was refueled, and then on to Tan Son Nhut airbase in Vietnam. There he was able to get off a letter to Katherine, informing her of his arrival. He couldn't give her a return address, as he had none.

He was immediately transferred to a smaller base and assigned as a co-pilot on a C-47 reconnaissance plane. There he was able to write Katherine a letter, giving her an APO address and such information as was allowed about his situation. On his third reconnaissance mission, Howard's plane was shot down.

Immediately, the wrecked plane was surrounded by North Vietnamese troops and armed civilians. His pilot was dead. Howard was severely injured. They took him on a stretcher to a nearby road, and by Jeep on to a field hospital. He had many injuries, including a broken leg, concussion and internal injuries. It pained him to breathe deeply.

He was semi-conscious. His leg was splinted. He was given a painkiller, and the next morning transported to a hospital about 10 miles up a little valley in the nearby mountains. There, he was put in a room by himself. It was a military hospital, with guards every where. Since Howard didn't speak Vietnamese, and none of them spoke English, he had to learn by just observing. His routine was simple. Besides two meals of cereal and bread or fish, sometimes potatoes or fruit, he had a lot of time to think of the death of his pilot and his own downright bad luck.

On the third day there, he was interrogated by a North Vietnamese officer who spoke broken English. Howard gave him only his name, rank and serial number. Constant plodding got the officer no other information. After three months, Howard was transferred to a small prison further up into the mountains.

It had been six weeks since Howard called her from Fairfield airport. Katherine still had not received a letter or another call from him. She was very worried. "Mother, I don't understand it. Howard said he'd send me an APO address for him right away. It has been almost two months, and I haven't received anything from him. That's not like Howard. I'm worried," said Katherine. "Something's interfered," said Mrs. Mims. "Maybe he's on the move, or somewhere he can't get mail out regularly. You'll probably get several letters together someday soon." "I hope so. This suspense is terrible." "Why don't you call the air base at Wichita Falls and see if they can get his address?" suggested Mrs. Mims. "They should have better ways of communication." "I think I'll drive up there. A phone call is so impersonal. I'll go tomorrow," said Katherine. The next morning Katherine drove up to the base in Wichita Falls. The airman at the base checkpoint directed her to the communications building. She entered and approached the service desk. "May I help you Miss?" asked the attendant. "I'm Katherine Mims. My boyfriend, Howard Reed, was sent from here to Vietnam six weeks ago. He was going to send me his address, but I haven't received a word. Is there any way you can get his address for me? It's very important." "The Captain will have to handle a request like that."

Katherine was escorted to Captain Gordon's desk where she was seated. "I'm Captain Gordon. What is your problem?" Katherine repeated her request. "It's very important, Sir." "Miss Mims, normally, we don't have much luck tracing our people in Vietnam from here. The communication lines are so busy. Why is your request so urgent?" asked the Captain. "He called me from Fairfield six weeks ago and promised to send an address right away. I'm worried that something happened. It's not like him not to write." "How long has Lieutenant Reed been your boyfriend?" "For about two years, Sir." "My daughter is about your age. Her husband is over in Vietnam. She has trouble with the mail, too," said the Captain. He showed her a picture of them that was on his desk. "They're a beautiful couple. I know you're proud of them." "Miss Mims, I'll send an inquiry to our base in Tan Son Nhut. You say that when he called you from Fairfield, he was going overseas.

He probably is in Vietnam. Chances are that he was transferred to some other base from there. Our mail is erratic. Ships get sunk. Mail gets lost in plane crashes. I should get a report back in 24 hours or so. If you'll give me your phone number, I'll call you when I receive it. We'll hope for the best." Katherine gave him her phone number. "Thank you, Captain Gordon," she said as she got up to leave

Late the following day, Captain Gordon called. They weren't able to locate Howard, but a Lieutenant Reid in a plane from a forward base failed to return after a flight over enemy territory. The report worried Katherine but was too vague to cause her to lose hope of hearing from Howard.

At the prison, Howard and the other prisoners were strictly guarded. Besides a few French, Aussies, Howard and two other Americans, the rest of the prisoners were all South Vietnamese. Howard's leg and arm were weak and poorly healed. He still had soreness in his chest. On the day of his arrival, the other two Americans managed to meet him. They met in an open area where prisoners were allowed to relax a few minutes in the evening before being locked up for the night. "I'm Captain Alonzo Fazio. We're sorry you're a prisoner, but glad to have your company." "I'm Sergeant Frank Berry. We'll help you all we can. This is not a happy place. We just try to get by until we can get out of here." "I'm Lieutenant Howard Reed. I'm glad to meet you." The three related the events that resulted in their capture, where they were from, their families, etc. Fazio was a career Air Force Captain. He had been shot down and captured three months earlier. He was married with a wife and two children. He was from Duluth, Minn.

Frank was an Army Sergeant and had been injured and captured in an ambush five months earlier. He was single and from Hawaii. "I assume you've been through plenty already. At this place they've about given up on their questioning," said Fazio. "They mainly concentrate on makin' it tough on us," said Frank. We don't get good food. Just enough to get by on. I'm sure we've both lost weight since we've been here," said Frank. "There's a large field of vegetables just up the valley. We have to help cultivate it, or we're shorted on our food. I don't mind. It's a break from being in a cell. It's hot and long hours sometimes, but I'm getting used to it," said Fazio.

One day about a month later, Frank and Howard came out to the "sit out". "Howie, you look bad today. Do you feel OK?" asked Frank. "I'm just worried, Frank. They won't let us send out messages or receive any kind of communication here. I want to let my folks and my girlfriend know where I am and that I'm alright. I'm just lonely and blue, I guess." "I understand. I get blue and then so damn mad I'd like to start a riot sometimes. Lonnie helps me get over it. He's older than me. He's 38. I'm 24," said Frank. "I'm 28. I'm going to get old fast here," said Howard. "I worry about my folks not knowing where I am, too. You said you had a girlfriend in Texas. I had a girlfriend, but we weren't steady. I worked in the pineapple fields in Hawaii. I couldn't afford the expense of college, so I enlisted in the Army. What does your girlfriend do?" asked Frank. "She works in a law office at present. She eventually plans to be a teacher. The problem, Frank, I don't know where I stand with her. We have dated for two years and were just now beginning to talk about getting married. At least, I was. She just hasn't decided to do it yet." "It's a shame you are separated by this war," said Frank. "I really love her," said Howard. "That's the kind of situation we were in when the Air Force grabbed me up on 24 hours emergency orders and flew me over here." "Boy, that's tough! I'm sorry, Howie!" "Some day, I think it'll all work out whenever I get back. Other times, I'm afraid I'll find her already married to somebody else. It almost drives me mad!" said Howard, clinching a fist, as a tear wandered down his cheek. Frank -to change the subject -, "I'd like to figure a way to escape this place." "Are you serious? I have no idea where we are." "Lonnie probably knows just where we are." "Let's think about it," said Howard. "Ask Lonnie what he thinks." When questioned about it, Lonnie said that none of them were in good enough physical condition at present to attempt it. There followed days of dull idleness. No radio. Nothing to read. The only break was the hour after the evening meal, when they were allowed to sit out in a large open space inside the quadrangle of cells.

CHAPTER TWO

Two months after Howard left, Katherine wasn't feeling well. She couldn't seem to shake it. "Katherine, you've been getting nauseated so much lately. Do you think it's something you've been eating? You've always been such a strong, healthy girl," said Mrs. Mims. I don't know, Mother. It must be a virus of some kind." "Well, I think you should go see Dr. Moore and let him prescribe something for it." "Maybe you're right. I need to get over it." She made an appointment with Dr. Moore. Later at Dr. Moore's office. Dr. Moore - after examining Katherine- "I think I know what your problem is, but I'm waiting to hear from the lab on the sample I sent. They'll call any minute now." "Is it anything serious, Doctor?" "I don't think so. It depends on your personal view." The telephone rang. Dr. Moore answered it. "Yes, I thought so. Thank you."

Katherine was getting nervous. She hoped she didn't have some disease. Dr. Moore turned to face her. "Miss Mims, congratulations. You are going to have a baby." Katherine was stunned. She knew it was possible, but it was a complete surprise. She sat back down, put her face in her hands, and thought. "Wow! What will I do now? How will I tell Mother? Oh, I wish Howard was here." "I see that you're surprised," said Dr. Moore. "Believe me, Katherine, it's a blessing to bring a new baby into life. You'll be thankful that you did, the rest of your life. As for being married, now that it's happened, don't let it bother you. You've got plenty of company. Go home and tell your mother. We're both here to help you." "Thank you, Dr. Moore. Its father will be back from the war soon, I hope." Katherine knew what Dr. Moore said was true. She was worried, but started their future on her way home. Of course, it included Howard. She became thrilled and excited, so much so that she almost had a collision with another car. She arrived home safely. "Well, what did he find wrong with you?" asked Mrs. Mims. "Nothing wrong. I'm pregnant!" "Oh, My! I suspected that, the way you were being ill.

When did he say it was due?" "Dr. Moore said July." "Then in July, we start a new era. I'll be a Grandmother!"

"I think I need a drink," said Katherine. "No! No! That's out now." They decided to go to a restaurant for dinner. A month later, Katherine and Mrs. Mims were making what plans they could for the baby, not knowing if it was a girl or boy. Katherine decided that its middle name, boy or girl, would be Louis or Louise. Louis was Howard's middle name. She decided to go a second time to the air base in Wichita Falls, to see if they could find out any new information on Howard. She still had no word from him. She drove the 60 miles to the air base. It was a cold, dreary day, and she hesitated about going until better weather, but she was already four months pregnant. She dared not put it off until later. Arriving at the air base about noon, she got in line at the service desk. Finally, it was her turn. "Oh, Hello! You were in once before. What can we do for you? Miss Mams, isn't it?" asked the attendant. "It's Mims. I want to see Captain Gordon again." "He's out somewhere for lunch. You can wait for him in our coffee shop down the hall, if you like." Katherine -disappointed- "Will he be back soon? I need to start for home before dark. It looks like it may snow." "It shouldn't be long. Al, will you show Miss Mims where the coffee shop is?" Al- behind her in line - "Sure, I'm going there myself. I'm Al Harper, Miss. Come along." Katherine followed him to the shop. He pulled out a chair at a table for her.

"Thank you, Sir," said Katherine. "Miss, can I get you something? Coffee? Cola?" asked Al. "Yes. Coffee would warm me up a bit. Seems the air is getting colder." "It is. I just came in. I'm a tow-truck driver here." Al brought her coffee and started to leave. "Come sit with me, Al, while you have your drink. I'd like to ask you a question." "Sure, Miss. What would you like to know?" He sat down. "Do you know how the non-official military mail is handled between here and Vietnam?" "Well, yes, I do. I spent a year over there. My job was helping to load and unload ships coming and leaving there. A lot of it was mail. There was a lot of it that was misdirected because of changed destinations of ships, relocation of units, ships sunk or damaged. Official mail went by air. Private mail went by air if there was space available. Delays were unavoidable at times." "Does mail just get lost for good?" "Eventually, all air mail and first-class mail is delivered, if correctly addressed, or returned to writer if it can't be delivered." "My boyfriend has been over there nearly six months. I'm sure he has written me, but I haven't received a single letter." "I'm not surprised at anything from over there. It's a real nightmare sometimes. You may get a fistful of letters at once soon. Just don't give up hope. I've got to go, Miss."

"Someone will call you when Captain Gordon comes in. He should be here soon," said Al. "Thank you, Al. I'll remember what you said." Al left. It was mid afternoon when Captain Gordon came back to his office. The attendant came for her and ushered her into his office. "Miss Mims, I'm sorry you had to wait. I had a meeting that lasted extra long. Please be seated. It's good to see you again. What have you heard from your friend, Lieut. Reed?" "Capt. Gordon, I haven't heard anything at all." "Really! I'm surprised. How have you been?" "I'm doing alright under the circumstances." "Meaning not hearing from Lieut. Reed, and . . .? "Yes, and I'm pregnant. I just need some answers," she said. "Miss Mims. I'm sincerely sympathetic with you and your problem. Let me send another inquiry to headquarters in Vietnam. Maybe they have more up-to-date information on Lieut. Reed by now." "I'd appreciate it, Capt. Gordon." "I'll send it today. I'll call you tomorrow, or as soon as we get an answer. Are you going back home today?" "Yes. My mother is expecting me back." "In that case, you should get started. The weather looks like it may snow, or sleet." "I will; thank you Captain Gordon." She left and was soon on her way home.

As Katherine reached the outskirts of town it began to snow. That didn't worry her, as she was an experienced driver. The air was getting colder, and night was coming on. About 20 miles farther, the snow turned to sleet. Traffic was getting sparse. Suddenly, as she was rounding a curve in the road, she felt that scary feeling when the wheels have lost traction. She jammed on the brakes. The car turned broadside and slid off into a three-foot ditch. Katherine wasn't hurt, but the motor died, and she couldn't get it started again. It would take a tow from a car or truck to get it out of the ditch. She needed help. She spied a farmhouse with lights on. Maybe they had a phone, or could somehow pull her up on the road. She walked over and knocked on the door. An older lady answered. "Yes? What do you want?" "My car just slid off the road into the ditch there. Can someone help me get it out? If not, do you have a phone?" "Lady, we don't have anything but an old truck," said the husband. "I'm sure it's not strong enough. It only hits on three cylinders. Maybe someone will come along the road that can help. We don't have a phone." "Young lady, you look like you're pregnant. You shouldn't be out in this cold weather. Where's your husband? He should have been with you," said the old lady. "He's in Vietnam." It was a little tiny lie, but it felt good to say it.

"If you can't get any help tonight, we can try pulling it up on to the road in the morning with my mules," said the man. "She can't stay in that car tonight, Lem. It's too cold. Lady, we have an extra bedroom that you're welcome to, if you can't get help tonight. I'm sorry. I didn't mean to lecture you. We have a son in Vietnam." "Have you heard from him?" asked Katherine. "Yes, but his mail is awful irregular. Nothing for a while, then we get several letters." Thank you for your kind offer. I'll go back up on the road. Maybe a highway truck will come along and can help." Katherine went back to her car and stood beside it. It was getting colder, and there was a brisk wind. It began snowing again and she was worried that the cold wind wouldn't be good for the baby. She had to stand outside the car, so a passing car would see her. She was beginning to feel desperate. Finally, a car came in view with a rotating light raking both sides of the road. They spotted her and pulled to a stop. It was Capt. Gordon and Al from the air base in a tow truck. "Capt. Gordon! Oh, thank you for coming. How did you know I was here, or was it just an accident that you found me?" "No accident. We were worried about you when you left, with the weather threatening. We had your home phone number. Later, when we thought you should be home, we called. our mother said that you hadn't arrived. She was worried. This road is awful slippery in this kind of weather. We're glad you're OK. I see that you need a hook back up onto the road. We'll take care of that."

"Capt. Gordon, you Air Force people are wonderful!" "We care of our own, Miss Mims. Lieut. Reed and you, we consider part of our family," said Capt. Gordon. The men got busy and attached chains to her car and soon had it back up on the road. They also got it running again.

"Thank you. I'll never forget your kindness," said Katherine. "We'll follow you for a few miles, just to be sure you make it home. Please call us when you get there." They followed her for about ten miles to where the road wasn't so obstructed with snow and ice, then honked a good-bye, turned around, and returned to base.

Katherine made it home safely and called the base to report her safe arrival. Mrs. Mims was ready with plenty of warmth and hot milk chocolate. After hearing Katherine's report of the trip, she got her into a warm bed for the rest of the night.

The next day, at the air base, they ran the best check they could to locate Howard, but came up with the same inconclusive report. A reconnaissance plane with two airmen- Capt. Nolen and Lieut. Reed - failed to return to base from a mission in January, 1973. No official report since. They called next evening and informed Katherine. Katherine was very disappointed. She wanted so much for Howard to know about the baby.

CHAPTER THREE

SIX MONTHS PASS...... On July 14, 1973, a beautiful baby girl was born. Katherine named her Mary Louise Mims. She decided to put her interests and emotions into raising her baby daughter, but still hoping that Howard was alive. Katherine waited patiently until a day in July, 1976. The war in Vietnam was ended for the U.S. One afternoon, there was a knock on their front door. Mrs. Mims answered it. Katherine was in her bedroom. "Katherine! Come here quickly! It's for you." Katherine hurried to the door. It was Capt. Gordon and another officer from the air base. "Miss Mims, we at the base finally got official word from the War Department regarding your friend, Capt. Reed. The Lieut. Reed that was shot down in January 1973 was from Lakewood, Texas. He was made a Captain after that; he is now listed as MIA. "Oh, No!" said Katherine, in surprise and shock. "Knowing his close friendship to you and Mrs. Mims, we wanted to inform you before you had to read it in the newspaper tomorrow. We at the base grieve with you. If we can help you in any way, please let us know." He tipped his cap and started to leave. "Thank you, Capt. Gordon!" She closed the door and fell to the floor in a dead faint. Mrs. Mims, seeing her fall, rushed to help her. She bathed her face in cool water and got her into a more comfortable position. She was revived and helped to her bedroom.

"Katherine, that was an awful shock to both of us. It doesn't mean that Howard was killed. A lot of our boys are prisoners over there, I've read. I know that you and Howard loved each other. I've learned to love him, too, in the two years that you two have been dating. Are you alright, now?" "Yes, Mother, I'm alright. It was such a shock. All this time, I've had hope of his return. This message seems so final." "I know, and I'm sad, too. Would you like me to brew you some tea now, Dear?" "No, Mother. I want to be alone for a while. I need to calm my emotions a little. I need to think. Will you take care of little Lou when she comes home from kindergarten?" "Yes, I will." Mrs. Mims left and went to the kitchen. In a few minutes, she heard Katherine softly singing the song "You Will Always Be My Sweetheart". Then silence.

It had been four years since they had said good-bye. Katherine had decided to say "Yes" on that next morning that never happened. She decided that Howard was most likely dead. She would have to get on with her life and concentrate on taking care of Lou. Mrs. Mims decided, and Katherine agreed, that they needed a change of scenery to shake the sadness of Howard's loss. She, too, thought that Howard was probably dead.

At the end of the term of the kindergarten school, Katherine and Mrs. Sims and little Lou moved to Rochester, N.Y. where Mrs. Mim's sister lived. Katherine could never get over the hurt of losing Howard. In Rochester, she renewed her college studies at a branch of New York University, with the aim of becoming a teacher. She received an MA degree and taught at the Oak Valley College for girls for two years, where she became operations manager. Then one day she was looking through an issue of a national education journal and noticed an advertisement of a vacancy for Superintendent of Sunrise College For Girls in Welcome, Texas. Mrs. Mims was sitting near. "Mother, how would you like to move back to Texas?" "That would be nice. Why do you ask?" answered Mrs. Mims. "There's a vacancy for the Superintendent of a girls college in Welcome, Texas. That's right next to the area where we lived before," said Katherine. "I love that area. What do you think?" said her Mother.

"I love the area," said Katherine, "I'd like to get Lou well established in a location that will serve her through high school. I think I'll apply for the job. It's a step up for me, and my credentials are adequate." Katherine applied for the job, and was accepted. They moved to Welcome, Texas in 1983. Lou was five years old. Katherine often wondered what happened to Howard.

CHAPTER FOUR

After several months, Howard's injuries were healed enough that he was asked to go with Frank and Fazio to work in the fields cultivating the food crops. It was hard, hot work sometimes, but it relieved the boredom of the cells. The days passed slowly. The monsoon rains came. Then it was summer again. Howard gradually lost his connection to the outside world. But he still thought, wondered and hoped that someday, the war would end and Katherine would be there waiting for him.

One day, about four years after being shot down, Howard noticed a new stream of ants crawling on the wall under the barred window. He checked their operation and discovered that they were eating away the wood base of the window. Gently pushing the bars, he realized that the bars could easily be forced out enough for him to get out. It would be easy to escape. He decided to talk to Lonnie and Frank about it. At the "sit-out" he described his discovery. "That's exciting! I don't want to stay another four years in this place. Where could we go if we escaped?" asked Frank. "We'd never make it on foot. We'd have to get help, or steal a car. That's unlikely," put in Lonnie. "I've been thinking about it all day," said Howard, "I've noticed that the driver of the laundry van makes his daily stop here while we're at our 'sit-out'. He eats his dinner with the camp officials. If we could slip out my window and steal his van, we could make a run for the coast."

"Let me examine your window." suggested Lonnie. "I can 'hot-wire' the van if I find a knife." He slipped in and examined the window. "You're right," he said. "We can get through it. Let's think about it tonight and decide if we want to try it, and what we would do then. We're about a mile from a river that runs to the coast. We could use the van all the way, or find an empty boat on the river." They all agreed. The next day at "sit-out", all three had decided to make the attempt. They set Saturday, two days later, as THE DAY. On Friday they went over their plan. Frank had sharpened a joint of bamboo into a sharp knife for Lonnie to use in "hot-wiring" the van. Everything was ready. On Saturday at "sit-out" they were all tense, and poised to go. The laundry van was parked and the driver was at dinner. "You two guys ready?" asked Lonnie. "I'm sure ready!" echoed Howard. "Slip those bars out, Howie. Let's go!" urged Frank. Suddenly, a convoy of three Vietcong army trucks arrived and parked, blocking the laundry van. An officer from the first truck got out and went into the camp office. "We'll have to wait until they leave," said Lonnie. Presently, he came back out, accompanied by the camp Officer. They approached the three Americans, who were standing together outside Howard's cell trying to look bored. The camp officer pointed to them.

Three guards quickly cuffed and shackled the astonished trio and put them in the middle truck with two guards, Frank - trying to address one of the guards -" Hey! Where we go?" He nodded to himself, Frank and Lonnie. The guard just raised his rifle and frowned. "I wonder where they're taking us?" wondered Howard. "I hope this isn't a 'shooting' party," said Frank. "If they're going to shoot us, why wouldn't they do it right in camp?" answered Howard. "You can't tell about these people. They are too unpredictable. I hate the bastards!" said Lonnie. "I think we'd better pray that they're taking us to another camp. With these shackles on we don't have a shot, if they plan to kill us." It was a long, rough road. "I just hope we get somewhere soon. My back's killing me, said Howard. At last, they came to a town and pulled into the loading dock of a small airport. "Wow! A plane ride. What's the farthest we can go back into Vietnam?" asked Frank. An airport employee came out and they were escorted to a small cargo plane. They were loaded in, the door closed and locked. A pilot and a VC officer got in the cockpit and the plane took off. The plane droned on for awhile. Fazio -looking out the narrow windows on each side -, "I see a seagull. I think we're going toward the water. I hope they don't drop us in it."

"I think Saigon is on the water. I hope it's that. We have a base there. I can see a lot of houses," said Howard. "At any rate, I'm glad to get out of the hole we were in." They were beginning to feel less anxious. In fact the hope of ending in Saigon sent a thrill through their skinny bodies. Then they felt a shutting back of the engines, then a bank to the left, a long glide downward. The three men stood looking out the narrow windows, trying to make out the town.

Then as it banked again, they saw the name of the airport on top of the airport building. It wasn't Saigon. It was Cam Rahn Bay. Now what? Why Cam Rahn Bay? Their enthusiasm was dashed. Uneasiness returned. The plane landed. They waited....and waited. Then the rear door was opened and two men looked in. "Are these men the ones?" asked one of the men. "Yes," answered the other, who appeared to be a Vietcong Officer. 1st Man - noticing the shackles on the three men - "Get these shackles off these men. - and to the three men: "I'm Gen. Francois Heep of the French Army. You are in my charge until I can turn you over to the U.S. Captain McAllen of your Navy is on his way here." Our heroes were speechless and excited. What a turn of events, and how fortunate, they were not to have had time to get out that camp window! All three men saluted Gen. Heep and thanked him warmly, as they were freed. "Before we got here, we thought we were going into Saigon," said Howard.

"Saigon is gone." We haven't been in Saigon in two years, said the General. "Where were you held?" "We never knew for sure. It was way back up in the mountains, somewhere," answered Fazio. Gen. Heep took them inside, where they used the office facilities to freshen up and enjoy a delicious soft drink. Soon Captain McAllen arrived and took charge of them. Next day they were flown to the United States. In the U.S., the three friends were separated, but not before they pledged to keep in touch, if possible, and to have a reunion someday. Howard was flown to the Oakland Naval Hospital at Oakland, California. Howard had heard nothing from Katherine while in Vietnam. When he arrived in Oakland, he tried desperately to contact her. Her phone had been disconnected. Mrs. Mims phone was also disconnected. He learned at the office where she had worked, that she and her mother had left several years ago to live in New York. They had no record of where. He was very discouraged. What was there to live for? He tried to forget her, but couldn't. He was hurt that she had moved away. Evidently she was not interested in him anymore. He decided that her answer would have been "No", since she had not answered any of his letters.

CHAPTER FIVE

In the Oakland Naval Hospital, Howard was given a thorough physical exam. He was found to be seriously undernourished, and his leg had not healed properly. It was re-broken and reset. The days had gone by slowly, as hospital stays so often do, until one day a new nurse came in. "Capt. Reed, I'm Margaret Snell. I'll be your nurse today." "I'm glad to know you. Are you a California girl?" "No. I'm from Oklahoma City." "Oh, so you're an 'Okie'. I'm from Texas, so we're natural enemies, aren't we?" "So they say. Anyway, I'll be watching out for you. Do you need anything this morning?" "Physically, I'm better. I'm not sure about other things just now." "Such as?" "Whenever I'm discharged from here, I'll be out of the Air Force, too. I've been away five years. I feel like I've been left behind; like I've been kicked off a train in a desert somewhere. I don't know where to start again." "My enlistment as a Navy nurse will be up in about eight months. I'll face the same thing, unless I reenlist. I have the same problem. Maybe we can help each other." "A Mutual Aid Society, huh? I feel better already."

"That's good. Here are two pills you must take, and turn over. I've got to give you this injection." "OK. Then will you see if you can hurry up my breakfast? I'm starved." They got acquainted, and for eight months, Howard and Margaret helped each other plan for the future. As it turned out, they fell in love. They decided to get married and go to Lakewood, Texas, where Howard would work for a law firm. That's exactly what they did. In Lakewood, Howard became a popular lawyer. He was elected to the office of County Judge of Whitby County in 1981. Tragedy struck him again in 1983 when Margaret was killed in a plane crash in Colorado. Then one day, after Katherine, Mrs. Mims, and Lou had moved back to Welcome to be headmaster of Sunrise College, the plane crash was reported in the Welcome News. It included a picture of both Margaret and Judge Reed. Katherine was reading a book. Mrs. Mims was reading the newspaper. "Katherine, did you ever know another person named Howard Reed from Lakewood?" "No, I never did. That would be unusual. Why do you ask?" "Read this report of the plane crash in Colorado, and look at the pictures of Mrs. Reed and her husband." Katherine studied the write-up and pictures. Suddenly, her face turned white, her mouth dropped open, and she stared at her mother. "Mother! That's him! That's Howard!"

"Oh, I don't know what to think," she cried, as she hid her face. "Well, I don't know what to think, either. But, Katherine, you must reserve judgment until you know the full story of what happened." "I'm sorry about his wife's death," said Katherine, still agitated. "I'm shocked and relieved that he's not dead or still MIA, but I'm angry." Her face reddened. "I'm angry that he didn't come back to me instead of her! It's awful all around. Mother, what should I do?" "Don't do anything today. Give yourself time to think about it. It would be nice to just drop him a simple card of sympathy. He's in sad times right now." "I think you're right. I need a new distraction; maybe a drink."

Next day, Katherine mailed a simple sympathy card to Howard at the address given in the newspaper. She added after her signature. Headmaster of Sunrise College. After the funeral of Mrs. Reed, Howard was looking through the many cards he received, when he opened the one from Katherine. Shocked and surprised, he stared at the card. "My Gosh! Can this be Katherine? I thought she was gone to New York forever! She's over in Welcome. I wonder what she thinks of me now? This sure brings back happy memories." He separated the card from the others. "I'd sure like to talk to that young lady. Why did she not answer any of my letters?"

NOW FOR THE REST OF THE STORY:

Chapter Six

Lakewood Texas High School was having its annual graduation ceremony. Judge Howard Reed, as guest speaker, was just ending his speech to the graduating class. "And in conclusion, boys and girls, I'd like to quote an old axiom I want you to remember: 'You'll never get a loan at a bank unless you try'. In other words, 'You Gotta Try', 'You Gotta Try'. Thank you all." After the ceremony was over, and as people were leaving or standing talking to the graduates and friends, Charles Dano and three of his friends, all graduates, stood together in the crowd. Judge Reed stopped by to congratulate them. "Are you boys going to stay together? Where are you going from here? I've heard your band play, and I think you're pretty good. You would be an asset to some college's music department." "We were just discussing that, Judge Reed. We want to stay together," said Charlie. "If I can be of any help to you, let me know," said the Judge. Judge Reed left. "Well, guys, we've got a problem," said Charlie. "I may have to stay out of school for a semester to earn a little money."

"My parents just can't afford the tuition, room, and board at Tech or State now. I don't see any alternative. How about you, Alfie?" "I'm in the same boat as you, Charlie," said Alfie. "My only chance would be to go to SMU and stay with relatives in Dallas." "How about Sunrise College over in Welcome, Tex.? It's close enough that we can commute, and it's only ten miles. That would save on room and board, if we can get in," said Cicero. "But that's a girls college," said Alfie. "I know it has been, but I think all colleges are to go co-ed since the Supreme Court ruled it legal in 1982," answered Cicero. "That would solve our problem. We need to find out if we have a legal right to attend there. I'd like to check it out. Remember Judge Reed said, 'You Gotta Try'," said Ted. "OK. Let's each of us go home and talk to our parents about it. Maybe we can enroll in Sunrise College next semester. Judge Reed said that he would help us," said Charlie. They all agreed. Sunrise College, a liberal arts college for girls was located in the town of Welcome, Tex., a town of about 3500 people. The campus was large with lots of towering trees and six to eight impressive buildings, almost covered with a green coat of ivy. Just off the side of the auditorium building was a large shaded patio. Easy Street ran by this area. Since the Supreme Court ruling, many similar girls colleges had gone co-ed. Sunrise College was one that resisted the trend. Established in the early 1900s, it had many prominent alumni throughout the area who were proud of the school and its 700 or so lively girls.

Charlie and his three friends discussed with their parents the possibility of attending Sunrise College. Their parents agreed that it would solve their money problems for a couple of years. They could lose nothing by trying. On a late August day the boys piled into Charlie's old Ford "Sea biscuit" and headed for Sunrise College. Just two blocks from the campus, "Sea biscuit" coughed a couple of times and rolled to a stop. Out of gas and no emergency can, they decided to just push it the final two blocks and get gas later. That's what the girls saw, as they came streaming out of the auditorium onto the plaza, just as the boys arrived pushing "Sea biscuit". The boys were a bit intimidated by all the girls. "Wow! Take a look at that!" said Cicero. "Hey, guys, let's sing something. Alfie get your guitar, quick!" said Charlie. Alfie ran to the car and came back with his guitar. The girls were wondering about the boys' intentions. "What are they up to?" asked Lucy. "I can't imagine. Are they crazy? They look like some roving garage group. I believe they're going to serenade us!" said Jane. The boys grouped around Alfie and sang their theme song, "Nellie Brown". "More! More!" screamed the girls. Katherine Mims, the Headmaster, hearing the singing and the applause and general commotion, came out to see what was going on.

"That was good, boys, but you better move on. The girls still have things to attend to. This is new term registration for them." "We know. That's why we're here. We came to register," said Cicero. The Headmaster was momentarily at a loss to answer. She pointed to a sign on the building that said "Sunrise College for Girls". "This is a girls college. You can't register here. We can't have any boys in this college." "I take it that you're the Headmaster," said Charlie. "We heard that the Supreme Court ruled recently that all colleges can now go co-ed." "It doesn't apply to us. Now go along or I'll have to call the police." She went back into the building.

Charlie couldn't take his eyes off one very attractive girl. Although she stood in the background, Charlie waved and directed a "Hi Ya" to her. She ignored him. Most of the girls were friendly and some crowded around them. Then a bell rang, and they all faded away. The boys, frustrated, pushed the car to a filling station, got some gas, and consulted about what they should do. They decided to go home, consult their parents, and find out if they really had a right to enroll in Sunrise College. They were a bit angry at their rejection. "The girls seem friendly, but that Headmaster She's a problem," said Ted. "Maybe Judge Reed can help us," suggested Alfie.

The boys, on the advice of Alfie's parents, called Judge Reed to get his advice. He told them to come over to his house and discuss it. Arriving there, they rang the door bell. Judge Reed answered it. "Come in, boys. Excuse the clutter. Since my wife died, I don't keep things too tidy. Please sit down, and tell me about this problem you're having at Sunrise College." "Judge Reed, we want to stay together in college," said Charlie. "Sunrise College is ideal for us, but we were turned down flat when we tried to register," added Alfie. "We think she's wrong. What can we do? We can't afford to go off somewhere else. We want to continue our band," said Ted. "Miss Mims, the Headmaster, is a very nice lady. I used to know her, but it's been years. What do your parents say?" "They'd like us to go there. They suggested we call you," said Charlie. "I know that many schools aren't co-ed yet, including Sunrise College, but they have to enroll you if you insist. Of course, they may challenge you in court. I think you'd win, but do you boys want to take on all that possible trouble?" "Judge Reed, we want to stay together. I, for one, would like to try again, if there's any way to do it. I don't want to upset the college, added Ted. I'll tell you what, my court isn't in session now," said Judge Reed. "I'll go along with you boys tomorrow, and we'll see if we can work it out with Miss Mims. I've been thinking I should call on her anyhow, to renew an old acquaintance, so to speak."

"That's great, Judge Reed," said Charlie, "What time can we meet you there?" "I'll meet you at the college at 10:00 A.M." "Sure thing, Judge Reed. We'll be there. Thank you." The boys left.

Judge Reed and the boys arrived at the college the next day at the same time. A lot of the girls were out on the plaza again. Charlie spotted Miss "X" again. She was prettier than ever. Their eyes met. Charlie smiled. She didn't. They walked through the curious crowd and into the building. They found the Headmaster's office, but the door was closed. "You boys stay here a minute or two. I'll go in and see if she can see us. I don't want to barge in at an inappropriate time." The boys agreed, and the Judge opened the door and stepped inside. He checked with the girl in the outer office. She went into the Headmaster's office. "Miss Mims, there's a Judge Reed here to see you. Shall I show him in?" "Oh, MY! MY! It's Howard! Just a minute," said Katherine. She collected her thoughts and smoothed her hair. "Yes, show him in." The receptionist, outside again, to Judge Reed: "She will see you, Sir." Judge Reed entered.

CHAPTER SEVEN

"Judge Reed! So nice to see you. What brings you to our little college today?...You still live in Lakewood, don't you?" "Yes, I do. ... Katherine, you look stunning! The years don't seem to have affected you at all... Can you help me to take care of a little problem regarding some of our local boys?" "Sure, if I can, Harold. May I call you Harold, for old times sake?" "For old times sake? Of course you can, Katherine.... Katherine, I had no idea you were here until I received your card after Mrs. Reed's death. I was very surprised. I wanted to see you to find out what happened to us. I wasn't sure you were married, or if you'd even want to see me," said Howard. "I didn't know you were in Lakewood until I read the account of your wife's tragic death. No, I am not married, but I have a daughter. I've made teaching my life's work.... After you left me, I went to New York University and got my MA degree in Education. I taught until I came to Sunrise College early last year. I never heard from you after you got to Vietnam. I tried to find out where you were. I felt abandoned. I was hurt, angry." "Katherine, I wrote you several letters as soon as I got to Vietnam, but never got any answers. Didn't you receive them?" "Not a single one. I couldn't write you, because I didn't have an address for you," she said. "How awful! It's no wonder that you felt abandoned. I'm so sorry! I wanted desperately to keep in touch with you. I was transferred right away, then I was shot down and captured. I was allowed no outside communication for four long years," said Howard.

"All I could find out was that you were missing in action. After the official notice in 1976 of being MIA, I assumed that you may have perished. It was awful, Howard! ...I was shocked to learn that you had returned to Lakewood and were married. I'm so happy that you survived. Did you escape? How did they treat you?" "I was injured when they shot me down. A broken leg and arm and some internal injuries. My pilot died in the crash. I was taken to a North Vietnamese field hospital where my leg and arm were splinted, then on to another hospital for four weeks. Then I was taken to a prison camp in the mountains where I was held until 1978, when I was turned over to the U.S. Navy." "Did you come back to Lakewood then?" "No. I was in such bad shape, I was put in the Naval Hospital in Oakland, Calif. I stayed there eight months." "Where did you meet Margaret?" "She was a nurse at the hospital. We were married the day I was discharged. Then we came to live in Lakewood. ....Katherine, I had lost all hope of ever seeing you again. I decided that your answer the morning I left was to be NO, since I had heard nothing from you." Katherine-tears brimming in her eyes- "Howard, you were wrong. The answer was to be 'YES'." She couldn't say any more. Howard -putting his arm around her shoulders- "Katherine, I'm sorry to have put you through such an emotional trial." "That's alright, Howard. It was something that neither of us had any control over," she said, as she struggled to regain her composure.

"Katherine, I'm not sure I heard you right," said Howard. "Have you adopted a little girl?" That's wonderful for you to do that. What's her name?" "Her name is Mary Louise. She likes to be called Lou." "That's what my friends called me in high school. Louise is my middle name." "I remember you mentioning that to me." "How long have you had her? I'd like to see her," said Howard. "I've had her since she was born. I'm her mother. She picked up a picture from her desk. "This is a recent picture of her. I'm very proud of her," Howard- as he looked at the picture- "Why, she's 9 or 10 years old. I was picturing a little girl of three or four." Katherine was silent with tears again in her eyes. "She was born on July 14, 1973. She's eleven now." Howard was suddenly struck with the truth. "*Oh*, Katherine! She's our child, isn't she?" Katherine—tears streaming through her fingers - "Yes. she is. Howard, I wanted you to know it all these years. She has been the saving of my sanity. I'm so glad you know about it now." Howard again had his arm around her. "I'm thrilled to learn about her. Does she know about me?" "Yes, she knows all about you and me. Even about you're marriage and your wife's death. She was shocked and angry, at first, but she considers you her father." "Where is she now? I can't wait to see her!"

"She's in a boarding school in Rochester, N.Y. She'll be here at Thanksgiving week vacation. You can meet her then.... Howard, we've forgotten the business you first called about. What was it?" "It's about some boys who want to enroll in your college," said Howard.

"But Katherine, I want to talk to you some more about us and Louise. I don't want to rush you. Can I make a date soon for dinner with you?" "Not just yet, Howard. This meeting has so surprised me, I want to take time to think what is best for me and Lou to do. I want to talk to Lou. Maybe, in about a week. Now tell me about the boys that you mentioned." "Alright. Four of our local boys have just graduated from high school. They've asked me to help them to enroll in Sunrise College." Katherine's smile faded. "That may be a problem, I'm afraid, Howard." "I know that Sunrise College was founded as a girls school, but many of the girls colleges are turning co-ed since 1982. I'm sure you've entertained the idea." "Yes, I've kept up with the trend, but ..." "It strikes me that this may be the opportunity you could use to ease your college into the co-ed class. There are some advantages in doing so. This is registration week, isn't it?" asked Howard. "Yes. There are some advantages, as you say, but there are many disadvantages, too. As we're set up, boys just wouldn't fit in here.. It's hard to keep some of our girls motivated as it is."

"Is your enrollment at capacity this term?" asked Howard. "No. We would have room for the boys. They were out here earlier, but I had to turn them away." "Yes, I know. They're waiting out in the hall now. But, Katherine, to be fair to you and also to the boys, how about you contacting your board of directors and see if they'd let these four boys enroll on a temporary, or trial basis. If it doesn't work out, then that's that. I know you'll have to make a few changes; a bathroom altered, lockers, etc., but I'll see if I can't get you some help on that." "The boys plan to commute, I believe?" she asked. "Yes, they wouldn't be here at night. They play together as a band. If it works out it would be a plus for your music department. I understand they are pretty good," said Howard. "Well, Howard, you're a good salesman. I'll contact the board and get their decision, but I'm not very hopeful." "Katherine I want to thank you. I knew you would help us if you could. I'll call the boys in. I want you to meet them." He went out to call the boys in. While Howard was conversing with Katherine, the boys waited patiently in the hall. Getting tired of standing, they ended up sitting on the floor and leaning against the wall. Miss "X" came by, walking carefully, as the boys pulled their legs up to let her by. She wondered what they were doing just sitting there. "Is that the girl you said you had dibs on, Charlie?" asked Alfie.

"That's her. I don't want to catch any of you guys makin' eyes at her," said Charlie. "I noticed you made her step around your legs. If I was her, I'd have stomped on 'em," said Cicero. "I was just tryin' to get her attention." "I wonder what's keepin' the Judge so long?" put in Ted. "She must be as tough with him as she was with us. I'm not sure I want to tangle with her again." "Here he comes now, finally!" said Alfie. The judge appeared. "Sorry for the delay, boys. Miss Mims, the Headmaster, wants to meet you. Come along." They entered the Headmaster's office. Judge

Reed introduced each boy separately, telling the Headmaster something about each one and his family. As they were leaving, Charlie addressed her. "Ma'am, we want to apologize for the commotion we caused the other time we were here. We don't want to be disruptive. We all need to attend close to home, and Sunrise is ideal for us." "We'll try to be fair, boys. We'll see how it comes out." As the Judge and the boys got to the door, Howard turned, "I'll call you, Katherine," he said. "Thank you for coming, Howard." "I don't know what happened, but she's not the tough lady I expected. That's encouraging," said Alfie.

Since time to register and start classes was short, the Headmaster canvassed the Board of Directors. They agreed to go co-ed, but only if she said it was feasible. It was practical in that the tuition would help balance their close budget, but Katherine demurred. She didn't want so important a decision on her shoulders, as she was aware that many of the parents and some of the students were opposed to going co-ed. The next day, the student body president notified the Headmaster that a majority of the Student Council had voted to oppose a co-ed school and would call a strike if need be to prevent it.

It was rumored that the boys planned a sit-in if a strike was called. Judge Reed, after being informed of the situation by the Headmaster, decided to take the matter to the court of Judge Stovall, in the same county as the college. Judge Reed was from the adjoining county. Judge Stovall knew that several families in his county would be benefited if Sunrise College went co-ed. It would be good politics, as well as helping his friend Judge Reed. He issued an order to allow the boys to register for one term "on a temporary basis." With a copy of the judge's order in hand, the boys jumped in "Sea biscuit" and headed for Sunrise College again. And would you believe it? Just two blocks from the plaza, "Sea biscuit" made a couple of coughs and went dead.

"This Easy street is a jinx! Same place as last time," said Cicero. Well two gallons only goes so far. We better put in more next time," suggested Ted. "Come on! Stop grumblin' and start pushin," said Charlie. They pushed "Sea biscuit" the two blocks to the plaza. As before, the girls were out in force. "It's those same boys again. Don't they ever put gas in that rattletrap?" asked Gail. "Boys are SO dumb!" said Lucy. Even so, the girls gave them a big cheer; or most of them did.

As the boys filed into the registrar's office, some calls of "Throw 'em out!" and "Call the police, again!" were heard from the hall. The Headmaster was called in for her OK. Katherine - who knew of the judge's order - "You have an order from Judge Stovall for one term. Let me see it." Charlie handed it over and the Headmaster studied it carefully, then gave it to the registrar. "It's OK. Go ahead and register them." Then to the boys: "My advice, boys, is to study hard, try not to cause any problems, and we'll see how things work out at the end of the semester." "We'll try our best, Ma'am," promised Charlie. Charlie got another glimpse of "That Gorgeous Girl" while he was registering. She was at a desk in the registrar's office.

The first day of classes there was no real problem. They were welcomed by most of the girls. They were assured of at least a semester of classes, by the court order. They were determined to make a good impression, study hard, and do their music practice at home. It turned out that "The Gorgeous One" was also a music major. Charlie found that out the second day as he went to the cafeteria between classes. He spotted her at a table by herself having a cup of tea. Two couples were at a far table. Charlie - aloud to himself - "Wow! There she is again! And all by herself! It's gotta be NOW. I gotta!" He turned to the vacant tables and sang "You Gotta Try" then ambled over and "accidentally" bumped her table, spilling tea on the table and her dress. "Oh, I'm sorry, Miss! I don't know what's the matter with me. Gee! I'm afraid I've spoiled your dress." "Well! I know what's the matter with you! I've been noticing you eyeing me every time I'm near you. It makes me uncomfortable," said Kelsey.

"I'm sorry, I'm Charlie Dano. I'll have to admit that I bungled it. I'm especially sorry about your dress. I was just trying to get your attention." "You mean you did it on purpose?" "I've been trying to find a way to meet you ever since I've been here." Kelsey - less angry and a bit flattered - "Why didn't you just hit me with a chair? Well, I'm Kelsey Mims. Now you know." "Your mother's the Headmaster?" asked Charlie, surprised. "No, she's my aunt." Charlie -as he wiped up the spilled tea - "May I get you another cup of tea?" "No. I don't need another. But sit down. I'd like to know why you would go to such trouble to know me. I'm no celebrity." "That's a plus, Miss Mims. I'll just have to admit I was so impressed the first time I saw you. I'm new here as you know. I don't have a girlfriend, and I just thought that maybe ..." "I'm amused,," said Kelsey. "I already have a boyfriend. Still, I've never had an introduction this clever before. You better get me another cup of tea." Charlie got two cups of tea. "My friends, Ted, Cicero, Alfie, and I are all music majors. We live in Lakewood. We have a band and Sunrise is an ideal place for us. Anyway, I'd like to be friends with you if you'd consider it. May I call you Kelsey?" "Sure. I'm a music major, too. I'll probably be seeing you in class, anyway. I'd like to meet your friends, too," said Kelsey.

"Maybe I was a little premature asking to be your boyfriend, so soon. But I just had to give it a try," said Charlie. "Well, you do get points for trying. Let's just say, you have a shot at backup. I don't know much about you yet, but I've got to run now, Charlie. I have a class. I'll see you around." Kelsey left.

Charlie sat for a few minutes while mulling over what had transpired. "So she has a boyfriend already. I should've known it, but Judge Reed said, 'You Gotta Try', and keep trying." As he started to leave, Deborah Hines, the Student Council president, came and sat down at his table. "I'm Debbie Hines. I want to meet you and explain what's happening." "I'm Charlie Dano. I'm glad to meet you. I hope we're not causing a big controversy. We just want to get an education. Sunrise College is ideal for us." "I understand, but some of the girls' parents are very opposed to Sunrise going co-ed. If we let you stay in, other boys will be sure to follow. It'll change the whole character of this school. My parents sent me here, because it was a 'girls only' school. Don't you realize what will happen?" "Yes, I understand what you're saying, but it's going to happen, anyway, maybe sooner than later. If I and my friends have to go elsewhere, it'll break up our band. We're hoping to be an asset to the school in that regard. We know that Sunrise's music department is A-1," said Charlie. "Charlie, I personally am not against going co-ed. It's my parents. I thank that's the feeling of most of the girls. But the Headmaster may be a tough one to convince," said Debbie.

"Debbie, you sound like you'd give us a fair shot. We'll do everything we can to not be disrupting." "As I say, I'm neutral. But I have to warn you. The Student Council has voted against going co-ed, and have threatened to strike. They heard a rumor that you boys threatened a sit-in." "That's ridiculous! We'd never do that," said Charlie. "That's what I thought, Charlie. I've got to go. Maybe this thing will work out well for all." "Thank you, Debbie, for enlightening me. I hope we can work it out, too. By the way, do you know Kelsey Mims?" "I sure do. She's my best friend. She's a music major, too. She's an excellent singer. Good-bye, Charlie. See you later." "Good-bye, Debbie. Thank you again." They both left.

A week passed and Howard, anxious to see Katherine again, decided to visit the college to see how things were going. The receptionist checked, then waved him into the Headmaster's office. "Come in Howard. How are you?" "I'm fine. I hope everything is going well with you. How are my boys doing?" "They're doing well. Not as much trouble as I feared." "That's good to hear. However, I've got some bad news. Three of the parents have filed an injunction to stop Sunrise from going co-ed. I think you'll hear about it tomorrow."

"I'm sorry. I was afraid of that. What can I do? I hate the idea of a court battle," said Katherine. "Judge Stoval of your county will hear the case. I understand that he insists on negotiation. He directs the status quo to stay until the end of this term, so it's not so pressing," said Howard. "Maybe they'll relent and withdraw," said Katherine. "Katherine, I stopped by mainly to ask if you would join me for dinner this evening. Will you?" Katherine -surprised, but pleased- "Well, Yes! I think it is nice of you to ask, Howard." "Fine. I'll pick you up at—say 7 pm. Is that OK?" "Sure. I'll be ready, Howard." At 7 pm Howard picked her up, and they drove to the Colonial Hotel and were seated on the dining terrace under a beautiful view of a gorgeous sunset. "Katherine, what do you hear from our daughter? When is she coming home?" "She's coming for the Thanksgiving holidays. I'll meet her plane at Wichita Falls. I know she wants to meet you. What her reaction will be when that happens is anybody's guess." "Do you mind if I go with you?" "Not at all. It'll be a good place for you two to meet."

A waiter came, and they ordered their dinner. "I love this hotel. We've spent many happy meals together here, haven't we, Howard?" "Yes, we have. We were younger then. Both of us have been through some sad traumatic times since then," said Howard. "It seems both have had to put our emotions deep inside. What a misfortune!" Do you think they're still there, Katherine? They are with me." "I don't know. The past is such a sad memory. It seems so long ago. - Do you remember our last dinner together at this hotel?" "I sure do! How could I forget it? You turned me down for the second time. You were so independent. But I've always heard that you won't get a loan at a bank if you don't apply. I like that!" "Ha! Ha! Is this going to be number three, Howard?" "You never gave me an answer to number two. I'm still waiting. We did have fun, though, didn't we?" "Yes, we did, and I'm still thinking it over." "You are? That's encouraging! Same 'hard-to-get' girl, are you? OK, I'm still available. Here comes our dinner. Are you hungry?" "I sure am! This is such a comfortable place and always good food."

Floor show announcer — "Our singer tonight is Miss Rita Parsons singing the reques *"An Autumn Breeze Brings Memories."* Howard, are you the one who requested that song?" "Yes, I did, Katherine. It fits us so well." She squeezed his arm. He smiled in return.

They enjoyed their dinner and were enjoying the cabaret program when an attractive couple approached them. The man slapped Howard on his back. "Hello, Howie, old friend!" Surprised, Howard quickly looked up. It was Frank his fellow prisoner in Vietnam. "Frank Berry! I can't believe it. It's wonderful to see you. What a surprise! "exclaimed

Howard, "We're on our honeymoon, Howie." He turned and introduced an attractive girl behind him. "This is Oona, my wife," he said.

"Katherine, this is one of the fellows I was in prison with in Vietnam, for four long years. Oh, I hope I'm not dreaming this," said Howard. "You must be the Katherine he moaned about so much in the prison camp," said Frank. "That's good to hear," said Katherine. "Sit down. I want to hear all about both of you," said Howard. They had a happy and friendly visit together. Katherine enjoyed talking to Oona, who was a teacher in a Honolulu school. "How did you happen to be in Lakewood?" asked Howard. "We were visiting Oona's sister in Lubbock. I remembered that you were from Lakewood, so we decided to drive over here and try to locate you."

"We're staying here at the Colonial Hotel. I spotted you while we were eating." "Where is Fazio? Have you heard from him?" "Lonnie is in Florence, Italy. He is still in the Air Force. He and his wife were originally from Italy. While he was an MIA, his family went back there."

"What about you, Frank. Do you live in Hawaii?" "Yes. I used my GI benefits to go to the University of Hawaii. I graduated with a degree in Business Management. I work for the Dole pineapple company." As Howard and Frank hashed over their activities, Katherine and Oona found plenty to talk about. It was Oona's first visit to the mainland, and Katherine had not been to Hawaii. Suddenly, the terrace lights blinked twice; a signal that it was closing time. As they were leaving, Oona invited each of them to visit her and Frank, any time they were in Hawaii. Howard and Frank promised to meet the next day for a golf game at Howard's club. They left.

Katherine and Howard were at the airport early to meet Lou. The weather was sunny, and a good crowd was present. Howard was anxious and restless. It was a special event meeting this "special" little girl. He had seen the picture of her. She was attractive like her mother. Would she be shy, cool, friendly? Howard hoped for the best. "Relax, Howard. You seem nervous. It's just a little eleven year old girl." "I know, but all girls are unpredictable to me." "Ha! That's one of our defenses."

A plane came in sight, circled and landed. Katherine and Howard waited anxiously as the passengers came out, but no Lou. A few minutes later, another plane came in and landed. People started flooding out. Finally, a pretty little short-haired girl dressed like a cheer leader hurried out. She spied and ran straight to Katherine, hugged and kissed her. Then she turned and faced Howard. This was the crucial moment for Howard. It only lasted a moment. Running and jumping into Howard's arms as she screamed, "Daddy, I'm Lou!" She hugged him around his neck. It was a happy scene. "How did you know me so quickly?" asked Howard excitedly. "I have a picture of you. Mother gave it to me on my first birthday." "How was your trip?" he asked. "Dull! I just sat and thought," she said. "About what? Anything new?" asked Howard. "Well, -I was wondering what it would be like if you and Mother were married, and I was back home." (WOW! Wanna take that question back, Howard?) "Young lady, you're getting over your head. You'll have your turn for things like that in about ten years," said Katherine. "Lou, you're a bright girl. I'd like to have you on my team," said Howard. "I was just thinking. I'm hungry. Can we get my bag and go somewhere to eat?" They picked up her bag and went looking for a good restaurant.

Chapter Eight

It was the second week of January, 1985. Several things had happened since Lou's arrival. Lou begged to stay in Welcome with her mother and grandmother, and near Howard. Katherine agreed, and Lou was transferred back to school in Welcome. The boys worked out so well in Sunrise College, their "authorization" was extended for another semester. Howard and Katherine had dined together almost every week since Thanksgiving. Charlie was still trying to date Kelsey. He caught her again in the cafeteria at a table by herself. "Hi Gorgeous! I found a new song. It reminds me of you." "What's it like? Let me see it." "I don't have a copy. I'll sing it for you." He sang "Maybe Yes, Maybe No". "Ha! I get it, Charlie. You're giving me a message. OK. The answer is maybe, yes, maybe, no. I can't sew, but I love to cook." "Darn! You're too cruel, Kelsey. But I'm not so easily discouraged. I'm still number two. I'll wait for a better answer." "I can't promote you, Charlie. You're too good a backup."

"What did you say your boyfriend's name was?" "I didn't say, Charlie." "That's right, you didn't. Well, names don't say much anyhow.? "Good try, Charlie. So you don't think I'm being too secretive, I call him 'Slugger'." "You don't say! I think I know him." The bell rang and they exited. Later in the day the weather became blustery, and it began to rain. The students were having a program in the auditorium. Judge Reed was in attendance. No one expected anything but a heavy rain. However, in the middle of the program a girl hurried from the office with a message for the Headmaster. "Miss Mims, there's a call from the police department for you. They say it's urgent." Katherine immediately left and went across the hall to her office. She noticed, as she glanced out the window, that it was raining hard outside. Katherine -on phone- "Hello. This is Katherine Mims, the Headmaster. What is it you want?" "This is Police Chief Phillips. We've just been advised that a tornado has been spotted only five miles away and is headed our way. I don't know if it'll hit Welcome, but we can't take a chance." "What should we do?" asked Katherine.

"We think you'd better get your students into the basement until this passes. I'm sending Officer Stokes out there to help if needed. Don't let the kids get too scared. It may miss us. That's it! I've got to go!" Katherine immediately got on the intercom. "Attention everyone! The weather has turned worse, and the Police Dept. has advised us, as a precaution, to go down into our basement until things get better. A tornado has been sighted and we don't want to take a chance. It'll be for just a little while, but get to the basement. I'll be with you right away." She hung up and went to supervise the change. There was a lot of excitement and speculation, but most of them were familiar with tornado scares, as Welcome, Texas was in the area sometimes called "Tornado Alley." When the two-story building was built, a full basement had been designed and outfitted as a refuge from tornados. Everyone from the auditorium was soon safely in the basement. Katherine found Judge Reed and the boys already there. "It may miss, I hope. Howard, will you go up with me just outside the building and help me to watch? You're more of an expert than I am." "It'll come from the West," said Howard, "if it continues toward us, it'll hit us in about 20 minutes. We'll need to keep the two exit doors held shut if it does hit us." Howard -addressing the boys -"Charlie, you and Ted man the back entrance. Cicero, you and Alfie man the one at the foot of the stairs. Otherwise, our ceiling will just be lifted off our heads if it wrecks the upper floor."

They all agreed, and Katherine and Howard went outside to watch. It looked bad. Strong puffs of wind seemed to go in several directions. Sometimes there was no wind. Dark clouds moved fast toward them. There was an eerie yellowish glow near the ground. The rain came down in angry sheets. "We've had these scares pretty often but we've been lucky so far. None have hit this town that I can remember," said Katherine. "You're right. I've lived in Lakewood a long time, too. So far, we've escaped. Maybe, we're lucky again," agreed Howard. "That darkest cloud is turning and getting lower," she said. Suddenly it happened. A whirling funnel took shape out of the bottom of the blackest cloud and was spinning. It reached down to the ground. Lightning and thunder increased. The rain came down hard. "That's it, Katherine. Let's get into the basement pronto. It's going to hit us in just a few short minutes."

They rushed down the steps. "Boys, man the doors. Don't let them be sucked open," said Howard. There was general confusion as the doors were being shut.

"Girls, stay quiet and stay calm." directed Katherine, "We're going to be hit with the main part of this storm. It should be over in about half an hour." Just as Cicero and Alfie started to close the heavy basement door. Bitsy, Lou's little dog bounded out the door, chased by Lou into the increasing wind and rain. "Bitsy, come back here!" screamed Lou, as she dashed after her little dog.

"OH, my Gosh! Lou, get back here! Let him go. The tornado is about to hit us," yelled Katherine. "Get inside, Katherine. I'll get her!" exclaimed Howard. He rushed after Lou, who had disappeared in the semi-darkness. Katherine went and stood at the door, anxiously watching. The wind and rain was getting really strong. Lightning and thunder got worse. Howard ran in the direction Lou and the dog had disappeared. There was no sight of either of them. He stopped and called. "Lou, where are you?" There was no answer. He ran a little farther. "Lou, where are you? Answer me, please!" Then he heard her. "Daddy, I'm over here." She was somewhere to the left. Howard ran over a little knoll and found them. Lou was kneeling at the entrance to a small drainage culvert that went under a footpath. "Daddy, Bitsy is in there and won't come out. I can't reach him." "Lou, we've got to get back to the basement. Right now!" "I don't want to leave him. He's scared of the thunder." Water was beginning to run stronger out of the culvert opening. It was obvious to Howard that the little dog would be washed out or drowned. He quickly lay down at the entrance and thrust his arm as far inside as he could. Luckily, he grabbed a leg of Bitsy and pulled him out, soaking wet and whining. "Thank you, Daddy! Let me have him." "I'll carry Bitsy. We've got to run, fast!" "I love you, Daddy!" she said.

They started running toward the basement shelter. Lou began to limp badly. "Come on, Lou. What's the matter?" "My foot's hurt. It's my ankle." Here, take Bitsy." He handed Bitsy to Lou, then picked her up in his arms and sprinted to the shelter. Katherine, Cicero and Alfie held the door open for them. The door was slammed shut, just as they scrambled in and the tornado reached the building. The wind became louder and louder until it became a roar. Then the sound of tearing and banging, as the tornado bore down on them. The boys at each door to the outside began to feel the push and pull of the winds and could barely keep them from being sucked open. Lightning and thunder were intense. Suddenly, the lights went out, accented by a terrifying roar of thunder. There was a loud scream from the girls. "Stay calm, girls. We're in a safe place," said Katherine. "Just stay where you are. We have some battery lamps here. I'll get them." Howard supplied a key-ring light to Katherine and she soon had three lamps shining. Then came a crashing, shuddering jolt, as the upper part of the building was ripped off. The doors to the outside were almost sucked open as the boys hung on to them. The rest held on to each other. It lasted only a few seconds and the furious part of the tornado passed on, leaving a steady rain.

Finally, Howard and Katherine ventured out the door and were greeted with the devastation. The auditorium building was gone, except the basement that they had been in. One other building, a classroom building, and a house next door were completely wrecked. Within five minutes, Officer Stokes arrived. It happened before he could get there. He was relieved that all the people at the college were safe. Soon, many of the parents and others from the town arrived. Luckily, both of the dormitory buildings weren't damaged. Other police and an ambulance arrived. The owners of the house next door that was destroyed, were away on vacation. The girls were shocked at the scene. The boys and Judge Reed were viewed as heroes. Under the direction of Katherine and the police, everyone was accounted for and settled for the rest of the night. The police placed a guard at the site to prevent pilfering. The boys and Judge Reed went back to their homes in Lakewood.

The next day, Katherine canvassed the school Board of Directors and they declared a two week delay of classes until plans were made to resume the semester. Debbie got up a petition to the Board of Directors, signed by a majority of the girls, for Sunrise to go co-ed. The Board decided that they'd go co-ed. With the rebuilding program, it was a good time to make the changes. They bought the lot of the destroyed house next door to build a new gym and a boys dorm, as funds become available. Classes were resumed using some temporary portables, and the old gym converted into classrooms.

At the end of the next semester, the new auditorium was finished. In a celebration to thank the townspeople and the parents, a concert was scheduled for a Friday night.

THE FRIDAY NIGHT: The newly finished auditorium was being filled. People came from all over the area. Charlie's Crazies were playing inside. Howard and Katherine stood outside and watched as the people passed them. "Well, Katherine, this has been a busy and happy nine months, excluding the tornado havoc." said Howard, "I've enjoyed working with you. You know, we make a pretty good team. I'm going to miss working with you." "Not so fast, Howard! I accept!" said Katherine. "You what? You do? Oh, Katherine, that's wonderful!" He grabbed her in an emotional hug and kiss. Katherine -catching her breath - "You said you were still available, and I told you I was still thinking about it." "Katherine, can we announce it tonight? When can we set a date. How about two weeks, before you change your mind?" "Yes, The sooner the better. I've learned my lesson about putting things off! I want to go co-ed, too."

INSIDE: During the uproar that followed the announcement of the projected wedding of Katherine and Howard: Kelsey came over to Charlie. "Charlie, I've changed my answer to 'Yes'. "You're #1 now." "That's wonderful!" He gave her an extra special squeeze. "What about 'Slugger', your other boyfriend?" "He took a powder, when I said you weighed 300 pounds." "I knew he was a smokescreen all the time." "It gave me time to size you up, Charlie."

THE END

Song Lyrics for "TRY"
Music & Lyrics by Tom Robb

YOU WILL ALWAYS BE MY SWEETHEART

You will always be my Sweetheart.
When you need me I'll be there.
You are my inspiration, dear.
You're the answer to my prayer.

You will always be my Sweetheart.
Oh, I love you! Yes , I do.
As the years come and go, with sunshine or snow,
You'll have me, Dear, and I'll have you.

MY HERO

Haunting mem'ries that won't go away.
I miss you Darling, every single day.
In my dreams, dear, I see your lovely face.
A pat, and then a tender kiss,
And feel your warm embrace.

All my thoughts are for you.
I'm lonely and blue.
Days seem to linger long;
Nights are awful too.

Now I've been waiting
the end of the war with glee,
To welcome home my own Hero —
When you come home to me.

* Music for equivalent of 1st verse played
without vocal by far off sax or clarinet.

Tom Robb

Now our war is over now,
But a sad mix-up somehow.
For my dear Hero,
Did not come home to me.

Strange things happen
to those we love today.
I learned the sad news, my Hero -
Is listed as M.I.A.
Haunting mem'ries that won't go away.
I miss you, Darling, every single day.
Strange things happen to those we love today.
I learned the sad news, my Hero -
Is listed as M.I.A.

NELLIE BROWN

Now the night birds are callin' and
Shadows are fallin' and the -
Late summer sun goes down, down, down, down
Hear Ye! Now it's time for my -
Saturday night date with Nellie Brown.

Boys and girls will all -
Truck down to the Ball;
Dance to music by Bo Bo's Crazies.
Red Hot! it's the onliest -
Place to be in this here town.

Nellie, she's a dream while dancin'.
I feel like a horse a-prancin'.
Can't get over that I'm so lucky.
She likes me and that's just ducky.

Think of her night and day,
And I am proud to say -
She means the world to me.
Any one can see.
Yes Sir! I'm in love with that dark-eyed Nellie Brown.

YOU GOTTA TRY

Those couples there, are gaily dining.
Here am I, alone and pining -
For a chance to meet the girl of my dreams.
She's sitting at a table near me.

(he turns and sings to audience)
Shall I try to make her see me?

(motions toward girl)

But I know she won't unless I try.

She's got charm and got class.
You can plainly see, and —
If she's NOT that Leaders' daughter,

(in a stern tone)

She's the one for me! (much softer tone)

(8 measure turnaround - no words)

Of all the girls I've seen on campus,
She's the one! I think she's fabulous!
So, I can not let this chance go by.

In Life's complicated state
You just can't be real shy.
I can't waste time in vain debate
Or Life may pass me by.

If I kinda bump her table;
Apologize and act like Gable;

(still singing to audience)

Will it work?—Here goes!—I'm gonna try!

(he saunters over and bumps her table-spills coffee)

Tom Robb

An Autumn Breeze Brings Memories

Chorus:

The Autumn breezes wafting thru;
The stars are bright and clear.
I sense a faint perfume like dew
And dawn will soon appear.
Sweet mem'ries from across the years
Come softly back to me,
When music filled our happy hearts
And we were young and free.

I close my eyes and see your face,
Your eyes, your hair, your smile.
I can't forget; they thrill me yet;
Your kiss, your warm embrace.
We shared our dreams, our crazy schemes.
We never Thought that life had heartaches, too.
And tho' our story had to end
I'm still in love with you.

The past is now our history.
Some things were meant to be,
And something happened to my heart
When you first smiled at me.
Tho' Autumn breezes come and go, with
Starry Skies above. — And we're apart; —
Somewhere, someway, sometime, somehow
We'll meet again, Sweetheart!

Maybe Yes, Maybe No

Maybe yes, maybe no.
That was her answer months ago.
Love her?
That's the reason I'm in this mental meltdown.

Easy come, easy go,
Just isn't this scenario.
Boy friends?
By the dozen in this here town. Now

She's so gorgeous.
Painted eyes and frizzy hair.
I go crazy,
Trying to work it so she will care; —and

She can cook, she can sew.
She's just the girl for me I know.
But whenever I "pop the question" it's
"Maybe yes" and "Maybe no."

THAT MAGIC NIGHT IN HAWAII

A Love Story

LIST OF CHARACTERS

TONY (Michael Michaivelli) - a Sailor in the Navy

SHIRLEY ROSE - a girl on vacation in Hawaii.

DORIS BOYD - Shirley's best friend.

HARRY BLAISE - Boyhood friend of Tony's.

FLORENCE BLAISE - Harry's Mother.

CHRISTINE BLAISE (CISSY) - Harry's young sister.

JOHN BLAISE - Harry's Dad.

PHIL PIKER - Office cohort and friend; suitor for Shirley's affection.

MR. GIBSON - a vice president of S.F. Port Authority

MR. WILSON - Tony's'1st floor boss.

TOM JONES - beat out Tony on 1st vacancy.

FRED WILLIAMS - beat out Tony on 2nd vacancy.

JOE ACOSTA - a fellow employee of Tony's.

MR. GRANT - Tony's new boss. YWCA receptionist.

SLIM - Bartender at "The Office" bar.

PAYMASTER - at S.F Port Authority.

JOEY - beggar at corner.

JUDGE REGINALD L. SMITH

JEFF MONTGOMERY - president of Jr. Professional Speakers Club.

MR. CARPENTER - Director of Personnel of Pacific Trade Co.

MR. FISHER - head of a department at Pacific Trade Co. (Tony's new boss.)

LITTLE SHIRLEY - at the park with her Mother.

JERRY FORD - a crippled boy in a bad situation.

MR. DREWER - Shirley's boss at the Chamber of Commerce.

HELEN - in love with Phil; didn't like Shirley.

SECURITY GUARD at Shirley's apartment complex.

DESK CLERK at the Reef Tower Hotel

STEWARD on North American Airlines plane.

CHAPTER ONE

<u>SUMMER OF 1998:</u> An older white haired woman sat knitting in a chair. Soft music to a song began to be heard. As the music became louder, the old lady put aside her knitting, arose and began to sing: "That Magic Night In Hawaii". As she finished, she walked away and the scene shifted to a telephone booth on the beach at Waikiki.

<u>BACK TO SUMMER OF 1948:</u> It was about mid day in Hawaii. Not many people on the beach at Waikiki. Roving rain clouds had made the air more humid; a young Navy male and a sun-tanned girl separately approached the lone telephone booth on the beach. As he noticed the girl approaching, he stepped back.

"After you, Lady," he said. "Thank you," she said, and stepped into the booth. The boy noted the friendly smile of the smartly dressed girl. After a couple of minutes, she opened the door a little. "I'll be just a little longer, Sir. I'm sorry." "That's OK. I'm in no hurry," he replied. The boy looked up at the darkening clouds, held his palms up, as it began to sprinkle. "It's about to rain out here," he said. There was a loud clap of thunder, and the rain began to come down hard. The girl opened the door, as she screamed - "You're getting wet. Get in here!" Not knowing what else to do, he crowded in, as she slammed the door shut. What a situation! A little embarrassed laughter from both. He -chancing to look in her beautiful, excited eyes, just about 14 inches away- "Wow! These tropical storms can surprise you. I'm sorry to crowd you like this." "It's

alright. I can stand it if you can." "My name's Anthony Michiavelli. Just
call me Tony." "I'm Shirley Rose. I understand these little squalls don't
last long. Do you want to make your call? I'll try not to listen." "It can
wait. I was just checkin' with my two buddies." "That's what I was doing;
calling my roommate at the hotel," said Shirley. "You're from the States?"
he asked. "Yes, from San Francisco. My girlfriend and I are on a five day
visit. I see you're in the Navy. Are you stationed here?" "No. I'm on the
USS Fargo. It's anchored in the harbor. We leave late tomorrow. I'm on a
24 hour pass from the ship." Both kept looking out at the rain. It seemed
to be letting up a bit. San Francisco is a great city. I'm from Chicago, I've
never been to San Francisco. One of my high school friends lives there.

Maybe I'll end up there too, said Tony. "It's getting kinda warm in here.
Can you crack that door a little?" asked Shirley. He opened the door a
bit. A few minutes later: "The rain's down to a sprinkle. Should we make
a run for it? asked Shirley. "OK, let's run for that coffee shop. I'd like to
buy you a cup for your kindness to a stranger," said Tony. "Alright. Let's
go!" she said.

They made a dash for the coffee shop. Shaking the excess rain off,
they found a vacant booth and sat down. A waiter brought them coffee.
Tony -for the first time noting her relaxed features, her beautiful brown
hair and dark eyes - "Is this your first day in Honolulu?" "No, it's my
third. My girlfriend and I will leave for home day after tomorrow. Is
your ship going back to the mainland from here?" "No. We're outward
bound; Tacloban, in the Philippines. I'll be over there for a year. Then I'll
be out of the Navy." They both smiled. Tony cleared his throat. "Are you
still single, Miss Rose?" "Yes. Nobody likes me. How about you?" "I'm
still single," said Tony. I can't believe nobody likes you. I can't get over
the fact that we met in a phone booth." "It is kind of romantic, isn't it?"
added Shirley. After the end of their second cup of coffee..."I have until"
8 am tomorrow to be back on my ship. Have you been to the dinner and
floor show at the Reef Tower Hotel here on Waikiki?" he asked. "No. I've
heard that Emma, their singer, is very good." "I have two of her records,"
said Tony. "I would like to take in their show and dinner there tonight. I
don't enjoy things like that by myself. Would you let me take you? Not to
be just a dinner partner, but I'd like very much to know you better."

Shirley-cautiously- "Oh, that's so nice of you, Tony. I'd love to hear
Miss Veary sing, but my Mom cautioned me about going out with
strangers." "I'm not a stranger," exclaimed Tony. "I'm from Illinois....
Here's my Navy ID. I'll give you the phone number of my Mother in
Chicago, if you'd like to call her. Please, Shirley!"

"Let me make a phone call. "I need to check with my room-mate.

We may have plans." ——— "Sure, you should do that," agreed Tony. Shirley went to a phone and called Doris, her roommate.

After hearing the details of Shirley's situation, Doris replied: "How romantic! I think he's OK, so go for it, Sher. If you have any problem, call me. See yuh!" Shirley -coming back from the phone- "I called Scotland Yard and they said they didn't have anything on you, so, what time should I be ready, Lothario?" "How about 6 pm? What's your hotel and room number?" "It's the Palace Hotel, room 1204. Six pm is fine." "Tony, I'd better go along if I'm going to be ready at six." "Do you want me to call a cab for you?" he asked. "No. I have some shopping to do, and my hotel is within walking distance. Thank you for the coffee, Tony. I'll see you at 6." "That's great! I'll be there, Shirley." They separated, turned and waved, then went on. Tony looked at his watch. It was 2 pm. He decided to go to his hotel and get everything arranged for the dinner, reservations, taxi, etc.

At six, Tony knocked on the door of room 1204 of the Palace Hotel. Shirley opened it. She looked gorgeous. Tony looked sharp, too, in his Navy dress blues. "Dottie, this is Tony Michaivelli, and Tony, this is my friend Doris Boyd. She wanted to meet you, to see what the Navy is putting out these days," said Shirley. "I'm glad to meet you, Miss. I'll try not to embarrass the Navy in your estimation." "Just take good care of Shirley. You both look super. Go have a good time," said Doris. Tony and Shirley left.

Tony and Shirley went to dinner and the floor show at the Reef Tower Hotel. It was both delicious and elegant. They were presented with leis of aromatic Hawaiian flowers. After they finished eating, the orchestra came back to play for dancing. Their first number was "The Molokai Waltz". "I suppose I ought to ask if you'd like to dance, but I'm not very good at it," said Tony. "I know a few of the basic steps of the fox-trot and the waltz. They are playing a waltz now. Come on, let's try it." She got up and held out her hand. "OK. I hope I don't disgrace the Navy doing this." Both soon got into the rhythm and flow of the dance, since both were better at it than they had indicated. As a result, they had a great time dancing to the beautiful Hawaiian music for an hour or so. Later, the band took a break, and they decided to leave. Tony paid the check, and they strolled the shops for awhile. "Tony, I should get back to my room. I don't want Dottie to worry about me." "Sure. Whatever you say. I've had a great time, all because of a little rain squall and a telephone booth." "Isn't that amazing! I've had a good time, too," said Shirley, laughing. Tony hailed a taxi, and they were taken to Shirley's hotel. "It's still early, Tony. Want to come up and say goodnight to Dottie?" "Sure. I'd like to see her again," he said. They took the elevator up to the 12th floor. Shirley -opening the door to room 1204 - "Dot. we're back." There was no answer. Then she saw a note on the door of the refrigerator: "I'll be back at twelve, Dot."

"Tony, it's only 10:30. Let's sit down awhile. I'd like to hear something about Chicago. I've never been there. I've lived all my life in California," suggested Shirley. "OK. I'd like to hear what you've been doing in San Francisco. I might even end up there after my discharge." Shirley turned on more lights, found some music on the radio, and they settled down on the sofa. They talked of Chicago, San Francisco, about each other's families, etc. Both loved music and the theater. Later, there was the sound of a key turning in the door, and Doris came in. "How time flies! It must be 12:00 o'clock. I didn't realize it was so late," said Shirley. "It's only 11:30," said Doris. "I've been to a movie. How did you kids do?" "We had a great time. At least, I did," said Tony. "I did, too. Even got some practice in dancing. Tony's very good," said Shirley. "Well, don't let me interrupt what you were doing. I've got to go downstairs and get some stamps and cards. I need to remember a few friends. I'll bring up something to eat if you two are hungry," offered Doris. "I think I'd better get on over to my ship," said Tony. "It's been good to meet you, I hope you enjoy your year in the Philippines. So, bye, Tony," said Doris. They shook hands and Doris left the room. "It's been so much fun, I hate to see you go, Tony," said Shirley. "Shirley, I'm so glad I met you, I wish we had another week.. We could check out all these islands together. ...Can you give me your home address? I'll let you know that I got there." "I'd like to hear how you're doing...If you'd like to be a pen-pal." "I'd love that," he said. They exchanged addresses. Tony got his hat and Shirley went to the door with him. It was an anxious moment for both. "Shirley, I'm going to miss you a lot. So, good-bye. I hope to see you again." "I'll miss you, too, Tony. I'll be anxious to hear from you." At the door, they leaned toward each other for a moment. Tony turned to go, but then he quickly turned back, took her in his arms and kissed her. She responded warmly. He left and she closed the door.

The next day his ship, the USS Fargo, left for the other side of the Pacific. The following day Shirley and Doris returned to San Francisco.

CHAPTER TWO

FAST FORWARD ONE YEAR...

SUMMER OF 1949. The USS Ticonderoga had just arrived at Treasure Island from Japan and the Philippines with returning troops. Tony Michaivelli was among the crowd of troops as they streamed off the big aircraft carrier. It had been a year since his memorable date with Shirley. As he started to use the only phone available in the Reception Center to call her, an Air Force Major also stepped up to use it.

"Excuse me," he said. "Could I make a quick call before you dial? It'll only take a second." "Sure, go ahead," said Tony as he stepped back. The officer had a little difficulty getting his connection, but was finished in about four minutes. "Thank you," said the officer as he left. Tony got on the phone and dialed Shirley's number in San Francisco. "Hello," answered a voice. "Is Shirley there?" asked Tony. "No. She just left a minute ago. Wait. I'll see if I can catch her," (a two minute wait) - "No. I'm sorry. You just missed her by a couple of minutes. I'm the maid." "Do you know when she'll be back?" asked Tony. "No. I don't know when she'll be back," she said. Tony was just back from his one year tour of duty in the Philippines. He had wanted to surprise Shirley. He'd have to call again later.

He went into the Reception Center coffee shop, got some coffee, and sat down to decide what to do Next he felt a tap on his shoulder. Looking up, he recognized his high school friend, Harry Blaise. "Tony, you rascal. Imagine seeing you here. Did you just get in?" "Yes, I just got off the Ticonderoga." "You did? I just stepped off it, myself," said Harry. "Where were you bunked?" "Our group was on the 3rd deck. Where were you?" asked Tony. "I was in a cabin on the 2nd deck. Where are you going from here? Anyone meeting you?" "No. No one knew I was coming in today. I'll put up at a hotel and call someone tomorrow," said Tony. "Tony, why don't you go home with me for tonight. Hotels are jammed, as you would expect, with 4000 service people coming in on the "Ti." My family hasn't seen you since our high school days in Chicago. How about it?" "Well, OK. That would be nice. I haven't seen any of you since your folks moved to California in 1944. But I'll need to call my girlfriend, Shirley, soon." "You can call her from our house in the City. These phones are all in use here now." "OK. Let's get our gear. I'll pay for a taxi," said Tony. "We won't need a taxi. Wilson, our chauffeur, should be here by now. I called as soon as we got in." "A chauffeur? Wow! Your family must be doing well." "Dad has hit it lucky on the stock market lately, and has done well on his other investments. I live at home, when I'm home, and work for him," explained Harry. "You're still single, are you?" asked Tony. "Nobody'll have me." "I don't believe that. I remember the girls were all crazy about you, our football quarterback. I didn't rate a ripple," said Tony. "You and I are only 22. What's the hurry?" Quipped Harry. Wilson, the chauffeur found them, and they were soon on their way to Harry's house, after getting their gear.

John Blaise, his wife, Florence, and daughter, Christine lived in a large 2-story house on Green St., near Telegraph Hill. Florence welcomed them at the door. She hadn't seen Harry for a year - his duty in Japan - and was especially happy to see her only son. Florence remembered Tony from the high school days, when he and Harry were good friends. The two boys were almost opposites. Tony was a quiet, calm boy who studied hard and got good grades. Harry, an extrovert, didn't seem to have to study much at all, but made passing grades. He was liked by everyone, including the teachers, and was president of his senior class. "Tony, what a fine looking man you turned out to be! You're in the Navy and Harry's in the Air Force. What a coincidence that you two meet again after high school, and of all places, at Treasure Island," exclaimed Florence. "Things like that happen to me. I'm just a very lucky guy," said Harry. "It's great to get back and see old friends like Harry and you folks," said Tony. Christina -Cissy- had been standing nearby. Tony - noticing her - "Cissy, I almost didn't recognize you. You're a very pretty young lady now. Are you still in high school?" "No. I've graduated. I'm waiting to hear from my application to enter Mills College in Oakland. I'm glad to see you again, Tony....I've got to go to my room. I have to make a phone call." Cissy left the room. "Tony, you may remember that Cissy has always been quiet, a bit of a loner. In grade school, some of the bigger kids used to tease her about having a big nose. Her nose is like her Dad's, a bit large for a girl," explained Florence. "A lot of women have large noses; I think when she gets in college and with a new crowd, she'll forget it," put in Harry. "Ed, who has a big nose, says it's an advantage; that she should forget it," said Florence. "I promised her that I'd take her to see a surgeon next year to find out what they can do about it if she still wants to," said Florence. I remember getting teased at that age, because I always carried a lot of books home. I was considered the class 'gnome'," admitted Tony. .We'll do whatever needs to be done. We don't want it to be a problem that will ruin Cissy's personality," said Florence. Tony -after a couple minutes - "I need to make a call to a girlfriend here in San Francisco, if you will let me use your phone." "That's no problem," said Florence. "Harry, take him to the phone in the office. It's more private." Harry took him to the office phone. Tony dialed Shirley's number. There was no answer. "She's not home yet. I'll have to try again later." Harry, - who had stood by to be sure he made a connection - "You can give her another try after dinner." Dinner was finished about 7:30, and Tony tried Shirley's number again. Still no answer, and no answering service. He tried again at 9:00 and 10:30 PM. "You sure she's still your girlfriend?" asked Harry. "Well, she didn't know I was coming in today. I'll give her another call in the morning, before I have to report for discharge at the Navy office on lower Market Street. I have 24 hours to do that." They had a pleasant evening together, including Cissy, and Ed, who came in late from some business in L.A. About 7:45 the next morning, Tony tried Shirley's number. Again there was no answer. It was frustrating. He left the Blaise's and registered at the Ambassador Hotel, just off Market Street. He then reported to the Navy office for discharge. It took all day. At 7 pm he tried Shirley's number again. This time she answered. "Hello," answered Shirley. "Shirley, this is your Pal from the Wild Blue Yonder." "Is this you, Phil? You sound different from last night," she answered. "No. This is Tony. Don't you remember me, the phone booth guy in Hawaii?" "Oh, Tony! Is it you? Are you calling from the Philippines?" "No. I'm here in San Francisco. I've been trying to reach you on the phone for two days." " Well, I've been here; either the apartment or the office. I can't imagine why you missed me. I did go out to a dinner last night....You've been here two days? I've been looking forward to you coming back. You should have let me know." Tony, feeling rebuked, -in spite of his efforts to contact her- "I wanted to surprise you. Who is this Phil guy you have? I'm sorry if I'm interfering in something that's none of my business." "Tony, he's just a casual friend. It's nothing serious." "Well, casual friend or not, do you want to see me?" "Yes, I do. But you seem angry, Tony. I didn't do anything wrong. When can we get together?" "Can you meet me in the lobby of the Hilton Hotel at 9:00 pm? I'm not quite finished here, but I can be there by that time," suggested Tony. "Alright. I'll see you at 9 o'clock," she agreed. They hung up.

Shirley was waiting in the lobby of the hotel when Tony arrived. After a hug and a hesitant kiss, they went into the "restaurant and were seated. "Have you had dinner?" asked Tony. "No. I knew you wouldn't have had time to eat, so I decided I'd wait for you." "Good. . ...Shirley, I'm just thrilled to death to be here with you. It's been a long year." "I'm thrilled, too," said Shirley. "I want to assure you that I haven't been running wild while you were gone. I can't just sit home for a year, so I've had a few dates while you were gone." (She didn't tell him that she had one with Phil on Friday.) "Did you date any of the natives while you were over there?" " Ha! We were kept pretty close to the base. Besides, the way they dress, I couldn't tell the girls from the boys," said Tony. "What are your plans, now that you are out of the Navy? Where are you staying?" she asked. "I'm at the Ambassador Hotel for the present. I'll be getting a job somewhere, preferably in San Francisco, with a company where I can advance. I like to work hard. What are your plans?" "I haven't thought about it much," said Shirley. "I have a good job at the Chamber of Commerce. I suppose I'll advance there in the future." "Shirley, I'm sorry that I screwed things up by trying to be dramatic and surprising you." "Oh, that's alright. It was just an odd incidence. If I had left my apartment five minutes later, the mix-up wouldn't have happened." "How is your friend Doris?" he asked. "She's fine. We play tennis together almost every week." And so it went. They seemed to have put the "surprise" thing behind them. They had been corresponding regularly, and were "up" on most events that each had encountered. (At least they thought so.) They enjoyed a good dinner, and since it was late, Shirley suggested that she should get home, as she had to work the next day. Tony hailed a cab that took them to her apartment. At the door: "Thank you, Tony, for the delicious dinner. I'm so glad you're here now." "When can I see you again? ...How about dinner again on Friday night?" -a moment's hesitation- "Friday night? ... Alright, I think I can make it," she said. "OK. I'll make the reservations for eight o'clock, and I'll pick you up at 7:45," said Tony. "I'll be ready," she promised. A genuine kiss, and Tony left. Shirley's date with Phil for Friday night was only tentative. She would just call him and beg off. Thursday night, Shirley dialed Phil's number, to inform him that she couldn't make the date on Friday night. She got an answering service that informed her that he was out of town. She left a message canceling their Friday night date. Shirley worked in the office of the San Francisco Chamber of Commerce. Phil Piker was a liaison officer there with an office on the floor above. He was an attractive young man, and was liked by everyone, including the CEOs whose offices were on the same floor. Phil was the coffee shop "flirt, kidder, prankster." It was through his influence with Mr. Booker, that helped Shirley advance to a better job and an increase in salary. She had just recently had a couple of dates with him, and had promised one with him for Friday night, the same night as with Tony. Since he was out of town and she had left a message of cancellation, she was confident there would be no problem. She didn't want to alienate Phil, after he had helped her advance in her job. Friday evening at 7:45, as Tony rang the bell at Shirley's upstairs apartment, a well dressed man appeared with a bouquet of flowers. "Hi, I'm Phil. Did you just ring Miss Rose's apartment?" "Yes, I did," answered Tony. "Are you delivering those flowers to her?" "I'm not a deliveryman. I'm a friend of Shirley's. You must be the Tony Something I've heard her mention." Tony, - a bit irritated - "Yes, I am. It's Michaivelli. I have a date with her at 8 pm, and it's that time now. I can take those up for you." Phil - realizing there was a mix-up somewhere about the date, agreed. "OK. Be sure to tell her they're from me." He took out his card and dropped it among the flowers, and left. Tony was admitted and greeted by Shirley. "Oh, Tony! You sweet guy! You brought me some flowers. Red roses are my favorite! Thank you." After the demonstration of happy appreciation by Shirley, Tony struggled to keep from mentioning Phil, but his honest nature overruled the temptation. "They're not from me, Shirley. Some guy named Phil showed up just as I rang your bell. He said they were for you. I promised to bring them up for him." "Why didn't you let him come up? I'd like you to meet him. He works for the Chamber of Commerce, too, but not in my department." "I didn't think of it," admitted Tony. "He seemed like a nice fellow." "He is. He's our 'Sir Galahad' of our office bunch." "Harmless type, huh? Well, are you ready for a good fish dinner at the Surfer? I've a car downstairs," he said. "Yes, I am. Did you buy a car?" "No. I rented one." Just at that moment the doorbell rang. Shirley pushed the release, and Phil walked in. He had had 2nd thoughts about the situation. After all. He had a date with Shirley, too. Shirley and Tony were dumbfounded. Everyone stood in silence for a moment, then: "I'm here, Shirley. Where would you like to go? Did you get my flowers?" asked Phil, looking at Shirley, then Tony. "There must be a mistake, Phil. I called your answering service and canceled our date. I couldn't reach you. Didn't you get my message?" she asked. She looked anxiously at Tony, who was just watching and wondering what Phil was up to. "I just got in from L.A.; didn't have time to do anything except buy the flowers and rush up here," explained Phil. "I'm sorry if I've cut in on your date," offered Tony. I'll leave and you two can go on and have your dinner." "No! No! Fellows, I'm sorry for the mix-up. It was all my fault. Let's work something out here," urged Shirley. "Why don't we all three go out to dinner together? I'd like to get acquainted better with you, Tony," suggested Phil. Shirley - who had no idea how to solve the mix-up - "That's OK with me. Tony, is that OK with you?" Tony - who was disappointed at the situation, and figured the evening was shot anyway, "Whatever you two say. I'm hungry. Let's go eat somewhere." "We have reservations at the Surfer, "said Shirley. "If we leave now, we'll make it; maybe just a bit late. Tony has a car downstairs. Let's go!" They got in Tony's car, Tony driving. Phil opened the rear door for Shirley, then got in beside her. Tony felt like a taxi driver. His dissatisfaction was rising.

They were a little late for the reservation, but Phil managed to get them seated right away. A waiter came to take their order. They examined the liquor menu. "What would you like to drink?" asked the waiter, as he looked from one to the other. "I'll take a "Pink Lady." That sounds mild," said Shirley. "I'll take a tall coke, you guys drink what you want. I'll be the driver" said Tony. "I'll take a vodka a la due," said Phil. "Loosen up, Tony, let's make this a 'Night To Remember'." "I love cokes. They were hard to get in the Philippines." "What's the 'a la due' part of your drink, Phil?" asked Shirley. "I have no idea. Just a fancy ending, I suppose," said Phil. They started sipping their drinks. Then their food came.

After a bit Shirley excused herself to go to the restroom. (Phil switched drinks with her. Tony didn't notice.) When she came back, she didn't notice either. After a bit, the usually quiet Shirley became very talkative. "Phil, are you sure this 'Pink Lady' doesn't have much alcohol in it?" "I don't know. I'm not a bartender." They were almost finished eating. Shirley finished her 'supposed' Pink Lady. The waiter brought their check. Shirley -"Boy! Oh Boy! Do I feel great!" She stood up. "Yee-Ooow! Hello, everybody! God Bless The U.S.A!" Phil got up from his chair to quiet her down. Both fell backwards with a crash and scream, as both chairs and the table were upset. In the confusion, the security staff came running. They rushed them out the door into the lobby. There they demanded payment of the bill of $64.00. Phil -who was getting wacky himself, as he had had several refills before he switched with Shirley-protested: "We haven't finished our dinner or dessert. We're not payin' yet!" "Come on, Phil. Fork over $32 dollars and let's get out of here," urged Tony. "Over my dead body!" he said as he struggled to go back in. Shirley was silent. She was unsteady on her feet and clinging to Tony's arm, to keep from falling. Suddenly, three policemen came through the front door, arrested them, and took them off to jail. There, they were lectured and paid a $25 dollar fine. Since they were now all nearly sober, they were sent in a taxi back to Shirley's apartment.

Phil and Tony argued over who should pay the $30 dollar taxi fare. "Get in. I'll take you guys home," urged the driver. "Drop me off at the Surfer Restaurant so I can pick up my car," pleaded Tony. Instead the driver took them back to jail, where the police sergeant made them pay the driver $15 each. They then paid him $10 to take them back to the restaurant for Tony to retrieve his car. Tony took Phil home. Shirley was glad to be alone again, and was soon snoozin' in bed. Monday, at the office, Phil caught Shirley in the coffee shop. "Sweetie, what happened to you on Friday night?" "I don't want to talk about it. You are in the 'dog-house' with me. Let's talk about something else." They tried to forget the "fiasco" at the Surfer Restaurant and later apologized to each other. It was a "Night to Forget" instead of a "Night to Remember". Shirley stayed friendly with Phil, but she didn't go on any more dates with him. She and Tony continued to date each week. Tony next turned his attention to finding a job. He enlisted the aid of an employment agency, suggested by Harry, and was sent to the San Francisco Port Authority.

At The Port Authority, Mr. Gibson, a Vice President, looking at a note he scribbled as he put down the phone, said, "Good morning.... You're Anthony Mich-i-vichi? Is that the way you pronounce it?" "Michiavelli. Just call me Tony, Sir." "Mr. Harry Blaise said you're just out of the Navy, and a very smart and capable person," "I'll do my best, Sir. I did this sort of work for the Navy in the Philippines." said Tony. "We are glad to have you, Tony. You're just the man we're looking for. So, if you'll come in tomorrow at eight o'clock we'll get you set up," said Mr. Gibson. Tony started work the next morning as a clerk in Section "A" of the San Francisco Port Authority.

THREE MONTHS LATER: Tony and Shirley were at the top of the tower on Telegraph Hill. It was a beautiful Sunday afternoon. A gentle breeze brought scattered white clouds drifting eastward against a bright blue sky. A few tourists were enjoying the view of San Francisco Bay and Alcatraz Island. A big ship was just coming in under the Golden Gate bridge. Tony -taking her hand and turning her to face him- "Shirley, somehow this setting reminds me of a little telephone booth in Hawaii. I'm thrilled to be here with you!. I don't want it to ever end. You're the one I want to spend my life with. Will you marry me? Please!" "Yes! Yes!" she answered. "I've been hoping you'd ask me." "I feel the same way about you!" She grabbed him in an emotional kiss and embrace. "You're wonderful, Sweetheart!" when he could get his breath. "Oh, I'm so excited!" exclaimed Shirley. "God bless that little telephone booth!" "When can we have the ceremony?" he asked. "Real soon I hope." "I agree," she replied. Let's go someplace and plan it." So they found a little restaurant down near Fisherman's Wharf and excitedly planned their wedding. Three weeks later, out at the end of Golden Gate Park, on the veranda of the Surfside Restaurant overlooking the Pacific ocean, Tony and Shirley were married. Dr. Everly, pastor of the church where Shirley attended, officiated. Harry Blaise was best man and Doris Boyd was the Bride's Maid. Other attendants were Ed, Florence and Christine Blaise, Mrs. Everly and three of Shirley's girlfriends from her church and office.

It was the end of another beautiful day. The sun slowly setting behind a tall white fog that would soon blanket the area.

After the ceremony, they all went inside for a fabulous fish dinner. It happened that Harry was seated next to Doris. They seemed to enjoy their conversations together. After the dinner and the breakup of the party, Tony and Shirley spent the night at the Hilton Hotel downtown. Next day the newly-weds went apartment hunting. They found a neat efficiency, out near the ocean on 42nd Street, and spent the rest of the day moving in. Two "HAPPY BIRDS" in a new exciting nest!

SIX MONTHS PASS: Tony and Shirley were happy in their little efficiency apartment. Soon there was a rumor that there was to be a vacancy in Section "A". Tony had been working for the Port Authority for 9 months. The vacancy was for the Assistant Manager of Sec. "A". Tony knew the duties. He was well liked and most expected him to get the job. But it didn't turn out that way. Tom Jones, whose father was a friend of Mr. Gibson, the Vice-President, was given the job. Tom Jones was from Section "B", and had been with the company about 6 months. Tony became suspicious that his name, Michaivelli, had been a factor in the selection. "Don't let it worry you so much, Tony. You've only been there 9 months. Just be patient. You'll get promoted soon, I'm sure," said Shirley. "You're probably right, but opportunities don't come up very often, I'm afraid." "I know you are, you are good at anything you do. I'm in your corner, Sweetheart," she said. "Thank you, Dear." Mr. Wilson, our 1st floor boss, assured me that I'd get the next promotion." They went to dinner at Dombey's. Phil was still around. He still liked to talk and joke with Shirley when they met at the coffee bar. "Shirley, just because you're married now doesn't mean we can't still be friends." "I know that, Phil. We're still friends." Later, when they left the bar: "Say 'Hello' to Tony for me, Shirley." "I will," she promised.

Four months went by and Charles Gray, Manager of Sec. "A" resigned to take a job in Long Beach. Tom Jones was promoted from Asst. Mgr. to Manager of Sec. "A". Tony, who was expecting to move up to Asst. Mgr., was asked by Mr. Wilson to fill in until the new Asst. Mgr. was decided on by the head office. A week later it was announced. Not Tony, as Mr. Wilson had recommended, but Fred Williams, a man from the Sacramento office. Williams' Dad, was a fraternity brother of the Vice-President of the San Francisco office. Tony was both surprised and angered. He complained to Mr. Wilson. "Mr. Wilson, you promised me I'd get the next promotion in this department. How come it's Fred Williams?" "Tony, I recommended you. Mr. Gibson just chose someone else. My influence only goes so far. Evidently, influence and POLITICS were in play, too. I'm sorry, Tony. We'll just have to wait for another opportunity." "I'm really disappointed, Mr. Wilson. I suppose I'll be the one to teach him what his duties are and how to do them." "I'll be out of town next week. I'll ask Tom Jones to give you a hand on that," promised Mr. Wilson.

Tony went home very discouraged. He didn't see any possibility of another vacancy in the near future in Section "A" or Sec. "B". He wondered if he was just in the wrong business. Shirley didn't seem to be bothered with his pass-over the first time. "I'm glad you're home. There's a good story on the radio tonight, 'The Happy Hoofer'. You mentioned you wanted to listen to that," said Shirley. "I don't want to listen to anything happy tonight. You remember, I was promised the Asst. Mgr. job, the one I'm filling right now? Well, I just got the shaft again. Some guy named Fred Williams from Sacramento got the job." "Is there a Port Authority at Sacramento?" she asked. "No. He's the son of one of the "Big Shots" in the office upstairs. He's just graduated from Georgia Tech, with a major in Business Management." "I suppose he learned all about this business there."

"I suppose he did," admitted Tony. "I'm sorry about the pass-over. But, Tony, don't let it ruin your life. You served in the Navy and have had two years in college. With your GI benefits you can finish some day if you want. In the meantime, we can get along fine on our two salaries.

All I want is a happy home with you, and maybe later a couple of darling kids."

"You Sweetheart! I wish I didn't bother you with my problems at the office. Do you really want two kids?" "Of course. Isn't that what marriage is all about?" "You are right, Dear," agreed Tony, as a smile replaced the worried look on his face. "What bothers me is that I work hard to prepare myself for a better job, only to have someone take it away from me because they have influence with the powers at the top. It's a snub to me, and very embarrassing." "Tony, that's the way the world is. In some places it's 'dog eat dog'. What was it that your 16th century ancestor warned about?"

"It was Niccolo Machiavelli in old Italy. He said: 'A man who should profess to be honest in all his dealings, would necessarily come to ruin among so many that are dishonest. Hence, it behooves every Prince desirous of maintaining his power to learn how to be dishonest, and to make use of, or not, of this knowledge according to circumstances," quoted Tony. "I don't get how that fits in your case. You're not dishonest." I try not to be," said Tony. "He was talking about Princes or Kings. Today, the game is 'politics', but it's not dishonest, necessarily. It's practiced by some to get ahead, as I've just witnessed." "It seems unfair," said Shirley. I think if Niccolo was living today, he would say 'If all your competitors are playing Politics, you'll have to do the same if you plan to succeed." "I suppose you'll have to learn to do it, too," she said. "That's just against my very nature. I don't think I could do it. How would I start? I've always thought that hard work was the key! I hate to think it's who you know!" "It looks like you are in a bad situation," said Shirley. "My Dad always told me: 'If you're in a bad situation, make the best of it and press on. It's the future that counts now'. I'll have to try to do that," admitted Tony. "That's a smart conclusion....What would you like for dinner? I'm dressed. How about going down to Dombey's?" she asked. "It's been a rough day and I've got a headache. I'd rather just have a hot chocolate and go to bed. Can you order something from Dombey's for yourself? They deliver." "I'll walk down there. It's only two blocks," she said. "OK. Be sure to take your key. I may be asleep when you get back." He gave her a hug and kiss and she left. Tony drank his chocolate, went to bed and was soon asleep.

At Dombey's, Shirley was about half through eating a Caesar's salad, when a man suddenly sat down opposite her. It was Phil. "Shirley, I'm surprised to see you here. Where is Tony?" "He's at the apartment. He had a headache and went to bed. How come you're in this neighborhood?" "I was on my way to the theater in the next block. Chinese Acrobats.

Have you ever seen them? It's a fantastic show." "No, I haven't. I've heard they're good," said Shirley. Why don't you go with me? If Tony's asleep, he'd never know," urged Phil. "He's expecting me back soon. He'd be sure to wake up if I came dragging in at 11:30." "Just tell him that you wanted to see the show. You wouldn't have to mention me," suggested Phil. "No, Phil. Tony knows you're a friend. I love Tony. I don't think he would approve." "Well, OK, Sweetheart. Some other time? I'll go." Phil was disappointed but he had lots of patience. He got up and left. There would always be "next" time. Shirley finished and went back to the apartment. Tony was sound asleep and didn't notice when she came to bed. Next day, Phil found Shirley at the coffee bar. "Did Tony wake up when you got home last night?" he asked. "No. He was sound asleep," said Shirley. "See! You should have gone with me. You're my kind of girl, Shirley. We can still find time to have fun together," said Phil. He gave her a friendly squeeze.

It was just 3 months later that a big reorganization occurred at the San Francisco office. The Port Authority at Oakland had been enlarged. Shipping across the Pacific of war supplies had declined. As a result, several jobs in San Francisco were eliminated. Tony's job was one of them. Mr. Wilson retired. Tony was demoted to a lower job with a pay cut. Since Tom Jones was in Hawaii and wouldn't be back for two weeks, Tony was asked to take on part of the Manager's duties until Tom came back. Fred Williams would take on the public relations duties of the Manager's office for the two weeks. It was a big load for Tony, but by working a bit of overtime he did it. On the Monday, when Tom Jones came back, Tony was moving his things to the floor below and a smaller desk. Joe Acosta, a fellow employee, was helping him. "This desk is too small. I need my big one," he complained. "Your job don't rate a big desk. Mine's small, too. See?" said Joe. He pointed to his own desk nearby. "I'm disgusted. I thought I was going up in this company. Instead, I'm going down. I've studied hard to learn all the jobs in this department. It was my dream to someday be the head of the company." "You're day-dreaming, Tony. Forget it. You either have to be born rich, or know the right people, or the powers-that-be will never notice you." Tony stared at Joe. "I don't believe that!" (He was taught in High School and Junior College, that superior knowledge, and hard work were the keys to success.) Tony went upstairs to protest to Tom Jones. "Tom, why can't I do my job from my old desk here? I need a large one like the one I had. That dinky one you're assigning me; with my long arms, there's no room for the work I have to do." Tony, your old job was eliminated. Your bigger desk was needed in the office above. That's all I know." "Well, I'm not being treated right by this company. I don't blame you, Tom, but I'm getting fed up with the treatment by the people upstairs." He pounded on the desk for emphasis. Mr. Grant, the successor to Mr. Wilson, had just walked up as Tony pounded on the desk and started walking away. Mr. Grant -to Tom Jones- "Is that 'Wop' complaining about his job downstairs again?" "It's Michaivelli, Sir," said Tom. Tony, who was still close enough to hear the reference to him being a "Wop", came back and addressed Mr. Grant. "Sir, I heard you calling me a 'Wop'. It's a demeaning term and I resent it," "Oh, you do?" shot back Mr. Grant. "I'll call you what you are. You'd better get back to your job or you wont have one." Tony was shocked and more angry. "Mr. Grant, I can see that I have no future here, working under you. I therefore resign!" announced Tony. "Tony, don't leave. I need you," pleaded Tom. "I'll get you another man, Tom. As for you, Mr. Shus-a-bitchi, you're through. You're fired!" responded Mr. Grant.

Without another word, Tony gathered up his possessions, bid good-bye to Tom, Fred, Joe and several others, and 1eft the building. When he got home, Shirley was still at work. He sat down and tried to decide what to do next. He thought over the way things had gone at the office since he had been hired. Time after time "outsiders" had been brought in to take the promotions that he was entitled to. The more he thought about it, the angrier he got. And to top it off, he had been publicly called a "Wop". About 6 o'clock Shirley came home. She could see that he was upset. "You beat me home. Have you been here long?" she asked. "I've been here all afternoon. I don't work there anymore. They put me down in the basement with a dinky desk. Besides that, they insulted me!" "Well, I've told you before, you have to have patience." "Patience! Patience! Do you expect me to have 50 years of patience?" answered Tony, angrily. "You don't need to shout. I'm not deaf!" "You are deaf to the problems I have been having down there. I get no real sympathy from you. Just - wait, and have patience!" "What do you want me to do? Go down there and fight your battles for you? I've had a rough day myself. I didn't come home to fight all night with you. I'd be better off going someplace else and find someone to talk sense with," exclaimed Shirley. "You would run out on me when I need you the most! I got along OK before I met you," countered Tony. Shirley was fuming. She had had enough. She went to the bedroom, threw some clothes into a suit bag and a briefcase, and stormed out the door, screaming: "I HATE YOU, TONY!" - taken by surprise - "Shirley, I'm sorry! Don't go! I love you!" But she was gone! Tony dropped to his knees and put his hands to his face.

Tony waited for her to come back, or call. She didn't that day, or the next morning by 11 O'clock, when he went out for breakfast. He was back by Noon. When she had not called by 9 PM on Tuesday, Tony went out again for a bite to eat and a drink at at a nearby bar. A couple of the girls there tried to engage him in conversation, but Tony was in no mood for them. He went back to the apartment. Tony's love soon turned to resentment, because she wouldn't listen, and had left him. At midnight he went to bed, but couldn't sleep until about 4 am (Wednesday). Meanwhile, Shirley, with tears streaming down her face, had walked to the corner with her bags. She expected Tony to call her, or to come after her. A taxi slowed, but she waved him on. She looked back at the apartment. A bus stopped at the corner to let a rider off. The driver waited for her to get on. She stepped away, and he closed the door and drove away. She was at a loss what to do. She had left in utter frustration. It had been a reflex, or emotional action. . . . But now, what should she do? "Evidently he didn't care that she had left, or he would have come after her. Maybe he was glad that she was gone. It would be embarrassing to go back if he didn't want her. Another taxi stopped. "Taxi, Lady?" He waited. "Come on, Lady. I've got to go." With a last look at the apartment, she got in.

"Where to, Lady?" he asked. "I ah... can you drive me to the YWCA?" "Sure can, Lady," he said. In a few minutes he let her out at the YWCA and carried her bags in for her. She paid him and he left. She approached the reception desk. "I'm not a member, but do you have a room I can have for tonight? I'm just caught without a place to stay for tonight." "Do you live in San Francisco?" "Yes. I just can't go home tonight." The attendant - assuming correctly that there was a domestic problem - "Yes, we can give you a room. You haven't broken a law, or anything like that, have you?" "Only my heart." said Shirley, tears coming into her pretty eyes. "Here's your key. Room 612," said the attendant, noting Shirley's emotional distress. "Now don't you go up there and torture yourself by crying all night."

"Come back here and we'll talk. It gets dull here late at night." "Thank you," said Shirley, taking the key. She went up to room 612, closed and locked the door and sank into a chair. Shirley was shocked, and felt terrible at the blowup of her marriage. She didn't know what to do next. Tony had been getting increasingly angry and dissatisfied with his treatment at his job the last few months. She couldn't seem to help him. In fact, he seemed to take her efforts to help him as criticism, like it was all his fault. They weren't happy together anymore.

Shirley got to bed about 3 am. She awoke at 9 am, when the maid came to clean the room. She quickly took a shower and went downstairs for coffee and a breakfast roll. She felt better than last night. She realized that most couples had problems, and most were able to work them out. She also felt that both She and Tony had acted irrationally and under pressure. She called the apartment at 11:30 am. There was no answer. She decided to stay at the "Y" and call again later. He was probably at work. At 9:30 pm, she called again. Still no answer. It worried her. She called the next morning 10:30. When she called again at 6 pm, the phone had been disconnected. Shirley was shocked! She didn't know what to do. "It suddenly dawned on her that her marriage may be over. Then she remembered that Tony had said that he had quit his job. It was a jolt! She was now on her own! She needed help. The YWCA office, on hearing her story, decided to let her stay on there. Shirley decided she needed to call Doris.

Shirley dialed Doris's number. "Hello?" "Doris, this is Shirley. I've got an awful problem. I don't know what to do." Doris noted the very serious tone of voice, when Shirley called her Doris instead of "Dot" or "Dottie". She set her coffee cup down and turned down the radio. "You sound scared. Are you OK? Where are you?" asked Doris. "I'm at the YWCA. I spent the night here." "Why the YWCA? Did you have a fire? Where's Tony? What happened?" "Oh, Doris. It's awful! I hate to say it. Tony and I had a big fuss, and I left the apartment. He's disconnected the phone. I don't know what to do" "Shirley, you're too upset right now. Tony is probably the same. It's going to take a few days for both of you to settle down; in the meantime, don't neglect your job at the Chamber of Commerce. It'll help pass the time. I'm sure you and Tony will work it out and be back together soon. You do want to, don't you?" "Yes. But he has been so angry lately about his job." "I'll come down to the YWCA. We'll go out to lunch and you can tell me all about it. OK?" "I'd appreciate it, Dottie. I can't think straight right now," said Shirley. They hung up and soon Doris arrived and they went to lunch. They talked about what Shirley could do until things got worked out with Tony.

MEANWHILE: On Wednesday morning, and no word from Shirley, Tony decided that she wasn't coming back. It would be too upsetting to stay in the apartment, besides being too expensive since he was now out of a job. The rent was paid for the rest of the month, but he called and had the phone and utilities cut off. Then he went and managed to rent a room at the YMCA. Giving up the apartment cast a feeling of frustration and anger over him. Why did this all have to happen to him? He felt like he was an unfair victim. He decided that, maybe a drink at the bar around the corner would help. Slim, the bartender there, had been friendly. He might understand. At least he had heard plenty of "problems" from customers. He needed to talk to somebody. So he went to the bar called, "The Office", where Slim worked. The bar was busy and Slim didn't have his usual help, but he greeted Tony as he came in. "Hello, Tony. Haven't seen you for awhile. How's the world treating you?" "Lousy, just lousy! Give me something with a little zip in it, Slim. I just quit my job and my wife just left me. I'm just about to explode, I'm so mad." "You need something stronger alright, but don't explode in here." Slim mixed him a drink and turned to wait on other customers. Tony sat quietly sipping his drink until it was gone. "Slim, give me a refill. That wasn't enough." Slim gave him a refill, and eyed him carefully. "You hold your liquor like an old-timer," he said. "Makes me feel real good, like I'm floatin' on high." Tony sat quietly sipping until it was gone again. "Slim, give me another. I'm not goin' anywhere." "Ok, but this is the last liquor; cokes from now on," warned Slim. Tony drank about half the glass, then without warning, he threw the glass of liquor against the huge mirror back of the bar, scattering and breaking about a dozen bottles, luckily not breaking the mirror. It was a mess. "To hell with everybody!" he screamed, as he raised a fist. Hearing the scream, Bronco, the bouncer, grabbed him and escorted him out into the lobby. "Don't you ever come back here again, you S.O.B.!" yelled Slim, as he surveyed the damage to his prized liquor supply. Soon, two policemen appeared in a squad car, and took Tony to jail.

Next morning, he paid a $50.00 fine for "disturbing the peace", and was released. Tony felt awful, but decided to drop by the Port Authority office to collect any final salary due him. When he started to enter the building, the guard stopped him. "See your pass, please?" "I gave it up when I resigned," said Tony. "I just want to check on the pay that I'm due." "I'm not supposed to let you in without your badge or pass, but I remember you. Don't stay long." "Thank you," said Tony. He went up to the pay office. The pay office was busy, but the pay officer recognized him. "Get out of here, Mich-i-votti! How come the guard let you in? I don't have time to figure what's coming to you today. You don't work here anymore. I'll send you your money, if you're due any, to your home address." Tony didn't feel like arguing. He left and went back to the apartment. There was no evidence that Shirley had been there. He didn't remember much of what had happened last night, but he felt like he owed Slim an apology. He went to "The Office" to do so. He walked in and sat down at the bar. When Slim saw him, it upset him so, he spilled a drink that he had mixed, on to the bar, splashing it on a customer. "Get out of here, Mick-i-vicci! Bronco, get him out of here!"

Tony was promptly hustled out. He was surprised and hurt. Why was all this happening to him? He sat down on the curb to try to decide what to do. Almost immediately, a street sprinkler came by, showering him liberally as it went by. Tony was so downcast, he put his hands to his face and cried. A beggar with a tin cup, sitting on the corner, saw it happen and threw a rock at the retreating sprinkler. "Are you hurt? What's your name? I'm Joey. I haven't seen you around here before. They don't have no respect for us street people. The idiots!"

CHAPTER THREE

Tony was devastated. He was worried. He realized that he had to do something to get himself out of the "tornado" of circumstances that had ruined his happy life with Shirley. He got up and brushed the water off his clothes. He thanked the beggar, split the $40. in his wallet with him, and went to his room in the YMCA. He was so sleepy. He couldn't think straight. He took a shower and went to bed. After a refreshing nap, he called Harry. "Harry, can you come over here? I'm at the 'Y'. I've got a problem I don't know how to solve." "Sure. I'll be glad to help, if I can. Anything serious?" "Yes. I've quit my job, and Shirley's left me," said a weary Tony. "Wow! That's a load! I'll be over, say, at 7 pm, said Harry. "Thank you, Harry. I'll see you at 7." He hung up.

Harry arrived promptly at 7 pm. "This is a nice place. I've never been here before," he said. "It is a nice place. There is a swimming pool in the basement, a gym on the 2nd floor, and a track on the roof," said Tony. "I could dig something like this," mused Harry. "The guys I see here look pretty successful," said Tony. "Well, what's the problem you're having?" asked Harry. "You said you had quit your job, and Shirley had left." Tony recited the details of his job end and the breakup with Shirley. "I'm sorry to hear about the breakup with Shirley. As far as the job's concerned, I don't think you'll have any trouble finding another. And I think that neither you nor Shirley have settled down enough to be rational about it," said Harry. "I know you're right. I was too upset and angry to be rational," admitted Tony. "Is there anything that is the real reason for your problems; any one thing?" asked Harry. "It wasn't Shirley's fault, although she seemed to think I was over reacting. It was the way I was treated at the office. Praised always for my work, but passed over twice on promotions to jobs I could easily handle, and then demoted. I felt like I was not appreciated or respected." "Well, then, don't think about divorce. Give her a chance to think about it. It's only been a few days. You need a little more time, yourself," advised Harry. You're right. I did give up the apartment too soon. But Harry, the real problem was at the office. I worked hard there. I wasn't respected there for anything except my 9 to 5 work." "Hard work is commendable. But to get to the top in business, there is also the ability to interact favorably with others. There is also enthusiasm; it's catching. Interacting; to meet others that will give you a break is important. I learned that, from watching my Dad, "said Harry. "I've never thought of it like that before. But I'm ME. How can I do any better? And my name always stumps people." "Tony, I remember reading -or maybe it was a movie- about Joe E. Brown, the actor, who was also a baseball player and good enough to be called up to the major league's St. Louis Browns. The Browns were in last place in their division when Joe was called up. He was a 'Ball-of-Fire' when he hit the field each game. It soon got all the rest enthused, and they improved their record a lot. I think they won their division."

"Then I just need to reinvent myself. That sounds very intriguing. How would I start?" asked Tony. "You could start by reading Dale Carnegie's book, 'How To Win Friends And Influence People'. You should also join the Junior Professional Speaker's Club. I used to belong to that and can get you in." "Good. I'll do both. I also want to do something about my name." "How about Tony Michaels?" suggested Harry. "I think I want to be an all new person. 'Bill Smith' sounds about right. I don't want Shirley to find out until I've made some progress." "It'll be interesting to see how you do. When are you going to start being 'Bill Smith'?" asked Harry. "I'll think about it for a couple of days and call you." "OK. I'll be expecting your call. Incidentally, do you need any help financially until you get a job?" "No. Shirley and I kept our accounts separate at our bank and I'll be OK for awhile. Thank you." "Can you tell me how to get in touch with Doris, Shirley's friend?" asked Harry. "She works in the downtown office of American Airlines," said Tony. Harry left.

Tony thought over his situation and the things that he and Harry had discussed. He decided that Harry and Niccolo were right. If he was to succeed in business, he would have to learn the other half of how to succeed. Only then could he be the successful husband that a wife deserved. The next day he called and informed Harry of his decision. He also bought the Dale Carnegie book and read it that night. He had a great feeling of excitement and enthusiasm. Why wasn't he taught this in High School? Tony decided the next thing to do was to change his name. He made an appointment with the court clerk for Friday of the following week. On Friday, Tony, a bit uneasy about the consequences of changing his name, sat twiddling his thumbs in the courtroom as he waited his turn with the judge.

When his name was called by the clerk, Tony got up and stood before the judge. It was then that he noticed the nameplate of the judge: Judge Reginald L. Smith. "You're Anthony L. Michaivelli? What a beautiful last name!" said the judge. "You don't like Anthony? What's wrong with it?" "It's not Anthony I want to change, Sir. It's my last name, Michaivelli," said Tony. "Michaivelli? I can't believe you want to give up a nice name like that, "said the judge." Why don't you like it?" "Sir, So many people can't understand it, or spell it. It's a handicap in my business dealings," explained Tony. I've been thinking of changing my name, too Do you know how many 'Smiths' there are in this country? There must be 90,000. It's ridiculous! What's your middle name?" asked the judge. "It's Luther, Sir." "Named after Martin Luther?" "You're lucky. My parents named me after my Grandma. Her name was 'Cleo', short for Cleopatra. My High School friends never let me forget it. What do you want to change your last name to?" Tony -hesitating a little- "Smith, Sir." The judge couldn't believe it. He sat and stared at Tony for a minute. "Don't you know there are too many Smiths already? Are you running away from some crime? Are you a member of a mob?" "I've never committed a crime, Sir. It's strictly a business decision. I like Smith. I think it will work for me." The judge motioned for the clerk to come over, and they held a short private conference. The clerk was amused and tittered, as she glanced over at Tony. She went back to her desk. Tony was uneasy. "The clerk checked you out. You're clear, so, I'll approve the change. Your request is granted," said the Judge. "To tell you the truth, I like Smith, too. My last name used to be -get this- Andropulos. So, congratulations Anthony Luther Smith! Next case?" Tony was relieved. He thanked and shook hands with the judge and the clerk, and left.

Harry had arranged for Tony to be admitted to the local Junior Professional Speakers Club. On Monday following the change of his name, Tony attended his first meeting of the club. He walked in, sat down and looked around. There were about 12 members present. Jeff Montgomery, club president came over and introduced himself, then stood up and called the club to order. "Attention fellows. We have a new member with us, Bill Smith. Come up here, Bill." Bill got up and stood by Jeff. There was a lot of applause. "The floor's yours, Bill. Tell us something." There was more clapping, as Jeff sat down, leaving an uneasy Bill with all eyes on him. What was he supposed to do? They expected him to say something. Bill had never made a speech like this in his life. What should he say?. The silence was scary! A motorcycle roared by, breaking the tension. Thank you, whoever that was! "said Bill ..."I suppose you want to know who I am, and where I came from. First,

I want to express my appreciation to you for my being here. As you can see, I'm not an eloquent speaker, but I hope I'll improve." Bill then gave a thumbnail sketch of his life - leaving out everything since his return from the Philippines. Then he sat down. There was general applause and congratulations. Jeff next took up the day's program, which was to be a three minute extemporary speech by each member, on a subject drawn out of a hat. It was to practice thinking on their feet. Bill was warmly accepted by the club. He tried to put in practice the things highlighted in the Carnegie book. The group met every two weeks, and Bill worked hard to learn. The next thing to do, thought Bill, was to set about finding a job.

He decided to put the lessons learned in the Carnegie book and Joe E. Brown's theory to the test. He selected the Pacific Trade Company's 20 story building on Market Street as his target. His past job experience should fit in with their operations. He found the Personnel Department, and after a short wait, was ushered into the office of Mr. Darrel Carpenter, Director of Personnel. "Good morning," said Mr. Carpenter, looking at Bill's card brought in by his receptionist. "You're Mr. Bill Smith?" "Yes Sir, I am. You're Mr. Carpenter?" "Yes. How'd you know my name?" asked Mr. Carpenter. "I asked the receptionist, Sir." "Why did you select this company to apply for a job?" "I did this kind of work for the Navy in the Philippines, Sir," said Bill. "You can drop the Sir. This is not the Navy. I was in the Navy myself for four years," said Mr. Carpenter. "Were you on shipboard, Sir? Oh, Sorry!" "Yes. The Magpie, a supply ship. ... I'm sorry, Mr. Smith. You seem a very serious and capable person, but we don't have a position that I can put you in today. You might check back in about a month," suggested Mr. Carpenter. "I'm sorry, too, Sir. I'd like to work for this company. Thank you, Mr. Carpenter," said Bill. As Bill was leaving, the receptionist came in to remind Mr. Carpenter, that Mr. Fisher would be by at 12 O'clock, to go to lunch with him. Bill heard her as he left. An idea jumped into his head. He wanted to cause Mr. Carpenter to remember him when a vacancy in his company did come up.

Downstairs, Bill looked around until he found the little closet where the brooms, etc. were stored. He selected a broom and a dust pan, and started sweeping the entrance and the sidewalk area in the front of the building. Soon, Mr. Carpenter and Mr. Fisher came out on their way to their lunch. Mr. Carpenter noticed Bill busily sweeping up the wind-blown debris. "Mr. Smith! What are you doing? You don't need to do that!" "Oh, hello, Mr. Carpenter. ...The wind blows all this stuff off the street and it winds up here. It looks bad. I thought I'd take a minute and clean it up for you. Doesn't that look better?" He waved his hand at the area. Bill started putting the broom and pan away. Mr. Fisher and Mr. Carpenter started on down the street. "who is that guy? What department does he work in?" asked Mr. Fisher. "This entrance does get dirty a lot."

"His name's Smith. He doesn't work here. He was in my office a few minutes ago, looking for a job. Former Navy. Worked in the Philippines. I just don't have room in my department to place him," said Mr. Carpenter. "I like his looks and his attitude," said Mr. Fisher. "I've got a problem in my department with work stacking up. We're behind up there. I could use a good man. Do you think you could work it so that I could get him for my department?" "I remember you're having the problem. Maybe I can squeeze him on the payroll. I think his card is in my waste basket. It's probably still there. If it's not, he lives at the YMCA," They went on to their lunch.

After putting away the broom and the dust pan, Tony walked a couple of blocks to a little park. He sat down on a bench to decide what next to do. He enjoyed the beautiful day; the birds searching for food and the people passing by. It should be a happy moment. He missed Shirley. He wondered where she was and what she was doing. How long had it been since he'd seen her? A surge of loneliness enveloped him. An attractive young lady with two cute kids; a boy and a girl came and sat down on a bench nearby. They looked about two or three years old and were dressed in the same colors. After a few minutes the little girl came over and stood in front of Tony, hands behind her back. "Hi!" she said." I'm Shirley." She waited for Tony to answer. Tony -taking her tiny hand -," Hi! I'm Tony. I'm glad to know you."

"Shirley, don't bother the nice man. Come back over here, urged her mother. The little girl ran back to her. Tony -addressing the mother- "You have two very fine little ones. Are they twins?" "Yes they are. They're the answer to our prayers. It's so much fun to watch them grow. Shirley, as you see, is very friendly." "She's a beautiful little lady," said Tony. "Thank you," said the mother. "Do you have any children?" "No, Not yet," answered Tony, as a tear formed in his eye. "Come on, kids. I'm rested. Let's go!" They took her hands and walked away. Tony remembered *his* Shirley saying she would like to have children. The little girl being named Shirley was kind of a shock. It would be wonderful if ....but he had to put 'what might have been' out of his mind. He got up and went back to the YMCA. Three days later, Bill got a call from Mr. Carpenter. A vacancy had just developed. Bill was hired in Mr. Fisher's department to help clear the backlog in outgoing shipments, at a salary better then the one with the Port Authority.

About a month later: Bill was doing well in his new job. He was enjoying the enthusiasm of the Junior Professional Speaker's club. Harry called him to relay his mother's invitation to a family dinner at the Green St. house, in celebration of Cissy's 19th birthday. Bill purchased a box of See's candy and drove to the Green Street address. Mr. and Mrs. Blaise, Harry and a couple of Cissy's friends were there. Cissy was expected any moment. Dinner was almost ready. Everyone was ready to scream "Happy Birthday" when she arrived. Finally, the door opened and they all screamed "Happy Birthday!". In the door facing them stood a surprised young man. He had long blonde hair, dirty rumpled jeans. He had a fuzz on his face instead of a real beard. His soft blue eyes looked tired. He was supported by a crutch under his right shoulder. The "Happy Birthday" died off quickly. Behind him was Cissy. "I'm here! Sorry I'm late. Mother. This is Jerry Ford. I met him on the bus. He hasn't had lunch. Can he eat dinner with us? He was trying to find a church in this area that served food." "Of course. Cissy, we have plenty," They all settled in the living room. "It'll be about 15 minutes. I'll set another plate for you, Jerry. Harry, will you show Jerry the bathroom, so he can freshen up a bit if he likes," said Florence. "OK. We'll use the office bathroom. Come on, Jerry."

When Jerry came out of the bathroom, Harry talked briefly with him. It appeared that Cissy's intuition was correct. Jerry did need food and help in a couple of ways. He had lived in South San Francisco until his Mother had died two months ago. He had no relatives that he knew of. He had to vacate the apartment where they rented. Jerry had been receiving a small check from a local charity, because of his club foot. It had been spent already for this month. He had graduated from high school. College was out of the question. He had been trying to find a job, but no luck so far. He had been sleeping in the basement of a church out off Geary St. Harry, with this information, felt that Cissy was right. They needed to help Jerry.

After the little talk, they joined the rest in the living room. Before sitting down to eat, Harry found Ed and Bill talking. He joined them and informed them about Jerry's problems. "Dinner is ready. Everybody find your seat." They did, and all had a delicious meal. Then the cake with 9 flaming candles was brought in. A birthday toast was made to honor Cissy. By this time, Jerry, who had never experienced such a family celebration before, was smiling and enjoying it. After dinner, Florence sought out Bill. "Tony -I can't get used to 'Bill'- What have you heard from Shirley? I worry about her. I'm so sorry about you two separating." "Florence, I don't know where she lives. I'm not satisfied with what happened to us. I still think she's a wonderful girl. I'm over my anger and disappointment between us. . . .I don't know how she feels about me. I'd like to know, but I don't know if she'd be interested." "There's been no divorce yet?" asked Florence. "No. I just can't bring myself to do that, and I haven't had any notice from her." "Are you dating anyone seriously now?" she asked. "No. I've been so busy with my new job and related activities, even if I wanted to I can't seem to bring myself to think about life without Shirley," answered Bill. "I think I understand." She gave him a sympathetic hug. Cissy came in to say that Harry was taking her back to her room at Mills College. "Cissy, I'm real proud of you," said Bill. "You're prettier than ever. It's very commendable what you did for Jerry. Is he leaving, too?" "No, Dad is taking him later to a place where he will have a room to himself. Mother is washing his shirt, jeans and socks. She will iron them for him. They have 'kind of adopted him." "All because you're such a sweet girl, Cissy. What are you studying at Mills?" "I'm taking courses to be a nurse." "You're a smart girl. Take care." He gave her a friendly hug, and she and Harry left.

About three months after Shirley had left Tony, she moved to a small apartment. She missed Tony, but now concentrated all her efforts on her work at the Chamber of Commerce. Phil had continued to chat with her whenever he got the chance. They went to lunch together a couple of times. He always insisted on paying for both. Finally, he persuaded her to go with him to a Dinner & Theater affair. Shirley enjoyed both. "Phil, you shouldn't spend so much on me," she protested. "Shirley, you're my favorite. You're worth it." At her apartment door, she hesitated. "Phil, it's so late, I think we'd better just say goodnight, here." "It's not so late, Shirley, I need to use your bathroom. It'll only take a minute." "Oh! sure. Go ahead," she said. They went inside. Shirley hung up her coat and slipped into more comfortable shoes. Phil was still in the bathroom, so she sat down on the sofa. Phil came out and sat down beside her. "Do you have some ice water in your refrigerator? My throat is so dry." Shirley -wondering if Phil is just trying to delay his leaving- "Sure. How about a coke? Wouldn't that be better?" She got up and got two cokes. They engaged in small talk while they sipped their drinks. - "What do you do these evenings? Do you have a lot of friends in for drinks, parties?" he asked. "I have a few friends over. Usually, I just listen to the radio, or read books. I like the 'Soaps' on the radio." "What kind of books do you like?" he asked. Oh, I like love stories, and I listen to the news. What do you do on your evenings?" "Same. Same as you. We're

71

a lot alike, Shirley. I'd like to see more of you." She didn't answer. "Don't you get pretty lonesome these long nights?" he asked. Shirley thought about it: The fact was, she *was* lonesome. It was awful sometimes. She felt like she knew what Phil was leading up to. He was nice company. But she didn't want to date him regularly. Her marriage with Tony had been wonderful, until the unfortunate break. She wondered where he was. Some things about marriage were hard to give up. In fact, tonight she had that 'feeling' again. When they were leaving the theater, Phil had put her coat around her shoulders, hugged her a little bit, and their eyes met. They both smiled.

"Shirley! Shirley! Wake up!" she heard Phil say. She must have been in a reverie. Phil had scooted against her and was leaning to kiss her. Her natural reaction would be to respond totally. Why not? What would it hurt? It would satisfy the urge that seemed to be so great right now. She felt helpless to resist.

Their eyes met again and held....She didn't see the love, the tenderness that she expected, like she saw in Tony's eyes. The urge disappeared. She turned aside and straightened up.

"I'm sorry, Phil! I know what you want, but I can't let it happen. I'm still not divorced yet." Phil -backing off- "What's that got to do with it?" "I'm still in love with Tony." "You're ridiculous, Shirley! "He got up, excused himself and left. After Phil left so quickly, Shirley sat back down to think. She knew Phil was angry with her. She had almost lost control there. She didn't like him a lot, ...but who else did she have? She realized that she loved only Tony. She sat for a long time thinking about the good times they had had together. Why couldn't they patch things up? If she only knew where he was. She got out a picture of Tony in his Navy uniform. Tears flooded her eyes as she held it to her breast. She decided to call Doris. She dialed her number..

"Hello?" "I'm sorry it's so late, Doris. How are you?" "I'm fine.... Shirley, are you OK? You sound like you're about to cry." "I am... I'm so lonesome. Have you seen Harry lately?" "Yes. I was with him last week. He took me to a dinner at his club." "Do you think he would know where-Tony is." "He might. I can ask him. What do you want him for? I thought he treated you pretty badly." "I just want to talk to him," said Shirley. "You are, crying, aren't you?" "Yes, I am. I'm just so.." "I see, you're still in love with him," said Doris. "OK. I'll call Harry. He may know where Tony is. I know he left his job at the Port Authority. I'll call you when I find out." "Thank you. You're the best friend I've ever had." "It's late. You should take a couple of aspirin and go to bed. Will you, Shirley?" "I will," promised Shirley.

The next day, Shirley decided she couldn't wait to hear from Doris. She would try to find Tony, herself. She called the Port Authority. They said that they had no idea where Tony was now. She even went down to the building where Tony had worked and stood outside, asking employees, including Joe Acosta, if they knew where Tony was. All they knew was that he didn't work there anymore. Shirley had done well at the Chamber of Commerce office. Phil, who was a friend of several of the company executives on the upper floor, had helped her get one advancement. Now there was rumor of a vacancy as a secretary in the office above. It was the kind of job she wanted, and she believe she had the best chance. Her immediate boss had hinted to her that she was the most likely selection. But when the selection was announced, it was Helen, a girl with less time with the company than Shirley. She noticed that Phil helped her move her things upstairs, Shirley was disappointed and angry. Now, she understood why Tony was in such an angry mood. It had ruined their marriage. She owed Tony an apology!.

Chapter Four

Bill Smith's job advance at Pacific Trading Co. was rapid. In six months he had learned the business so well, that he was Mr. Fisher's understudy. Mr. Fisher's department handled the foreign trade, with branches in Singapore, Manila and Sydney, Australia. Tony's duties concerned the Australian trade. Tony had kept working to better himself in public speaking, making new friends, and boosting the business of The Pacific Trading Co. When a big trade Conference was scheduled for July 16th in Honolulu, Mr. Fisher asked Bill to go along as his assistant. So on July 12th, we find Bill in attendance at the conference in the Reef Tower Hotel. The hotel and being in Hawaii constantly reminded him of Shirley and the happy times they had together there. He decided that his life would never be happy again until he and Shirley were back together. He planned to find her as soon as he got back to San Francisco, and try to win her again. It was the last day of the Conference; Bill had had time to visit the telephone booth, the little coffee shop, and of course, the Reef Tower Hotel where he was staying. The visit to the telephone booth was especially emotional for him.

A week after Shirley's conversation with Doris, Doris called her at work. "Shirley, I just found out that Tony is in Honolulu. He's attending a trade conference. That is all I could find out." Shirley was excited! "Dottie, I'm going to Honolulu, tomorrow! I'll get my boss to let me off." "I'm on my 2 weeks vacation. Can I go with you?" pleaded Dot. "Yes! Yes! You can help me find him. I'll order two tickets and call you the flight time. You be ready!" urged Shirley. Shirley went immediately to her boss, Mr. Drewer, and requested a week off to go to Hawaii. "Shirley, I can't let you off now," said Mr. Drewer. "You have to make your request two weeks in advance." "Mr. Drewer, If I had known earlier, I would have asked you then," pleaded Shirley. "I have two employees off already this week. I can't do it." "Then I'll have to go without your permission," she sighed. "Then you're fired! What can be more important than your job?"

"My happiness, Mr. Drewer. I'm sorry!" Mr. Drewer -relenting- "Shirley, you're a good employee, if not my best. I don't want to lose you. Call me when you get back. I'll get by, somehow." "Thank you, Mr. Drewer! I'll call. Good-bye." She left. Shirley phoned an airline ticket office, and reserved two tickets to Honolulu for 11am the next day. Then she called Doris the time of departure.

Helen, who happened to be picking up some papers from Mr. Drewer's office, heard the conversation between Shirley and Mr. Drewer. Helen was jealous of Phil's dates with Shirley. She reported the event to Phil. Maybe Phil would pay more attention to her. Phil decided it would be a good opportunity to get a little revenge for Shirley's embarrassing "turn down" at her apartment recently. He decided to foil her reunion with Tony. He checked with the airport. Northwest had a flight next day leaving for Hawaii at 11am. That would be the one Shirley would be taking. He would just make her miss it! About midnight, he drove to her apartment complex, parked his car a half block away, and walked over to her building. There was a light in her apartment window. She was probably getting things packed for her trip. He crawled under her car and loosened the drain plug in the gas tank, so that it drained slowly. It would be about empty by morning. She would run out of gas in a few blocks, and miss her plane. He grinned in glee, as he thought of her problem. As he crawled out from under the car, a security guard saw him. "Hey there! What are you doing?" Phil -surprised- "Oh, ah...I was checking the drain plug of my car. It's been leaking." "It's still leaking pretty bad. Are you sure you fixed it? May I see your driver's license, please?" Phil produced it. Security Guard -looking at the license - "Your address on this license is for a street way across town." "That's right. I was here to visit my friend in the apartment there." He indicated the apartment with the light burning. "I know the lady who lives there. I'm not sure she knows you," said the security guard. Phil -desperate now- "She knows me. We're friends." "OK, let's go up and see what she says," said the guard. Phil didn't want to, but he'd explain it to Shirley, somehow. They went up and rang her bell. There was no response. The guard rang the bell again. Still no response. "She's not at home," said the guard. "Now I remember! She left this afternoon and asked that the newspapers be picked up until she gets back. . ." "You're under arrest, Mr. Piker. You'd better go down and plead with the policeman at the jail in the morning. "He took Phil to jail, where he spent the rest of the night. The reason for no answer to the bell was that Shirley had gone to spend the night with Doris, so they could go together next morning to catch their flight to Hawaii. Phil called Helen next morning, to come and bail him out.

When Shirley and Doris arrived in Honolulu they registered again at the Palace Hotel. It was about 3 pm when Shirley took Doris to see the historic telephone booth that had started the romance between she and Tony. Shirley had a 'feeling' that drew her to see the booth first. Doris -stepping into the booth- "So this is the magic phone booth that you two met in? I can't see two people getting in here with the door closed." "Sure they can," said Shirley." Move in a little further." Doris moved in a little and Shirley stepped in and closed the door. "See", said Shirley. "Plenty of room." Doris - gazing at the writings on the wall - "Here's your name on the wall. Did you write it?" Shirley - looking at the writing - "No, I didn't. Some other person named Shirley, I suppose." Then her eyes widened, as she read the message under the name: "I love you! I just had to stop by! Tony -July 11, 1951." "Oh, Doris! Tony wrote that!" exclaimed Shirley. "Are you sure? The date is yesterday. How peculiar!" said Doris. "Oh, where could he be? Let's go check the coffee shop and see if he's been there," urged Shirley. They hurried across the beach to the shop. No one remembered him. "Maybe he's gone back to the mainland, but I've just got to check the Reef Tower Hotel," said Shirley. "I need to go back to the hotel, said Doris, "I have an appointment there within an hour to get my hair done. You go check the Reef Tower. I'll see you when you get back at the hotel." Doris took a waiting taxi, and Shirley left for the Reef Tower Hotel, which was about six blocks away.

At the Reef Tower, the desk clerk checked her registry. No one was registered as Anthony Michaivelli. Shirley described Tony to her. Clerk -thinking over the description- "Hmmm. That's almost an exact description of a man listed here as Bill Smith. He checked out about an hour ago." "Do you know where he was going from here?" asked Shirley. Clerk -checking registry again- "The note here just says: 'tkt.pur. S.A. N.W.' ". "I suppose that was meant to be SF, for San Francisco. I'm almost certain that's my husband, " said Shirley. "A few of our customers register under assumed names," volunteered the clerk. "What airline is his ticket for?" asked Shirley. The clerk eyed her suspiciously. "You're not going to shoot him, are you?" "No! No! I love him!" "It's Northwest Airlines," said the clerk. "Thank you," said Shirley. Shirley took a taxi for the airport. It was crowded. She searched through the crowd. Tony was not in the group of people around the Northwest Airlines departure gate.

Shirley was standing at the top of the escalators, when she spotted him on the floor below, buying a newspaper. She quickly got on the escalator going down, just as he stepped on the one coming up. As they passed, Shirley yelled - "Tony! I want to see you!" Tony looked up in surprise. "Shirley!" he yelled as they passed. When he got to the top, she was at the bottom. Both quickly reversed directions (She going up; he going down.) As they passed again: "Stay up!" he cried. This time she did. Tony was behind a man with two large suitcases. He couldn't get down and then back up fast enough so he scrambled over the dividing rails separating the escalators onto the "up" escalator. At the top, they fell into each other's arms. "Shirley! Where did you come from?" "From everywhere! You are SO hard to find. Tony, I love you!" She was breathing hard. Thank you, Sweetheart. I love you, too! . . .I was just about to catch my plane," said Tony. He seemed worried. "I can't leave you, Shirley! What can we do?" "Let's go. I have my return ticket." They rushed to the Northwest Airlines boarding gate and onto the plane, just as the door was being closed. They quickly found seats. She was out of breath again. The plane took off. In a few minutes, a Steward came by checking tickets. Tony gave him his. He tore off a stub and handed it back to Tony. Shirley gave him her ticket. He looked at it carefully. "This ticket is for San Francisco," said the Steward. "I know. That's where I'm going," answered Shirley. "Lady. .This plane goes to Sydney, Australia!" Shirley looked in awful surprise at Tony. Tony had a big smile on his face. "Sir, said Tony. "We almost missed the plane. We didn't have time to get her a ticket. She is my wife. I'm a regular traveler on your airline." (Tony showed him his Northwest Airlines travel ID.) "Can you put her fare on my account?" "No problem," said the Steward. He did, then moved on. "I'm not sure I know the new 'You', but I love it! What should I expect in Sydney?" she asked. "We'll be there only a week, then back to San Francisco. How about a kiss to seal our reunion?" She complied warmly. Is Doris going to be surprised," giggled Shirley. "We'll call her when we get to Sydney," promised Tony. Shirley -hesitating-! "Tony, I've got something to tell you." "I think I know what it is," a big grin on his happy face.

Shirley - uncertain of what to say - "What?" Well, you get out of breath so easily, you've gained a few pounds, and looking into your beautiful, dreamy eyes, is.. Are you ...?" Shirley -eyes brimming with tears-

"Yes I am. I .... " When is it due?" He gave her a kiss on her wet cheek. "In three months." "You sweet, wonderful girl! I love you! I'm so proud of you!" Tears of happiness and relief flooded her eyes, as she buried her face in his shoulder. He put an arm around her. "Thank Goodness, we found each other. We'll never be separated again!" promised Tony-Bill/ Michaivelli-Smith. The plane droned on.

END OF STORY.

Tom Robb

POSTLOGUE: Bill changed their names to Mr. and Mrs. Anthony Michaels. Cissy had an operation on her nose, as a graduation present on her graduation from Mills College. She is currently engaged to a very nice young man! Jerry was adopted by the Blaise family; had an operation on his foot, and is now in college; crutch was eliminated. Harry and Doris, decided to get married. Phil and Helen ran off to Reno and were married. Phil transferred to the company's Los Angeles office. Helen went along. A beautiful baby girl,, was born to Shirley and Tony. Tony is still successful in his job. Shirley works two days a week for Mr. Drewer. The other days you can find her at home with little Doris.

HAVE FUN.
TGR

THAT MAGIC NIGHT IN HAWAII

Music & Lyrics by Tom Robb

That Magic Night in Hawaii
Dark roving clouds in the sky,
I was a Girl, all alone, at a telephone booth.
He came and stopped, just nearby.
A shy little smile as he waited.
Lonely heart missed a beat.
And then it Started to rain all of a sudden,
So we shared the phone booth retreat.

(key change, to B-flat)

"What do you do when you don't know what to do?
We both were asking that question.
Soon, we were laughing and feeling O.K.
Rain, it stopped; we ran to a near cafe.
Lucky was I, when that rain came pouring down;
'Else I'd have not met my Tony Boy.
For it was just that passing "chance"
—- that sparked a long romance,

On that Magic Night in Hawaii.
He was a boy from the Navy. A sailor ashore on a leave.
We spent the day and the night Making "Hay" 'til near mid-night-
That Magic Night in Hawaii.
Years come and go but my memory—
Still thrills my heart like long ago.
That's when a girl and a boy—
Seized a future full of joy,
On that Magic Might in Hawaii.

Jack Loves Lucy

A Three Act Play

LIST OF CHARACTERS

JACK — Top cowboy at ranch

LUCY — Jack's girlfriend

BOB — Jack's best friend

MIRABEL - Lucy's, mother

JOSEF — Taxi driver. Formerly of N.Y.C.

SOFIA —   Josef's niece from Russia

VIOLA — Nurse for Sofia

HOSS — Cowboy at ranch

MOONBEAM — Hoss's girlfriend

CALLER — Square dance caller

KGB guys

MOB guys

TEXAS RANGER

ACT 1

Ranch just outside Ft. Worth, Texas. Large family room of main ranch house. .1940's. Early morning. As curtain goes up it reveals a square dance in progress. At end of dance, the Caller dismissed the class.

CALLER — "That's it for today guys and gals. Don't forget to be early Saturday night, Bye."

Just as they all cleared out, a cowboy, Hoss, chased Moonbeam, his girlfriend, across stage, catching her with his lariat rope.

HOSS — "I gotcha!"

MOONBEAM - "Whatcha gonna do wit me, Hoss?"

HOSS — " I donno yet."

Moonbeam suddenly ran free again. They disappeared off stage, with Hoss in pursuit, swinging his lariat. As they disappear, the phone rang.

A minute later it rang again. Finally, Jack came in lugging a saddle, threw it in a corner, and answered the phone.

JACK — on phone- 'Oh, hello, Baby. Glad you called. Where are you?... You are? ...OK. I'll see you when you get here." He hung up phone as Bob came in.

JACK — "Hello, Bob. What's up? You goin' with the group on the cook-out today?"

BOB — "Not today. I've got a golf date. Can I borrow your clubs again? I'll bring 'em back tomorrow.... Anything new with you and Lucy?"

JACK — "I've got some great news, Bob. We're engaged! We haven't set a date or anything yet. In fact, she just called. She's on her way out here."

BOB — "Then I'd better vamoose. I don't want to screw up your plannin'." He took the clubs and left.

Lucy arrived.

LUCY — "Hello, Jack, Darling. I couldn't wait to get here. Why did they put the ranch so far out from town? The taxi man said it was two miles."

JACK — "They didn't put it out two miles. The town just grew out this way."

LUCY — "Well, they should move it in closer....Anyway, Jack, I'm thrilled and excited about our marriage. Let's plan it right now!"

JACK — "That's what I was hopin', Sweetheart. The sooner the better for me."

LUCY — "Well, it'll take time to get things together; like my wedding dress chosen and made, invitations printed, friends and relatives notified, preacher and organist hired, newspapers notified,..."

JACK — "That's a lot of expense. Couldn't we just run in to the Justice of the Peace and get married in our Levis?"

LUCY — "You cowboys don't have an ounce of imagination. A quick ceremony would be OK, but this is January. Nobody plans a wedding in January. Mother follows the Zodiac calendar closely. She says April is the best month, and the 25th is the 'lucky' day."

JACK — "Sweetheart, I'm not going to marry your mother. Tomorrow, next week would suit me fine."

LUCY — "Yes, but Mother would be so disappointed. Anyway, that's only 3 months. We could hardly get everything arranged much faster, Darling."

JACK — "OK. Whatever makes you happy, is fine with me. I don't plan to do this but once."

LUCY — "Where would you like to go on our honeymoon, Darling?"

JACK — "I haven't thought that far ahead. Where would you like to go? I'll leave it up to you. Anywhere your little heart desires, we'll go, Sweetheart."

LUCY — "I knew you'd say that, you sweet man! Thank you, Darling. I've always wanted to see Paris. I've dreamed of seeing the Eiffel Tower, the Louvre, the River .. Seine, the Rue de la Pais and all that. One of my friends who went there on her honeymoon, said it was fantastic."

JACK — surprised- "That's a dream, alright. I was thinkin' more like a week-end in San Antonio or Cloudcroft, but we'll work it out."

A honk of a car horn is heard -a peculiar honk.

LUCY — "Oh, that's my taxi. He's going to take me to mother's, and then home. Bye, Sweet. I'll see you later."

She left. Bob came back in.

JACK — "You back already, Bob? You didn't play very long."

BOB — "We didn't play. Sammie didn't show up. He was supposed to pick me up. Here's your clubs back." Jack took the clubs.

JACK — "Better luck next time."

BOB   "Have you and Lucy set a date yet?"

JACK — "Her mother, Mirabel, did. She's a Zodiac follower. So we've set the date for April 25th. That's supposed to be the lucky' date to get married this year. That's alright with me. I may need a lot of luck."

BOB — "Mirabel sounds more like Jezebel. Better watch your behind there, Jack."

JACK — "There IS a problem that I'm worried about."

BOB — "Like what?"

JACK — "Our honeymoon. I left it up to Lucy, and she enthusiastically chose Paris, France."

BOB — "Holy Cow! Is she crazy? How can you afford a vacation for two people to Paris, France? It would cost at least $5000. What did you tell her?"

JACK — "Nothing. I didn't know what to say at the moment. She's a sweet girl, and I love her very much, but I can't possibly take her to Paris, France."

BOB — "Jezebel, or Mirabel, must have talked up the Paris thing, hoping to tag along as an escort or helper."

JACK — "I hope it was just a 'spur-of-the-moment' thing by Lucy."

BOB — "Why don't you two go to Reno? I've been to Reno. Good honeymoon city. You might even win enough to pay for the trip."

JACK — "That's a great idea. Why didn't I think of that? Lucy will agree, I'm sure. She's a sensible girl. That eases my mind. I couldn't swing a trip to Paris."

BOB — "You'll work it out. I've got to go, Jack. See you later."

Bob left. Jack got the saddle, set it up on a saw-horse and began to energetically polish it. Lucy came by on her way from work.

JACK — "Hello, Sweetheart. How was your day at the office?"

LUCY — bubbling over with enthusiasm- "Oh, Jack! Guess what? I told them at the office all about it. They are planning a sending-off party for us on April 25th. Isn't that wonderful? I'm so thrilled! Are we going by boat or plane?"

JACK — "I've been thinkin', Lucy. How about Reno? That's a real fun place. You know, 'America First.'"

LUCY — "Oh, Jack. You're so wonderful! Paris first, then Reno! I'll be the envy of all my friends. I can't wait to tell them at the office! I've got to go tell Mother. Bye, Darling."

They kissed and she left very excited. Jack was speechless. He didn't know what to do. Hoss came in.

HOSS — "Jack, what's a good present for a girl like Moonbeam?"

JACK — "How about a ticket to Paris, France? No. forget that, Hoss." Jack wiped his brow.

HOSS — "I don't want to get rid of her. It's her 19th birthday."

JACK — "I was just kidding when I mentioned Paris....Let me think.... What would please your horse Suzy? Oats or hay? Something to eat's a good bet.?

HOSS — "Moonbeam wouldn't go for anything like that."

JACK — "I mean, take her to dinner at a nice restaurant and then buy her a box of chocolates."

HOSS — "I can do that. Thank you, Jack. I'll see you later."

Bob came in. Jack was pacing the floor.

BOB — "Jack, what's the matter? You look like a sick horse."

JACK — "I'm havin' a big misunderstanding with Lucy, Bob."

BOB — "You mean you had a fuss?"

JACK — "I wish it was as simple as that. It's all over town now, that I'm takin' Lucy to Paris on our honeymoon."

BOB — "Gee! I'd enjoy a visit to Paris, myself. You had me fooled, Pal. I thought you said you couldn't afford it. Where did you get the $5000?"

JACK — "That's the problem, Bob. I haven't got it."

BOB — "I guess I'm kinda dumb, Jack. Where are you goin' to GET $5000?"

JACK — "I don't know. How about you? Can you loan me 5 G's?"

BOB — "Jack, if I had 5 G's, I'd be in Paris, myself."

JACK — "It's goin' to be a big disappointment to Lucy, if we can't go to Paris on our honeymoon. I can't let her down, Bob. Where can I get a quick $5000?"

BOB — "Credit cards?"

JACK — "Maxed out already, because of my foot operation and the down payment on my car."

BOB — "How about your bank?"

JACK — "Not a chance."

BOB — "Maybe Lucy has $5000 she can spare."

JACK — "Don't be ridiculous, Bob. You're my best friend. Think of something!" (...a couple of minutes silence...)

BOB — Sat up; snapped his fingers. "It may be a long shot, Jack, but I was talkin' to Josef my taxi driver last week. He's from Vladivostok, Russia. His niece, Sofia, who's 24 years old, well off, needs to leave Russia. The government is getting nosey and she's afraid of being arrested for political reasons. She'll pay $5000 to marry a U.S. citizen."

JACK — "What's that got to do with my problem? I'm in so much trouble already, I don't want any thing to do with the Russians."

BOB — "They're not goin' to bother a cowboy on a ranch 2 miles outside of Ft. Worth, Texas. They have problems over there."

JACK — "They have spies everywhere. With my luck I'll end up on their 'hit' list."

BOB — "Look at it this way. You've got a chance to pick up $5000 by doin' a lady a favor. Do you know where else you can pick up 5 G's right now? You've heard the old sayin' - 'A bird in the hand is worth one in the bushes.'"

JACK — "I think it's 'two in the bush'. But we're getting off the subject... This girl from Russia; how do you know it's not just a rumor your taxi driver heard?"

BOB — "It's his niece. A member of his family."

JACK — "It would probably take forever to arrange it. They don't do business like we do over here. I wouldn't want to end up with two wives. Why did you say she wanted to come over here?"

BOB — "She wants to emigrate to the U.S. It will take a three year wait by normal U.S immigration procedure. She's very discouraged. The only quicker way for her to get here, and be a permanent resident, is to marry a U.S. citizen but she has no prospects for that. Vladivostok is a little far off for someone shopping for a bride."

JACK — "I don't see the connection. If I marry Lucy, I can't marry this Sofia, too. I'd end up in Leavenworth."

BOB — "You've got a good point, but here's how we could work it. You're not marrying Lucy until April. That's 3 months away. Sophia gets here and you marry her temporarily. You or she would get an annulment or divorce in a month or so, and she could stay here in the U.S. A friend of hers did it."

JACK — "Hey, that might work. You marry her for the fee of $5000 and loan it to me."

BOB — "I can't marry her. I still live with my parents. I wouldn't have a place to put her. Anyway, it's not my problem, but it would work out for you."

JACK — "How?"

BOB — "Easy. I'll have Josef contact his niece, Sofia. She'll pay her way here. You'll put her up at a hotel, marry her the next day and collect the $5000., then she or you will have the marriage annulled in two months, and Lucy will never know. She's kinda' lacking' anyway."

JACK — "She's not 'lacking'. You say that because she wouldn't fall for your crummy attempts to date her. And, what do you mean 'Lucy would never know'. How would we ever keep them apart? Lucy is by here every day."

BOB — "It's simple. Sofia will go along. I'll keep her busy. Josef said she's a homebody, likes to watch the 'Soaps' on TV. She's not a celebrity. You'd be doing the poor lady a great favor, Jack. How often do you get a chance to be a real hero to some unfortunate person? You know how fast two months go by. Just two rent payments."

JACK — "You putting it like that, makes it sound like I ought to do it. I suppose it wouldn't hurt to check into it. Ask Josef if his niece is still interested."

BOB — "I'll see him tomorrow. I envy you, Jack. Paris in the Spring is beautiful." He started singing the song.

JACK — "Shut up, you moron!" Bob left, shoved by Jack.

LATER - Lucy and her mother came by.

JACK — "Come in, Sweetheart; and Mother! How are you, Dear?"

MIRABEL — "I'm fine. As ornery as ever. I just want to say 'Bravo' to you, on your decision to take Lucy to Paris for your honeymoon. It's been her dream since she was 10 years old. She told me all about it. You're a fine gentleman, Jack."

JACK —subdued, worried- "Thank you, Mother."

LUCY — "We've been shopping. We just came by so Mother could say hello to you. We can't stay long."

MIRABEL — "I've just been shopping for some new clothes. I want to look good at my only daughter's wedding."

JACK — "You always look good, Mother."

MIRABEL — "Thank you, Jack. It's no wonder Lucy loves you."

They left. Jack resumed polishing the saddle.

TIME PASSES — LIGHTS FLICKER.

NEXT MORNING Jack and Hoss are in the Big room. Hoss is trying to untangle a lariat rope.

JACK — "Hoss, what did you give Moonbeam for her birthday present?"

HOSS — "I gave her a box of chocolate candy, like you said."

JACK — "I'm sure that made her happy."

HOSS — "Well, yes and no. She didn't like it 'cause I sampled a couple pieces before I wrapped it up."

JACK — "Is she mad at you for that?"

HOSS — "No, but she wouldn't let me have but one more piece."

JACK — "Women are not as easy to get along with as horses, Hoss. I'm having trouble figuring them out myself, sometimes."

HOSS — "I hear you're getting hitched, Jack."

JACK — "Yes, I am. Man! News gets around fast on this ranch. How'd you know? We haven't put out the word yet."

HOSS — "Moonbeam works at the telephone office in Ft. Worth. She mentioned it. Is it that little black headed filly I've seen you with lately?"

JACK — "That's her. We haven't tied up the details yet, so go easy on the gossip, old Pal."

HOSS — "You can count on me, Pard." Bob comes in.

BOB — "Hi, Hoss. You gettin' ready for the rodeo next week?"

HOSS — "Rarin' to go! I'll see you guys later." He left.

BOB — "Jack, Josef called his niece last night -it's day there- to learn if she's still interested in the temporary deal."

JACK — "That's really a long shot, I figure."

BOB — "She called him back, later to say that she was accepting the deal and was sending the $5000 to Josef by cable. The money should be here any time now."

JACK — "We didn't offer any deal. We just asked her a question."

BOB — "What do you care? $5000 is $5000. Isn't that what you need? Grab it!"

JACK — "I'm just surprised at the speed of it all."

BOB — "That's high finance, Jack."

JACK — "High finance or whatever. I don't want to get into something over my head."

BOB — "There's a little bit of chance in everything. It's like entering your horse in a race. You have to enter it to win. In this case, the prize is $5000, and the odds are all in your favor."

JACK — "You confuse me, Bob. Anyway, what's the next step? When do I get my $5000.?" A raucous sounding car horn was heard.

BOB — "That's Josef now. I recognize his car horn."

Shortly, Josef appeared.

BOB — "Josef, what's the matter with the horn on your taxi? It sounds awful."

JOSEF — "I don't know. It's a 'short' in the line somewhere. It just honks when I turn the engine off."

BOB — "Jack, this is Josef Bronsky, Sofia's uncle; my taxi driver. Do you have the check yet, Josef?"

JOSEF — "Yes, here it is." He gives it to Bob, who examines it.

BOB — "This check is for 500,000 kopek; it's supposed to be $5000 in U.S. money. It's made out to you, Jack, and Josef. Josef will sign

93

it as soon as the wedding is completed. Then it's all yours, Jack."
He let Jack examine the cable check.

JACK — "Kopeks? I can't use any kopeks."

JOSEF — "It's the same as $5000 in Russia. You just have to get a bank
to change it to dollars."

JACK — "Can you get it changed for me, Josef? I don't think my bank
would know how to do it. They'd probably have me arrested as
a communist."

JOSEF - " I can do it. I have my connections."

JACK — "Thank you, Josef. She's a fast action dame. Do you know
her?"

JOSEF — "Yes, I remember her. She's quiet, but very smart and business
wise. That's why she wants to come to the U.S. Business is
slow in Vladivostok."

JACK — "What kind of business, Josef?"

JOSEF — "I think it was ... I'm not sure."

BOB — "Josef wanted to meet you and show you the cable draft, so you
can start the planning of the wedding. Sofia will arrive by plane
tomorrow."

JACK — "She's already on her way? Gollywumpas!... Josef, will you
photo that draft for me and give it to Bob?"

JOSEF — "Sure. I'll take care of it."

Josef left. Jack was very worried.

JACK — "Wow! I don't see any way to go except to go through with
the deal and hope for the best. If this plan doesn't work out
perfectly, I'm ruined with Lucy."

BOB — "We'll work it out. Jack, don't worry."

JACK — "OK. Bob, will you go rent a room for Sofia in a nearby hotel, and arrange for a license and a preacher?"

BOB — "Sure. I'll take care of it."

JACK — "Josef will meet her and bring her here and we'll plan the details of the wedding."

BOB — "Fine. This is going to work out like a charm."

Bob left. Jack went over to work on his saddle, but he was so worried he threw the chamois in the corner and left.

"Jack, why are you always polishing that old saddle?"

ACT 2

NEXT DAY: Jack is in the Big room polishing his saddle. Hoss enters with Moonbeam.

HOSS — "Moonbeam, this is my friend, Jack Dillard. He's head honcho here."

MOONBEAM — "Me glad to know you. Hoss say you know everything. He tinks you be smart like a professor."

JACK — "That's a bit exaggerated. Hoss says you have a very important job at the telephone company."

MOONBEAM — "I do. I keep place clean."

JACK — "Did you know that Hoss is our champion bare-back rider?"

MOONBEAM — "He have to teach me that. He be good teacher."

HOSS — "We gotta go. I just wanted her to meet you."

JACK — "I'm glad you came by, Moonbeam."

MOONBEAM — "Bye."

She and Hoss left. There was that awful honk again. Josef, Sofia and Bob arrived.

JOSEF — "Jack, this is Sofia Bronsky, your future and ex-wife."

JACK — "I'm glad to meet you, Sofia. How was your flight?"

SOFIA — "It was a hassle getting out of Vlad. I'd never have made it except for my disguise."

JACK — "You don't look like you'd need a disguise. You look like an ordinary person."

JACK — "I hope you understand this is to be a temporary thing."

SOFIA — "Yes, I understand. One of my friends did it."

JACK — "Sofia, this is Bob Simms. He will take you to your hotel room. It's only a block away."

BOB — "I'm glad to meet you, Sofia. You speak English well."

SOFIA — "I was an interpreter for the Trotsky party in Vlad. Can I go to my room, now? I'm very tired."

JACK — "Sure. I understand. Bob, take her to her room, please. We'll have the wedding tomorrow here at 3 pm. OK?"

SOFIA — "OK. I'm game. I've been looking forward to this."

BOB — "Let's go, Sofia." They left.

JACK — "Well, she looks OK. The peasant type. Doesn't look like the intelligent business lady you mentioned. But that makes no difference. I don't anticipate any problems, now that she is here, and you have the money in hand."

JOSEF — "I think things should go smoothly from here. I'll go along, too, Jack. I'll see you tomorrow. I'll have the check."

He started to leave. Just at that time Lucy and Mirabel walked in. Mirabel recognized Josef immediately.

MIRABEL — "Oh, Hello! You're Mr. Bronson, aren't you? I remember you. You were my taxi driver in New York City two years ago when I was there. I was staying at the Ritz. I'm Mirabel. Remember?"

JOSEF — "Sure, I remember. Quite an experience, wasn't it? My last name is Bronsky. I used the name Bronson in New York as a precaution. A couple of bad guys there didn't like me."

MIRABEL — "Oh? Anyway, we got stuck in the Holland tunnel, under the river, because of some accident."

JOSEF - excited at the recall— "The tunnel lights went out. We were stuck for about two hours."

MIRABEL — "Nothing to do, so we told each other all about each other's lives. Did the Mob ever find out who blew up their hide-out?"

JOSEF — "Not yet. I keep my fingers crossed."

LUCY — "Well, it's like 'old home week' for you two. Why did you leave New York, Mr. Bronsky?"

JOSEF — "It's much healthier out here. Do you live here?"

MIRABEL — "Lucy and I live in apartments in Ft. Worth. We were on our way home, and just stopped by to say hello to Jack. He and Lucy are engaged."

JOSEF — "I'm goin' back to town. I'll take you there if you are about ready to go."

MIRABEL — "Sure Lucy, let's go. We have a ride with Josef."

LUCY — "OK. Bye, Jack, Darling."

The three started to leave.

JACK - caught Josef's sleeve and whispered: "No news about Sofia." —then louder— "Thank you for dropping by, Josef."

JOSEF — "I getcha, Pal. See you later."

They left. Bob came back in.

JACK — "Did you get her settled in the hotel OK?"

BOB — "Yes. No problem. She complained about the quality of the room a bit, but I told her it's just until the wedding."

JACK — "So far, luck is with us. Did you get the license and the preacher lined up?" (he starts work on the saddle)

BOB — "I'm workin' on it. I'm workin' on it. Don't worry...Why are you always polishin' on that old saddle?"

JACK — "I'm going to sell it, and buy myself a fancy one."

The telephone rang. Bob answered it.

BOB — after hanging up the phone- "That was Josef. The bank said that the 500,000 kopeks was worth $4000. Their service fee is 10%, or $400., a finder's fee of 10%, or $360. They are issuing a check for $3240."

JACK — "Darn! That'll leave me with only $2440. How'll we get to France on that? And there's still Sofia's hotel bill."

BOB — "Do you think Sofia might come up with a little more?"

JACK — "It's cost her $5000 already. It's not her fault. We'll just have to make the best of it."

BOB — "OK. I'll get Sofia here at 3 pm tomorrow with the preacher."

JACK — "Josef said he'd be here at 3 pm with the check, so don't be late."

They left.

NEXT DAY: Jack and Bob are talking. An ugly car honk, Josef and Sofia appear.

JACK — "OK. Let's get goin' on our wedding. Sofia, you feel OK?"

SOFIA — "I'll feel better when it's over."

JOSEF — "Where's the preacher? We're ready to go."

BOB — "He's just arrived at the back. I'll get him."

He left. Presently, a tall man with long hair, mustache, large glasses and wearing a long coat came in.

PASTOR — "I'm Bro. Hobbit. Who are the lucky people I'm goin' to marry today?"

SOFIA — "It's me and Jack, there." She pointed at Jack.

PASTOR — "Stand together, please."

They did. Jack and Josef looked at each other and shifted nervously on their feet.

PASTOR — "May I have the license, please?" No one answered.

PASTOR — "Oh, I have it already. I forgot."

He opened a folded paper and read from it.

PASTOR — "Please join hands" They did. "Do you take this girl, Sofie Grunsky, to be your wife, Jack? I mean Jack Dillard."

JACK — "Yes, I do."

Some more shifting of feet by Jack and Josef.

PASTOR — "And do you, Sofie Grunsky, take this fellow to be your husband?"

SOFIE — "Yes, I do."

PASTOR — "Then I hereby pronounce you to be husband and wife. Bye, folks, I've another appointment right away". He left.

SOFIA — "WHEE! YIPPEE! HOORAY! God bless the U.S.A."

She yanked off her wig, revealing a bunch of beautiful red hair, and threw her colored glasses against the wall. Really, she was a beautiful girl. Bob came rushing in, knocking over a table of dishes.

BOB — "What's the fuss? Marriage over already? Dang!. I missed it. Sofia, what happened to you? You're beautiful!" JACK — "Bob, I need to have a little talk with you."

JOSEF — "I've got a couple of questions to ask you, too, Bob."

When Sofia was in the bathroom, they cornered Bob.

JACK — "What kind of a shenanigan are you pullin' ?" -worried- "This whole thing is goin' to blow sky high, and instead of a honeymoon, I'm gonna be arrested for sponsoring illegal immigration."

JOSEF — "It wasn't a real wedding by any standard."

BOB — who was beginning to sweat- "I'm sorry, fellows. I had hired a preacher. He called me about 1 o'clock and said he was sick with the flu. I didn't have time to hire another."

JACK — "The way Sofia's celebrating, she thinks it's all legal."

BOB — "At the license office, they insisted that both parties to be married, should appear with identification. I was afraid the immigration authorities would arrest Sofia. I had to do something, and what you saw is what I did."

JOSEF — "Well, I can't blame you for what you did. I think you were a pretty good actor."

JACK — "You're forgiven, Bob. You earned the $100 I was goin' to pay the preacher."

JOSEF — "It's too risky to Sofia to depend on this marriage to protect her from the Feds. I think you'd better hire a lawyer, just in case she comes to their attention. I know a good lawyer who will help us."

JACK — "I suppose that's our safest direction, but don't tell Sofia."

At this point Sofia came out of the bathroom.

JACK — "Sofia, you're gorgeous! I almost wish this was for real."

JOSEF — "Without the disguise, you look like my favorite niece from Vlad. We'll start the annulment right away."

JACK — "Can you get your lawyer friend on this at once? He can decide which grounds; divorce, annulment, or maybe danger of persecution."

JOSEF — "I'll do it tomorrow. Sofia, you should just lay low, while this plays out."

SOFIA — "I will, except for an occasional trip to shop. I need some new clothes. I barely got away with what I had on."

There was the noise of a car stopping at the front.

JACK -excited- "That's probably Lucy! Bob, get Sofia out of here. Take the back door."

Bob and Sophia rushed out.

JOSEF — "I'll go along, too."

He went out the back door as Lucy and Mirabel came in the front.

JACK — "Hi, Lucy, Sweetheart! Hello, Mother. Come in." They did.

MIRABEL — "We're on our way to do some shopping, again. We're not satisfied with the wedding dresses the shops have on hand. We've decided to have one custom made."

LUCY — "It'll take two weeks to make it. We'll have plenty of time. We hope to select the style today."

JACK — "Anything will look good on you, Sweetheart."

MIRABEL — "I don't understand why you two want to wait three months to get married. It seems ridiculous to me."

LUCY — "Mother, you told me we should get married by the Zodiac calendar, and the best month for me is April. Besides, that's Springtime in Paris. Isn't that right, Jack?"

JACK — "I think that's right."

MIRABEL — "Well, that's up to you two. I'm not the one getting married."

JACK — "You should get married, too, Mother. you're still a young woman."

MIRABEL — "I'm too busy right now. If I find a handsome man I can't resist, I might make the plunge again."

LUCY — "We just stopped by to say hello, Jack. We'd better get on our way. So, bye Darling. I'll see you later." They left..

ACT 3

THE NEXT MORNING: Bob went to check on Sofia. She wasn't there.

BOB — "Jack, I just checked on Sofia. She wasn't at her hotel. I suppose she's out shopping."

JACK — "Well, she said she needed some things."

By evening, she hadn't returned; nor the next day. Bob and Jack were very worried.

JACK — "Bob, Sofia's been gone two days. You've got to find her. I've got to drive the Boss into town."

BOB — "Don't worry. I'll find her. She probably just got lost, I hope."

He set out searching. LATER, Jack came back to the ranch. He opened the door and, tried to step inside. The door was partially blocked by a sofa. He had his arms full of packages. He gave the sofa a hefty shove with his foot. It caused him to lose his balance and fall, scattering the packages over the floor. He got up limping. The room smelled funny. Things didn't look right.

JACK — "Damn! Who moved that blasted sofa against the door?" As he started picking up his packages, he spied the nurse and Sofia in the darkened corner of the room. They had been silently watching him.

NURSE (VIOLA) — "You Jack?"

JACK — "What's this? Who are you?" Then he recognized Sofia.

JACK — "Sofia! What happened? How did you get here?" She shrunk away from him.

SOFIA — "I don't know you."

JACK — "Sofia! I'm your...Don't you remember me?"

VIOLA — "She has amnesia. She doesn't know anybody. She doesn't even know who she is. She's your cousin, Mr. Bob said."

JACK — "My cousin? Well Sure. She's my cousin, Sofia." Bob came in with some groceries and supplies.

BOB — "Oh, Hi, Jack. I thought I'd get back before you did."

JACK — "Fill me in, Bob. I can't believe things have got this complicated. It's like a bad dream."

BOB — "I finally located her in the Ft. Worth Hospital. The doctor there said that she was in a car wreck. She has a broken leg and a concussion. She also has amnesia, a type called psychogenic fugue. She doesn't remember who she is."

JACK — "That's awful. Didn't she have a purse or something on her that could identify her?"

BOB — "Her purse with any identification had disappeared in the excitement of the wreck. The taxi driver had no idea who she was. He had picked her up at a street corner and was taking her to a shopping center."

JACK — "How did she get back here?"

BOB — "When I found her, I told them to discharge her to the ranch, and that she was your cousin. I had to tell them something."

JACK — "Thanks, Pal. I guess I'm the rational scapegoat."

BOB — "The hospital was short on patient's rooms. They decided to send along a nurse attendant for a week, since she is in a wheelchair. Viola, the nurse decided that the room was too bright, so she closed the curtains and rearranged the furniture a bit. Then I went to the store to get groceries and supplies that Viola suggested."

JACK   "I'm glad you found her and managed to get her back here. Our first priority, now, is to take care of Sofia, and to get h e r memory back. Poor Girl!"

BOB — "You're absolutely right, Jack. She didn't deserve this!"

Viola goes to the kitchen to stow away the supplies. Just at this moment, Lucy and Mirabel walked in.

JACK — surprised- "Oh, hello, Sweetheart; and Mother! I wasn't expecting you. I just got here a little bit ago, myself."

MIRABEL — "We just stopped by for a minute. Josef brought us. He's still out there in the taxi. He's my favorite driver now.... Did we catch you at the wrong time, Jack? Is that another girlfriend there?" She pointed at Sofia.

LUCY — "Jack, who is she? I'm surprised at you!"

JACK — "She's Bob's girlfriend, Lucy."

MIRABEL — "Let the lady speak for herself. This is not Bob's apartment. Looks like we walked in on something. Who are you, young lady?"

Both Jack and Bob were feeling the pressure.

SOFIA — "I don't know." She started crying. Bob rushed over to comfort her.

BOB — "she has amnesia. She was in a taxi wreck."

LUCY — "When was this?"

SOFIA — "They said it was two weeks ago. I don't remember."

LUCY — "I remember that. I read of it in the newspaper. It said she was unable to remember who she was."

JOSEF - coming up from the taxi- "What's the hold-up? You said you'd only be a couple of minutes."

Sofia rushed over and hugged her uncle.

SOFIA — "Uncle Josef! Oh, you're Uncle Josef. I remember now. I was in a hospital. My husband, that's him." She pointed. Jack and Bob were standing close together.

MIRABEL — thinking she pointed to Bob- "Bob, you scoundrel. Why didn't you tell us? Congratulations!"

BOB —surprised- "...Well, I..."

SOFIE — "No, not him." -she pointed at Jack. — "Him."

Jack was stunned. His plans were coming apart.

JACK — "This thing is getting so mixed up, I don't know what to say"

LUCY — "Well, I do! You two-timing scum! I can't believe this! Come on Mother, let's go."

MIRABEL — "You rat! Both of you. You're traitors to both of these girls."

JOSEF — "Hold it, everybody. This is all a simple misunderstanding."

He explained the whole scheme.

Tom Robb

JOSEF — "Sofia was in a car wreck, as Lucy read in the paper. The hospital is crowded. These young men, Jack and Bob, have been trying to help her get established in this country."

SOFIA — "I remember now. It was all my fault. I only wanted to come to your country to live. Things are bad in Vladivostok. Your friend was doing this to please you, Miss Lucy."

JOSEF — "That's true, ladies. Jack was doing this to earn money for your honeymoon trip to Paris. They already have the annulment scheduled. It will cost them $1500. Lawyers don't come cheap in this country."

Jack winced.

LUCY — "I'm amazed at all of this. Jack, why didn't you tell me you couldn't afford a Paris honeymoon. We don't need to take a trip. Let's just go camping."

JACK — "Thank you, Lucy, for that."

BOB — "Sofia, I'm so glad you're remembering things now. When you're better, we'll have a job for you at the ranch."

MIRABEL — "Jack, you're wonderful! And, Bob, If Sofia needs any help, let me know."

BOB — "Thank you, Mirabel. I hope to take care of her myself from now on, if she'll agree."

MIRABEL — "We need to go. Josef is taking us to dinner at the Ft. Worth Fat Stock Show. Come along, Lucy."

LUCY — "You go on. I'm staying with Jack."

JUST THEN, two Russian KGB guys rushed in.

1st KGB guy —pointing at Sofia- "That's her!"

2nd KGB guy — "You're Sofia Bronsky, Secretary of the Trotsky party in Vladivostok. We're the KGB from Moscow. You're under arrest!"

They quickly handcuffed her.

JUST THEN, three MOB thugs dashed in and grabbed Josef.

MOBSTER #1 — "We gotcha now, Pal. You're Joe Bronson of the East Side Gang. You won't blow up any more of our hide-outs. Put your filthy hands up."

JUST THEN, a tall guy appeared in the door with a Texas Ranger badge on his chest.

MOBSTER #2 — "Lord, help us! It's Lone Wolf Gonzalez!"

GONZALEZ — "Drop yer guns and raise yer hands high, and I mean HIGH!"

There was a clatter of guns hitting the floor.

GONZALEZ — "Now line up and march out to that van outside. We'll teach you not to come to Texas to commit your crimes."

They marched out, leaving an astonished group praising the Texas Rangers.

SOFIA — "How am I going to get these handcuffs off?"

JOSEF — "I have a key. I used to be a member of the East Side Gang, but I'm with the FBI now. We work closely with the Texas Rangers. Drivin' a taxi is a good ruse for me. My headquarters is in Chicago. I'll be leavin' for there right away."

MIRABEL — "I'm going with Josef. We're getting married there."

JOSEF — "You're all invited to dinner and the show at the Ft. Worth Fat Stock Show. Dinner's on me."

They left. They all took him up except Jack and Lucy.

JACK — "I love you, Lucy!"

LUCY — "I love you, too, Jack!"

JACK — "I'll still have $940 after the annulment. That's enough to go to Paris, Texas. They have an Eiffel tower there, too, and a beautiful lake nearby."

LUCY — "Oh, good. Let's do! We can go to France later, maybe."

Just at that moment, Hoss came rushing through the room, followed by Moonbeam, swinging a lariat.

JACK — "Moonbeam, what did he do?"

MOONBEAM — as she disappeared after him- "He kissed me and ran."

LUCY — "Isn't love wonderful?"

FINIS.

P.S. If you're wondering what happened to Jack's saddle ? ?
Somebody stole it.

THE RELUCTANT GROOM

A Two Act Play

LIST OF CHARACTERS

HERBERT COLLINS - Head of household

JUDY COLLINS - His wife

HORTENCE - Judy's older sister. 24 yrs. old

JOE TUTTLE - Hortense's boyfriend. 29 yrs. old

CHIP COLLINS - 18 yr old son

SHIRLEY COLLINS - 16 yr old daughter

BRO. LESTER (preacher) - Hired for ceremony

FUGITIVE - on the lam

FIRST POLICEMAN

SECOND POLICEMAN

MISS TWADDLE - Joe's other girlfriend

BUDDY - Herb's golf partner

NELLIE WITHERSPOON - Gossipy neighbor

FRED - Friend of Herb

THE GG'S - Joe's fraternity buddies

ACT ONE

As the scene opens, Judy is on the telephone at the far side of the room.

JUDY - "No. We're not Republicans OR Democrats. We're Independent. Yes, we'll be voting in the election. I'm not sure yet. No. I won't make a contribution. I disagree. I don't think our country is going to the devil in a hand bucket. Thank you." She hung up phone. Herb came in.

HERB - "Judy, have you seen my golf cap? Where did you put it?"

JUDY — to Herb, as the phone rings again- "I don't wear your golf cap. I haven't seen it."

While Judy was on the phone, there was a knock on the door. It was Buddy.

BUDDY - entering- "Hi, Herb. Ready to go?"

HERB - "As soon as I find my cap. I put it right there. Somebody moved it." He looked behind the sofa.

JUDY -on phone- "Yes, I'll be there. That's Friday, 10 am? I'll bring a salad. OK. Bye."

HERB - "Who were you talkin' to? I'll be home early, Friday."

JUDY - "It was Helen, from the church. We ladies are having lunch together. I'll be home by the time you get here, Herb."

BUDDY - "Judy, you really are a good wife. If I ever find another like you, I'll get married myself. Herb, you're a lucky guy."

JUDY -still on the phone- "Thank you, Buddy. That was a nice compliment. If Herb ever gets tired of me, I'll look you up."

HERB - "Let's not get carried away with this mutual admiration business. I need to find my cap. Hurry up and get off the phone, Judy. We need to get on out to the club."

At this moment, Chip comes in followed by Shirley. Both are greeted by Buddy.

BUDDY - "Hi, Chip. Hi, Shirley. What's doin'?"

CHIP - Hello, Buddy. We're goin' out for a game of tennis as soon as she gets her things together." Shirley is putting on her tennis shoes and checking her purse.

SHIRLEY - "Hi, Buddy... Judy, can you spare me a few tissues? - and a couple of quarters for the coke machine. I know it's going to be hot out there." Judy found the tissues and quarters for her.

JUDY - "Don't stay in the sun too long, Shirley. You know you blister easily."

CHIP -as Shirley is cramming the tissues in her small purse- "Why don't you get a bigger purse? You women are ridiculous!"

SHIRLEY - "Let's go, Crabby. I'm going to beat you today."

As they were leaving, there was a knock on the door and Mrs. Witherspoon, a neighbor lady, walked in.

JUDY - "Hello, Nellie. How are you?"

NELLIE WITHERSPOON - "I'm fine, Judy. Do you have some aspirin? We're all out, and Bob's got an awful headache."

JUDY - "I'm getting a headache myself. We have some. I'll get them for you." She found a half dozen for her.

NELLIE -observing all the activity- "Gee! It's like Grand Central Station in your house. How do you stand it?"

JUDY - "Time heals everything. In about 15 minutes, it'll be like a church in here. Nellie, I hope Bob's headache gets better."

Nellie left. The rest also left, except Judy. Judy started dusting the furniture. As she busily went about, she hummed a tune; then broke out singing, "I ain't Got Nobody, And Nobody Cares For Me". She danced a little jig, then resumed dusting as Herb came back in. He stopped and listened.

HERB - "Why are you always singin' that song? Makes me feel left out or somethin'".

JUDY - It's just a tune. I like the melody. You're not left out, Herb, I'm real proud of you. I just haven't mentioned it much lately. I'm sorry."

HERB - "Aw, that's alright, Judy. I'm not jealous, I forgot to go to the bank yesterday. Do you have any cash? I need $5.00 for the greens fee."

JUDY - giving him the $5.00 from her purse- "Have a good game. Dinner will be ready by the time you get back." Herb left.

5 HOURS LATER: There was a knock on the door.

JUDY -aloud- "Now who can that be?" She quickly opened it.

JUDY -surprised- "Why, hello, Hortence. I didn't know you were in town. I thought you were in Sacramento. Come in."

115

HORTENCE -shedding her coat and hat and stepping inside- "I was last week, but I'm home now. I just wanted to say hello to you while I was in this part of town. Where's Herb and the kids?"

JUDY - "Herb's playin' golf and Shirley and Chip are out playin' tennis at the Tennis Club. There's 2 years difference in their ages, but they like to compete against each other."

HORTENCE - "I thought you might be alone today. That's one of the reasons I came this afternoon."

JUDY - "I can't imagine what it's about. Is someone in trouble?"

HORTENCE - "No. No trouble. I just had a great inspiration and I want to get your reaction to it."

JUDY - "Well. You're so mysterious! Let's hear it. I'm all ears."

HORTENCE - "Judy, while I was up in Sacramento, I was invited to a beautiful wedding ceremony. It was a couple who've been married for 30 years. They had been married by a Justice of the Peace, just like you and Herb. They had always regretted not having a real wedding with family and friends. It was beautiful! I just cried!"

JUDY - "That was nice. Is that all?"

HORTENCE - "Don't you get it, Judy? I know you've said many times, that you missed the pretty formal church wedding."

JUDY - "Yes, but it's a little late now for us, don't you think?"

HORTENCE - "Of course not! It was a 'Renewal of Vows' ceremony. People do it all the time. I read about it every week in the society section of the paper."

JUDY - "I'm not sure Herb would go for anything like that."

HORTENCE - "Men are naturally not sentimental, and Herb's no exception."

JUDY - "But he's a sweet man. I consider myself lucky. We eloped instead of having a formal wedding - But we're happy like it turned out."

HORTENCE - "I was too young then, but I love to dress up for things like that."

She was almost crying at the thought.

HORTENCE - "Why don't you think about it. I'm sure the kids would like it. I'll help you plan it and we'll spring it on Herb on one of his weak moments."

JUDY - "When is one of his weak moments?"

HORTENCE - "Just after a good meal when he's relaxing with his cigar in his easy chair. He may even like the idea. We could have it on your 25th anniversary. That's 2 weeks from now."

JUDY - "I kinda like the idea. It'll all depend on Herb. Sometimes I think we need something like that to get us out of the rut we're in. To kind of rejuvenate us. It's been 25 years. I doubt that Herb will even remember the anniversary. He doesn't put much stock in celebrations."

HORTENCE - "You keep thinking about it. We'll plan it together on the phone. I'll come back next Saturday and we'll spring it on Herb after his golf game and dinner.

"JUDY - "If it would be just a simple rededication ceremony at the church on Sunday afternoon, he might go for that...Where's your friend, Joe? Is he still around?"

HORTENCE - "Oh, we broke up a couple of months ago. He's got a drinkin' problem. I told him to quit drinkin' or stay away. I haven't seen him since."

JUDY - "I always liked Joe. He's such a nice gentleman. I remember when you two first started going together. You were just out of college and went to apply for work. Where was it?"

HORTENCE - "The Crane Co. It was a large mercantile company. Joe was head of the advertising department. The vacancy was in his department."

FLASHBACK:

HORTENCE - "I'm Hortence Fling. I'd like to apply for the job your company advertised in today's paper."

Joe didn't answer. He just stared at her.

HORTENCE - "I'm Hortence Fling. I'd like..."

JOE — -(recovered from the shock of seeing "The Girl Of His Dreams" - love at first sight; whatever.) "I heard you, Miss. I'm sorry. I was distracted there for a moment."

He found an application blank and watched her fill it out. When she was finished, he studied it carefully.

JOE — "I see you're single. That's good."

HORTENCE - "What difference does it make if I'm single?"

JOE — "It's just that this company prefers married people. More stable. Personally, I don't agree with that.."

HORTENCE - "Then why did you say 'That's good? Are you married, Mr. Tuttle?"

JOE — "Did I say that? No. I'm not married, yet. Sometime soon, I hope."

HORTENCE - "What about my application? Do I get the job?"

JOE — "I'll have to let you know after I check with the head of the department. Let's see..," he looked at the completed application, "We have your address and your phone number. When is the best time to call you, Miss?"

HORTENCE - "I'm usually home in the evenings."

JOE — - "Fine. You'll hear from me soon, Miss."

He escorted her to the door. Hortence left, not very hopeful, but she remembered how gentlemanly Joe was. He seemed flustered about something, however. The reason Joe was worried was that his company had a policy of not allowing their supervisors to date the regular employees in their own department. The vacancy was in his department. If he hired her, he wouldn't be allowed to try to date her. So Joe arranged to have the vacancy listed as accounting, instead of his sales department.

On the following evening, Joe showed up at her house with a large bouquet of flowers, to tell her that she had been officially hired. Hortence was pleased, especially as Joe took her out to dinner to explain the routines of her new job.

JOE — "You'll start work each day by punching in on a time clock. You'll have to join the clerk's union. The dues will be deducted from your salary each month."

HORTENCE - "If that's the case, I'm not takin the job! I'm not joinin' any union and punchin' a time clock. It's demeaning. I've had two years of college."

JOE — "Miss Fling, you can't do that. You already have the job. The company put you on the payroll as of yesterday, the date of your application. You'll have to give us 30 days notice. As for punchin' a time clock. We all do it."

HORTENCE - "Your company is some flim-flam, fly-by-night, bunch of crooks. I'll hire a lawyer!"

JOE — "Miss Fling, please don't cause a problem the first day with your company. We have been in business for 55 years. We're one of the largest companies in the city. The pay is good; you'll have 20 days vacation after a year, and health benefits. Jobs are not easy to get these days."

Hortence remembered that she hadn't been able to find a job of her liking since her graduation from the community college, and there was an economic recession in progress.

HORTENCE - "Well, I was a bit hasty and critical. If it's like you say, I'll do it. When do I start work?"

JOE — "You'll start tomorrow, Hortence, if you can make it."

HORTENCE - "I'll be there, Joe."

JOE — "I'm especially glad to welcome you into the company. I'll keep in touch, to see that we treat you right."

From that beginning, their romance flowered, except for a couple of dips.

END OF FLASHBACK.

HORTENCE - "I could tell he liked me. In spite of his frustration, he was so polite and gentlemanly. I really wanted that job. After I started working, he was promoted to an outside sales job. I worried that he wouldn't still call on me for dates, but he did."

JUDY - "Romance is wonderful, scary sometimes, and exciting."

HORTENCE - "Yes it is."

JUDY - "I always liked Joe. He's such a good, friendly person."

HORTENCE - "Judy, I need to get on home. I'll call you and I'll see you next Saturday, if nothing happens to interfere."

JUDY - "Alright Hortence. I'm glad you came. I'll keep thinking about a plan for the anniversary."

At that moment, there was a knock on the front door. Hortence peeked out the window.

HORTENCE - "Good Heavens! It's Joe Tuttle."

JUDY - "Your old boyfriend?" -she peeked out the window- "It's Joe, and he's got a bunch of flowers."

HORTENCE - "I wonder how he knew I was here? I told him, until he quit drinkin', I didn't want to see him again."

JUDY - "Maybe he's quit. We'll have to see what he wants."

HORTENCE - "I suppose we have no choice. You open it. I'll hide in the bedroom."

She left and Judy opened the door.

JUDY - "Oh, hello, Joe. How are you? I haven't seen you for awhile."

JOE — Evidently sober. A distinguished, sharply dressed man, about 29 years old. - "Hello, Judy. Is Hortence here? I saw her get off the bus down at the corner. I just happened to be in the neighborhood. I thought she may be visiting you."

JUDY -not knowing what to do, stammers- "Well, I..."

HORTENCE -coming to the rescue from the bedroom- "Hello, Joe. I'm surprised to see you. I thought you were in Florida, soaking up some of their brand of sunshine."

JOE — "Hor, I've been lookin' for you. I wanted to tell you that I'm on the wagon now. I brought these flowers for you. I can't pass a flower shop without thinkin' of you."

HORTENCE -taking the flowers- "That's sweet of you, Joe. Thank you. What kind of wagon are you on? You mean the one with those pretty draft horses?" They sit down in the living room.

JOE — "Hor, you and your wit! No, I've been goin' to meetings of the GG's. They've settled down now, Hor."

JUDY - "What's the GG's?"

HORTENCE - "It's Joe's fraternity. He's a founding member. Their idea of fun is breakin' up marriages."

JOE — "It stands for Good Guys. It's a social club. We have fun and help each other with our problems. We also sponsor a boys' baseball club."

JUDY - "Herb should join something like that. He doesn't believe in trying to change. He's still back in the 60's."

HORTENCE - "What have you been doing lately, Joe? How's your friend, Miss Twaddle, the waitress at the bowling alley?"

JOE — "Aw, Hor. I wasn't serious about her. She doesn't compare to you. She married the cook. They're a happy couple now."

HORTENCE - "I thought she married him the last time."

Chip and Shirley came in, just back from a tennis game.

JUDY - "Well, hello! Who won this time? You both look exhausted."

SHIRLEY - "Mr. Superstar, as usual. But he cheats. I did pretty good in spite of it."

CHIP - "She needs new contacts. She thinks everything she hits is in bounds, and mine are all 'out'. But she's my 'little' sister, and I love her." He gave Shirley a hug.

JUDY - "Joe, you remember Shirley and Chip, don't you?"

JOE -getting up and bowing and shaking hands with both- "Sure I do!. It was about two years ago. I think it was a piano recital, wasn't it Shirley?"

SHIRLEY - "That was a disaster! I'm better now."

CHIP - "I've got to hurry and take a shower. Got a hot date at 6:30. Glad to see you Mr. Tuttle, and you, too, Aunt Hortence."

Chip and Shirley left.

HORTENCE - "Speaking of 6:30, it's getting late. I need to get going. It'll be 7:30 by the time I get home."

JOE - "Hor, you don't need to catch that lousy bus. Let me take you home. I want to talk to you some more."

JUDY - "That's nice of you, Joe. I'm sure Hortence will appreciate that."

HORTENCE -between a rock and a hard place- "Well, Joe, if it's not too much trouble."

JOE — "Nothing's too much trouble when it concerns you, Hor, my Dear."

Hortence gathered her things and started to leave with Joe.

JUDY - "Wait, Hortence. Your flowers."

HORTENCE - "Yes, the flowers." She took the flowers.

JUDY - "Take good care of her, Joe."

JOE - "It's my life's ambition."

HORTENCE - "Judy, I'll call you."

Joe and Hortence left.

LATER Judy is sitting in a chair. Herb comes in, looking tired. He plopped down on the sofa.

JUDY - "Herb, dinner is almost ready. How'd the game go today?"

HERB - "I shot 102 today. I would have shot 99 if I'd been the scorekeeper. Buddy was keeping score today."

JUDY - "Hortence dropped by today. She reminded me that next Saturday week is our 25th wedding anniversary."

HERB - "Why doesn't your sister get married herself? She's 24. She keeps up with everybody else's anniversaries. Joe's a nice fellow. I don't see what she's waitin' on."

JUDY - "They've set a date twice, and both times Joe didn't show up in time. He was out celebrating, she said."

HERB - "That was what Hortence thought. Actually, his GG buddies got him to drinking and convinced him that the current date was Friday - it was really Saturday, the day of his wedding. They even turned the clock back two hours.."

JUDY — "I remember that. She didn't believe any of it. The second date they set, after Hortence settled down was even more bizarre. Joe claimed that the GG's got him groggy, kidnapped him, and dropped him off out in the country, in just his shorts. His buddies rescued him later, but it was too late for the wedding."

HERB - "That was two months ago."

-A pause in the conversation-

JUDY - "Herb, our 25th anniversary is supposed to be special."

HERB - "What's special about it?"

JUDY - "We should do something different. We have had a happy 25 years together. Our kids would enjoy it, too."

HERB - "OK. It's fine with me. We could all go to dinner at Norco's 'All-You-Can Eat' restaurant, or something like that. I'll leave it up to you and the kids."

JUDY - "Alright, we'll come up with something. I've got to check on the roast in the oven." She left.

JUDY -on phone- "Hortense, I've talked to Herb about our 25th Anniversary. He said that it's up to me and the kids. So you come over Saturday and when he comes back from his golf game, we'll spring it on him. I'll have his favorite dinner. You're invited to dinner with us, so I'll see you then. OK?" She hung up.

SATURDAY-PRESENT TIME: Judy-Herb-Hortence-Chip-Shirley. They had just finished Judy's "special" dinner and as they streamed into the living room from the dining room:

HERB -patting his stomach- "Boy! That was a good dinner. It beats Norco's a mile. Judy, you're the best! Nobody can top your chicken and dumplins and pecan pie." Judy escorted Herb over to his regular easy chair, fluffed up the cushions, and fixed his feet on the ottoman. Chip got him a cigar and helped him light it.

JUDY - "There you are, my sweet husband for the last 25 years. Isn't he the best, kids?"

SHIRLEY - "I'm looking for someone just like you, Daddy."

CHIP - "He's the greatest! Just needs to be a bit more generous with my allowance."

HORTENCE - "If I could just get Joe to be more like you, Herb."

HERB - "I don't know what's goin' on here, but somethin' is! All these compliments! What's up?"

He started to get up but Judy restrained him; sat down on the ottoman at his feet.

JUDY - "It's about our 25th wedding anniversary, Herb. You said I could plan it. Remember?"

HERB - "Well, what's the big deal about that? Where do we eat?"

JUDY - "We'll eat later. We've planned for a 'renewal-of-vows' ceremony next Saturday at the church. Brother Lester will be the pastor."

HERB -stunned- "I ain't goin' through nothin' like that! All those people, publicity and such. I'd be embarrassed to death."

JUDY - "It'll only be family and a few friends like Joe, Buddy, and a few more from the church."

HORTENCE - "Herb, there won't be any press if you object."

SHIRLEY - "Come on, Daddy. I missed your other one."

CHIP - "We'll fix you up like Clark Gable, tux and all."

HERB - "That's too expensive."

JUDY - "We got a bargain. Hortence and I will split the fee." Herb thought. it over for a minute.

HERB - "I might do it if you'll have it here at home, in the living room. It's plenty big for that."

Judy and Hortence held a short conference.

JUDY - "OK. Herb. We'll have it here in our living room."

HERB - "I think it's silly, but I'll go through with it. Just plan to make it short and quiet. I don't want to wear one of them monkey suits any longer than I have to."

During the next week, Judy and Hortence made all the preparations for the event.

Act Two

SCENE: IN THE LIVING ROOM - SATURDAY 5 PM.

Lots of activity in the Collin's household as they were preparing for the ceremony. Chip came in with a suit box. He approached Herb.

CHIP -Taking a tuxedo out of the box- "Here you are, Dad. Just your size."

HERB -surprised- "It's brown! Who ever heard of a brown tux? And it's got tails! I ain't wearin" nothin' like that!"

SHIRLEY - "That's the style now, Daddy. Black's kind of old fashioned. I picked out the color."

CHIP - "Too late to change now. The shop's closed already."

HERB -reluctantly- "OK. I'll take it off as soon's this thing is over. Why did I ever agree to this, anyway."

There was a knock on the door. Shirley opened it. It was Fred, a friend of Herb's. He walked in.

HERB - "Hello, Fred."

FRED - "Wow! Did I walk into a wake or somethin'? What's the get-up for, Herb?"

HERB - "Fred. It's just for a wedding ceremony we're havin' here tonight."

FRED - "Who's gettin' married?"

HERB - "I am. Can't you see?"

FRED - "I thought you and Judy were already married. You had me fooled, Herb."

HERB - "It's a 25th anniversary 'Renewal-Of-Vows', Fred. They say everybody's doin' it now."

FRED - "No kiddin'. Don't tell my wife about it! I'll see you later. Sorry to interrupt."

Fred left. There was another knock on the door. Judy opened it. It was Nellie Witherspoon, the gossipy neighbor from across the street.

NELLIE - "Hello, Judy. I've been seeing all the comin' and goin' here this morning. Is somebody sick?"

JUDY - "No, Nellie. We're just having a private 25th anniversary 'Renewal-Of-Vows' ceremony in a couple of hours. Nobody's sick. I'll tell you about it later. It's just a family affair."

NELLIE - "Who's the preacher?"

JUDY - "It's Brother Lester. We're all OK, Nellie. Thank you for checking on us. I'll see you later." Nellie left.

HERB - "Why did you have to tell her all the details about it? She'll have the news all over town in 30 minutes. I'll bet the newspaper guys will be knockin' on our door before we're through."

JUDY - "I don't think we're that important, Herb. Don't worry. Everything should go smoothly at the ceremony. You'll see."

SATURDAY 7 PM - IN LIVING ROOM.

Everyone was assembled in the Collin's living room, all dressed in their finest. Herb, uncomfortable in the rented tux, and Judy in a beautiful pink bridal dress she borrowed from the upscale dress shop where she worked. Hortence wore her best; the same one she wore to all special occasions -weddings, funerals, etc.- It had been a hot day, and was still warm at 7 pm. Herb was sweating in the tux and a tight bow tie.

BUDDY - "You look like a preacher yourself, Herb. Those tails!"

HERB - "I'm just about to explode in this outfit."

CHIP - "You look real good, Dad. No kidding."

SHIRLEY - "I'm so proud of you, Daddy."

BUDDY - "I'm goin' to get one of those to wear at the golf course."

HERB - "You won't be playin' with me."

JOE — "I envy you, Herb. If I can get Hor to say 'Yes', I might be wearing that suit next."

Finally, everything was about ready for the ceremony.

BRO. LESTER - "Everybody please take your places. We can start our ceremony now."

The organist played "The Processional". Chip escorted Herb across the room to in front of the "flowered wedding arch". Shirley escorted Judy and stood her beside Herb.

BRO. LESTER - "We are gathered here this evening to unite in Holy matrimony..."

Suddenly, a loud police siren was heard. It got louder and louder. Everyone froze.

BUDDY - "Golly! Sounds like they're comin' here."

Then without warning a trampy looking man burst into the room through the front door. Evidently frightened, he hesitated, then dashed out of sight through the kitchen door. Immediately after, there was a loud knocking on the front door. Buddy opened it and two policemen quickly entered.

1st POLICEMAN - "Where did he go? We saw him come in here."

HERB - "He just rushed in here and rushed out. Who is he?"

2nd POLICEMAN - "He was breaking into a house down the street. When he saw us, he ran this way. He came in your front door."

JOE — "He went through that kitchen door. There's a back door that goes outside."

The policemen rushed through the kitchen and outside, where with their flashlights, they made a search of the backyard and surroundings.

BRO. LESTER - "This used to be such a safe neighborhood."

JUDY - "It still is. We just need to keep the crooks out."

CHIP - "He probably jumped over our back fence and is gone by now."

The policemen came back in.

1st POLICEMAN - "He's not out there," -pause- "Since we're not sure that he did leave the house, we'll have to search it for your protection."

They made a quick check of the rooms.

2nd POLICEMAN - "Where is the little door to the attic?"

JUDY - "It's in the kitchen ceiling." She showed it to them

HERB - "You won't find him up there. He disappeared too quickly. He must have gone outside."

Nevertheless, they insisted and one of the policemen ascended into the attic.

HORTENCE - "If he's not outside or in here, where did he go?"

HERB — This is a waste of time!"

BRO. LESTER - "We need to get on with our ceremony." Herb tugs at his tight collar; wipes his forehead.

2nd POLICEMAN -from the attic- "Bill, he's not up here, but I've found some thing very, interesting."

1st POLICEMAN - "Bring it down." The 2nd Policeman handed down a large brass bell.

2nd POLICEMAN - "If I'm not mistaken, this is the bell that was stolen from the church belfry down the street about 10 years ago."

BRO. LESTER - "That's our bell alright. I'm surprised at you, Mr. Collins. I don't know what to think of you, Sir."

HERB - "I didn't know that thing was up there. I've never been up in that attic."

1st POLICEMAN - "It's still an open case. I'm sorry, Mr. Collins, but we'll have to arrest you for stealing this bell."

He proceeded to handcuff Herb and to read him his rights. Everybody was stunned and began to protest at once.

JUDY - "Not Herb! You can't do that. We've only lived here for eight years. It must have been the owner before us."

2nd POLICEMAN - "Can you prove that, Mrs. Collins?"

JUDY - "I sure can. Wait just a minute." She left.

BUDDY - "Herb might fudge a bit in a golf game, like myself, but he'd never steal a church bell."

Judy came back in with some papers.

JUDY - "Here's a copy of our purchase agreement from Mr. Jeb Brock, the former owner. It's dated 8 years and 2 months ago."

1st POLICEMAN -examining papers- "Jeb Brock. He's dead now, but I remember him. He complained several times about the church bell keeping him awake on Sunday mornings. I suppose he just up and stole it and stashed it in his attic."

HERB - "Well, you can find old Jeb down in the cemetery. Go arrest him and let me go."

BRO. LESTER - "They used to start ringing it at 7 am on Sunday morning. I was glad when it stopped ringing, too."

1st POLICEMAN -taking the handcuffs off of Herb- "You're right, Lady. It's too late for Mr. Brock, but we'll have to take the bell. We're very sorry we interrupted your affair." They left with the bell.

BRO. LESTER - "They should have left it up there. We don't need a bell anymore....Well, can we resume our ceremony?"

Finally, everyone was settled down again and Bro. Lester and the organist were ready.

BRO. LESTER - "We are gathered here this evening to unite in Holy Matrimony.."

WHEN — SUDDENLY — the same trampy looking man appeared from the kitchen area. Screaming "Get out of the way!" He ran back across the living room and out the front door.

HERB - "Judy, lock that door!"

Judy quickly locked it. Immediately there was a banging on the door from outside.

VOICE - "Let me in!"

HORTENCE - "That's Joe. What's he doing outside?"

Judy unlocked the door and Joe came in.

JOE — I went out to my car. That guy almost knocked me over. He's gone for sure now, out of sight down the street.

Hortence was suspicious. Later she noticed Joe put a small brown sack on top of the grandfather clock. While Bro. Lester and the organist were getting things arranged again, she snitched the bag and took it just inside the kitchen. It   was a bottle labeled "Old Crow". She sniffed it.

HORTENCE -aloud to herself- "I wonder why Joe likes this stuff so much?" She took another sniff; took a sip; smacked her lips; took another sip.

JOE — - "Hor, where are you? We're ready to go out here. Horrors!"

Hortence, on hearing Joe's call, quickly tried to decide what to do with the liquor.

JOE — - "Hor, we're waiting for you."

HORTENCE -aloud to herself- "I've got to get rid of this somewhere."

Not knowing what to do, she drank the rest that was in the bottle and put the empty bottle in her brassiere, just as Joe   found her.

JOE — "There you are. Come on. We're ready to start."

Hortence couldn't speak for a moment, but managed an ..."OK." They were all ready again to begin the ceremony. The organist played "The Processional". Chip escorted Herb across the room to the "flowered wedding arch". Bro. Lester beamed a wide smile at Herb. Suddenly, there was a blinding flash.

HERB -startled- "What's that?"

BUDDY - "It's a newspaper reporter."

HERB - "This is so ridiculous!"

He yanked off the bow tie that was choking him, threw it and the boutonniere to the floor and stalked out the back door. Everyone was stunned.

BRO. LESTER -recovering from the shock-" Well, somebody owes me
    $100.00. I came prepared to perform a wedding ceremony!"

HORTENCE - "Lucky there wasn't much left in that bottle. Joe!"

JOE - "What, Hor?"

HORTENCE - "Yes!"

JOE — - "Yes, what?"

HORTENCE -"hic"- "You asked me to marry you," -"hic"- "I wasn't
            ready then. Well, I am now."

JOE — "You really mean it? That's wonderful! When can we do it?"

HORTENCE - "Right now!" She led him up to Bro. Lester. " Here we
            are."

JUDY -Flabbergasted- "Well, I never! Wonders never cease!" She went
    to the back door and yelled: "Herb, come back. You're safe now."

Bro. Lester lined up Joe and Hortence in front. He spied the bottle in
Hortence's brassiere. He took it out; looked reprovingly at her; tried to
take a drink. It was empty. He looked around for a place to put it. No
place handy, he put it back in her brassiere. Joe on seeing that, took it
out and put it in his coat pocket.

BRO. LESTER - "Ahem! Can we please go with this ceremony, before
            something else happens?" As the organist played "The
            Processional" for the 3rd time.

BRO. LESTER - "We are gathered here this evening to unite —etc."

Herb quietly slipped back in. He led Judy to be next to Joe and Hortence
and went through the motions of being married. He hugged and kissed

Judy as Bro. Lester pronounced both couples husband and wife. As congratulations were being given to the two couples:

HORTENCE -speaking to Judy- "Joe is such a sweet man. He needs someone to help him stay sober."

Suddenly there was a loud knock on the front door. Judy opened it.

LADY AT FRONT DOOR - "Is Joe Tuttle here? I see his car outside. I've got a package for him."

HORTENCE -from across the room- "You're too late, Miss Twaddle. He doesn't need a bootlegger anymore. Just drink it yourself. He's all mine now!"

BUT THEN — ANOTHER knock at that front door! Buddy opened it. It was three men. "Joe!" called out one.

JOE —seeing them- "Heaven help us! It's the GG's. Quick Hor."

They dashed out the back door.

THE 3 MEN - "We just wanted to congratulate our buddy."

CURTAIN.

CHELSEA GIRL

LIST OF CHARACTERS:

BILL ROBBINS — A student in Audubon College.

MARCIA — Waitress in school cafe.

SUSIE BIGGE — Also a student, Bill's girlfriend.

CHELSEA SHAW — Susie's best friend.

FLO — A student.

RITA — A student.

MR. BIGGE — Susie's father.

PIERRE LE FOLLETTE — Employee of Mr. Bigge.

MESSENGER — (POPEYE # 1)

GYPSY (Mr. Stambosky) — Passenger on plane.

DESK CLERK — At hotel in Plainfield, N.J.

MRS. JONES — Temporary roommate of Bill and Chelsea in hotel.

MISS SWEENEY — Another roommate "

TAXI DRIVER — (Popeye # 2) Takes Bill and Chelsea to Central
        Park.

PARK NATIVE — Welcomes them to N.Y.C.

POLICEMAN #1 — A good guy, knows Mr. Bigge.

MARY — Housemaid in Mr. Bigge's house.

POLICEMAN #2 — At Central Park, arrests fighters.

JAILOR — Stern but good guy, since he's a friend of Mr. Bigge's.

SUSIE'S FRIENDS In N.Y.C.

MESSENGER #3 — Also looks like Popeye.

JOE — 1st robber.

MUGGY — 2nd robber.

FRANK AND ROCKY — 3rd and 4th robbers.

MR. BIDDLE — Owner of old house.

CHELSEA GIRL

Chapter One

Time was 9:00 AM at Audubon College, Columbia, Pa. It was a dark, cloudy day, and a slow drizzle was falling. Sheltered by the overhang of the roof of the Cozy Corner Cafe, sat an old man. He looked ragged and frail. Beside him on the sidewalk was a small cup holding a few coins. He paid no attention as Bill Robbins approached the entrance of the cafe. Bill dropped a quarter in the cup, as the old man turned his weary eyes toward him.

"Thank you, Sir," said the man, as Bill entered the cafe. Inside, Marcia the waitress poured Bill a cup of coffee.

"Marcia, who is the old man out front? He looks pretty frail to be out in this weather," said Bill.

"I don't know except he said his name was Howdy, she said. "You look worried, Bill. Where's Susie, your girlfriend? She's usually with you for breakfast. You two are among my best customers," said Marcia.

"I know, Marcia. Susie's always right on time."

"She's probably like I am," said Marcia. "Girls can't afford to be too predictable. It's likely not too serious. This campus life is a bit hectic at times."

A FEW MINUTES LATER: "Do you want to order now, Bill?"

"No, Marcia. I think I'd better go and check on Susie. Something must have happened. I'll see you later, but fix me a large sandwich and another coffee to go. I'll give it to the old chap out front. He looks like he could use it."

Marcia fixed the sandwich and coffee for Bill and he left. The old man appeared to be asleep. Bill tapped him on the arm.

"Here's a little something to help you fight this lousy weather, my friend," said Bill, as he gave the man the food and dropped a $5.00 bill into the cup.

"God bless you, Sir," said the man.

"You're welcome," said Bill. Bill thought of how his dear deceased mother was noted for always helping people who needed it, especially those who were hungry. After trying to contact Susie again, he called the pastor of his church and asked him to check on the old man known as Howdy. Then he tried again to reach Susie. Still no answer at her apartment. Bill was troubled.

LATER. 2:00 PM. A light rain was falling. In the school library, several students were loitering about.

"I think I flunked that test," said Flo. " I'm glad it's only three weeks left in this semester."

"Thank Heavens!" said Rita.

"Did you hear the scuttle about Susie?" asked Flo.

"Now what? Is she in some kind of trouble or something?"

"That depends," said Flo. "She left school and flew home to New York City last night. Her boyfriend, Bill Robbins, is going to be shocked when he finds out. I hear they had a spat yesterday. She's an awfully sweet girl, but a little mixed up about something."

"I saw her just before the last class yesterday. She seemed angry about something. I think she's just lonesome for her dad and friends in New York City and some fellow named Pierre."

"Whoa! Here comes Bill now; I don't want to be the one to break the news," exclaimed Rita.

"Me either!" agreed Flo.

They both left the library, which was now vacant. Bill Robbins entered. He threw his hat, umbrella and raincoat on a chair.

"What a gloomy day! I didn't sleep a bit last night. I wonder where Susie is? She didn't meet me for breakfast and doesn't answer her phone. Nobody seems to know where she is. I hope she didn't take offense from our little disagreement yesterday." He looked around. "Where is everybody?" he asked. He got a coke from a vending machine and stood wondering. He sat down on the edge of a table and said to himself, aloud: "Susie, where in the world did you go? I'm sorry Susie. I thought you understood...." His voice trailed off.

Chelsea Shaw came in. Bill knew that Chelsea was Susie's best friend in school. Everyone seemed to like Chelsea. She was like a breath of fresh air.

"Chelsea, I'm glad to see you. Have you seen Susie? She seems to have vanished."

Chelsea hesitated. "I think she went home to New York City last night. I thought you knew. I'm sorry, Bill. I know that you and she are good friends. She's my best friend and I'm worried about her, too."

"Chelsea, Susie hasn't said much to me about her family in New York City. Do you know anything about them?"

"Yes, I've met her dad, Mr. Bigge. I spent Christmas week there with Susie and her family."

"What's Mr. Bigge like? What about her friends, especially the one she calls Pierre, the French guy?" asked Bill.

"Mr. Bigge, her dad, is a widower," said Chelsea. "Her mother died several years ago. I don't know what Mr. Bigge does. He was gone most of the time I was there. He's a very nice man but a bit stern, and a kind of 'take-charge' guy. Susie is his only child and he loves her very much."

"What about her friends, and the one called Pierre?" he asked again.

"They're OK. A pretty 'hep' group. As for Pierre, he's a lot more traditional. He's a very nice looking person. I liked him a lot," she added.

"You don't say! Do I smell a mouse? What about Henry, your recent boyfriend?" "Oh, him? We were never very serious. He's a nice guy, but I like someone more like you, Bill."

"Oh? Thank you, Chelsea. That's a real compliment. Chelsea, I'm afraid that Susie's dad and friends in New York will persuade her to come back there to finish college. I'm really fond of that girl and she needs to get back here and finish this term."

"Mr. Bigge sent her here to be away from the influence of her friends there. He thinks that they are too much of a distraction. He's anxious for her to finish college. I think she likes it here," said Chelsea.

"Darn! This is awful!" exclaimed Bill. "It's a bad time for her to leave here. I'll bet Pierre had something to do with this. I'm not going to let him take her away from me. I love that girl too much, Chelsea."

"It must have been a sudden decision, Bill, maybe, to talk with her dad. I think she was worried about something, but she didn't mention it to me."

"You girls keep too many secrets," said Bill. "Boys never know what's on your mind." "Ha! You'd be surprised, Bill. I think she'll be right back. The term exams are in three weeks," said Chelsea."

"You may be right, but I think she had other things bothering her than the exams," said Bill.

"Bill, I've got to run out for a few minutes. I'll be right back." Chelsea left.

Bill finished his drink and sat down. Worried, he drummed his fingers on the table. He got up, kicked a wastebasket in frustration, just as Chelsea came back in, accompanied by a red-headed fellow who looked like Popeye of the funnies.

"Bill, this fellow has a message for you from Susie."

"Oh, great!" said Bill, greatly relieved. "I knew things would be alright." Bill took and signed for the message. He read it. He seemed stunned.

"What did she say, Bill? Is she OK?"

Bill read the message aloud. "I'm going home. That's all I can say now. Good-bye. Susie."

"Oh, no! That's trouble!" moaned Bill.

"I've got a brother in The City. If you ever have any trouble there, just contact him. He'll help," volunteered the messenger. Bill was so stunned he didn't answer and Popeye left.

Just at that moment there was a commotion just outside the door. A hefty older man and a younger, well-dressed man strode in. They almost knocked Bill over as he stumbled out of the way.

"Oh, hello, Mr. Bigge!" exclaimed Chelsea— And Pierre! Surprise! Where did you come from? It's so nice to see you."

Mr. Bigge, seeing her— "Hullo, Chelsea Girl! We just stopped by to see Susie Girl for a few minutes. We've been down to Philly and are on our way back home. We're in my plane and thought we'd surprise the little rascal. How do we find her, Chelsea Girl?"

"Mr. Bigge, you just missed her. She flew home to New York last night."

"She did? Well, that's not good. She should stay in school. Was there some problem?" He was very disappointed and showed it. Chelsea, to kind of cool his rising temper, turned and started introducing Bill to them.

"Mr. Bigge, this is Bill Robbins, Susie's friend; and Bill, this is Pierre le Follette." They all shake hands. Bill had just been standing by, taking it all in.

"Oh, yes," responded Mr. Bigge. "Susie mentioned you, Mr. Robbins. I want Susie to concentrate on her education. She doesn't need any distractions or she'll lose interest. I hope you'll understand. I can't have her leaving school." There was an uneasy pause all around.

"Well, we'll go," said Mr. Bigge. "The weather looks bad up toward New York City. Sorry we missed her. Glad to see you again, Chelsea Girl." Bill was so surprised, he didn't say anything in his defense.

"I'll walk a little way with you," said Chelsea. She left with Mr. Bigge and Pierre.

Bill, having formed a jealous opinion of Pierre, wasn't pleased with the closeness of him and Susie's father. Pierre had remained silent except for giving Chelsea a friendly sign of recognition when they first came in. Bill was puzzled by it all. It seemed to him that Mr. Bigge had ordered him to stop seeing Susie. From puzzled to angry, he was in a state of needing to do something. But what? "Mr. Bigge doesn't understand," said Bill aloud. "I'm not a distraction, but I'm serious about Susie. Forget her? No way! I'll call her on the phone right now." He went to a phone and dialed her number in New York. Chelsea came back in.

"Bill, who are you calling?"

"I'm calling Susie. I want to talk with her before she makes a wrong decision. I'm not going to just drop out of her life." Someone answered in New York.

"May I speak to Susie, please?" asked Bill. He received an answer and hung up the phone. "Out with some friends? Well, There is no other choice. I've got to talk with Susie in person," muttered Bill.

"Bill, if she were to decide to finish college in New York, it would be a mistake, but I don't know what we can do."

"Well I do! I'm going up to New York City! Chelsea, what's her address up there?"

"I don't know her address."

"You're a big help. How'd you find her place when you went there?"

"I went with Susie. I spent Christmas weekend there last year. I didn't notice the address, but I'd know how to get there if I was in New York City," said Chelsea. "Just how? Are you psychic?"

"No, but she lives in the fourth house on her street that ends at Central Park. There is a statue there at the edge of the park. I think it's of Abraham Lincoln."

"Chelsea, that would be like trying to find Popeye's brother in New York City," said Bill.

"Maybe the school office has her address," suggested Chelsea.

"It's closed until Monday. Chelsea, will you go with me to help find her house? I don't know any other way. I'll pay your fare."

Chelsea hesitated. — "Yes, I'll go, but I'll have to get back right away." Chelsea had a problem. She didn't want to follow Susie to New York City, but since Bill was determined to go, she thought she should go along. Who knows what might happen.

"Susie is fortunate to have a friend like you, Chelsea," said Bill.

"I'm your friend, too, Bill."

"Yes, I know. I appreciate your friendship, too, Chelsea."

Bill checked his billfold. "Darn! Two tickets to New York City will just about drain me and the bank is closed."

"I've got a little cash and my credit card," said Chelsea brightly. "We'll manage, Bill. This is exciting! I've never done anything like this before."

"OK. We may need a little luck. I've never been to New York City. We'll have to hurry. I'll call the airport for tickets. We'll grab a few things we'll need and I'll meet you at the taxi stand in front."

"OK. I'll hurry." She left.

Bill got on the phone to the airport. "Mmmm kkk press one. Mmmm nnn press two, etc. "I don't have time for that," said Bill. "We'll have to get our tickets at the airport." He left. They took a taxi to the airport.

At the airport there was a long line at the ticket counter. They got behind a grumpy couple with two unruly kids. When he finally got to the inspection contraption, Bill was buzzed twice. He had a pat-down, then back through and was buzzed again. He decided it was his belt buckle. He took his belt off and went through holding his pants up with his hands. No buzz. Great! Just at that moment an announcement over the intercom, "Last call for flight # 642."

"That's our call! Inspector, please hurry. We're about to miss our plane."

"OK. You're clear. Better hurry," said the inspector. Bill and Chelsea started running through the crowd. Chelsea stumbled and grabbed her ankle.

"Oh, Bill, help me! I can't run. It's my ankle."

"Darn! What'll we do?" exclaimed Bill, as he stared at the limping girl. Bill looked frantically around. He spotted an empty wheelchair and grabbed it. He picked up Chelsea deposited her in it and dashed through the crowd for gate #14, still holding up his pants with his left hand. They arrived just as the entrance to the plane was being closed.

"Hold it! Don't close it. That's our plane!" cried Bill. But the door to the plane was closed.

"I'm sorry, Sir," said the flight official, "but all seats on the plane were already filled."

"Damnation!" said Bill. "What will we do now, Chelsea?"

"We have our tickets already. Let's see if there is another plane to New York City soon." They found out that there was another plane in two hours.

"Since we have two hours to spend, let's get a bite to eat," suggested Bill. They went to a food counter and bought drinks and sandwiches and sat down to waste the two hours.

"Chelsea, I've never learned much about you. Where were you born?" asked Bill.

"I think I was born in New York City, but grew up in Rochester" she replied.

"What do you mean, you think you were born in New York City? Didn't your mother tell you where you were born?"

"I never knew my mother. When I was a few days old I was left in a basket at the entrance of a hospital on the edge of New York City."

"That's terrible. How did you get to Rochester?" he asked.

"I was adopted by a young couple from there when I was six weeks old. They are my adopted parents and have been wonderful to me. I love them very much."

"I'm astounded," said Bill. "I'm glad it has turned out so well for you. Do you have any brothers or sisters?"

"Not that I know of. — -How about you, Bill? Are you a native New Yorker?"

"No, I'm from Montana. My dad and mom own a cattle ranch outside of Bozeman. My history is not as extraordinary as yours," he said.

"Oh, you're a cowboy! How exciting! How did you end up at Audubon?"

"My mother graduated from there," said Bill.

"I think I'd love to live on a ranch. Are you going back there when you graduate?"

"That would make my family happy," said Bill. "My major at Audubon is Business Management. I could end up anywhere, even in New York City." They smiled at each other. They were both impressed.

"Bill, take a look at that old foreign looking fellow at that table," She pointed. "What do you make of him?"

"Hard to tell," said Bill, looking at the man. "If it isn't a disguise, he's probably a gypsy from Hungary or there-abouts. The earrings and beads may be fake. He seems to be carefully eyeing people as they pass by." The old man soon finished his food and left.

After awhile they noticed that people were already lined up for the New York City plane. "We'd better get in line for our plane, Chelsea. We don't want to miss this one." They got in line and were soon allowed aboard. Bill and Chelsea were the last to board the new plane. They were directed to the two seats at the front, usually reserved for the elderly or those with infants. To their surprise, they were seated on each side of the mysterious gypsy looking man they had seen in the snack area. Facing them on the other seat were two young women with infants. Bill and Chelsea kept talking across the old guy between them. He looked like he resented it, so Bill moved across to the seat between the mothers. This allowed Bill and Chelsea to talk directly across to each other. But the eight month old girl next to Bill kept hitting him with her rattler. The one on the other side kept clawing his ear.

"Bill, switch seats with me. I love little babies," said Chelsea. Bill was grateful to comply. However, the old gypsy guy seemed to be uncomfortable with that arrangement, too. Then came the hostesses serving drinks, cookies and bags of peanuts. After a little bit, Bill noticed that the old man couldn't open the peanut bag. He tried and tried.

"Let me help you with that, Sir," offered Bill. The man handed it over. "They must seal these bags with super glue," said Bill, as he worked to open the bag. He succeeded in opening it and handed it back to him.

"Thank you. My hands don't work too well any more," said the gypsy guy. With that little "ice breaker," Bill and the strange, dark and mysterious old fellow began an interesting and friendly conversation. "Thank you. Do you and your wife live in New York?" he asked.

"She's not my wife. She's just a friend," said Bill.

Chelsea, hearing Bill's comment— "I'm a friend of a friend. Not quite an understudy to the leading lady, but I'm an optimist."

"I'm sorry. I'm new in America," explained the gypsy guy.

"That's OK. I'm Bill Robbins and this is Chelsea Shaw." He indicated Chelsea. "I'm Bela Stambosky," he said. "I'm from Romania. You two just looked like you should be together."

"We saw you in the airport at the food counter, Sir," said Chelsea.

"You did? I was just watching the people. Americans are so interesting. I like to speculate on what kind of a person each one is and what they do," said Mr. Stambosky.

"Isn't Romania where fortunetellers are from?" she asked.

"That's just a myth, Chelsea. Romania is a modern country now," said Bill.

"We're a modern country now," said Mr. Stambosky, "but we still have our old traditions and diversities. My grandmother was a fortuneteller and a medium. People came to her for advice. I still remember some of her 'truisms', as she called them."

Chelsea, very interested: "What are some of them, Sir?"

Mr. Stambosky - eyes wide as if in a trance - "'Things are not always like they seem' and 'Don't look for diamonds through colored glasses.' Those are a couple of my favorites."

"Oh, that's exciting! You should write a book," exclaimed Chelsea.

"I have. That's why I'm going to New York. It's where my publisher is," said Mr. Stambosky.

"What's the title of your book?" asked Chelsea.

"It's title is 'The True Story Of Dracula's Family.'"

Bill, not as excited as Chelsea — "You've got lots of competition. Seems like everybody's writing a book these days."

Suddenly, the pilot's voice came over the intercom: "Ladies and gentlemen, I've just been informed that the storm has closed all airports in New York City. We have been instructed to land at Plainfield, New Jersey, about 40 miles from New York City. We regret and apologize for this delay, but this storm is pretty bad."

They soon landed at the Plainfield airport. The rain was pouring down. They were bussed to the Olympic Hotel. It was crowded. Another plane had been directed there before them.

"It's getting dark already," said Chelsea. "If we make it to New York City today, it's going to be pretty late."

"We'll have to get a taxi to take us into The City and to the park. Once there, everything should be fine, though it will be late, as you say," agreed Bill. They searched for a taxi but found none.

"It looks like we're stuck here for the night," said Chelsea. "At least we can have a room to freshen up and rest." They approached the check-in desk.

Bill, to clerk: "We'd like a room. We're from the plane that was just diverted from New York City."

"I've got only one room left, but it's large," said the clerk. "It has a double and a single bed. We have room service available."

A Mrs. Jones from Baltimore was standing with them. "For the three of you, I can put in a cot if you'd like."

"I, for one, say 'Yes,'" said Mrs. Jones. "I'm not sleeping on the floor somewhere. We have to wait out this storm. We can sit and drink coffee if we can't sleep."

"I think we'd better take it," said Bill. "I don't know of any other solution. OK with you, Chelsea?"

"I think you're right, Bill." They were assigned and sent up to room 23. The desk clerk sent up a cot and pot of coffee.

They sat down to relax and to contemplate on their situation and the weather.

"Are you two Mr. and Mrs.?" asked Mrs. Jones.

"Yes," said Chelsea.

"No," said Bill. They both answered in unison.

"Ah! I understand," said Mrs. Jones. Bill looked quizzically at Chelsea. She just smiled. "Before I settle in, I want to check on some friends that were on the plane. I want to be sure that they were able to get a room," said Mrs. Jones. "Sure, go ahead. We can be freshening up a bit," said Bill.

Mrs. Jones left. Bill, a bit unsettled by Chelsea's reaction to Mrs. Jones's question, said, "Chelsea, why did you tell her we were married?"

"On the spur of the moment, I couldn't think of what to say. It just came out," admitted Chelsea.

"Chelsea, you're going to get me in trouble yet!"

"She probably didn't give it a second thought. I'm hungry."

"OK. Let's go down and see if we can get in the dining room."

The dining room was crowded, but they were finally seated.

Waiter, -looking them over- "We have a special today. Half-price to all newly-weds, married in the last six months. Do you qualify?"

"What shall I say, Bill?" Chelsea said meekly.

"Waiter, we're just friends," said Bill.

"Oh, sorry! Maybe later, huh?" volunteered the waiter.

Chelsea -after the waiter leaves with their orders— "Seems everybody thinks we're a married couple. Do you think we look like we're married, Bill?"

"Oh, I don't know. We probably look like two lovebirds."

Chelsea giggles — "That's a nice compliment, don't you think, Bill?"

"Well, Chelsea, you are pretty nice company."

"I like you, Bill. This is fun." The waiter brought their food.

"Chelsea, I need to find you a new boyfriend."

Chelsea, a bit surprised and pouty — "I don't want a new boyfriend! I'll just be a Nun, probably."

"Ha! I'm sure you'll find 'The One' for you soon enough."

"I've got strict requirements, Bill."

"I know, Chelsea. You're a lot like Susie."

Just after they returned to their room, Mrs. Jones came back.

"My good luck!" she said. "My friends are here and want me to spend the night with them, so I'll be in room 30."

"Good luck to you two. I hope this horrible weather clears tomorrow."

"That's nice of them. We're sorry to lose you," said Chelsea. Mrs. Jones took her things and left.

Bill —after a few moments of thought — "It just struck me, Chelsea. What's Susie going to think when she learns that you and I spent the night together in a hotel in Plainfield? Especially after the little argument that she and I had the day she left."

"Well, do you think spending the night with me is such a bad thing?" asked Chelsea, surprised and a bit irritated.

"Of course not, Chelsea, I think you're ahh, a real sweet girl. Great!"

"That's encouraging. What were you and Susie arguing about?"

"Oh, she was just a little jealous, I think," admitted Bill.

"Jealous? That's odd. She never mentioned anything of it to me. Who was she jealous of? Madonna?"

"No. It's so ridiculous! It was you. I told her that you were the last person I'd be having an affair with."

"Oh, Bill! You said that?" said Chelsea, astonished, shocked and a bit hurt.

"You think I'm that bad, do you? Maybe I should not have come on this trip!"

"No! No! I meant — because you are her best friend. I think you are terrific, Chelsea!"

"That's more like it, if you really mean it."

"Of course I really mean it," said Bill.

"Which do you really mean?"

"Chelsea, I didn't mean to infer that you weren't a very desirable girl. I appreciate you very much."

"I don't want you to appreciate me. Don't you like me?"

"Of course I like you, Chelsea. You're...."

"I'm afraid to ask you how much," said Chelsea.

Bill, not knowing how to get out of the predicament, sighed and said — "My big mouth! That's what caused the argument with Susie yesterday. I'm in love with Susie, Chelsea. That's why we're on this trip."

"I know," said Chelsea, ruefully.

"You sound disappointed. What's the matter?"

"I don't know," said Chelsea. She realized that she had been falling in love with Bill.

149

Bill —a light suddenly hit his brain — "I'm sorry, Chelsea. I didn't mean to hurt you."

"That's OK. Bill."

Bill —after a couple of minutes — "Looks like we're stuck here until this storm lets up. At least for the rest of the night."

Chelsea —her spirits perking up a little, — "Speaking of the rest of the night; how are we going to sleep?"

"Well, there are two beds; a double, a single,...and the cot. Which would you like?"

Chelsea — hesitating — "I'll....take the double. Which would you like?"

"There's only one left, so I'll take the single," said Bill.

"If you'd rather sleep in the double, I'll..."

"No, it's settled. I'll string up a couple of sheets so you'll have your privacy."

"I can't ruin these clothes by sleeping in them, so I'll change to my pajamas. I hope you won't be embarrassed."

"I'll try not to look," said Bill. Bill found a couple of sheets and erected a semi-partition between the beds.

By this time it is about one am. "There you are, Chelsea. I hope you can sleep well."

"I'm usually a sound sleeper, but sometimes I may walk in my sleep. Do you?" asked Chelsea.

"It's funny that you should mention that. I have a few times," admitted Bill.

"Well, just remember, I'm not Susie. Goodnight, Bill."

"Goodnight, Chelsea." They each prepare for bed. Bill, from beyond the partition, "Are you in bed? I'm turning out the lights."

"Yes, I am."

"OK, goodnight, Chelsea." "Goodnight, Bill." (Click. The lights go off.)

About a minute later, "Bill, it's awful dark. Can you turn the lights on dim just a little?"

"Oh, alright! Do you want me to come and read you a story?" Bill turned the lights on dim. It's quiet for a few minutes and Bill hears Chelsea softly singing "Cloud Nine". It startled him. He realized that Chelsea may be in love with him. What a dilemma! He lay there thinking. "I wish I had a twin brother. Chelsea is such a sweet girl." He understood Chelsea better. He had thought of her more like a young sister than a lover. A warm feeling surged through his body. He quietly got up and sneaked over to where she was now asleep. He looked at her a long time. Did he love her, too? What a beautiful picture.

Just at that moment, there was a knock on the door. Bill- startled -opened the door. It was the desk clerk.

"I'm sorry," he said. "Can you possibly let another share your room? Everything else is full."

Chelsea- coming awake -"Male or female?"

"It's a young lady whose car stalled in the storm."

"Yes, of course," answered Bill. The desk clerk stepped aside and a drenched young lady appeared.

"This is Miss Sweeney. Thank you kind people," said the clerk. He left and Miss Sweeney was invited to share the double bed with Chelsea.

Miss Sweeney- hesitating -"Let me take the single, and you can sleep with your husband."

"He's on some kind of 'sweat' tonight. He used to be a hermit," said Chelsea. "I'll revert to being a hermit tonight, Miss Sweeney," replied Bill.

"You got caught in this heavy rain? It's no wonder that you are wet and cold," remarked Chelsea, as they prepared for bed.

"My car was drowned out about a mile down the road. A lot of crazy things have happened to me today. I'm ready for a quiet warm bed. I'll sleep like a log." They all get to bed. Lights are on dim.

LATER: —It was 4:00 AM. All was quiet. Then a slight noise; a gurgling sound. It was Miss Sweeney. She had begun to snore. Bill stirred. He sat up and looked around. He went over and stood at Chelsea's bed. She opened one eye, but didn't move. She sensed that someone was standing there and that it was Bill. She still didn't move. She remembered their comments about sleep walking. Was Bill awake? Suddenly, Bill went back to his bed. She sneaked a look. Evidently he was going to stay. She wasn't sure that he had been asleep, so she settled down and tried to go back to sleep. Miss Sweeney continued to snore. Suddenly, he was there again at her bed. She closed her eyes and waited. When he bent down to kiss her, she suddenly grabbed him around the neck, pulled his head down, kissed him passionately and held on tight. Bill, losing his balance, fell heavily onto the bed, causing it to collapse with a loud noise.

Bill and Chelsea, laughing, screaming and tumbling, finally managed to get off the pile of bedding onto the floor.

Miss Sweeney, now on the floor and terrified, quickly got up, grabbed her things and was out the door. "Good-bye! Don't mind me!" she yelled, as she slammed the door on her way out.

"What happened?" asked Bill, as he switched on the lights.

"You were supposed to be walking in your sleep."

"What happened to your bed?"

"It just caved in when you fell on it," said Chelsea.

"Poor Miss Sweeney! I'm sorry she didn't get her 'quiet, warm sleep,'" said Bill.

"Chelsea, that was a wonderful kiss. You surprise me!"

Coyly — "Would you like another?" she asked.

"Don't tempt me. I don't think I'll ever forget that one."

"I wonder if you were really asleep?" accused Chelsea.

"Let's go down and see if the coffee shop is open." said Bill. They did.

"I take it you folks are from out of town"

Chapter Two

7:00 am the next morning. The rain still poured down. Their plane was still grounded until about six PM that evening. They were then allowed to board and take off. They had not seen Mr. Stambosky since registering at the hotel. Evidently he'd made other arrangements. They landed at La Guardia airport. They had lost a full day because of the storm.

"Thank Goodness, we're here!" exclaimed Chelsea, as they hailed a taxi.

Bill- to taxi driver- "Take us to Central Park; to the area in the park where Abraham Lincoln's statue is."

"OK. I think I know where that is," said the driver. They took off into the traffic. The rain had stopped and after about 30 minutes they were let out at the edge of the park. Chelsea paid for the taxi ride with her credit card. "This is about the middle of the park," said the driver. "I think there's a statue here somewhere, I remember. Good luck, and I hope you enjoy your visit to The City." He drove away. As he disappeared in the dark distance, Chelsea screamed.

"Stop! Stop! —Bill, he's still got my purse and your backpack. They're on the floor of the back seat. Call the cab office quick. Have him come back."

"I didn't notice what kind of cab it was," said Bill.

"What can we do? I still have my credit card in my hand. Lucky me!" Both stood staring into the darkness toward where the taxi disappeared. "Bill, did you notice that this taxi driver looked almost exactly like

153

Popeye, except that Popeye's hair was red, and this fellow's hair was black?"

"Strange things happen sometimes," said Bill. "So, this is Central Park?" mused Bill. "I wish I had a flashlight. It's too dark to appreciate it. I suppose I can do without a change of socks and underwear for one night."

"Bill, here comes a fellow. He looks like he may be a native around here. Ask him where Lincoln's statue is."

"Sure — I say, Sir, is there a statue of Abraham Lincoln near here in this park?" asked Bill.

"I don't know about Mr. Lincoln, but yonder is a statue. It may be the one you're looking for." He pointed to a statue in the distance. "I take it that you folks are from out of town. Well, Well! I'm sorry, but I'll have to take your cash, and that watch.

I'll take that jacket and those shoes and socks, too, Sir." He pulled out a pistol and pointed it at them.

Bill, after handing over the articles, including the socks — "Please don't take my shoes. My poor feet couldn't stand it!"

"I'm a kind-hearted person," answered the man. "I can see those shoes are too big for me. So, Bon Jooie! Lady and Sir. Have a nice day." He vanished into the darkness.

"Have a nice day! I suppose it's day for him. What else can happen on this miserable day?" muttered Bill. They headed toward the statue in the distance.

"Bill, that statue may not be of Mr. Lincoln, but it may be the right one," said Chelsea,

"I hope so. We can't have any more distractions." As they approached the statue, a man appeared on horseback.

"Here comes a policeman, Bill. They are always helpful. Maybe he can get our things back from that robber."

"He's probably not even near here by now. We might as well forget about your purse and my backpack," replied Bill.

The policeman stopped his horse in front of them. "Just a minute, please. It's past curfew in the park. May I see your identification? What are you doing here this late? It's almost 11:00 o'clock."

"We're trying to find a friend who lives near here," said Bill."

"A lot of people live near here, but none are supposed to live in the park," replied the policeman.

"Officer, a man just robbed us of our money and identification just about five minutes ago. He went into the trees back there." said Chelsea. She pointed back toward the trees.

"She's right, officer. He took my wallet with all my money and identification. Also my watch, jacket and socks."

"That's a likely story. Just what are you up to?" He got off his horse and gave Bill a pat-down.

"Officer, do you know Mr. Anthony Bigge, who lives just four houses off this park and near this statue?" asked Chelsea.

Policeman, puzzled, "As a matter of fact, I do. What are you doing in this park; and what do you know about Tony Bigge?"

"We're friends of his daughter, Susie, and we don't know her home address. We just know that she lives the fourth house from this statue. A taxi from the airport let us out near here about 30 minutes ago and we were robbed back there," said Chelsea.

"Well, I think you're OK," said the officer. "I'm sorry you were robbed. Tony Bigge does live just four houses from here. My horse and I will accompany you there, just to be sure they know you. Tony is on our Police Commission. He's a great guy!"

They walked to the fourth house. The policeman stayed at the curb. Chelsea rang the doorbell. The house was dark inside. After a long wait, someone turned on the porch light. A dog set up a loud barking inside and a female voice answered on the door speaker— "Who's there?"

"Mary, it's Chelsea, Susie's friend from college." Mary, the housekeeper, opened the door as Susie, putting on a robe, came up behind her.

"Chelsea! Where did you come from?" Susie exclaimed. Then she saw Bill behind her. With surprise and irritation: "Bill, what are you doing here?"

"You folks come inside," urged Mary. "It's cold outside." She closed the door behind them.

Mr. Bigge, hurrying up to see what the commotion was about, saw Bill. "You again! Didn't I tell you to stay away from my daughter?"

Chelsea, noting the sudden confrontation, interceded. "Mr. Bigge, we came because we were worried about Susie. When she left we thought she was depressed; and Bill wanted to apologize, didn't you, Bill?"

This statement of Chelsea's was out of the blue for Bill. He had said nothing about apologizing. He didn't understand her statement. It put him in a delicate spot, especially at this time.

Mr. Bigge - who thought the proffered apology was for him — "Uh, that's nice. You folks come on into the living room and sit down. I was a little upset there in Columbia." They were ushered into the living room. Sitting on the sofa was Pierre. He appeared both surprised and displeased. Mary brought some hot chocolate and they all settled down.

Susie was puzzled at the statement of Chelsea's, and of her father's answer. She wondered what they were talking about. "What happened at the college? Who's apologizing to whom? Do you mean me, Bill?"

Chelsea realized she needed to intercede again. "Wait! I'll explain, we had an awful time getting here. Our plane was forced down at Plainfield by the storm."

"I know about the storm," said Mr. Bigge, "We barely got back ahead of it."

"Yes, I know. We left the same day that you did, only later," said Chelsea.

"I'm a bit confused," said Susie. "What happened last night and today?"

"We spent last night in a hotel in Plainfield," said Chelsea.

"You did! Chelsea!" - disbelieving - "Well, now!"

"Susie, the rain was so bad our plane was ordered to land there. It couldn't resume the trip until late this afternoon," explained Bill.

"We were lucky to get a room at the Olympic Hotel last night," added Chelsea.

Mr. Bigge seemed pretty concerned - "So you two spent the night together in a hotel in Plainfield?"

"It was the last room available. We shared it with a Miss Sweeny, whose car had drowned out," explained Bill.

"Well, I suppose you couldn't do otherwise under those unusual circumstances," admitted Susie.

"That's not all," said Chelsea. "From the airport a taxi brought us to Central Park, and then drove off with my purse and Bill's backpack in the back seat. We didn't know your street address, but I knew how to find the house, from the statue in the park."

"Then we were robbed," continued Chelsea, "by a gunman in the park. After he left, a policeman who knew you, Mr. Bigge, brought us here."

"Chelsea Girl, you're still excited. You and Mr. Robbins, Bill, have had a bad day. Since it's so late, and I'm sure you're both tired, let's all get to bed and we'll thrash out our problems in the morning. Mary, will you arrange for their quarters? I'm going back to bed. Goodnight all." Mr. Bigge and Pierre left.

"Chelsea, you can go with Susie. Bill, I'll fix up the sofa for you," said Mary.

Bill, to Susie as she left — "Susie, I do want to apologize to you. I want you to know that before you go back to bed."

"Alright, Bill, I need to talk to you, too. We'll talk in the morning, OK?" "Sure. Goodnight to both of you." Chelsea and Susie left.

Mary, coming in again, "Bill, here are some pajamas that you can use. The bathroom is just down the hall." She pointed. Bill got in bed. Lights were low and the house was quiet. He couldn't get to sleep, so he got up and headed for the bathroom. He stumbled over an ottoman. The dog appeared, growling. When he got back to the living room, Susie was sitting on the sofa.

"Susie, thank you for coming back. I couldn't sleep. I am so embarrassed at the way this has gone. I realize that you were right and I was wrong yesterday morning, and I want to ask your pardon."

"Bill, I couldn't sleep either. When I left school I was so mixed up. I wanted to talk to Daddy. He is so solid in his judgment. I've never been sure where I should finish my schooling. My friends here want me to come back here, but I like my friends at Audubon, too. And of course, Bill, you're special. — Why did you come here so soon?"

"Susie, I was shocked that you had gone; and your message just scared the daylights out of me. I was afraid that you were angry and would not be back. I just couldn't lose you without a fight."

"Bill, I was angry when I left, but I soon realized that I was wrong. I'm surprised and pleased that you care for me so much. I think I'll be coming back to Audubon right away. I'll talk to Daddy in the morning. Now we'd better get back to bed."

"OK, this talk has lifted my heart. I feel much better."

"I feel much better, too," said Susie.

"Then I'll see you in the morning," said Bill. They kissed and Susie went back to her bedroom. Bill settled down on the sofa, and with a smile on his face, was soon asleep.

Early the next morning, Mary came in, opened the front door and retrieved the morning paper. Bill awoke, got up and headed for the bathroom, just as Pierre went in it and closed the door. They nearly collided when Pierre came out, but said nothing. Not even a "Good Morning". When Bill returned and sat down on the sofa, Mary noticed that he had no socks on.

"I'll get you some socks," she said. She left but was soon back. "These were hanging in the furnace room. I think they are extra."

"Wow! Red socks! A good conversation piece," exclaimed Bill. Bill put the socks on and Mary left. Pierre came in. Neither seemed to want to say anything. Finally, Bill did. "You seem to be at home here. Do you live here?"

"I don't think that's any of your business," answered Pierre.

"Well, I think I've got you figured anyway," said Bill.

"Is that so? What's your verdict, old chap?"

"I'd rather not say. Anyway, I'm no 'chap' of yours."

Pierre spotted the red socks on Bill, he walked over and pulled up a pants leg and exclaimed, "Those are my socks. My monogram. I just washed them and hung them in the furnace room. You're stealing my socks" There was a quick scuffle.

Bill shoved him away, pulled off the socks and threw them at him. "Take your old socks," exclaimed Bill. He started to leave.

"Wait a minute," demanded Pierre. "We need to settle something."

"What do you want to do about it? Have a fight right here?"

"You're a coward, too. I thought so!"

"I'm not afraid of you." retorted Bill. "Lets go to the park and settle this. I don't want Susie and Chelsea to know about it."

"Alright! There are some gloves in the furnace room. I'll get them."

"We'll go right now, before the rest get up," said Bill. He put his shoes back on and they rushed off to the park, bumping into each other as they left.

AT THE PARK: "It was pretty immature of you, barging in here last night," said Pierre. "I know Susie was embarrassed by you following her, and making such a commotion. You should have accepted the fact that she didn't want to be with you, you cheapskate."

"It's none of your business, and I don't discuss my private affairs with a clod such as you. Let's get this thing on," retorted Bill.

"Alright, I'm ready! We'll separate, according to the rules, ten feet apart and then come together. You'll get yours!"

They stepped off ten paces, turned and rushed at each other. In a wild flailing and punching that lasted all of two minutes, both were almost exhausted. Neither had succeeded in overcoming the other. A police officer who was patrolling the park saw them and promptly put an end to their battle.

"Hey! You two. Stop it! You're under arrest for fighting in a public park." Both were loaded into the paddy wagon that soon arrived. Who was observing these actions as they left the park, but the "native" who had robbed Bill and Chelsea the night before.

Bill, - screaming and pointing - "Officer, stop! That's the guy who robbed me last night!" He got no reaction from the officer.

AT THE CITY JAIL: Jailer -putting Bill and Pierre in separate adjoining cells, - "You guys might as well settle down for a long stay here. I'm too busy to attend to you right now. I'm getting tired of you bums causing problems in that park." He gave them some water and some old magazines to read.

LATER: Bill and Pierre, bruised and tired, had cooled off, lost their anger, and now even had a measure of respect for each other.

"Bill, I want to apologize for my hot temper. I should have known better. But I do want to say, you're a pretty good boxer."

"You're good yourself," answered Bill. "I'm glad it didn't last any longer. This is embarrassing. What will Susie, Chelsea and Mr. Bigge think?"

"You're right. We're in a pickle. But I'd like to know just what is eating you? You've acted like you disliked me from the first time we met," said Pierre.

"Just who are you, anyway?" asked Bill. "Are you the family guardian?"

"I work for Mr. Bigge. He has an office in his house there, so I'm there a lot. I want to be fair with you, Bill. Susie and I have been dating the last year or so. However, we haven't had much chance to be together since she's been in Audubon."

"Pierre, I appreciate your telling me this. As I understand you, we are competitors for Susie's affection. In the end, it's her decision, as it should be. But I want you to know, I love her."

"I love her, too. So may it work out for the best. Can we shake on that, Bill?"

"Yes, I will," said Bill. They shook hands through the bars. "Pierre, I'm sorry for the mess we're in. Mary brought the socks to me. I didn't know they were yours."

"That's OK, Bill. Forget it. That's all past now."

"We've got to worry about what the girls and Mr. Bigge are going to say. How are we going to get out of here? That jailer sounds pretty tough," said Bill.

"The police chief, I think, called Mr. Bigge and left a message about us. I just hope he got it," answered Pierre.

Meanwhile, back at the house, Susie and Mr. Bigge sat down to discuss her future.

"Susie Girl, you know that I love you and want the best for you. Tell me why you came home; and what are your feelings toward your friend, Bill? Are you in love with him? I was a bit rough talking to him at the college, and here last night."

"Daddy, I came home because I needed to talk with you. As for

Bill? I'm not sure. I know that he loves me. He said so last night. The little disagreement that we had a couple of days ago isn't a problem. We settled that last night, too." "Disagreements are a part of life. Who's perfect?"

"I was a bit depressed," said Susie. "I wanted to know, for sure, if you wanted me to finish there in Audubon. I like it there."

"Susie Girl, I called the college this morning, just to reassure myself about Bill. I also mulled it over last night before I went to sleep. I've changed my mind about that boy. I like him. He's got lots of spunk. He'll take good care of you, if it turns out that way. And, of course, I like Pierre, too. As for your other friends here, they're all good kids, but not too serious."

"Daddy, I appreciate your concern for me. They're all dear friends of mine."

"What I want you to do, is to go back to school there in Audubon," said Mr. Bigge. "You have one more year there. In the meantime, your affair with Bill, or Pierre, will evolve as it should, one way or the other. Just remember, anytime you're worried about anything like this, just call me and I'll come down."

"Thank you, Daddy! I love you!" She gave him a loving kiss.

"Now, we'd better go get those toughs out of the slammer," said Mr. Bigge. "I got the message earlier about them, but I thought I'd leave them in for awhile, just to teach them to control their tempers."

BACK AT THE JAIL: Just after noon, Mr. Bigge, Mary and the girls arrived.

Mary brought sandwiches and cokes for Pierre and Bill. She didn't trust jail fare. Mr. Bigge was in high humor. He congratulated the jail officials and bailed the two culprits out.

Jailer —who knew Mr. Bigge well — "Mr. Bigge, here are your two prize fighters. They seem pretty subdued since this morning. You can have them. I'll get their possessions." He did.

Mr. Bigge —facing Bill and Pierre — "You guys should have woke me up. I'd loved to have seen it. Who won?"

"It was a one-round 'no decision', Mr. Bigge. I want to thank you for bailing us out. It was stupid on my part," said Bill.

"I wasn't very smart either," said Pierre.

"That's alright, if you two learned something from it. You two should be friends," advised Mr. Bigge. The jailer called Mr. Bigge over to sign the release for the boys.

Susie —giving each a hug — "You crazy guys!"

Bill, nodding toward Mr. Bigge, "Did you talk to him yet?"

"Yes, I'm going back. Daddy said he'd take us."

"That's wonderful! When?" asked Bill.

"Tonight." Susie went to help Mary.

Chelsea, who was standing by, "Are you alright, Bill?"

"Yes, I'm OK."

"I was awake when you went to the park. I was worried about you."

"Thank you. - You really are a sweet girl, Chelsea. I wonder about you," said Bill.

"About me, Bill? What about?"

"Only good things, Chelsea. I'll tell you sometime. Some other time."

"Everybody, let's go. Back to the house!" announced Mr. Bigge, with a flourish. They all left.

Susie's friends had found out that she was back home. When the group arrived from the jail, they were waiting for them in the living room. As Susie and party filed in, Frankie and his group began singing. "Blue-Jeaned-Baby", referring to Susie's favorite item of apparel.

Susie introduced all of them to Bill and Chelsea. Chelsea had met some of them before. "You guys are great! I love all of you," she said. "This is a short visit. I'm going back to school this evening. Daddy is flying us back. I can't promise anything except, I'll see you at mid-term and Christmas."

There were many groans, but they understood. They weren't stupid. They decided to serenade her again and sang "I Would Love To". Mr. Bigge was happy and confident, knowing that Susie was back on track to complete her education at Audubon College.

LATER: —It came time to leave for the airport. A "toast" was made for all. Then the doorbell rang. It was a messenger for Bill Robbins or Chelsea Shaw. Bill signed for it. Opening the package, he found his backpack and Chelsea's purse. As the messenger turned to leave, they noticed on the back of his jacket, the initials "FBI".

They started once more to leave for the airport. Pierre held up his hand, "Hold it! Please! I want to sing a song." Pierre sang "Lonely".

Susie ran over and gave him a big kiss. "Pierre, I'll be back when school is out. Wait for me!"

Bill — To himself, surprised at Susie's action, "Hmmm. I don't like the looks of that." Bill remembered that the argument with Susie at school was not just about Chelsea, but about Pierre, too. Bill - still to himself - "Where does that leave me? Maybe we were both partly right back at Audubon."

Chelsea also noticed. She realized that Susie's action was a shock to Bill. She moved over to his side and took his hand. Bill squeezed it in response. He looked over at her as she dropped her eyes and blushed a little. Neither spoke, but something did pass between them- unexplainable — but thrilling? Warm? Bill -to himself- "Chelsea, sweet Chelsea. Such a puzzle. But then I don't understand myself either."

CHAPTER THREE

At the airport, Mr. Bigge's plane took off into a beautiful golden sunset. As it gained altitude the sunset dissolved into a system of low dark clouds in the direction of Columbia, Pa.

"Looks like we have a little rain up ahead," said Mr. Bigge. "Doesn't look too bad. Maybe we'll get to Columbia before it does."

"I hope so. I've had enough of flying in the rain," said Bill.

"Ha! I'm along this time to see that you don't get into any trouble," chided Susie. Don't celebrate yet; I'm along. I seem to be 'Miss Jinx,' or the 'Odd Man Out' on this trip," warned Chelsea.

"I was just kidding, Chelsea. You're my very best friend," said Susie.

ABOUT A HALF-HOUR LATER: — "The rain has beat us to Columbia," announced Mr. Bigge. "Put on your seat belts. We're going through some rain clouds." They flew into the clouds. The turbulence was pretty rough. There was a flash of lightning and an immediate blast of thunder. The plane shuddered as it was forced downward suddenly. Mr. Bigge struggled to control the plane.

"Stay steady folks. We just got zapped by lightning. We'll be OK if we don't get hit again," said Mr. Bigge. Just at that moment the left motor started coughing, then the right. Mr. Bigge struggled to keep the motors going. "We're going to have to land somewhere real quick if one of these motors doesn't pick up. Brace yourselves for a rough landing. I'm aiming for that bare spot in the trees."

The three passengers were frozen with fear. They braced for a crash.

Mr. Bigge managed to bring the plane down in a clearing. He clipped a small tree with a wing causing the landing to be rough and wobbly. It also caused Mr. Bigge to jam his foot on the floor, severely spraining or breaking his ankle.

Susie was the first to find her voice. — "Oh, Daddy, are you alright?"

"It's just my ankle," said Mr. Bigge. "Help me get this seat belt off."

All three shed their seat belts and Susie assisted her father.

"Mr. Bigge, you saved our lives," said Bill. "That was a very good job of getting this plane down safely, so fast."

"We're lucky. There may be some damage to the right wing or the landing gear. Otherwise we're alright, if I can find out what caused our motor failures," said Mr. Bigge. It was getting dark as they got out of the plane. They looked, but could see no house or other evidence of people. "I can't walk on this leg," said Mr. Bigge." One of us should scout around the area and find someone to come and pick us up. Bill, will you do that? Also someone should go with you and help keep you from getting lost. There should be a road near here.

"Sure. I'll get started right away, before people start going to bed and turning out the lights," said Bill.

"I'll stay with Daddy," said Susie. "He needs a bandage on his ankle. Chelsea, you will have to go with Bill."

"I'm ready. Let's go, Bill, before it gets too dark," said Chelsea.

"Bill, take this flashlight. You may need it," said Mr. Bigge.

Bill and Chelsea left and Susie started searching for things to doctor and bind her dad's swelling ankle. Bill and Chelsea headed toward the area of fewest trees.

"I think we're going South, Chelsea. Remember that. This looks like a pasture. We may find some cows or horses, if that's true, and also a ranch house or something."

"There's a fence. Bill."

"It sure is. That should lead to a house. Which way should we follow it? Let's try to the right. Remember that, too, Chelsea."

They followed the fence for what seemed like 30 minutes. It was dark now and the flashlight was a necessity. The rain had stopped before they had started and the moon shone only now and then through the clouds. They were getting scratched up on their arms and legs by the bushes. Finally, the fence intersected another one going off to the left and right at 90 degree angles. —- "Now what, Chelsea? Should we go right or left?"

"Listen! I hear something!" said Chelsea. They listened. It was a squeaking sound. Really eerie!

"Oh, Bill! That's scary! What do you think it is?"

They listened attentively for several minutes.

"It's not an animal. It must be something mechanical," Bill decided.

"It's to our left," said Chelsea. "In this new area."

"Chelsea, I think I know what it is. It must be a windmill, turned by the wind. If so, there must be a house nearby."

They cautiously climbed through the new fence and headed toward the sound. They found it. It, WAS a windmill, laboring in the darkness, despite the need for a little grease.

"There's the house, just ahead," said Chelsea. "Sure thing! We've come up to it from the rear. There's the road just beyond."...Chelsea, whispering as they approached the house — "it's all dark. I wonder if anyone's here?"

"It may be vacant, but I hope they're just asleep," said Bill.

"What can we do? We can't just stand here 'til daylight."

"You're right," answered Bill. "If there's somebody here, we'll have to wake them. I don't see a car though," said Bill.

They walked around to the front steps, on to a little porch, and looked for a bell. No Bell. Bill knocked on the door. They waited. Bill knocked again, this time louder. Another wait.

"It must be empty," whispered Chelsea.

Suddenly, the door was jerked open and Bill and Chelsea were confronted by two men, one with a pistol. They were quickly ushered inside and trussed to chairs.

Their mouths were taped. It was then that they saw another person, also taped and trussed to a chair. They were pushed against the wall next to him.

Joe, the 1st robber, spoke — "You people just take it easy. Give us no trouble and you won't be hurt."

MEANWHILE, BACK AT THE PLANE: Susie applied ice and bound up her dad's injured ankle. She also treated a cut on his forehead. Luckily, no one else had been injured.

"Things happened so fast I forgot about my radio-telephone. I need to call the Columbia airport and report what happened," said Mr. Bigge.

"Have them call Pierre for you, too," said Susie.

"Yes, I need to let Pierre know. He was to pick me up at the airport on my return. I hope my radio isn't damaged."

The radio was OK. He connected with the Columbia airport and

165

described his landing. They promised to call Pierre.   "Daddy, do you think the plane is damaged very much?"

"I don't know. That was a rough landing. Help me out and I'll check that wing and the landing gear."

She helped him out and he made a check.

"The wing has a rip in it but should be OK. I can't tell about the landing gear. It took an awful bounce, but it looks OK, too. My big worry is what caused our engines to fail."

"If they failed at the same time, the trouble must be somewhere else, don't you think?" suggested Susie.

"That's a smart deduction, Susie Girl. Vibration must have caused a loose fuel line. No, they're separate. It's the ignition."

With Susie holding a flashlight, he spent the next 30 minutes checking the ignition system. Finally, he found it; a "short", caused by a worn wire scraping on the battery box. He quickly taped it. When he got back into the plane and tried the motors, they briefly sputtered, then caught and ran smoothly.

"Thank Heavens, it was something that simple," said Mr. Bigge.

"It's dark already. If Bill and Chelsea were here now, you couldn't take off. What will we do?" asked Susie.

"Maybe they can find someone who can take us somewhere to spend the night. We'll do that. Otherwise, we'll just have to spend the night in the plane," said Mr. Bigge.

"It's been a couple of hours since they left. I wonder where they are? It's getting cold. I'm worried about them," said Susie. "They may have become lost. They should have come back by now. It's so dark out there, even with a flashlight."

They waited another two hours.

"Well, I'm sure they're just lost," said Mr. Bigge. "We might as well try to get comfortable, even if we can't sleep. There are some blankets and pillows in the upper compartments." Susie got them out and they settled down to wait.

MEANWHILE, IN NEW YORK CITY, Pierre received the phone call from the Columbia airport about the downing of Mr. Bigge's plane. There was no mention about injuries. Pierre worried about his employer, Mr. Bigge, as well as Susie and Chelsea; especially Susie. Pierre decided that he should try to help them. He called the Police Dept. in Columbia to report the crash and asked them to try to find the crash site. Next morning early, Pierre flew to Columbia. Arriving there, he took a cab to the police dept. They had already located the plane and found Mr. Bigge and Susie safe. Mr. Bigge had repaired the plane and they were expected to fly into the airport sometime soon. Pierre decided to wait for them at the airport.

BACK AT THE OLD HOUSE, "We need to get out of here, Muggy," said Joe. "People droppin' in here like flies. I thought this was an old abandoned house. Then the guy who says he owns it shows up. Now these two. Next it'll be the cops."

"As soon as Rocky and Frank get back with the car, we can split," said Muggy. "We've already got our share of the loot."—-"I'm goin' out front to watch," said Joe. "You stay here and keep an eye on these creeps."

Joe went out front to watch. Inside, after a bit, Chelsea tried attracting Muggy's attention. Finally he loosened her mouth gag so she could talk.

"I need to go to the bathroom," she pleaded.

"You should have thought of that before you came," said Muggy.

"Please!" pleaded Chelsea. "What would your mother think?"

"I never had no mother," answered Muggy.

"Please, Muggy, You can tie me up again. Hurry! I've got to go." urged Chelsea.

"You damn women!" he growled.

Not knowing what else to do, he untied Chelsea to allow her to go to the bathroom, the rope dangling from her arm.

"You hurry up. No funny stuff," he warned.

Chelsea, in the bathroom, slipped the rope off her arm and hid it in the wastebasket. After a couple of minutes, she flushed the toilet and came back outside.

"OK. Sit down. What did you do with the rope?"

"Oh, it came off while I was in there. It's on the floor."

"You stupid idiot!" said Muggy.

He stepped into the bathroom to retrieve the rope. Immediately, Chelsea jumped up and jerked the bathroom door shut. "Bill," she cried. "Quick! See if you can get loose! Hurry!" Bill, who had been watching closely, knew that she was up to something. While Chelsea was holding the bathroom door shut, Muggy was trying to pull it open from the inside. Bill quickly backed his chair up against the back of the other captive's, so that his hands could help Bill's get loose. It worked. Both were soon free. While Bill and Mr. Biddle, the other captive, were struggling to free themselves, Chelsea was having a hard time keeping Muggy, who was yelling for Joe to help, from opening the bathroom door. Suddenly, the doorknob came apart, leaving Chelsea with a knob and the innards. Muggy, with only a knob, was trapped in the bathroom. Bill and Mr. Biddle tackled Joe as he came rushing in to help Muggy.

They wrestled him to the floor, managed to disarm him and quickly tied him to a chair, just as Muggy managed to break down the bathroom door. They did the same to him.

The robbers had cut the phone lines to the house. Bill found the cut and repaired it. Mr. Biddle called the police and they immediately sent a detail to the rescue.

"You'll never get away with this?" announced Joe. "Before Rocky and Frank get back you'd better be gone or you guys will be dead."

"Who's Rocky and Frank," asked Bill
"You'll see!"

"Chelsea, go watch at the front. I'll watch these two."

Chelsea went to the front window to watch. In just a few minutes she yelled, "Here they come! Both of them.

Two police cars coming from the left, and a car coming from the right. Now they're stopped and are shooting at each other!" "Quick, Chelsea, let's get out of here!" yelled Bill." Back to the plane!"

Bill and Chelsea, followed by Mr. Biddle, rushed out the back door just as Rocky and Frank came in the front.

Mr. Biddle went in one direction; Bill and Chelsea ran toward the plane. They ran until they came to the wire fence. They were out of breath. Bill went through the fence first, then turned and held the wires apart for Chelsea. As she came through and straightened up, their eyes met and held for a moment. It was a MAGIC moment!

Without saying a word. Bill pulled her up into a loving embrace and kiss. Chelsea responded totally. When he released her, both were a little embarrassed.

"I love you, Chelsea, more than anyone else! I've been wanting to say this to you ever since that night in Plainfield. You're the one I want to spend my life with."

"Oh, Bill! I thought you'd never say it! I love you, too. I'm so thrilled."

"I'm thrilled, too, Sweetheart!" — and they embraced and kissed again. They started hurrying toward the plane.

Bill —after a moment — "Chelsea, how am I going to tell Susie? The way I've acted, I feel like a louse."

Chelsea stopped him and kissed him again. "Bill, don't feel badly. Susie has been a mixed up girl. You were jealous of Pierre. Well, Mr. Bigge sent her to Audubon because he believed that Susie and Pierre wanted to get married right away. He wanted Susie to finish her college first, then she got involved with you. It was agony for me! I've been trying to get your attention ever since."

"Sweetheart, you've got it one hundred per cent from now on," affirmed Bill. Holding hands, they resumed running and soon came to the plane.

"Thank Goodness, you're back," said Mr. Bigge. "The plane is OK. We're ready to take off. Help us get the plane down to that level area and we're off again."

They all helped and soon had it ready for take-off.

"Everybody hold your breath. Here goes!" said Mr. Bigge.

He gave it the gun and without the least problem they were in the air again.

"We've got lots to tell you," said Chelsea. "So exciting!"

"I was worried sick about you. I couldn't sleep," said Susie.

During the flight to Columbia, Bill and Chelsea related their experiences to Mr. Bigge and Susie. As the plane neared the airport, Mr. Bigge went through the normal routine for landing. As he approached to land, there was a blinking on the instrument board; a malfunction of the landing gear. Mr. Bigge aborted the landing. He circled around and came in to try again. Same result. He called the tower to report the problem. He tried a third attempt. The tower reported that no wheels were down. It was a crisis - AGAIN!

"Everybody brace yourselves. We're going to have to make a belly landing. When we're down, get out as soon as you can," urged Mr. Bigge.

"Oh, Daddy! Are you going to be alright?" asked Susie.

"I think I know how to do this," said Mr. Bigge.

"Bill, hold my hand. I'm scared!" whispered Chelsea.

"Don't worry, Chelsea. We'll make it OK." He took her hand.

"Here we go, kids. Hold tight!" said Mr. Bigge. As the plane came gliding down onto the runway, the little front wheel section collapsed with a "crack". Then came a terrible thud, then a bounce up and another hard jolt. Finally a loud screeching and grinding, as the plane scooted on it's belly to a stop. Immediately the plane was enveloped in smoke and dust. It was stifling hot as everyone strived to get out. All four made it out, just as the plane burst into flames from the friction and spilled gasoline.

Mr. Bigge —looking around — "Are we all OK? Don't worry about the plane. It's insured."

Running up to meet them was Pierre. He grabbed Susie in an emotional embrace. Bill wasn't close, but he could see the love expressed by both. He suddenly realized that it was a good time to explain his change of heart to Susie. So when he saw her alone, he went over to her.

"Susie, this plane downing and crash, and all the other events have caused me to rethink and understand better a lot of things. I've made mistakes and I'm sorry, but I now realize that you and I are destined to be more in love with other people."

"It's Chelsea, Isn't it Bill?"

"Yes, it's Chelsea."

"I'm happy for both of you, Bill."

"I'm happy for you and Pierre, too," said Bill. They embrace and separate.

As the group started to leave the airport lobby, they ran smack into a big man at a bridge table with a stack of books.

"Buy my book," he said. "All about that mystery man, Dracula."

"Hello! Mr. Stambosky, it's you!" exclaimed Chelsea.

"Hello, Little Lady. Your gentleman seen the light yet?"

"Light as day, Sir."

"And you helped me see it," said Bill.

"I want you should have my book. A wedding present to you." He autographed a book for them.

"It's not until next month," said Chelsea.

"I could have told you it would happen when we were on the plane," said Mr. Stambosky. "I'm a fortuneteller, too, - part time."

"Thank you, Mr. Stambosky, for the book," said Chelsea, giving him a kiss on his ruddy cheek. I'll tell my children and my grandchildren all about you and that exciting plane trip." Just then, their taxi pulled up and they took their leave. Mr. Stambosky resumed selling his book.

END OF STORY.

Music

Cloud Nine

It was just a dream I have each night I can't erase.
You and I were floating on a cloud way up in space.
We were so in love, and such a thrill
To have you there by my side All alone.
I was a bride and you were a groom.

When I'm full awake and wonder how
Can it be so ?
I love you, adore you Sweetheart!
Tell me that my dream is true,
And that you will be mine,
And we'll be together on Cloud Nine!

Blue-Jeaned Baby

VERSE —1
VERSE —2
VERSE —3
TURN AROUND —
VERSE — 3 (repeat)
Blue-jeaned Baby with the flashing eyes —
Stole my heart away.
She's got that certain thing.
She's such a cutie and I'm here to say:
Heavenly Days! What did Santa Claus bring?

Tom Robb

In the evening when the sun goes down
We both come alive.
Chills run up my spine.
We start with " The Jitter" and then the "K.C. Jive ",
Holy Gee! My Blue-jeaned Baby and me.

Pale moon shinin' and the night is young,
And we'll dance the whole night through.
The place is swingin' with the music.
It's great fun the things we do.
 Yow-ee! My Blue-jeaned Baby and me.
(16 measures of music here, no words, then:)
The world, it keeps on turnin';
Summer, Winter, Fall.
Lovers, they keep a yearnin'
Wedding bells, they call,
Thinkin' 'bout my Baby;
My Blue-jeaned Baby-Ooo.
 'Think I'll pop the question soon.
Just to see what she will do.

Pale moon shinin' and the night is young,
And we'll dance the whole night through.
The place is swingin' with the music.
It's great fun the things we do,
I'm talkin' 'bout my Blue-jeaned Baby and me.

I Would Love To

I would love to take you dancing
On that ritzy avenue.
You'd be gorgeous. I'd be jealous.
All the guys there would wish
They could dance with you.

I would love to hear you whisper;
"Dear, I love you. Yes I do!"
From ecstatic, to dramatic;
I would tell all guys there
To just skidoo.

It's a secret with my pillow, and it says to me
You're the only one for me. Believe me.

I would love to pop the question
If you'll promise to say "Yes."
We'll make Disney, have a party
All the rest.
Darling, I may not can give you
Diamonds that are blue,
But dear Sweetheart, I'd love to!

LONELY

I'm just a lonely romantic who's minus a girl (guy).
That's worse than having the flu.
My lonely heart keeps telling me
"Some lovely female will come in view."

No doctor can help me. There's nothing wrong with me-
Except I'm lonely and longing for a kiss.
Now sooner or later she's bound to appear,
Some sweet Heaven sent Miss.

But now when night comes with millions of stars in the sky,
I sit alone in my room.
That old devil Moon keeps taunting me.
I need a sweetheart to lift this gloom.

So somewhere I'm hoping that fortune will be kind
And I will find her, The girl I'm longing for.
Now if you're a girlie and you're lonely too,
I'm looking for you!

Music and Lyrics by Tom Robb

THE TICKET

A Three Act Play

LIST OF CHARACTERS:

HERB — Main character

MARGE — Herb's wife

MRS. HOOKER — Owner of cottages

BUTCH ANDRIOPOLOUS — Mrs. Hooker's chauffeur

HANK — Another tenant of cottages

VOICE ON RADIO

DR. SMITTY — Local veterinary

MR. LOTTERY MAN — In charge of lottery office

LIZ —Young divorcee running for City Council

DAISY — Herb's mother

FRED — Plumbing repairman

ACT ONE

SATURDAY MORNING: COLLIN'S LIVING ROOM.

HERB — "Marge, turn on the radio. Let's get the news."

MARGE - Turning on the radio- "There's nothing interesting on these days that affect us, unless it's a threat of higher taxes, or politics."

HERB — "Maybe there'll be something different."

MARGE - "Everything keeps going up because of inflation."

HERB — "I know. Old Mrs. Hooker is just itching to raise our rent again."

RADIO VOICE - "We're at the lottery office, folks. In just a few minutes, we're to have the drawing for our big $1,000,000. prize. Stay tuned."

MARGE - "I think that's a waste of money. You keep buying tickets but we've never won a thing. Anyway, what would we do with a million dollars if we won? Have you ever thought of that, Herb?"

HERB — "Oh, pay off our credit cards and buy a new car. That's about all. Maybe take a trip. What would you do?"

MARGE - "I'd like to move to a nicer place. Mrs. Hooker hasn't spent a penny on these cottages since we've been here. And I'd like

Tom Robb

> to help some of the poor people who are homeless. I feel so sorry for them."

HERB — "You're right. We aren't too bad off like we are, are we Marge?"

Just then, the doorbell rang. Marge answered it. Facing her was a tall, slender, dark-haired young lady.

MARGE - "Hello?"

LADY - "I'm Liz Holloway. I'm running for the City Council of our city of Lumpkin. I'd like for you to vote for me in the election next month."

MARGE -taking and studying the card- "What party do you represent, Democrat or Republican?"

LIZ — "I'm Independent. Those two parties never get anything done. I believe in action!"

HERB — "It's about time somebody got on that Council and shook things up."

LIZ — "Sounds like you're on my side. I hope you'll vote for me."

HERB — "Oh, I'm not registered. My one little vote wouldn't count for anything."

LIZ — "Sure it would; just as much as anyone else's."

MARGE - "He doesn't keep up with politics. I'll consider your campaign. I always vote."

LIZ — "Thank you. I have to go along."

But just then Hank the next door neighbor came by leading a little white goat on a leash.

MARGE - "Hello, Hank. What have you got there?"

HANK — "It's a goat."

MARGE - "It's a pretty little thing. Where did you get it?"

HANK — "It's been wandering around loose near the building where I work... Herb, you work at the animal shelter. Can you take it with you when you go to work tomorrow?"

LIZ — "I wish I had a place big enough to keep it. I need something to pet."

Hank didn't like her comment.

HANK — "I plan to adopt it, myself."

HERB — "I can't take it with me. I ride the bus. I doubt they'd allow it. Marge takes the car to her work."

HANK — "OK. I'll take it with me tomorrow when I go to work.... Herb, do you have a short rope I can borrow. This leash is too short. I want to graze Hector, that's his name, in my back yard."

Herb got him a rope.

MARGE - "Liz, this is Hank Sims, our next door neighbor. Hank, this is Liz Holloway. She's running for our City Council."

HANK — "Oh? I didn't know there was an election."

LIZ — "I'm glad to know you, Mr. Sims. Yes. There is an election on the 25th of next month. I'll bring you some literature the next time I'm by here. Are you married, Mr. Sims?"

HANK — "No. Just put it in my mailbox."

Hank left with Hector.

LIZ — To Marge- "He's a handsome man. He's single? Is something wrong with him?"

MARGE - "No. He's just a bit bashful, is all."

HANK — Coming back- "Here's your rope, Herb. I didn't need it. I just hooked the leash over my clothes line. That's better."

HERB — "Hank, Mrs. Hooker is taking rent raises around, now. She just left here. If she sees that goat, she'll scream."

HANK - "Golly! She'll be at my place, maybe next. Can you keep Hector in your garage until she's been by my place, old Pal?"

HERB — "It's a chance to put one over on old Mrs. Moneybags. Put him in my garage, and as soon as she leaves your place, you can come and get him."

MARGE - "He's a cute one. He won't be any trouble."

HANK — "Thanks, Pal."

LIZ — "I'll look forward to seeing you again, Mr. Sims."

HANK - (He just mumbled something.)

LIZ — "I've got to go, Marge. I'll see you later."

MARGE - "Drop by any time you're in this neighborhood, Liz."

LIZ — "I will. I like this area."

She left.

MARGE - "Well, she's a 'fresh breeze' for the politics of this town. I like her."

HERB — "Ha. Her 'fresh breeze' will shake a few people up, I bet."

HANK — "She's 'fresh' alright. Fresh behind the ears!"

Hank and Herb put Hector in the garage and Hank left.

HERB - When he came back in-"I think Hank's afraid of girls, the way he acted toward Miss Holloway."

MARGE - "I think you're right. He seems comfortable around me. He just needs to be around females more."

MARGE - "Herb, I think that Hank and Liz would make a good couple. I don't think Hank would ever initiate anything to be with her. What do you think about my having a good dinner and inviting them?"

HERB — "Hank would probably beg off, if he knew why you were having it."

MADGE - "I won't tell him Liz will be there."

HERB — "That might work. Hank likes good food, as myself. Go ahead and plan it."

Herb settled down to read the newspaper, and Marge started preparing dinner. After a bit Hank returned for Hector.

HERB — "Did she get by, Hank? Probably lowered your rent $20."

HANK — "You're kiddin'. The old weasel RAISED my rent $20. a month. It's just me there. I'm the most economical tenant she has."

MARGE - "She raised our rent $30. You're lucky, Hank."

HANK — "What can we do about it? Gimme the goat. I'll take it out on him."

MARGE - "Don't you dare! Hector looks like a model pet."

HANK — "Just kiddin', Marge. Thanks for keepin' him."

Hank took Hector and left.

MARGE - "I need to iron a dress that I washed and hung in the garage. I want to wear it tomorrow."

181

She left but was soon back angrily holding up a chewed, tattered dress.

MARGE - "Look at this! That darn goat has ruined my dress."

HERB — Laughing, slapping his knees— "Ha! Ha! Your little darlin' won't be any trouble, huh? He looks cute but he's just being' a goat. Relax, Marge, I'll buy you another. If we win the lottery, I'll buy you a dozen."

Herb went back to reading the newspaper and Marge to trying to repair her mutilated dress.

RADIO VOICE - "Here we are again folks.. Some lucky person will like this. The winning number for this week's lottery is 7-4-15-21-6. The mega is 13."

HERB — "Something sounds familiar. I think our mega number was 13. What did you do with the ticket?"

MARGE - "It's up there on the bulletin board."

HERB — "I'll check it. On the bulletin board, you say?"

MARGE - "Yes. It was there yesterday. I remember seeing it."

Herb searched the bulletin board.

HERB — "There's no ticket here. Are you sure you put it here?"

MARGE - "Yes, I'm sure."

Marge got up, and both searched the board items.

MARGE - "It was right there, next to the edge. I can't imagine what happened to it."

HERB — "Maybe you picked it off and put it someplace else. Look in your purse. Anything can get lost in there."

The phone rang. Marge answered it.

MARGE - "Hello? —Oh, hello Mother." -to Herb - "It's Daisy, your
    mom."

HERB — "Hello, Mother. Yes, I'm behavin' myself. Where are you? -
    Amarillo? —What are you doing there? —You're on a speakin'
    tour of your League?" —to Marge- "She's comin' for a short
    visit" —back to Daisy — "When will you be here?" — "When
    you can spare the time?"

HERB — "Let us know when you'll be here. We look forward to seeing
    you. —Yes, I'm fine. —Yes, I still take my vitamins. — OK, bye."
    — "What were we doin'? Oh, yes, the lottery."

They searched the purse, sweater, the room, etc. No ticket.

MARGE — "The only explanation I can think of is that the rotating fan
    blew it off. In that case, it may have fallen into the garbage
    can. It sits just in the right place to catch it, if that's what
    happened."

HERB — "You shouldn't have put it in such an unsafe place."

MARGE — "Well, you took the garbage out this morning. You should
    have noticed it. Go out and check the garbage tub."

HERB — (He started out to comply. As he got to the door, he yelled.)
    — "Hank's goat has turned over both tubs and is on top of the
    mess eatin' the stuff."

They both ran out to shoo Hector the goat away. Herb and Marge
searched the strewn garbage with no luck finding the ticket.

**** a loud speaker relayed to audience the voices of Herb and Marge at
    the garbage tubs, and running Hector away. Herb and Marge came
    back into the cottage.

HERB - "We didn't find it. I'm sure that goat ate it. It had to be in that garbage tub, and it was our tub that he was grubbin' on before we ran him away."

MARGE — "Well, it would be a miracle if our ticket won anyway."

There was a loud knock on their door. Marge opened the door and Hank stormed in. He had seen them kicking the garbage around and had rushed out to protest just as they went back into the cottage.

HANK — "What were you doing out there. You've made a mess of my garbage. A man's garbage isn't safe here anymore."

HERB — "Your lousy goat turned those tubs over and was eating the garbage. We had somethin' missin' and were checkin' our garbage for it. I wish you'd get rid of him. He's turned out to be a problem. I wouldn't have one."

HANK — "Hector is a prize goat. He's like a member of my family."

HERB — "What family? You should get married like you're supposed to"

HANK — "I like animals. They don't yell at you and give you a bad time."

HERB — "Last week, when he was in my garage, he chewed up one of Marge's best dresses. I'm goin' to have to buy another because of that prize goat of yours."

HANK — "OH? —Hector was sick that night. It must have been that dress."

MARGE - "I'm sorry if he got sick on my dress. We didn't hurt him today. We just chased him off so we could search our garbage."

Hank left and they resumed drinking their coffee.

HERB — "The ticket is not in that pile of garbage. I'm pretty sure that goat ate it. It had to be in that garbage."

RADIO VOICE -"As mentioned earlier, someone in the Meadowbrook district bought the lucky $1,000,000 ticket in the lottery." He gave the winning number again.

MARGE - "We're in Meadowbrook. It's a good chance it's our ticket, and Hank's goat has it in his stomach. We could sure use the money, rather than some little old rich lady like Mrs. Hooker, who owns all these cottages. What can we do, Herb?"

HERB — - "For $1,000,000? I just saw Hank leave. He was probably going to the gym. We could take the goat to our vet and have it X-rayed. It won't hurt the goat, and Hank won't know. We'll have the goat back here in less than an hour. What do you say?"

MARGE — "For $1,000,000? It's risky, but I'm sure Hank will understand when we explain it to him. He'd do the same thing. Let's do it."

HERB — (looking out the window) — "Hector's back out there again, trying to get a tub overturned. Let's grab him and go."

They rushed out, and amid the screaming, bleating and scuffling, they grabbed Hector and headed for the vet's office.

**** — Loud speaker again relayed voices of Herb, Marge, and Hector.

AT THE VET'S OFFICE —Pictures of dogs and cats on wall—Herb and Marge hurry in and deposit Hector on the counter.

HERB — "Dr. Smitty, can you X-ray this goat for us?"

DR. SMITTY - "What's his problem?"

HERB — "It's us that has the problem. He ate our lottery ticket, and it's a winner."

DR. SMITTY - "What good would an X-ray do if it's all 'chewed up'?"

MARGE - "Don't you see? It's worth $1,000,000. We need the X-ray to claim the money.."

DR. SMITTY - "O.K. Let's take a look. We'll X-ray him and maybe see what's in his stomach."

The vet X-rayed the goat and they took a look at the negative.

DR. SMITTY - "That's a lottery ticket alright but a bit chewed up. I can't get it out without endangering the goat's life. In about 6 hours his strong stomach acids will obliterate the numbers anyway."

MARGE — "Don't kill the poor goat. He was just doing what comes naturally."

HERB — "No. Don't hurt the poor beast. It's not my goat. Do you think the lottery office would take this X-ray and the goat as enough evidence to pay the prize ?"

DR. SMITTY - "I don't know. If that's the right ticket it may be the only solution. They close in Sacramento at 5:00 o'clock and it's 2:00 o'clock now. You may have a shot but you'd better hurry."

HERB — "O.K. Thank you, Dr. Smitty. Let's go Marge. Sacramento is 90 miles away."

They took Hector and the X-rays and rushed out.

MEANWHILE:

**** (This scene could be just outside curtain where Frank, the neighbor boy, tells Hank about Herb and Marge taking Hector.)

HANK (calling) — "Hector? Hector? Where is that blasted goat?" He saw Frank nearby. "Frank, have you seen Hector, my goat?"

FRANK — "Yes. Herb and Marge caught him and took him somewhere in their car. I heard them say something about the Vet and Hector eating a lottery ticket, or something.

HANK — "When was this, Frank?"

FRANK — "About 30 minutes ago, I think."

Hank, putting 2 and 2 together, figured that somehow Hector had eaten a lottery ticket that belonged to his neighbor. He remembered that the lottery prize was $1,000,000.

HANK — "Wow! If Hector has the winning ticket in his stomach, it ought to belong to Hector and me!" — (He jumped in his car and headed for the local vet's office.)

AT THE VET'S OFFICE - 15 MINUTES LATER. Hank rushed in.

HANK — "Did a man and a woman bring a goat in here?"

DR. SMITTY - "Yes, they did. They left just a few minutes ago."

HANK — - "That's my goat. They think it ate a winning lottery ticket. Where did they go?"

DR. SMITTY - "I X-rayed the goat. It did have a lottery ticket in it's stomach. They left here for the lottery office in Sacramento."

HANK — "That's my goat, and if that ticket is the winning ticket it should be my $1,000,000.. I'm going to Sacramento. Bye."

Hank rushed out on his way to the lottery office in Sacramento.

AT THE LOTTERY OFFICE IN SACRAMENTO: (Picture of new car on wall.) — Herb and Marge rush in with Hector and X-rays.

HERB — "We've got the winning ticket, Sir."

MR. LOTTERY MAN — "Well, it's about time somebody brought it in. Congratulations, you lucky people; let me see it. PHEW! Will you get that smelly goat off the counter, please?"

MARGE — "He ate the winning ticket. See. Here's an X-ray. It shows the ticket in his stomach."

MR. LOTTERY - "Let me see that X-ray." He checked the X-ray. "This is ridiculous. It looks like a ticket in the X-ray film, but I don't think it's legal. I don't think the state would go for anything like this. We may have to get a court ruling on it."

HERB — "How come? You can see the ticket in his stomach."

MR. LOTTERY — "That middle number is pretty blurred. I can't tell if it's a 15 or a 16. The correct number is 15."

HERB — "It has to be a 15. I can tell it's a 15. All the other numbers are plainly correct."

Just at that moment Hank burst through the door.

HANK (shouting) — "Stop! Those people are thieves. They stole my goat with the lottery ticket inside. It's my goat and my ticket -or at least half of the prize."

MR. LOTTERY — "Please calm down, all of you. This is a very complicated problem. We need positive proof that the ticket inside the goat has the number 15. We don't know it for sure."

HERB — "Holy Cow! Don't you know a 15 when you see it?"

Just then old Mrs. Hooker and her chauffeur came through the door. She looked at her tenants in surprise, over her gold-rimmed pince-nez.

MRS. HOOKER — "What are you people doing here?"

HERB — "We came to claim the $1,000,000 lottery prize. We have the winning ticket and we're going to move out of your crummy cottage the first thing."

MRS. HOOKER — "You can't have the winning ticket. I have it right here." She presented a ticket to the lottery official who examined it carefully.

MR. LOTTERY — "Well, this looks like an exact match. May I offer you my congratulations. Your name please?"

HERB — "There ought to be a law against rich people winning lotteries."

HANK — "Aw Gee! That's a shame, Herb, old friend."

MR. LOTTERY — "I'm sorry, folks. Will you get that goat out of here. Now, again Lady, your name, please."

MRS. HOOKER — "Butch Andriopolous."

HERB — "That's not right. We know her, Mr. Lottery Man."

MRS. HOOKER — "It is right, isn't it Butch?"

The little chauffeur stepped forward.

BUTCH (in a high squeaky voice) — "Yes. That's me."

HERB (angrily) — "Hank, take your old goat. I've had it!"

HANK — "Serves you right for mistreating Hector. Come here, Hector, Baby."

MR. LOTTERY — "Will you people with the goat please clear the room!"

MRS. HOOKER — "Herb, I'm raising your rent another $10.00 a month starting in 30 days. And Hank, you get rid of that goat, or your rent goes up $20.00 at the same time."

Just then, a young couple rushed in.

YOUNG COUPLE — "We have the winning ticket! Can you cash it?"

MR. LOTTERY (throwing up his hands) — "How many winning tickets did they print this time? I've got one right here."

YOUNG COUPLE — "Ours is the right one. See?" He held up a ticket for the lottery man to see.

MR. LOTTERY (examining his ticket) — "I can't believe this! Mrs. Hooker, let me see your ticket again." He examined it carefully. "Mrs. Hooker, the last number is supposed to be a 6, with a dash under it. Yours is a 9. It doesn't have the dash. So this young couple has the right ticket. His has the dash. Now will all of you please leave except this young couple."

JUST THEN, a man stuck his head in the door and yelled to Mrs. Hooker — "Lady there's a man trying to steal your car out here"

HERB (looking out the door) — "He sure is. Hank, help me stop him!"

HANK — "Hold Hector, Marge!"

He gave Marge the leash and ran to help Herb. There was a lot of excitement in the room. The lottery man quickly called the police. The group stood at the door and watched as Herb and Hank struggled to stop the theft. Finally, Herb came back in. His clothes were torn and dirty and he was out of breath.

MARGE - "Are you hurt Herb? Where's Hank? What happened?"

HERB (still excited) — "We got to the car just as the man was racing the engine and takin' off. I managed to get inside and grabbed the steerin' wheel. I couldn't stop it; Hank was hangin' on the door on the other side. Then we hit that tree. It knocked the thief dizzy. Hit his head on somethin'."

MARGE - "Where's Hank?"

HERB — "He was flung forward. He's hurt. Badly bruised. I don't know what else. The police took the thief to jail, and an ambulance took Hank to the hospital. They sure got there in a hurry!"

MRS. HOOKER — "Thank you, Mr. Collins, for your and Mr. Sims' trying to save my car. I take back what I said about raising your and Mr. Sims' rent. I'm sorry Mr. Sims got hurt."

MRS. HOOKER — "I've got to get my briefcase from my car, lock it, and see about having it towed to a garage."

While Mrs. Hooker was out seeing about her car, Herb whispered to Marge:

HERB — "Marge, don't offer to take her home."

MARGE — "You ought to be ashamed, Herb. Her car's ruined. It doesn't cost us anything to offer them a ride."

HERB — "Aw, geez, Marge. You're too kind hearted."

When Mrs. Hooker returned, she accepted the offer of a ride back to the cottages for her and her chauffeur. They stopped on the way to check on Hank at the hospital. Mrs. Hooker was very grateful for the effort of Herb and Hank trying to save her car. Herb and Marge cared for Hector the two days that Hank was in the hospital. They learned to like Hector and were again good friends with Hank. Marge set the dinner for the benefit of Liz and Hank, to be Saturday at 6:30 pm.

ACT TWO

3 DAYS LATER.

It was 6 pm. No one was in the living room of the Collin's little cottage. Herb came in; threw his jacket and cap on the sofa. He walked across the room, holding his back, and eased himself into a chair.

HERB (aloud) — "Oh, Man! I'm glad this day is over."

Marge breezed in. She hung her coat on a hanger.

MARGE — "You here already? I've got some good news for a change. I'll put on some coffee, then I'll tell you."

HERB — "Pitch me one of those pillows. My back's hurtin'. What's the good news? We ain't had nothin' but bad since my job was outsourced and I had to take this job at the animal shelter."

Marge handed him a cup of steaming coffee, which he nervously spilled in the handover.

HERB — "OW! Look what you've done! Ruined my pants. I need to wear them tomorrow."

MARGE - "I'll clean 'em. Take 'em off. I'll get you another cup of coffee."

Herb took his pants off. Marge got him another pair, which he put on.

HERB — "What's the good news that you are so happy about?"

MARGE (brightening up) — "Oh! I was voted the 'Teacher-of-the-Month' at our kindergarten. Wasn't that nice?" She clapped her hands and danced a little jig.

HERB — "Big deal! That doesn't pay you anything. They'll just expect more out of you."

MARGE - "It may bring in more later."

HERB (struggling to get something out of his pocket) — "Here's some good news for your birthday." He gave her a lottery ticket.

MARGE (chagrinned) — "A lousy lottery ticket! My birthday was last week. Why do you keep buying those worthless things? It's a complete waste of money."

HERB — "Well, somebody's gonna win it. It's our only chance to get on 'Easy Street'. We almost won it last time, remember?"

MARGE — "Yes, I remember. One in forty million. Fat chance!"

The phone rang. Marge answered it.

MARGE — "It's Daisy, your Mother."

Herb takes phone.

HERB — "Hello, Mother. How are you? - I'm fine. Where are you? - Texarkana? What are you doin' there? - You're speakin' to who? - The Women's Confederate League? Isn't that kind of out of date? - You're goin' to visit us? Good, let us know when you will be here. —Yes, I still brush my teeth every night. - OK. Bye Mother."

MARGE (opening the morning mail) — "How was your day?"

HERB — "I spent half the day cleaning cages. That's why my back went out on me."

MARGE (still opening mail) — "Here's the water bill. Gee! Look at this! It's for $115. That can't be right."

HERB — "Let me see it. I ain't payin' no $115." He took the bill. "It has to be a leak somewhere. Get on the phone and have them send a man out here, pronto, to fix it."

MARGE — "What's their phone number?"

HERB — "I don't know their phone number. It's in the phone book."

MARGE — "It's right there on the phone bill."

HERB — "Oh." - he checked the bill - "78-7120."

Marge dialed the number; spoke into the phone.

HERB — "What did they say?"

MARGE — "They were closed. I left a message."

The doorbell rang. It was Hank.

HANK — "Here's your vacuum cleaner back. Thank you, Marge."

MARGE — "OK. . . .What did you think of Liz, the girl I introduced you to last week?"

HANK — "Her? She's too fresh. Makes me nervous. Girls like that are dangerous. My Mother was a girl. I never knew what to expect of her."

HERB — "What about your Dad?"

HANK — "I never knew him. He left when I was a baby."

MARGE — "Don't you get lonesome there all by yourself?"

HANK — "I get lonesome sometimes. I have Hector and a couple of birds that keep me company."

MARGE — "You should join a club and meet a nice girl."

HANK — "I've been thinkin' about adoptin' a cat. As for girls? I donno. I like more your type, Marge."

HERB — "Marge is already taken, Hank."

HANK — "Oh, I didn't mean."

Just then, the doorbell rang. It was Mrs. Hooker.

MRS. HOOKER — "Hello, Marge. Hello, Mr. Sims. I just dropped by to ask if you're having any trouble with squirrels living in your attic. A couple of the tenants have complained."

MARGE — "No. We haven't noticed anything like that. We do hear a woodpecker hammering away somewhere near, and every morning there is a mockingbird serenading us from the telephone pole across the street. We love that."

MRS HOOKER — "Mockingbirds are no problem, but the woodpeckers can cause damage....Hank, you need to dry your clothes with your dryer, instead of hanging them outside on that long clothesline. It looks so 'country'! Lumpkin is a high class city."

Hank didn't answer.

MRS. HOOKER — "I've got to go, so, I'll see you later." She left.

HANK — "I'll make my lines shorter, but 'sun-dried' clothes are cleaner and feel better...as for the mockingbird, it's my house he's been workin' on. He'll quit when the hole is big enough to store his winter food in."

HERB — "A little hole under the eaves ain't gonna hurt the house."

MARGE - "Hank, I'm cooking a turkey for dinner Saturday evening. Would you like to come and help us eat it?"

HANK — "Sure, I'd love to. It's been a while since I've had a turkey dinner."

MARGE — "Good. We'll expect you. Dinner will be at 6:30 sharp."

HANK — "Thank you. I'll be there."

LATER, Marge invited Liz, who gladly accepted the invitation when she learned that Hank would be there.

NEXT DAY Liz came by to leave some political material.

MARGE - "Hello, Liz. What's this?"

LIZ — "Just some info on the sloppy way the present Council keeps records of our expenses."

MARGE — "Have you been by Hank's place yet?"

Tom Robb

LIZ — "Yes, but he peeked out the window and wouldn't answer his doorbell. I just left the bulletin behind his screen."

MARGE — "Hank's a fine man. Not a lot of experience with girls."

LIZ — "I can see that He's very manly and handsome. I've been married once. It was a disaster. A person like him is interesting to me."

MARGE — "He's lonesome, I'm sure, by himself like he is. I feel sorry for him."

LIZ — "I've got to get on. I'll see you later. I'm looking forward to your dinner Saturday night."

She left. A few minutes later, Mrs. Hooker knocked on the door.

MARGE — "Hello, Mrs. Hooker."

MRS. HOOKER - "Hello, Marge. Here's your water bill. The postman delivered it to my cottage by mistake."

MARGE — "Oh, good! The one we got must be yours." She examined the one that they had received.

MARGE — "It's yours alright. We were discussing what to do with it." They exchanged water bills.

MARGE — "Won't you come in, Mrs. Hooker?"

MRS. HOOKER — "No, thank you. Not this time." She left.

HERB (who was in the kitchen, but heard it all) — "I hate that woman! She's rich. Owns all these cottages; always promising to upgrade 'em, but never does."

MARGE - "I've heard that she has a big mortgage on them, so she may not have much extra to play with."

HERB — "Well, at least we don't have to pay a $115. water bill."

THE DINNER: - Marge cooked a delicious dinner. Everything was ready at 6:30 on Saturday evening, and we find Hank, Herb and Marge ready to sit down to the roasted turkey and all the goodies that make up a sumptuous meal. The aroma was gastronomically irresistible.

MARGE — "OK. Everybody take your place. Herb, you and I will sit on this side. Hank, you sit on that side."

They all sat down at the table. Hank noticed another place setting by him. He wondered about it, but didn't say anything. Just then the doorbell rang. Marge answered it. It was Liz.

MARGE — "Hello, Liz. You're just in time for dinner. You sit down here by Hank."

Liz sat down.

LIZ — "I'm sorry if I'm late...Oh, hello, Mr. Sims. I'm glad to see you again."

HANK — (surprised, trapped) - "Glad to see you. Did you just drop in?"

LIZ — "Yes, I was just walking by, and smelled this delicious turkey. I was hungry and stopped in. Am I glad I did?"

HANK — "Do any of you girls ever tell the truth?"

LIZ — "Sometimes."

Hank decided to just make the best of it. Liz did smell good. He liked that. They ate in silence a minute or two.

LIZ — "I'm Liz."

HANK — "I know."

LIZ — "How've you been, Mr. Sims?"

HANK — "OK."

LIZ — "How's Hector?"

HANK — "He's OK."

LIZ — "Would you reach the butter for me, Mr. Sims?"

Hank reached it for her.

LIZ — "Thank you, Mr. Sims. Do you like music? Do you play tennis or golf?"

HANK — "NO! Please, could I just eat for a couple of minutes; I'm starved. I'll have a question and answer session later."

LIZ — "I'm sorry. I'm hungry, too."

They ate in silence, except for passing the salt, pepper and butter back and forth. Finally —

LIZ — "Do you like to dance?"

HANK (exasperated) — "Are you workin' for a newspaper or somethin'?"

Liz dropped her fork. It went under the table. Hank retrieved it for her.

LIZ — "Thank you. Clumsy me!"

HANK — "Umm."

Marge was a good hostess. She refilled Hank and Liz's wine glasses when they were still half full.

LIZ — "Do you mind if I call you by your first name?"

HANK — "I was born with this one. I've never had another."

LIZ — "I know you're Mr. Sims. What did your Mother call you?"

HANK — "I don't think I'd like you callin' me that."

Just then the doorbell rang. Marge went to check. It was Mrs. Hooker.

MRS. HOOKER — "Marge, I just dropped by to tell you....Oh, what a delicious smell! Turkey?"

MARGE — "Yes. Won't you come in? Have you had dinner yet?"

MRS. HOOKER — "Why,...No, I haven't. Gee! That turkey smells good."

MARGE — "We've plenty. You just sit down here by Herb, and I'll get a plate and a helping of everything."

She sat down by Herb, who cringed and edged a bit away. She noticed, but ignored it. A good home cooked meal was worth a subtle snub. Anyway, she enjoyed the chance to aggravate her chief critic.

MRS. HOOKER — "How are you this evening, Mr. Collins?"

HERB — "Well, so far, it's been OK. You been out passin' out rent raises again?"

MRS. HOOKER - "No. I've been cleaning cottage #9. They skipped out last night, owing two months rent. The inside was a wreck. It'll take me a month to rent it again."

HERB — "Tough luck, but you can take it off your income tax."

Just then, Liz dropped her fork again. It went under the table. She looked guiltily at Hank. He reluctantly crawled under the table and retrieved it.

HANK — "It's your turn next, Miss. You don't like to eat with a fork?"

The wine was making both a bit tipsy. His answer set her laughing. He was amused at her funny hi-pitched laughter. He almost laughed himself.

HANK — "What's funny. Your laugh sounds like a police siren." He laughed. "What were you asking me?"

LIZ — "I asked you what your first ..." Hank, who was getting quite uninhibited...

HANK — "I told you...."

He knocked his own fork off and it went under the table. They were oblivious to the fact that they were the center of attention for the others at the table. Liz crawled under the table and retrieved Hank's fork.

LIZ — "There's your fork, Mr. Sims." She tickled him under the chin, as he was merrily laughing at her.

HANK — "Just call me Hank, Lizzie. You're a very funny girl."

Just then a fire truck roared by; siren blaring. Mrs. Hooker rushed out. It was cottage #1. She had only eaten a few bites of her meal.

MARGE — "That's too bad. I'll fix up her dinner in a sack and Herb can take it to her. She's standing by the fire truck."

HERB — "Aw, Marge. She's got a refrigerator full of food in her cottage."

MARGE — "Just the same, it's the nice thing to do."

Herb took the sack of food. In a way, he felt sorry for her. She was having a really bad day.

HERB — "Here's the rest of your dinner, Mrs. Hooker."

MRS. HOOKER — "Thank you, Herb. Tell Marge I'm sorry I had to leave. I appreciate her sending this."

Just then the doorbell rang again. Marge answered it. It was a young black man wearing a tool belt around his waist.

MARGE - "Hello?"

MAN — "I'm sorry I'm late. I'm Fred, from the water company. You have a leak some place? My, that turkey shore smells good!"

MARGE — "That was two days ago. It turned out to be a mistake. I'm sorry you having to come out on a false report, and, right at dinner time. I'll bet your wife won't like that."

FRED — "I'm not married, Ma'am. I just eat when I get the opportunity."

MARGE — "You haven't had dinner yet?"

FRED — "No, Ma'am. Not yet."

MARGE — "Well, just take off your tool belt and have dinner with us. You can sit right here by me."

Fred agreed and Marge helped him fill his plate. Just then, Daisybell Collins, Herb's Mother walked in.

MARGE - "Oh, hello, Mother, come in."

DAISY - "I'm already in."

MARGE - "I didn't hear the doorbell ring."

DAISY — "I don't use them new fangled things. Where's my son, Herbert?"

MARGE - "He went to take a dinner to a friend. Have you had dinner yet, Mother?"

DAISY - "No. I was hopin' I'd get here in time." She looked at the table of diners. "Are you runnin' a boardin' house now, Margaret?"

MARGE — "No. They are just friends. Take off your hat, coat and scarf and have dinner with us. You can sit here by Fred."

She and Fred eyed each other.

DAISY — "I'm used to sittin' at the end, account of my elbows."

Marge fixed her a setting at the end and filled a plate of food for her. Then Marge introduced her to the others. In a few minutes Herb came back.

HERB (surprised) — "Mother! When did you get here? How are you?"

DAISY (between bites) — "Just now. I've been attendin' a convention in Dallas." I thought I'd drop over here to see how my little Boy Scout, Herbert, was doing."

HANK — "Herb was a Boy Scout?"

DAISY — "Yes. I see he's still being a good patriotic Scout, taking food to a poor neighbor."

Herb sat down again and began eating. Suddenly, the music on the radio broke into "The Stars and Stripes Forever". With the clatter of falling knives and forks on plates, Daisy and Herb jumped erect in a patriotic salute to a small flag on the wall. Everyone else stopped eating in amazement until the song was finished and Daisy and Herb had sat back down.

FRED (addressing Daisy) — "Where you from, Lady?"

DAISY — "I'm a rootin', tootin', shootin' gal from Texas! I was born and raised in Ft. Worth."

FRED — "You in the cow business?"

DAISY — "No. I'm an officer of The Women's Confederate League."

FRED — "I see."

He decided he wouldn't ask another question. Finally, the dinner was over.

DAISY — "It's my bedtime. Margaret, where do I sleep tonight?"

MARGE — "All of you excuse me while I get Mother to bed."

HERB — "Goodnight, Mother."

DAISY — "Goodnight, Herbert. Goodnight everybody."

They left. Marge was soon back.

LIZ — "It was a delicious dinner, Marge. I'd better get home."

MARGE — "It's dark out there. Someone should escort you home. Hank, will you do that?"

HANK — "It's not far. She'll be OK."

LIZ (disappointed but defiant) — "I can take care of myself. I used to be a Rangerette."

HANK — "What's that got to do with protectin' yourself?"

LIZ — "Got me in good shape. I still am. See . . . ."

She tried a handstand. Her dress fell down, revealing her bright red panties. Hank, embarrassed at the sight, first turned away and put his hand over his eyes; then rushed over and tried to hold her dress down, er, up.

LIZ — "Oh, I'm sorry. I'm just a little out of practice."

HANK — "I think you need a lot of practice."

But he agreed to escort her to her apartment and they left. Just then, the ground began to shake and sway. It was an_EARTHQUAKE. An uncertain and scary feeling! Hank and Liz came running back in. Herb turned the radio up.

RADIO ANNOUNCER — "We've just had an earthquake, folks. It was centered about 30 miles South of Lumpkin, near the town of Sulfur Springs, where it is reported to have caused considerable damage. Imagine that! An earthquake in Texas!"

LIZ — "Wow! My uncle Dub Holloway lived there. He was my favorite uncle. He had a great big house on a hill above the town. His wife was dead. We kids used to love to visit him. There were lots of trees. It was spooky! He liked to tell us ghost stories. It was rumored that he was connected to some underground group before he died. They say the old house has been vacant since."

HERB — "I remember that house. My Dad used to go to Sulfur Springs for the sulfur baths. The house had a high fence around it."

LIZ — "That's right. It's supposed to be haunted, now."

HANK — "Who owns it now? Old houses like that shouldn't be left to rot and fall down."

LIZ — "I have no idea who owns it now. Uncle Dub died about two years ago."

RADIO ANNOUNCER — "It's just been reported that the old Holloway house in Sulfur Springs was badly damaged by the quake; some damage to the rest of the town. An old man with 12 cats and 5 dogs had been living in the house. He was evicted by the police."

MARGE — "Well, I guess that's the last you'll hear of your Uncle Dub's old haunted house."

Evidently Daisy slept through the earthquake, since she didn't appear again that night. Since the aftershocks had ceased, Liz and Hank left again for her apartment.

MARGE — "Hank's changing. I believe he really likes Liz. He just doesn't want to admit it. You can see that she likes him."

HERB — "I think you're right. I'd better advise him about women, so he won't get hurt."

MARGE — "BOO! When did you become an authority on women?"

HERB — "Well, I won you didn't I? I've lived with you for...seems like 50 years. That's somethin."

MARGE — "You didn't win me in a raffle! I had my heart set on you. It was easy."

HERB — "Well, anyway. We've had a happy life together, haven't we?"

MARGE — "Yes, we have." He gave her a loving hug.

Early next morning, Herb took Daisy to catch her bus to Dallas, so she could attend the rest of her convention.

After taking Daisy to the bus, Herb and Marge were having coffee. The phone rang. Marge answered. It was Liz.

MARGE — "Hello?"

LIZ — "Marge, I left my coin purse at your house last night. It must have dropped out of my...OH! OH!...."

There was a lot of noise like a scuffle - then only silence. Marge tried to get the connection again, but the line remained silent.

HERB — "Something must have happened. Maybe she fell."

MARGE (still holding the 'open' phone) — "Herb, run over to her apartment and see if she's alright."

HERB — "I don't know where she lives."

After a few minutes, the doorbell rang. Herb answered it. It was a policeman.

POLICEMAN — "I'm policemen Nevers. Are you Mr. and Mrs. Collins?"

MARGE — "Yes. Has something happened to Liz?"

OFFICER NEVERS — "Yes. Two men just a few minutes ago, tried to kidnap her. Luckily, my partner and I were driving by and saw them trying to put Miss Holloway in their car. She was fighting them with all her arms and legs. When they saw us, they dropped her and fled.

We radioed for help, but they got away. It's not known, at present, where they are."

HERB — "Why would they want to kidnap a girl like Liz?"

OFFICER NEVERS - "Our sources say that she is inheriting her uncle Dub Holloway's estate. We've been watching for these two guys. We knew they were in town."

MARGE - "Is Liz OK?"

OFFICER NEVERS — "Apparently, yes. She's at the hospital being checked over. She was not seriously hurt, but was bruised badly, and had a swollen lower lip. I'll go along, now. Miss Holloway asked me to tell you that she's alright." He left.

HERB — "Geez! Wait 'til Hank hears about this. Liz, a hero an' a 'airess now. An' he was accusin' her of not growin' up."

The next day Liz was brought up to the Collin's cottage. Marge put her to bed. When Hank learned that Liz was at the Collin's place and was injured, he rushed there to see her. He realized that he had begun to like her, and she liked him. He generally was ill-at-ease around girls, but Liz was different; like Marge.

LIZ — (on seeing him) - "Oh, Hank! How nice of you to come see me. I can't talk very well. I have a busted lip."

HANK — "Are you alright? OH! Your lip does look bad! I wasn't gonna kiss you, anyway. I'm sorry you're hurt. I'm sorry for the way I've treated you. I like you. You're a nice girl."

LIZ — "Hank, I'm not going to die. Thank you for what you just said, except for the kiss. I'd like to have one of them, sometime."

She took his hand. He didn't withdraw it. He didn't know what to say, so they just looked at each other for a minute. Just then, Marge came in.

HANK — "Well. I better go."

LIZ — "Thank you for coming, Hank. You're Special!"

HANK — "Bye." He left.

A<small>CT</small> T<small>HREE</small>

TWO DAYS LATER

Liz had recovered enough that she wanted to get back to her apartment. Marge took her. On the way home, Marge stopped at the grocery store. Hank seeing her come back, decided to check on Liz.

HANK (knocking and entering) — "Anybody home?"

MARGE — "Hello, Hank. How are you?"

HANK — "I'm OK. Where's Miss Holloway?"

MARGE — "I just took her back to her apartment. She's better... Have you heard the latest on Liz? She's an heiress now."

HANK — "What did she inherit?"

MARGE — "You remember the day of the earthquake, we were talking about the old house in Sulfur Springs that her uncle owned?"

HANK — "Yes, I remember. What about it."

MARGE — "Her uncle died and left it to Liz. The earthquake wrecked it. Liz wants to go and take a look at it. It sits on 20 acres. Since you have done remodeling work, she wants you to go along."

HANK — "Sure. I like that kind of work."

MARGE — "Mr. Nevers, the policeman, said there is a rumor in certain circles, that old Dub Holloway had a huge sum of money stashed somewhere, maybe there. The Mob learned at the inquest that his niece, Liz Holloway, is inheriting his property, including the old house in Sulfur Springs. The police think that they plan to kidnap her to find out where the money is. That's why they grabbed her the other day,"

HANK — "It's too bad the house was wrecked. I'm just thankful she's safe after her fight with those crooks. She's a fighter; I like her."

Hank wondered if Liz would be different toward him when she found out that she was rich? It worried him. He realized that he had fallen in love with her. How did that happen? He had written a poem that he thought would convey his feelings toward her. He had it in an envelope. He didn't want to deliver it himself. Maybe Marge would deliver it for him.

HANK — "Marge, I've got to go, will you take care of this for me?" He waved the envelope for her to see.

MARGE (still putting away groceries and thinking it was a letter to be mailed) — "Sure." She took it and stuffed it in her purse.

HANK — "Thank you." He left.

HERB (just coming in from work) — "Marge, I need to get gas for the car. Let me have the keys and I'll do that now."

MARGE — "The keys are in my purse there on the counter."

Herb, searching for the keys, pulled out the poem from Hank. The envelope had come off it in the stuffing. Herb stared at the poem. It read:

"To the one I admire the most."
I think of you, in the early Morn,
When the sky breaks brightest blue,
I think of you, on the darkest Night,
And one lone star shines thru —That's You!

Sincerely, Hank..

Herb was shocked. What's goin' on with her and Hank?

HERB — "Marge, what's the meaning of this?"

MARGE — "What are you talking about?"

HERB — "This note, or poem from Hank. I just got it out of your purse."

MARGE — "I haven't read it. Hank asked me to deliver it for him. Go on and get the gas, and I'll read it when I get these groceries put up."

HERB — "I think I deserve an explanation."

Herb left. As soon as Marge put away the groceries she read the note (or poem.) She was surprised, puzzled. Did Hank mean it for her? She had kind of favored him and tried to get him to be more attentive to Liz. Maybe Hank had meant it for Liz. Just then Liz came in, as the door was still open.

MARGE — "Hello, Liz. I want you to read something."

Marge showed her the poem. Liz's face turned red.

LIZ — "Why are you showing me this? Is it to taunt me? I see you and Hank are carrying on behind my back. I'm surprised at You, Marge. I thought you were my friend!"

MARGE — "Liz, I don't know what this is all about."

Just then Hank came in. The door was still open.

HANK — "Hello, everybody. What's new, today?"

LIZ — "News. You ought to know! I can't believe you would do this to me. I'm hurt. I thought you cared for me."

HANK — "I haven't done anything. I've been downtown all day."

Tom Robb

Just then, Herb came in from getting gas.

HERB - "What have you got to say for yourself, Hank, you traitor!"

MARGE - "Wait just a minute. I remember that note was in an envelope." She searched her purse and retrieved the envelope. "The envelope says, 'To Liz.'"

HERB (gazing at the envelope) — "Well, it says, 'To Liz'; so the poem is meant for Liz."

Marge gave the poem to Liz.

LIZ — "Oh, Hank. I love you, too!.. I'm sorry Marge."

Hank went over and hugged her.

HANK — "You're the only one for me, Liz."

HERB — "I'm sorry, Marge. I just couldn't stand the thought of you being in love with somebody else."

HANK — "Take it easy, everybody. We've all been through so much lately, I think we need a relaxer. I've got a bottle of California's best, here. Let's have a toast!"

He took a bottle out of his coat and popped it. Marge supplied the glasses, and they did.

HANK — "Nobody's perfect. Long live our friendship! YEA!"

LIZ — "I have to leave now, but I want to go to Sulfur Springs this weekend to see the condition of the 'old house'. I want all of you to go with me."

They all agreed. Hank and Liz left

MARGE — "Those two seem to be very good friends, now. Our little 'dinner' was a success. I wonder what's in store for Liz in Sulfur Springs?"

HERB — "Who knows. Liz is the one havin' all the good luck now."

NEXT DAY: Hank came by.

HANK — "Have you seen Liz, today? She doesn't answer her phone or her doorbell."

HERB — "We haven't seen her today."

There was no word the next day either, nor the next. That evening Mr. Nevers, the policeman, came by.

OFFICER NEVERS — "I've just had word that Miss Holloway is safe in Sulfur Springs. She was kidnapped by the Mob and taken to Sulfur Springs in an attempt to find a cache of money. In events that I don't know yet, the Mob was arrested and Miss Holloway is free. She's on her way up here now. She asked me to inform you of this."

He left. About an hour later, Liz arrived. She looked unharmed.

HERB — "How did you get away? Did they find any treasure?"

MARGE - "How did they treat you?"

HANK — "What happened? I was worried sick about you."

LIZ — "It's a long story. I'm glad it turned out like it did. After the mobsters failed to kidnap me the first time, they hightailed it out of town. They came back three nights ago and sneaked in while I was asleep. I don't know how they got in. They slapped a cloth saturated with chloroform over my face and held it until I was unconscious. They took me to the 'old house' in Sulfur Springs. When I came to, I was tied up and sitting in a chair."

"In spite of their badgering and threatening, I made them realize that I had no idea where any treasure or cash was hidden. After it was dark, I managed to free myself of the bonds and slipped out of the house. I drained most of the gas from their car, then slipped away and alerted the police. When the Mob discovered my escape, they knew that the police would be there shortly. They jumped in their car and headed out of town toward Dallas. Since the gas gauge showed almost empty, they pulled in at the nearest gas station. Waiting for them there were four policemen and me. Almost out of gas and outgunned, they quickly surrendered. The police put the three mobsters in jail. By this time it had become daylight and I had a chance to take a look at the 'old house'. The water tower had fallen. The windmill, garage and stables, although in bad shape, were still standing. The rear part of the house had collapsed. The beautiful circular stairway to the second floor and two bedrooms, including the master bedroom and bath, were intact. Another stairway to the attic was blocked. There was a basement under the middle of the house that was partially filled with wreckage. Uncle Dub never let us kids go into the basement."

HANK — "What a shame, a beautiful house like that wrecked. Do you think it can be restored?"

MARGE — "Aren't you getting hungry? When have you eaten?"

LIZ — "Yes, I'm starved. I did grab a sandwich on the way up here, but let me finish my report."

HERB — "Go on! This is like a movie."

LIZ — "OK....To complete the inspection, I descended to the large basement. It appeared to be a combination office and storage. There was a desk, telephone and several cabinets. There was a bed in a corner. Two kitty sand boxes were in a corner." I pulled on what appeared to be a loose brick in-the wall. A large section of it collapsed, revealing a small niche. Inside the space was a rusty metal box. I lifted it out. In the half-light it appeared to be filled with bundles and bundles of money. What a sight!"

HERB — "Oh, Man! I wish I'd been there!"

MARGE — "Weren't you in danger there, with all that money?"

HANK — "It couldn't happen to a nicer person. I'm happy for you, Liz. I hope you'll let me have the job of restoring the house. I can't wait to get down there when you get around to it."

LIZ — "Oh, Hank. You've got the job! Can we put a seal on that agreement? My lip's well now."

HANK - "Yes! I've been looking forward to this." He took her in his arms and kissed her. He didn't want to let her go.

LIZ — "There's more, yet. I took the chest of money to The First State Bank in Sulfur Springs for counting and safe keeping. Mr. Edmonds, a vice-president, gave me a receipt for it. He told me to come back in an hour and he'd have it counted for me. He took a glance in the box to see that it was money."

MARGE — "Whew! This has been another week to remember! Inherited property, your kidnapping, captured by the Mob and escaping; and to top it off, finding a real treasure."

LIZ — "Wait. Let me finish.. While Mr. Edmonds counted the money, I went to a little cafe to eat. When I got back, Mr. Edmonds had the money all counted and stacked in bundles. It was a stunning sight. I had never seen such a pile of money."

HANK — "I'm surprised someone hadn't found it before."

MARGE — "I can't imagine that much money. The biggest I've ever seen was a $50 dollar bill."

HERB — "How much was it? Was it in $100 bills?"

Liz didn't seem to be as excited as the rest were.

LIZ — "I was stunned when Mr. Edmonds handed me a paper itemizing the money. He said there's $382,000 in Confederate money and 50 pesos of Mexican money. It's of no value, except a lot of people like to have it as a souvenir. Of course, I was disappointed, as you probably are."

Her friends were dumbfounded. After the first shock, it got to be funny; a good joke on Liz and themselves. This might be a good ending of a story.

but, NOT THIS ONE.

THE CLIMAX IS STILL AHEAD!!

HANK — "In a way I'm relieved, Liz, I was afraid with all that money I wouldn't get to see you anymore, unless I went to New York City or Hollywood."

LIZ — "I'm not sorry it happened like this. It brought me closer to my Sweetheart."

Hank gave her a hug as she looked at him.

HERB — "Well, we live and learn, don't we?"

LIZ — "I brought the chest of Confederate and Mexican money back to Lumpkin and it's in the vault at my bank. I'll decide what to do with it later."

Two weeks after things settled down from the aforementioned events, Herb gave Marge a beautifully wrapped "gift" package.

MARGE — "What is it?"

HERB — "Open it and see."

She carefully unwrapped it.

MARGE — "Another lottery ticket! Herb, you're a Dear!"

This time Marge wasn't angry. The last one had brought about many memorable events. She wondered about this one.

HERB — "Somebody's gonna win it. We almost did last time."

Liz came in 2nd in the City Council race. It wasn't a disappointment, since things happening had very much altered the future for her, but.... She had a big problem! She saw Hank out in front of his cottage watering his flowers.

LIZ — "Hank, I've got a problem that you'll have to help me solve."

HANK — "Sure. What's the problem?"

LIZ — "I'm supposed to report to Washington, D.C. in 10 days."

HANK — "Washington, D.C. What for?"

LIZ — "Washington is my headquarters. That's my problem. That's why I need your help. I'm an FBI agent, Hank."

HANK (stunned) — "I don't understand. Why didn't you tell me?" Hank turned off the water, and came back.

LIZ — "Hank, I couldn't tell you. I was on this case to catch these criminals, who had shown up in Lumpkin. We had a tip about what they were planning. I'm sorry to mislead you. I still love you, Hank!"

HANK — "I love you, too. You can't just go away!"

Tears were in both their eyes. Hank was desperate. He didn't want this to happen.

LIZ — "That's not all of the problem, Hank. It gets worse."

HANK — "What could be worse than that."

LIZ — "I'm not Liz Holloway."

She knew she was hurting him, but she had no choice but to get through it. If only he could understand.

HANK — "You what? I don't understand. I can see you with my own eyes. Oh, I hope I'm just dreaming!"

LIZ — "I'm Marie Dawson, Hank. But I still love you! I had to take the name of the owner of the old house in Sulfur Springs and play a role to protect her from those gangsters. Then I fell in love with you!" She lowered her weeping eyes.

HANK — "This is so shocking to me. I don't know who I'm in love with."

LIZ — " I know. I'm sorry, Hank, but I'm still ME!"

HANK — "I know you are. Thank God, for that!" Hank straightened up and took her hand. "When do you have to leave for Washington?"

LIZ — "In 10 days, but I don't want to go."

HANK — "You're not goin'. Will you marry me, Liz-Marie?"

LIZ-MARIE - "Yes! Yes! I thought you'd never ask me. I'm so happy!" He took her in his arms and kissed her.

HANK — "Liz, you're so beautiful when you cry! I'll always call you Liz...Let's get married right away."

LIZ — "Yes! Tomorrow?"

HANK — "That's a great idea. If the owner, Miss Holloway will sell the old house and acreage with it, I'll buy it for us. I have enough in my savings accounts."

Hank and Liz did get married the next day. It was a happy occasion. Liz resigned her job with the FBI. The next week they bought the old house and acreage from Miss Holloway and they moved to Sulfur Springs. Hank is busy restoring the old house. They live in the undamaged front part. Liz -(it's still Liz)- opened a gift shop near the springs, where she sells the Confederate money given them by Miss Holloway, for $2.00 per bill, along with many other things sold in a successful gift and antique shop. Hector and his new partner, Becky, now have 19 acres to graze on in the rear of the newly remodeled Holloway house, now owned by Mr. Hank Sims and his beautiful wife, Liz-Marie.

END OF STORY.

POSTLOGUE:

Daisy Collins now lives in the cottage formerly occupied by Herb and Marge. She got it repainted and some new furniture, including a new sofa. Mrs. Hooker, because of ill health, moved to a house that she owned in Santa Cruz, California. She hired Herb and Marge to manage her cottages, and let them move into her luxurious cottage that she vacated, rent free, plus $800 per month salary.

THE END.

LOUISA

A Love Story

Tom Robb

<u>LIST OF CHARACTERS:</u>
LOUISA — Immigrant to U.S. from Italy in 1920
TONY — Louisa's brother
JUDITH — Friend of Louisa's-brother of Howard
HOWARD — friend of Louisa's
LUIGI — Cousin of Louisa & Tony's
MRS. ANGELO — Apartment owner near Ellis Island
SAM BRADY — Salesman friend of Louisa's
PHIL GREEN — Attorney friend of Louisa's
NOLA DELANO — Aunt Mary's daughter
AUNT MARY DELANO — Louisa and Tony's aunt
RITA — Tony's girlfriend
MR. MOSCHETTI — Official at Ellis Island
BENNY — Shoeshine stand operator
FANNIE — Rag Lady
MR. BAKER — Owner of The News
MAN — (CARJACKER)
GERTIE — Housekeeper for bootleggers
BRUCE — Bootlegger
LEM — Bootlegger
NURSE — (AT HOSPITAL)
AMBROSE — Porter on RR
CAROL SCOTT — Friend of Howard's from Tarrytown
BUSTER — Taxi driver
MR. WILBURN — Owner Premier Men's

CHAPTER ONE

It was mid-summer in the year 1920. The steamship "Belloma", 3 days out of Portsmouth, England, was cruising along toward America with 850 anxious and excited passengers. The weather on the Atlantic was good; waves only moderate. It was a sunshiny day. The main deck was crowded with people enjoying the wide expanse of the ocean. They had just had the exciting experience of seeing a couple of whales surfacing repeatedly near the ship. Suddenly there was a cry of "Help! Boy Overboard!" Louisa Delano, 20 years old, was leaning over the railing at the side of the ship. She saw the boy, about 12 years old, as he fell into the water. Without thinking; she ripped off her coat and shoes and dived overboard. The crowd was screaming. When she surfaced she looked around. He was not in sight. Louisa quickly swam over to where the boy went under. She managed to locate and support him. He could swim but was scared and had swallowed quite a bit of the salty water. The ship stopped as soon as it could and put out a boat to pick them up. She kept him afloat until the little boat rescued them and carried them back to the "Belloma ".

A nurse, Edith Google, escorted them to the dispensary where the boy was checked over. Still scared, exhausted and soaked, he was turned over to his parents who thanked Louisa profusely for rescuing their son. The nurse helped Louisa to get into some dry clothes.

NURSE — "You did a fantastic job of rescuing that boy. He's lucky that you jumped in so quickly. You're a good swimmer, what is your name?"

— "I'm Louisa Delano. I'm from Naples, Italy. I've had some experience in life-saving. I was a part-time lifeguard at the South Shore Beach in Naples."

— "I'm Edith Google. I'm a nurse. I'm working in the dispensary here to pay for my passage. My brother, Howard, is also on the ship. We're from London. Is your family also on board?"

— "Just my brother, Tony. He's 14. My parents died in the flu epidemic that has been raging in our country. We're on our way to live with our Aunt and Uncle in New York," said Louisa.

"Are you in a cabin?" asked Edith.

— "No, we're in 'tourist'. We couldn't afford a cabin."

Just at this time the Captain of the ship came in, along with the deck officer on duty. They thanked Edith, and especially Louisa, for their part in the rescue. Later Edith brought her brother down to "tourist" to meet Louisa. Howard had been impressed with Louisa's quick rescue and requested that Edith introduce him to her. They were in the lounge. Tony was present.

EDITH —(introducing Howard)— "Louisa, this is my brother, Howard Google. He wanted to meet you. He thinks he wants to be a newspaper reporter. This is a 'story' to him."

— "I'm very glad to meet you, Louisa. That was a wonderful job you did rescuing that boy. I'm sure that it saved his life. Are you and Tony going to stay in New York City in America?" asked Howard.

— "No, we're going to live with our Uncle and Aunt in Middleton, N.Y. It's a town of about 5000 people." "We're not going to stay in New York City either. We prefer a smaller town," put in Edith.

— "I hope to work for a newspaper somewhere. Tony, you're a big husky boy. Did you play soccer? How old are you?" asked Howard.

"I'm 14. Yes, I played soccer. I also played in the band."

Suddenly the ship's bell rang for lunch time. Louisa and Tony started to leave for their "tourist" area.

EDITH —(as they parted)— "Louisa, I'd like to talk to you again. We don't have any friends on this ship. Could we get together later?"

HOWARD — "That's right. I'd like to get more information for my 'story' about the rescue. Might sell it to a newspaper. Make you famous Louisa."

— "That would be nice, Edith. We don't know anyone on this boat either. As for being famous, Howard. That isn't one of my ambitions."

— "Ok. I'll fix us a lunch tomorrow and we'll have a picnic on the deck somewhere. We can talk and watch the waves," said Edith. They separated.

TONY— (as they walked to their area of the ship.)— "Louisa, while we were all watching you rescue that boy, I think I saw Luigi. I just got a short glimpse, but it sure looked like him. Is he supposed to be on this boat?"

— "I don't think so. I know he mentioned once that he would like to go to America. Probably someone similar. I'm sure it's not Luigi."

— "Maybe you're right. I didn't get much of a look. He was all bundled up with a big coat, hat and scarf. But it gave me a start to see him

223

on this ship." said Tony. — "Don't worry about it. If it's him, it's not going to sink the ship."

Luigi Castavo, 20 years old, was the only son of Grandpa Cicero Delano's second wife. Since he was 12, he had lived with Grampy and his mother in Naples. Grampy, patriarch of the Delano family, owned an upscale restaurant on the beautiful South Shore. They lived on opposite sides of a little valley from the family of Louisa and Tony and their parents. Sometimes Luigi would practice on his sax in the evenings, the beautiful clear tones to be answered by Tony with his trumpet. Both liked American jazz and both were getting to be very good at their instruments. But Luigi dropped out of school and joined a local band, against the advice of Grampy. Being the same age as Louisa, he liked to take her to events the band played for. They also played tennis together. Louisa had lots of friends, both girls and boys, but didn't like some of Luigi's friends. Luigi became jealous, which resulted in a break in their association just two months prior to the untimely death of Louisa's parents and her and Tony's leaving for America.

Scene 2

The following day Edith guided them to an area on the upper deck where they had a good view and it wasn't crowded. She had coaxed a good assortment of sandwiches, etc. from the galley. The weather was pleasant.

HOWARD — "Louisa, are you planning to go to college in America?"

— "I would like to, but first I need to get a job. I've had two years of college in Italy, before my parents died."

— "Is your Uncle meeting you in New York?"

— "No. we'll send him a telegram when we arrive in New York."

— "What kind of a job will you be trying for?" asked Howard.

— "I don't know yet. I've heard jobs are easy to get there."

HOWARD — "To get a job that pays well, you'll need some experience or specialization unless you just plan to get married, in which case you wouldn't have to know much. Did you have a boyfriend in Italy?"

— "Yes, I did. But he wasn't really a boyfriend. He was a distant cousin, same age as me. We played a lot of tennis together."

— "Howard, you're not working for a newspaper yet. Those questions are too personal," cautioned Edith.

LOUISA — "That's alright Edith, I don't mind. I've never had anyone so interested in me before. Howard, smarty, a mother has to know a lot of things besides how to run a newspaper, I may study law when I can get to a college again."

— "Ho! That's man's work. Who would hire a lady lawyer? Women's occupations are nursing, teaching, waitresses, etc. You're aiming pretty high." said Howard in a teasing voice.

EDITH — "You're wrong, Howard. In America it's different. Women can vote. They made it legal last year. They can do anything they want, even if they're married. I've read of Hetty Green. She's a financial success in the New York Stock Market."

— "She's an exception, Edith. You and Louisa are no 'Hetty Greens, but you'd both make some poor struggling guy a good wife."

He laughed as Louisa gave him a protesting shove.

LOUISA — "I like you, Howard, but I wouldn't want to work for you. I'd probably never advance. Edith, you need to tone him down a bit."

— "Don't take him seriously, Louisa, he's just my ignorant big brother."

— "I'm not a tyrant, Louisa, but to get a good salary you should finish your college and specialize in something. My major is communication. Women can't handle that, I'm afraid." said Howard.

Their attention was diverted by people crowding into the area near them. Suddenly the "Belloma" was passing a huge, beautiful, glistening iceberg. It was much bigger then the ship and rose up at least a hundred feet above the water. A foggy haze seemed to hover above it. It was a good distance away but was a very exciting sight.

TONY — "Wow! That's a huge chunk of ice. Where did it come from?"

— "It probably broke off the ice shelf of Greenland; what you see above water is only about l/7th of it's total mass. The biggest part is under water. Ships don't pass them too close as the under part can't be seen." said Howard.

— "It's summertime. What's it doing here?" asked Louisa.

— "It's slowly drifting South and melting at the same time. Ships have to watch out for them, specially if it's foggy." said Howard."

— "It's beautiful!" said Louisa.

It was the morning of the 8th day out of Portsmouth. The Captain of the "Belloma" had just informed everyone that in about an hour the ship would be docking in New York. All passengers were to get their things together and be ready to leave the ship. There was great excitement and anticipation, knowing that the end of their journey was near. Within a half hour there was a crowd on the decks to watch. Many other ships came into view as they neared the busy harbor. The dim coastline became visible. They passed in view of the tall black and white Montauk lighthouse with it's light sweeping. As they came in view of the beautiful "Statue Of Liberty", a great cheer came from the crowd as they gazed in admiration at the huge copper statue. Louisa, Edith, Tony and Howard stood together watching as the ship approached.

— "Well, Louisa, what do you think? " asked Howard.

— "It's beautiful. I think I   want to cry from happiness."

— "Nowhere else in the world is there a welcoming symbol like that for people who need a new start in life." added Edith.

SCENE 3

The "Belloma" finally was able to stop at an unloading dock at Ellis Island off lower Manhattan. The passengers streamed into the reception building with their suitcases and bundles of possessions. Louisa and Tony got in line for last names starting with "D". Finally it was their turn.

OFFICIAL — "Your name please."

Louisa responded and presented all her papers for passage and the letter from her uncle in Middleton who was sponsoring them. He checked her money also.

OFFICIAL — "Everything seems to be alright. You'll need to get in line for a medical check. I'm glad to see you. I see you're from Naples. I came from Bologna 12 years ago. I'm Mr. Moschetti. You'll find some discrimination against Italians here but don't let it discourage you. This is a free country and you'll be OK. Do you have a place to stay here in New York City?"

— "No. We'll have to find a place for tonight," said Louisa.

MR. MOSCHETTI— "If you do have trouble finding a place, come back and see me. We have a few extra beds here for emergencies."

— "Thank you, Mr. Moschetti."

— "Miss Delano, don't forget to get your money changed to American money before you leave here. You're free to go after your medical check."

Louisa and Tony went through the medical checkups and had their money changed. They had not seen Luigi again while on the ship, but in the big room as they were about to leave, Louisa spotted him. She approached him.

— "Hello, Luigi. I see that you weren't kidding when you said you might go to New York. Where did you board the ship? I didn't see you in Naples."

— "I came aboard at Portsmouth. I've been playing in a band in London. I just felt like I needed a change of scenery; I didn't know you were on this boat."

— "Luigi, I'm sorry for our recent disagreement; where are you going in America?"

LUIGI— "I have an offer to play in a band in New York City. Can we get together there? You're still my favorite partner. Lots of tennis courts in New York City I'm sure."

— "Luigi, Tony and I are going to Middleton to live with Uncle Cicero and Aunt Mary. So I won't be near a New York City tennis court. Does Grampy know you're coming to New York?"

— "Yes. He wasn't pleased. But he doesn't need to worry. I'll be making lots of money."

Tony saw them and came over.

TONY — "Hi, Loog! I thought I spotted you. Have your sax?"

LUIGI— "I'm married to it since your sister turned me down."

LOUISA — "I'm going to marry a rich American oil man."

— "You're both goin' to end up in the 'Nut' house." predicted Tony.

A call for Louisa and Tony Delano on the intercom to report to line "B". It was for their official immigration papers which were now ready.

LOUISA— "Luigi, prohibition on liquor has recently gone into effect in America, so be careful. It's not like Italy."

— "Don't worry about me. New York City is a big city. I'll fit in."

They separated and reported to line "B".

TONY— "Louisa, was he trying to get you to marry him again?"

— "Not this time. But he's just not the one for me, Tony."

— "I don't know why you're so particular. I think I'll get married as soon as I'm 18."

LOUISA — "Ha! We'll see."

Scene 4

Their boat fare had cost them $80.00 and they had $180.00 left as they stood on the street outside with Edith and Howard. Taxis, busses, etc. jockeyed to pick up and carry the new arrivals to the hotels, etc.

— "Louisa, I wish the best for you and Tony. We've got to go now, we're going to catch that limo over there. We'll stay here a few days while I check out some of the smaller towns for employment. Maybe Middleton, who knows?" said Howard.

LOUISA— "We can't go to a hotel. They're too expensive. The newsboy on the corner said that there are some rooming houses about 4 blocks from here. We're going there. So, good-bye, maybe somewhere we'll meet again. As you say, who knows?"

EDITH— "Oh, that would be great. I've enjoyed very much knowing you. God bless you both. Good-bye."

Howard and Edith left. As they were going away, Howard looked back at them and waved. Louisa waved back and then a signal (index finger sticking up—thumb out; the other 3 fingers of hand closed), she smiled and gave the signal again.

HOWARD—(mumbling to himself) "I wonder what she meant by that?"

EDITH — "What did you say?"

— "I Was Just mumbling to myself. Edith, Louisa is a very interesting kind of girl, don't you think?"

— "We're all a bit mysterious and unpredictable, Howard. But you were pretty critical of Louisa there. I hope she didn't feel hurt."

HOWARD— "Oh, she's Italian. She's used to it."

Scene 5

As Louisa and Tony started to walk away from the Ellis Island receiving building, they got their first impression of New York City. Everybody seemed to be in a hurry or at least busy about something. Lots of well dressed men in suits, smart felt hats. Some with straw hats, since it was still Summer. Young ladies in short skirts, bobbed hair topped with a saucy little hat, all hurrying on some important mission. On the corner as they left was a street organist playing "On The Sidewalks Of New York". His little monkey companion holding out his cup for donated coins.

TONY— "You like Howard, don't you Louisa?"

LOUISA— "Why do you say that? I love Edith. But him? He's pretty critical of women. But underneath, he's a very interesting person. Did you like him, Tony?"

— "Yes, I did."

They walked the rest of the four blocks and selected a modest looking building and rang the bell.

MRS. ANGELO—(answering) "Yes, what is it you want?"

LOUISA— "We would like to rent a room, we're from Ellis Island."

— "What is your name? You look like you're Italian."

— "I'm Louisa Delano. This is my brother, Anthony. We're from Italy."

MRS. ANGELO— "I'm Italian, too. I'm from Livorno. All of my rooms are rented. You may find it hard to find a place. There's a lot of prejudice against us in a lot of places in New York."

— "This is for short time, we will go to our uncle in Middleton. We have to telegraph him first."

MRS. ANGELO— "I do have a small attic room that you could have, but only temporarily."

— "Thank you. How much to rent it?"

— "It's $3.00 per week or $10.00 per month."

LOUISA— "Thank you. We would like it."

She paid Mrs. Angelo $4.00 for two weeks and were shown to a small attic room. Mrs. Angelo supplied them with two cots and the necessary bedding, etc. and they were settled. Louisa immediately sent a telegram to her uncle in Middleton informing him of their arrival in New York. Three days went by and they had no word from her uncle.

MRS. ANGELO— "Are you sure your uncle was expecting you? He may have been out of town. Maybe the address that you sent it to is not correct."

She seemed worried. Louisa showed her the letter from her uncle. The address was correct.

MRS. ANGELO— "Your telegram should have been delivered to him the next day. His letter to you is dated three months ago. Something may have happened. If you don't hear from him in the next week, I would advise you to get work somewhere while you wait. Living is expensive here in New York these days."

Louisa realized she was right and agreed.

Scene 6

The reason why Louisa had received no reply from her telegram was that a family tragedy had occurred in Middleton. Her uncle had been killed when the horse pulling him in a wagon had become terrified by a passing train as both approached a crossing. The horse panicked, upsetting the wagon and throwing Mr. Delano out and breaking his neck. The horse broke loose from the wagon, then disappeared back down the road toward home. Mr. Milano did not survive. After the funeral, Mrs. Delano went to another town to live for a while with a brother and his family. Nola, their daughter, had returned to the college in Pennsylvania where she was studying to be a nurse.

Scene 7

After another week and no news from her uncle and her shrinking finances, Louisa decided to try and get a job. Mrs. Angelo decided to help her, since she was well informed of the businesses in the area. She took Louisa to a candy factory, where she once worked and still knew the office manager. Louisa was employed at $1.00 per day in the chocolate dept. boxing the delicious goodies as they came down the line on a conveyer belt. Mrs. Angelo also helped Tony get a job selling newspapers on one of the busy street corners. Tony enjoyed the job. A natural extrovert, he was soon acquainted with Benny, the shoeshine stand man at the corner, as well as a lot of Benny's regular customers— including a Rabbi, a banker, several salesmen, and a mysterious guy that Tony figured to be a member of the Mafia that he had read about. Then there was the "rag lady " who came by to chat. Never a dull moment on Tony's corner. So they settled in for the present while they were awaiting word from their uncle in Middleton.

Two months went by and then one day a letter came from Louisa's Aunt Mary (Maria) Delano, inviting them to come on down to Middleton to live with her. She explained that Mr. Delano had died and she had been temporarily with her brother and family. A few days later Mrs. Angelo helped Louisa and Tony get their things together for the trip to Middleton. Louisa sent a telegram to her Aunt Mary that they were on their way. Passengers for the train to Middleton from Ellis Island had to first take a ferry across the Hudson River to Hoboken on the Jersey side.

MRS ANGELO — "I'll go with you on the ferry to Hoboken where you'll catch your train to Middleton. I want to be sure that you don't have any problems getting to your train."

LOUISA— "New York is such a huge place. I appreciate you going with us."

Scene 8

With Mrs. Angelo's guidance they took the ferry and finally arrived at the train station in Hoboken. After purchasing their tickets, they were standing outside awaiting the train's arrival.

MRS. ANGELO— "Louisa, I'm glad that you're finally getting to go live with your aunt. I've learned to love you and Tony in your short stay with me. It will be kind of lonesome without you."

LOUISA— "You've been so wonderful to us. I'm almost sorry to go. But it is best for us. I'm looking forward to more open country. I want to keep in touch with you, and I'll write to you soon after I get to Middleton."

There were lots of people at the train station. The concrete area between the stationhouse and the tracks was crowded with many dollies piled high with crates, packages, produce, etc. to be loaded for destinations down the line to Passaic, Peterson, Ridgewood, Suffern, Chester, Middleton and points beyond. Two dollies with U.S. mail were ready for loading, guarded by a man wearing a pistol. A whistle was heard and around a curve in the track came engine #27. With it's bell ringing, it eased to a stop in front of the waiting crowd, with a hiss and a gush of steam to adjust the pressure in the brake lines; the conductor stepped off the train. The loading was ready to begin. The train was eight cars long behind the engine, a coal-tender carrying coal for the engine, then two baggage cars for produce and mail, dining car, parlor car, and four passenger cars. The engineer leaned out of his cab and waved to the kids. The brakeman stepped out with his red lantern to supervise the loading and unloading. The station agent hurried out to the baggage man with waybills that described the merchandise to be loaded, and their destinations.

Two porters, dressed in their tailored black uniforms, white shirts and fancy caps stepped out of the passenger cars. They put down their little step-ups and started checking the tickets of the boarding passengers.

PORTER — (addressing Louisa and Tony as they started to board.) "What's your destination, Ma'am?"

LOUISA — "We're going to Middleton."

PORTER-(checks tickets) " OK. Go on."

They went aboard. — Meanwhile, activity up and down the length of the train is brisk. The unloading came first. Not much of it since this was the starting point of the run. Mostly a few supplies for the station. Next, the merchandise is loaded, the farthest destination first. The mail is loaded into the second baggage car, a combination mail and baggage car. The mailman in the car also wore a pistol. After everyone and everything was loaded, the porters picked up their steps and boarded. The brakeman signaled to the engineer with his lantern and also boarded. The train gave a couple of blasts of the horn, the bell started ringing. A cloud of steam, a loud JOLT from each successive car, and #27 left the station .

It was 120 miles to Middleton and the train made about 12 stops between Hoboken and Middleton. Leaving at 10:00 A.M. sharp, it would be shortly after 4:00 P.M. when they got to Middleton. Louisa and Tony got into one of the cars named "Niagara Falls". There were double seats on each side of a center isle. A big window for viewing the scenery as they pass through the countryside. After they got through Hoboken's lower side with it's backyards, factory warehouses, etc. they finally got into the beautiful countryside.

The scenery was so exciting; much different from where they had lived in Italy. After a few minutes, a porter came through. It was the same one who had checked them at boarding.

PORTER— (basket of items suspended from his neck) "Fruit? Candy? Crackerjacks? My name's Ambrose. Like some fruit or candy, Lady? Souvenirs?"

LOUISA— "Not now. Thank you."

He went on through the coach. At 12:00 noon, the porter, Ambrose, came through to announce that the diner was open from 12:00 until 2:00PM. He stopped at Louisa's seat.

AMBROSE— "Lady, the diner is the next car up. (he points) - Good food. Hot coffee."

LOUISA— "We brought our lunch. Thank you."

AMBROSE— "You folks from the City?"

TONY— "No. We're from Italy. We come from Naples."

AMBROSE— "I Was in Naples once. It's a beautiful city. I worked on a ship before I got this job."

TONY— "Why did you quit the ship job? I think that would be fun."

AMBROSE— "I didn't like being away from my family so much. I have a wife and two children. My wife is not well. I've been on this job two years. It's better for me."

Ambrose left, but was shortly back pushing a little cart loaded with sodas, fruit, souvenirs, ham and cheese and pimento-cheese sandwiches.

LOUISA— "We would like a couple of sodas and some fruit." They selected a creme soda and an orange soda; also an apple and an orange.

AMBROSE— "How about a souvenir for your trip. Here's a little glass cat filled with candy. Only twenty cents."

LOUISA— "It IS pretty. I'd like it. You're a good salesman, Ambrose." She paid him for the item.

AMBROSE— "Thank you, Miss. I'll be back later."

It was a pleasant ride as they sat eating their lunch and watching the countryside glide by. The sounds of the clicking of the rails, the different sounds going over bridges...the sudden darkness of the tunnels, the peculiar smell of the train smoke and the lonely sound of the engine puffing and the whistling stays in the memory for a lifetime. The stops at the various towns were repeated like that at Hoboken (the crowds, produce, mail, etc.) Shortly after the train had left Suffern and after getting out into the countryside, the train suddenly slowed and stopped. Ambrose came through to say that there was a brush fire on the right of way up ahead and the train crew was out fighting it.

SCENE 9
_____

Looking out the window Louisa could see a field of grain of some kind. There was a lot of smoke that swirled past her window. She couldn't see where the fire was.

TONY— "There's plenty of smoke; where's the fire?"

LOUISA — "It must be up ahead. That's where the smoke's coming from." She wiped a cinder from her eye. The conductor appeared reassuring the passengers that they were in no danger.

The fire was in the grass that grew along the sides of the track. Some of the creosote soaked ties that the rails were laid on were indeed afire up ahead, but the train crew was putting them out. A half dozen of the passengers were helping the train crew fight the grass fire. The smoke cleared a bit and Louisa and Tony could see the men with wet tow sacks and buckets of water beating the flaming grass. In about thirty minutes, the fires were out and the train resumed the trip.

LOUISA — "I wonder how the fire started? This is way out in the country. Nobody around much."

GENTLEMAN-(who was seated across the isle, on hearing Louisa's comment)-"It was probably started by the freight train that we passed about fifteen miles back. Usually from a fire in a lock box."

LOUISA— "What's a lockbox?"

GENTLEMAN — "That's the enclosure that is around the end of the axel of each wheel of a boxcar or passenger car. It's packed with rag material which is soaked with oil for lubrication. Sometimes the oiled material gets dry and the friction causes it to catch fire. Some of the burning material drops out and starts the fire."

TONY— "That's interesting. How'd you learn all that stuff?"

GENTLEMAN — "I'm a drummer. I sell dress shirts and ties wholesale all up and down this line. Fires happen occasionally. Where are you two going?"

LOUISA — "We're going to Middleton. Our Aunt lives there."

GENTLEMAN — "Do you live in New York City? I work out of New York City."

TONY — "No, we're from Italy. We will be living in Middleton with our Aunt,"

GENTLEMAN — "My name is Sam Brady. Italy must be a beautiful country, America is beautiful also. I think you'll love it here. Middleton is one of my stops; I have clients there that I see several times a year."

LOUISA — "I'm Louisa Delano and this is my brother, Tony."

SAM BRADY — "Maybe we'll run across each other there sometime. I have to get off at Chester, which is the next stop. Tony, let me give you something."

Sam Brady opened a small brown suitcase that he carried, looked carefully at Tony, and selected a white dress shirt and a couple of bright ties.

SAM BRADY — "Tony, I'd like you to have these. I think you'll like them. They're samples. I carry dozens of them. Most are in my trunk in the baggage car. They've never been worn. You look like a very deserving boy. So, with my compliments!" Tony took the shirt and ties.

TONY — "Thank you, Mr. Brady. They're beautiful!"

LOUISA — "That's very nice of you, Mr. Brady. Thank you."

There was a train whistle and the train started slowing down.

SAM BRADY — "I've got to get off here. It was a pleasure to meet you. As I say, maybe we'll cross trails in Middleton sometime. Who knows? Sam got off at Chester. Louisa took note of how sharply dressed and professional Sam Brady was. He seemed so confident and friendly. A bit of a contrast to Howard. What made her think of him?

TONY— "I think I'd like to be a traveling salesman like him."

The next stop after Chester was Middleton. Ambrose came in to Louisa and Tony's seat.

AMBROSE — "The next stop is Middleton, lady. You two have a happy visit there."

LOUISA — "Thank you, Ambrose. I hope your wife gets over her illness soon."

They prepared to get off the train.

"I was just hoping someone would come by and buy me one"

CHAPTER TWO

SCENE 10

When Louisa and Tony stepped off the train and started looking around at the big crowd of people, a lady about 50 years old stepped up to them.

LADY — "You're Louisa Delano, aren't you?"

LOUISA — "Yes. How did you know? You're Aunt Mary?"

LADY (Aunt Mary) — "Yes, I am. You look so much like your mother did. I remember seeing you in Milan when you were about eight years old. And this is Anthony? How are you, young man?"

TONY — "I'm fine, Aunt Mary."

LOUISA — "I'm so glad to get here. I want to thank you for inviting us. We do appreciate it so."

AUNT MARY — "Well, it works both ways. I'm by myself now since Mr. Delano died. Nola, she's your age Louisa, is in school in Pennsylvania. I need some people near me to help me keep up with the world. My car is waiting, so let's get your luggage and we'll go to my house."

After a little wait they secured the luggage, got into Aunt Mary's late model car and drove through Middleton to her house. It was on the outskirts of town and had been the center of a five acre horse set-up, but Mr. Delano had sold off all but the one acre that the house occupied. Aunt Mary had recently sold the last horse; the one that had run away with Mr. Delano. The house was an older but pretty, white, two-story with a smooth green lawn in front and a white picket fence. It looked homey and spotlessly clean. The lot still had remnants of it's larger use. There was a windmill and water tower and a garden house topped with a weathervane. Electricity had recently been brought to the house and both bathrooms and the kitchen had been remodeled. A wood plank sidewalk ran from her house up to a new red brick street that ran into the center of town. The street in front, while kept well graded, was in line to be paved in the near future.

Scene 11

After unloading their sparse luggage, Aunt Mary showed them to their bedrooms to rest a bit while she went to a grocery store for some things she needed. So they were finally there and settled. It was a very satisfying feeling for Louisa. She could hardly wait to start planning this new life. She was so excited.

After Aunt Mary came back from the store, they all sat down in the large living room.

AUNT MARY — "Louisa, how is Grandpa Milano and the rest of the relatives in Naples? I don't hear from them often. Is Luigi still there?"

LOUISA — "Grampy is fine and still runs his restaurant. Luigi came over to New York on the same boat as we did. He is playing in a band in New York City. Aunt Mary, we were so shocked and saddened to hear about Uncle Cicero's death. I'm sure it is still a great sadness to you."

AUNT MARY — "Yes, it is. I'll tell you about it sometime soon. It was so unexpected. Louisa, tell me what you would like to do. You're twenty now. Do you have plans for college or do you want to work? I'll help you do either. Anthony, I'm sure you'll want to enroll in school. This is August, so you would be starting in about three weeks."

TONY — "What sports do the schools have here? I love sports. I played soccer in school in Italy. I also played the trumpet in the school band."

AUNT MARY — "The main sports played here are basketball, football and baseball. We'll have to see about soccer."

LOUISA — "Aunt Mary, I need to work somewhere, we don't want to be a financial burden to you. I'd like to enroll in a college night class if there's an opportunity. I've had two years college in Italy."

AUNT MARY — "We'll try to find you a job soon but you don't need to rush. I work for an insurance company as a secretary. Also, I'm secretary of the local Democratic Support Group. We're pretty active here. This town is about equally divided between Democrats and Republicans."

LOUISA — "That's interesting. You'll have to tell me what the difference is."

AUNT MARY — "We have two newspapers here: *The Middleton Times* which generally supports the Democratic agenda, and *The Middleton News*, which is staunchly Republican. I have good connections here, especially with our local Democrats."

So within a week Aunt Mary had helped Louisa get a job as a telephone switchboard operator, which entailed sitting before a switchboard wearing earphones and connecting incoming calls to the correct numbers dialed, then disconnecting them when the conversations were completed. Not an exciting job but a start.

Aunt Mary instructed Louisa in the local political scene and Louisa began to help her Aunt with the Democratic Support Group. In three weeks Aunt Mary took Tony to the local high school where he was enrolled as a freshman student. The school was not far, so Tony walked back at the end of classes.

LOUISA — "Well, Tony, what was your new school like? What did you do?"

TONY — "Not too different from Italy, except more crowded. I signed up for a full course, including band and football."

LOUISA — "Did you make any new friends?"

TONY — "No, but I saw a girl that I'm going to try to meet."

LOUISA — "So soon? Girls may be different over here. She may already have a boyfriend. What's her name?"

TONY — "I haven't found that out yet, but I will."

Tony wasn't the bashful type. Within a week he managed to meet her. She was also in the band and was taking singing lessons. They seemed to be attracted to each other from the start. Her name was Rita.

Scene 12

During the next two years Louisa became a real Middleton booster. She advanced in the telephone company to the advertising department. Her duties were to solicit advertising from the local merchants. In this job she became well acquainted with most of the local business men. During this time she also enrolled in a night school law class sponsored by Columbia University. It was held at the local high school. One evening, a young man sat down next to her and introduced himself.

YOUNG MAN — "I'm Phil Green. May I sit by you?"

LOUISA — "Sure. I'm Louisa Delano."

PHIL — "This your first class?"

LOUISA — "Yes. Is it yours?"

PHIL — "No. I'm already an attorney. I'm just reviewing some of the classes I had several years ago."

LOUISA — "Isn't that kind of a waste of time?"

PHIL — "Not really. I'm not very busy right now. Time on my hands. I play tennis a lot. Do you play tennis?"

LOUISA — "I have played in Italy, before I came here. I love to play."

PHIL — "I belong to a tennis club, we should get together for a game or two."

LOUISA — "I'd like that."

So they did begin playing tennis together at the club. Phil picked her up regularly in his 1922 yellow Ford sport car. They also "partnered" in various "official" events that each needed to attend. Soon, the *Middleton Times* hired her away from the telephone company to do the same job for them. It was then that Louisa changed her major at night school from law to communications. Howard had said women couldn't handle it she remembered.

SCENE 13

It was now the Spring of 1923. Walking on the busy downtown street one day, as she turned a corner, Louisa ran smack into a man. Who was it? Then she recognized him. It was none other than Sam Brady!!!

SAM BRADY — "Oh, I'm sorry, Lady I'm such a clumsy cow!" He helped her pick up a few things she'd dropped.

SAM — "Oh, you're Miss Delano! Do you remember me, Sam Brady? I met you and your brother on the train when you were coming to Middleton about two years ago."

LOUISA — "Yes, I remember you. You gave Tony a dress shirt and ties. He liked them very much."

SAM — "I was just going to the ice cream store, for a soda. could you join me? I'd like to hear how you and Tony are faring."

LOUISA — (hesitating at first) "Yes. I'd be glad to. Today's a warm day and a soda sounds good."

Sam escorted her to a seat at an inside table and a waitress took their order: strawberry sodas.

SAM — "Miss Delano? If you are still Miss. It's been a long time since our train ride together. I've thought of you often since then. Are you working in town here now?"

LOUISA — "Yes. I'm still Miss Delano. I'm in charge of the advertising department of the *Middleton Times*. We're happy here."

SAM — "I'm still with The Royal Shirt Company. I worked in the office for a couple of years but am back on the road now. I hit Middleton about twice a month. How is Tony? I'm sure he's outgrown the shirt by now."

LOUISA — "Yes. He has outgrown it but he still wears the ties. You look prosperous. Is the shirt company doing well?"

SAM — "It's booming! I hope men never quit wearing shirts. We're trying to design a shirt that ladies would wear. Feminine type, of course. Would you like a refill on that soda?"

LOUISA — "Sure, why not?"

They had another soda and Louisa prepared to leave.

LOUISA — "Thank you, Mr. Brady. That was delicious!"

SAM — "Just call me Sam. I'm still single, too. And may I also call you Louisa? AND may I treat you to another soda when I come through again in two weeks?"

LOUISA — "Sam, I have a regular boyfriend. Not too serious. But sure, if you can find me. I love sodas!"

SAM — "That's great, Louisa. I'll look forward to it. Please say hello to Tony for me." They both left.

Two weeks passed. Sam was again in town. He wondered if Louisa would remember that he would be there. He was hopeful but realized that it might be a long shot It was 10:00 A.M. and already getting warm when he went by the Ice Cream Store on his way from his hotel to his first customer's store. There were a lot of people in the street. He didn't see anyone that looked like Louisa. He went back and went in the Ice Cream Store and purchased a couple of good Cuban cigars to give to customers. She wasn't in there, so he went on to his customer, The Premier Men's Clothiers. Mr. Wilburn, the owner, was busy with a customer so he waited near the street door, just in case he saw Louisa out on the street somewhere. When Mr. Wilburn was free, Sam displayed a couple of new style shirts and ties just out for the market.

MR. WILBURN — "Sam, I'm pretty well stocked up right now. However, I do need a dozen of your #2 white dress shirts. Show me the new ones later."

SAM — "Alright I will. I'll bring the #2 whites by this afternoon. Mr. Wilburn, do you know Miss Louisa Delano who lives here?"

MR. WILBUBN — "Oh yes, I do. I see her quite often. Very fine lady. Very friendly. Do you know her?"

SAM — "I've met her briefly twice. I was hoping I'd see her while I was here today."

MR. WILBURN — "She works for the *Times*. She's a good sales lady. Attractive, too. She might make a good shirt salesman for you, Sam."

SAM — "Well, if you see her, Mr. Wilburn, just mention that I was in."

Sam left. That afternoon about two O'clock, after delivering the #2 white shirts to Mr. Wilburn, Sam decided to walk by the Ice Cream Store again. Was it just luck, or was she waiting for someone? Standing and looking in the show window of the Lady's Delight Dress Shop next door to the I.C.S., was Louisa. He slipped up behind her:

SAM — "BOO!"(scary but not too loud)

Louisa turned quickly.

LOUISA — "OH! Sam! You scared me. You're an old meany. Imagine seeing you here."

SAM — (after the laughing died down) "My apologies, Louisa. Imagine seeing *you* here. I'm famished for a cool soda. How about you?"

LOUISA — "I was just hoping someone would come by and buy me one."

They went in and were seated at a table.

SAM — "Louisa, I've been looking forward to seeing you again since I was here two weeks ago. How have you been?"

LOUISA — "Very busy. I saw Mr. Wilburn just now and he said you were in town. I was hoping to see you before you left."

SAM — "Were you, really? I'm pleased to hear that."

LOUISA — "I like to hear the latest from New York City. You're a good source of information. And of course, you might want to advertise your shirts in *The Times* or subscribe to it."

SAM — "I'll consider it later. Mr. Wilburn was right. He said that you were a good salesman. How about coming to work for my shirt company?"

LOUISA — "If I ever lose my job with the *Times*, I might consider it."

SAM — "I'll see if I can get you fired."

Their sodas came and they enjoyed about forty minutes of banter and conversation before they had to separate. As it turned out it became a pleasant break for both every two weeks. Louisa still kept up her tennis, etc., with Phil, but Phil had other interests that limited his time with Louisa.

Sam was such a warm, well mannered gentleman that Louisa felt comfortable with him. A successful salesman had to be like that. Competition was strong. Sam was top notch!

Scene 14

Howard and Edith didn't stay long in New York City. After an extensive search, Howard got a job with a newspaper in Tarrytown, N.Y. And Howard *did* sell his "story" about the boat trip and the rescue to a New York City newspaper. In fact it helped him get the job in Tarrytown. Edith went along with him to Tarrytown. In time he became Assistant Manager of the paper.

Howard had not forgotten the sign that Louisa had flashed at their separation at Ellis Island. One day while walking in a park, he noticed a group of deaf students and their teacher. The teacher was flashing signs, including the one that Louisa had flashed.

HOWARD — "Pardon me, lady. Can you tell me what this sign means?"

He gave the sign.

TEACHER — "That sign is for "L", as in lost, love, louse, etc."

HOWARD — "Thank you. I was just curious."

He resumed walking and turning over in his mind the mysterious signal that Louisa had made. He felt that it was a deliberate message to him, but what?

HOWARD (to himself) - "Something beginning with "L". Love? No. Lost? No. Like?"

That fit his own feelings for Louisa. A warm feeling surged through his body as he contemplated the possibility of Louisa sending him that message. It was for him, wasn't it? Edith wasn't looking. Well, it was something that he'd never know for sure. Best try to forget it.

SCENE 15

In the Fall of 1923, the *Middleton News* had a vacancy and put an add in the News Register for a replacement for Assistant Manager.

HOWARD (Perusing the ads at breakfast with Carol Scott, a clerk) - "Carol, here's an ad from a newspaper in Middleton. They have an opening for an Assistant Manager. That's a bigger town than Tarrytown."

CAROL — "It should pay more, too. Are you going to bid on it?"

HOWARD — "I think I'll write them for the job description and ask for a bid application. I used to know a couple of people there."

CAROL — "I'd like to get out of this place, myself."

HOWARD — "If I get the job, maybe I can bring you along later."

CAROL — "*That* would be nice."

HOWARD — "It's not so far away. We can still keep in touch."

And so, Howard wrote the *Middleton News* about the job. It ended up that he was hired.

SCENE 16

Louisa, at the time, learned of Howard's new job at The News. What a surprise! She was both happy for Howard and, well, something else. Kinda like a thrill or was it a chill? She had often wondered about him and Edith. The beautiful Edith was probably married. But what about Howard? Were those goose bumps she felt? Nonsense! Howard was just a typical Englishman. Someone had said the problem with England was the Englishmen. How did Howard fit in that? He liked to put down women. Maybe he was just sarcastic.

When she mentioned to Tony that Howard Google was coming to work for The News, Tony was thoughtful.

TONY — "I'd forgotten about him. Do you still like him? You've got so many boyfriends: Sam, Phil, and there was Loog. And now comes Howard Google. You're like 'The Girl Who Can't Say No.' I don't know what to think of your generation."

LOUISA — "Your generation is the same as mine, Smart Alec! None of my friends are really serious. They are all just good friends. I don't think I'm flighty or flirty as you infer."

TONY — "You ought to narrow it down to one, like me and Rita. Have an elimination contest."

LOUISA — "Tony, you're impossible!"

Scene 17

So it was that on Monday Louisa decided to go over and give Howard the surprise of his life. She went into the restroom, brushed her hair, applied new lipstick, just a touch of perfume behind her ears and headed across the square and down the block to the *Middleton News* office. They knew her in the *News* office and called a "Cheerio" as she headed to the Assistant Manager's office. The receptionist raised her eyebrows at her as she neared the closed door.

LOUISA — "Clara, I'm an old friend. I just want to surprise him."

CLARA — "Sure, Louisa, go ahead."

Louisa opened the door and slipped in. Howard was standing looking out of the window with his back to her.

LOUISA (In a raised voice.) - "SURPRISE!"

HOWARD (without turning around.) — "Hello, Louisa." He turned around, smiling.

LOUISA (chagrined) — "Howard Google! How'd you know it was me?"

HOWARD — "Louisa, I just remembered your cheerful voice. I knew you were here. I've been thinking about you and planned to see you. I even kinda expected you."

LOUISA — "How did you know that I was still in Middleton?"

HOWARD — "Before I accepted this job I checked out our competition, *The Times*. I was surprised to see your name. But sit down, I'm very pleased to see you. How long have you been with the *Times*?"

LOUISA— "Two years. Tell me where and how is Edith?"

HOWARD — "Oh, that girl! She got married the first year. She has two children. Now lives in Paterson, N.J. Not like you, who apparently doesn't plan to get Married."

LOUISA — "I never said anything like that!"

HOWARD — "Oh, I'm sorry! Was I mistaken? Are you married?"

LOUISA — "No, I'm not and not planning to any time soon. Let's talk about something else. Why did you choose the *News*? They're such a radical conservative newspaper."

HOWARD — "They chose me. I'm just an ordinary newspaperman. I'm really not conservative except in a few things."

LOUISA —"I remember one. Back at Ellis Island you said that women should not be given the right to vote. You didn't think we were smart enough."

HOWARD — "Louisa, I was just ribbing you then. I really didn't know the situation over here. But women do have the right to vote since 1919, and you're probably using it with a vengeance."

LOUISA — "Tony and I still live with our Aunt Mary, who is a serious worker for the Democrats."

HOWARD — "Louisa, that reminds me. You and I work for opposing newspapers. Please remember, when you read our paper and we blast the *Times*, the Democrats, or their platform, it's not *little me* against *you*. We're still friends."

LOUISA — "I'll try to remember that. Incidentally, I should have asked you earlier. *You're* not married yet are you?"

HOWARD — "Yes, I am. I have a wife and three children."

LOUISA (astonished) — "You have?! Why didn't you tell me?"

HOWARD — "That was a joke, Louisa. I'm not married yet."

LOUISA — "Howard Google! I never know when to believe you."

They talked several minutes more.

LOUISA — "I've got to get back to my office. It's almost 9:00 o'clock."

HOWARD — "Thank you for coming, Louisa. I'm looking forward to seeing you around."

Louisa was somewhat disappointed with her meeting with Howard. He didn't seem serious like she had expected, hoped. Later when she saw Tony:

TONY — "How did your meeting with Howard go?"

LOUISA — "Oh, so, so. He's the same old Howard."

TONY — "Is he a reporter, or what?"

LOUISA — "He's still an enigma to me, Tony. I think he's a reporter at heart. But we're still friends."

SCENE 18
_____

Louisa had maintained contact with Mrs. Angelo by letter and had promised to visit her in the Spring. So as school was out in May, she and Tony took the train back to New York City for the visit. Mrs. Angelo was delighted to see them.

MRS. ANGEL0 — "It's so good to see you again. You look so pretty, Louisa; Tony, you have grown so!"

LOUISA — "We're the same, although it's been about three years since you helped us so much. We're so glad to see you again."

MRS. ANGELO — "You can stay here with me and I'll help you to go or see whatever you've planned."

LOUISA — "Besides our visit to you, I'd like to visit Ellis Island again."

TONY — "I want to go by my old 'corner' again, if possible."

MRS. ANGELO — "We'll do both. You can stay with me in my apartment. It's plenty big. Three bedrooms as you'll remember. It may interest you to know that your little attic room is rented to a young man who is a writer. I seldom see him."

And so, they settled in for a pleasant week with Mrs., Angelo.

SCENE 19
_____

On the second day they decided to revisit Ellis Island. Mrs. Angelo, who had also come through Ellis Island many years ago, decided to accompany them. So about 10:00 A.M. they walked the six blocks to the entrance. After getting visitor's passes at the entrance, they entered the Big Room. The first person that looked familiar was Mr. Moschetti.

LOUISA — "Hello, Mr. Moschetti. I see that you are still on the job."

MR. MOSCHETTI (very surprised) — "Heavenly Days! It's the kids from Naples! What a surprise! Young man, you are almost as big as your sister. You both look great! Now who is this fine looking lady with you?"

LOUISA — "Mr. Moschetti, this is Mrs. Mary Angelo. We're visiting her. We stayed with her when we came through Ellis Island three years ago."

MR. MOSCHETTI — "I'm glad to know you, Mrs. Angelo. How long have you been in the U.S., or were you born here?"

MRS. ANGELO — "My husband and I came through Ellis Island seventeen years ago. We came from Trieste. He died nine years ago. I have some apartments about six blocks from here."

MR. MOSCHETTI — "Is that so? I can help you keep them rented with good tenants. Many people coming through have to rent an apartment. If you'll give me your phone number, I'll keep it on file and maybe we can help each other."

MRS. ANGEL0 — "Yes. That may work out well." Mrs. Angelo gives him her phone number.

There was a new crowd of people just coming in from a ship that was unloading and Mr. Moschetti turned to help them.

MR. MOSCHETTI (as they separated) — "Mrs. Angelo, don't forget. Let's keep in touch."

TONY — "I'm hungry. Let's get a sandwich somewhere."

They did find a soda fountain that also served sandwiches, and with a milkshake, they sat down to watch the crowd.

LOUISA — "All these people streaming through here; every one of them would have an interesting story to tell."

MRS. ANGELO — "It was nice to meet Mr. Moschetti. He reminds me a lot of Mr. Angelo, when he was alive."

TONY — "It reminds me of Luigi. We haven't heard anything of him lately."

LOUISA — "(Grampy said in a letter to Aunt Mary that Luigi was doing well, but holding down two jobs.)"

After touring the other buildings, the docks, etc., they walked back to Mrs. Angelo's apartment.

Scene 20

During the next two days, they joined tour groups to visit Coney Island, the Statue of Liberty, Central Park and the City Aquarium. The next evening, they went to dinner at an upscale restaurant.

While waiting for a waiter:

TONY (looking around) — "Louisa, there's Luigi! He's waiting tables. Over there!"

Tony pointed.

LOUISA — "It sure is. I knew he was doing something besides his band job. I don't think he's serving our table area, I'd like to talk with him."

MRS. ANGELO — "If you'll go and ask for him to serve this table, they will arrange it."

Louisa quickly went and made the request. Presently Luigi came over-sharply dressed, a very handsome young man- with water glasses, napkins, etc.

LUIGI (passing around the menus) — "Welcome to The Rose Room."

Then he recognized them.

LUIGI — "Oh, My Lord! Louisa, Tony! Where did you come from? Do you live here now?"

LOUISA — "No. We're just visiting. Luigi, this is our friend, Mrs. Angelo. She lives here."

LUIGI — "Let me take your order, and when you leave, I want to talk to you a minute, Louisa."

He took their orders and spent as much time with them as he could, having other tables to serve.

LUIGI — "Tony, you got a girlfriend yet? I remember you sayin' you hated all girls."

TONY — "Loog, was I stupid? I've got a girlfriend that puts Mary Pickford in the shade!"

LUIGI — "Good for you. I can see you're growin' up." (they laughed)

When they paid the bill, Louisa and Luigi stood apart for a few minutes.

LOUISA — "How are you *really* doing, Luigi? I hear you're working two jobs."

LUIGI — "I'm doing fine, I make plenty of money, Louisa. Why don't you come to New York City. You'd fit in here great. I've got good connections. My two jobs are both five hours each. You'd make a lot more money than you can in Middleton. We'd have fun together, Louisa."

LOUISA — "I'm sorry, Luigi. No. I'm happy where I am. And Tony is settled there as well."

LUIGI (admitting defeat) — "Well, Louisa, I think you are a wonderful person. I just had to try again."

LOUISA — "Luigi, you'll find your wonderful 'someone' someday soon. Don't be discouraged. Come down to Middleton sometime.

Aunt Mary would be glad to see you. I hear Grampy would like you to come back and work for him."

LUIGI — "Yes, I know. That's a possibility for the future. But not now."

LOUISA — "Luigi, I've got to go. It's been good to see you and to know that you're doing well."

LUIGI — "Goodbye, Louisa. Say Hello to Aunt Mary for me." He went back to work and they left.

Scene 21

The next day Tony decided to visit his old "corner". So at 8:00 A.M. he walked the ten blocks to the site. Arriving there, he climbed into a seat in Benny's shoeshine stand. Benny looked at him quizzically, as if trying to place him.

TONY — "What're you lookin' at me like that for. Somethin' wrong with me?"

BENNY — "I didn't recognize you at first. But when you spoke, I knew. You're the little shrimp who used to sell papers on the corner, and worry the hell out of me, wanting change for customers. How are you, Tony, Boy? Glad to see you. My! You've grown!" They embraced as old friends.

Benny's stand had three seats. Tony sat in #3. Between customers, he and Tony enjoyed catching up on gossip of the "corner's" unique customers.

TONY — "How's business, Benny?"

BENNY — "It's good, I've lost some and gained some."

TONY — "How about the guy we thought was in the Mafia?"

BENNY — "He was in the mob, alright. He's in the pen. Murder: 25 years."

TONY — "How about the banker who always pulled a five or ten spot on you? And the Rabbi who always paid you in pennies?"

BENNY — "The banker's gone. The Rabbi still comes by about once a month. Still pays in pennies."

After about an hour, Benny held up his hand for silence.

BENNY — "Watch this." Crossing the street carefully and guiding herself with her cane, was Fannie, the "Rag Lady". With her rag bag on her little cart, she approached Benny's stand. Benny barked loudly, like a dog. Fannie stopped quickly. Benny barked again.

FANNIE — "Mis'r Benny, I knows that's you. Ain't no dog bark lak dat."

BENNY (laughing) — "You're right, Fannie. I apologize. Guess who's this sitting here with me?"

Fannie came real close and gazed at Tony.

FANNIE — "Mus be tha newsboy's big brotha. Looks lak him anyhow."

BENNY — "It *is* Tony, Fannie. He's just grown up."

FANNIE— "Well, I declare! Hello, Tony."

TONY — "Fannie, I'm glad to see you're still on the job. Have you been keepin' Benny here on the right track?"

FANNIE — "He ain't on no track. He's bin off a long time."

BENNY (Pulling a large sack out from under a seat) — "Fannie, here's the cloth and things from the cans at this corner and the two in the next block. You won't have to check them this time."

FANNIE (Taking the sack) — "Thanks, Benny. If ev'rybody was as hepful as you, this ol' wor'l 'ud be awright. Nice ta see you agin, Tony."

Fannie ambled off down the street with her cart. Tony decided it was time to go back to Mrs. Angelo's. So, with a hug and a good-bye to Benny, he also left.

On the following day, Louisa and Tony went home to Middleton. This time, Mrs. Angelo didn't go with them to Hoboken to catch the train. The train ride was much the same as before, minus the track fire and not meeting a swell guy like Sam Brady. Aunt Mary met them at the station."

SCENE 22

Soon after Louisa and Tony returned from New York City, she was walking along Main Street when she passed an attractive young lady who was wearing The News identification button on her dress. She had never seen her before. Louisa turned and watched her enter The News entrance. She wondered who she was.

A few days later, the Tennis Club was having their annual dinner/dance. Phil had brought Louisa, It had been a gala and fun affair. Just before the end, Phil and Louisa found themselves alone at their table. Phil took a paper out from his coat pocket and handed it to Louisa.

LOUISA — "What's this?"

PHIL — "It's a combination Investment Bond and Insurance Policy. I hope you may be interested in it. Read it, Dear."

LOUISA (Opened the gilded document and read it aloud) — "I Louisa Delano promise to marry Phil Green-(signature)- I, Phil Green promise to marry Louisa Delano-(Signed by Phil Green)- P.S. Please! I promise to love and care for you for life." Signed by Phil Green.

LOUISA (surprised-tears in her eyes) — "Oh, Phil! You are a very dear friend. I'm so mixed up right now. I'm not sure of anything. But I'll think about it, Phil. I'm sorry."

PHIL — "That's alright, Louisa. I understand. I just had to ask you. Maybe later? You're still my best friend."

LOUISA — "Thank you, Phil. Yes, we are still very good friends."

Later, on the way home, Louisa thought of the new girl she saw.

LOUISA — "Phil, do you know the new girl that's working for the *News*. I saw her on the street recently."

PHIL — "Yes. I've met her. Her name is Carol Scott. She came from Tarrytown. She arrived while you were in New York."

LOUISA — "That's where Howard Google came from."

They drove on to her home, and since it was late, they parted after agreeing to meet the next week for tennis.

Scene 23

few days later Sam and Louisa were again together at the soda fountain.

SAM — "Louisa, I wish I had known you were in The City, I would have liked to have taken you and Tony through our shirt factory, including a new unit for making ladies shirts and blouses. We would treasure your comments on it. I'm involved in the project."

LOUISA — "That would have been very interesting. I thought about you. We were there only a week and very busy. We'll have to go again, maybe next year. Will you be selling the ladies shirts, too?"

SAM — "I just got word yesterday that we're ready to build a new plant in Paterson, N.J. for the manufacturing of ladies shirts and blouses. I'm to be the Vice-President in charge of sales!"

LOUISA — "Oh, Wow! That's so exciting! I'm happy for you."

SAM — "It is exciting news, but what I really came down here for today was to ask you a question."

LOUISA — "Me? I'm not sure (as she studied his eyes)."

SAM — "Louisa, I'm madly in love with you. Will you marry me?"

LOUISA — (shocked, thrilled, overcome with emotion - tears in her beautiful eyes.) "Oh, Sam! How sweet of you to ask me that!"

SAM — "I can see that it is unexpected, Louisa. I don't want to press you."

LOUISA — (wiping her eyes) "Sam, you did surprise me. I feel honored. But I don't quite know what my real feelings are. I'll need to have a little time to think about it."

SAM — "You're right. I've been wanting to ask you for weeks. You think about it, Louisa. I'll be back next week. O.K?"

LOUISA — "Yes, I will Sam."

She didn't know, but Sam had a beautiful engagement ring in a little white box, waiting in his inside coat pocket. As they hugged and kissed on leaving, Louisa dropped her hankie. Sam picked it up, and as he did, the little white box fell out of his coat. He quickly picked it up and put it in the side pocket of his coat. Sam hoped she didn't notice. — But she did; and wondered about it.

Scene 24

Sam did come back the next week. The town was in the throes of an election. But there was a tent show in town and Louisa had four tickets to it. She invited Sam and Tony and Rita as her guests. Tent shows were popular entertainment for the medium- sized towns of the U.S.

Louisa and Sam sat on one of the high seats for better viewing. As they sat down Louisa noticed a little bulge in the side pocket of Sam's coat. Was it the little white box she had seen him drop last week? She was curious. Tony and Rita sat lower down on the long plank seats. The crowd soon filled the seating area. The band came inside and played a few Sousa marches. Then the show's owner came onstage and welcomed the crowd to the show. A comedian came out to the front of

261

the curtain to crack jokes and tease the crowd, while hawkers worked the crowd selling bags of roasted peanuts, crackerjacks and soda pop. The hawkers disappeared and the curtain went up and the performers were greeted by clapping and whistling from the audience. The play was "The Widow's Revenge", a typical kind of plot, but the crowd enjoyed the story as "Toby" bested the "villain". Then came intermission, while they enjoyed more peanuts and sodas, Louisa wondered if Sam was going to pull the little white box out? How exciting. She was on pins and needles. She knew she loved him, but she couldn't say "Yes" just yet. Finally, Sam broke the tension.

SAM — "Louisa, have you thought any more about the question I asked you last week?"

LOUISA — "Yes, Sam. I've been thinking about it all week. But this week has been so hectic. I know you're anxious for an answer. Sam, I'm just not sure yet. I need a little more time to think about it. It's about the rest of my life, and what would happen to Tony?"

SAM — "You're right, Louisa. I was selfish to ask you to answer so soon. I'll wait. And Tony's future would be my top concern, after you."

LOUISA — "Thank you, Sam. I'll try to let you know soon."

The curtain went up again and they enjoyed the rest of the show. Sam was disappointed. He realized that an attractive lady like Louisa had other friends. He hoped not serious, however. She had mentioned playing tennis with a guy named Phil. He wasn't exactly jealous, but anxious. Yes, very!

SCENE 25

So that's the way things stood as the election of 1924 now approached. Louisa and Howard both becoming involved through the newspapers that each worked for. Locally, The *Middleton News* supported the Republican candidate for Mayor, Mr. Clarence McKinney. The *Middleton Times* supported the Democratic candidate, Hal Minor. For months, the candidates for the various offices had been campaigning by speeches, handing out cards, newspaper ads, etc. Both newspapers boosted their favorite candidates. As the election approached, a final special speaker's night was planned for the candidates. On a Friday night, on the lawn of the courthouse, a well lighted platform was erected for the event. The voting would be Saturday, the next day. On this Friday night in November in 1924, a huge crowd was there for the debates. Several candidates for lesser offices made their appeals for votes. Then came the time for the mayor's office candidates. It was always a hotly contested race. Howard Google, speaking for The News, introduced Mr., Clarence McKinney for mayor of Middleton. Mr., McKinney gave an emotional speech asking for the votes of everyone. (Enthusiastic applause!)

Next, Mr. McCord of the *Times*, introduced Mr. Hal Minor as a candidate for the office. As Mr. Minor got up to speak, he cleared his throat. It was squeaky. He cleared it again and was seized with a spell of coughing. Finally, before he could get started, he developed an embarrassing case of hic-ups. The crowd held their breath. A cup of water didn't cure It. It became evident that he was not going to be able to continue, so he asked Mr. McCord to read his speech. Mr. McCord demurred. Louisa volunteered. After reading Mr. Minor's speech, Louisa had some other things to say...

LOUISA — "And I'd like to add while I'm up here...some of our problems are the responsibility of all of us. Both parties. We need a new fire truck in this town. Some of our citizens have been waiting for years to get their streets paved in front of their houses. Our schools need more money for musical instruments for the school band, and for building repair- especially the Negro school down below the ice house. We should be ashamed not to help them more." (applause)

HOWARD — "Miss Delano, are you running for this office?"

LOUISA — "No, but I just want to remind all of us of something. All of our parents grew up somewhere. They paid what was necessary to give us an education and keep us safe and healthy. Now it's our turn to do the same for our families and the kids in our schools." (more applause)

HOWARD — "Are you through, Miss Delano?"

LOUISA — "One more thing. I hope Mr. McKinney and Mr. Minor will agree with me on this. Since 1919 prohibition is supposed to be the law here in the U.S.. In New York City and Chicago it's a huge problem. Our sheriff is overwhelmed keeping the bootleggers out. He needs another deputy to help. Finally, you women. Now that it's legal for us to vote, let's do it!"

HOWARD (taking the floor again) — "Well, I don't know if that was a sermon or a political speech. Sounds like she wants more taxes." (applause from a few)

LOUISA (from her seat) — "But I didn't say that." (applause)

HOWARD — "Free speech is one of the corner stones of our country. Most of the things Miss Delano mentioned are favored by Mr. McKinney. It's just a difference of when, how and to what degree. Some of you may not know Miss Delano. She is a new citizen and a very loyal one. She and I both came to the U.S. almost five years ago on the same ship, the "Belloma". I came from England; She came from Italy. She saved a young man's life who fell overboard. I have a lot of respect for her. That's all. Be sure to vote tomorrow. Thank you."

As the crowd dispersed, Tony and Rita appeared.

TONY — "What happened? I heard the crowd clapping and whistling."

LOUISA — "Where've you been? You should have been here listening."

RITA — "We were just over at the ice cream store."

LOUISA — "Nothing special happened."

When Howard was alone, Mr. Baker, owner of *The News* approached him.

MR. BAKER — "Howard, you're fired!"

HOWARD — "Fired? What for?"

MR. BAKER — "For letting that girl get the best of you tonight. I was very embarrassed. I know she works for the *Times* and you should have shut her down. Instead you praised her."

HOWARD (subdued) — "Mr. Baker, I just couldn't be harsh to her. She's a friend. In fact, I love her."

MR. BAKER — "Dad Burn It! How can politics get so complicated?"

HOWARD — "I'm sorry, Mr. Baker. I'm not very good at politics. I'm just a newspaperman and a reporter."

MR. BAKER — "Well, I suppose what happened didn't hurt us too much. I still think our man will win. So, forget what I said about being fired. But that girl is a winner. I've noticed her work the last couple of years. I don't know what the *Times* pays her, but we need someone like her on the *News*. You're her friend. See if she would consider coming over to the *News*, at a raise in salary."

HOWARD — "After tonight's fiasco I doubt she'll even speak to me."

MR. BAKER — "Well, give it a try, women are unpredictable anyway. Maybe that's one of the reasons we like them so much."

Scene 26

The next day was voting day. Both Louisa and Howard cast their ballots, as did Aunt Mary. Howard realized that he may have hurt Louisa's feelings, so he went to The Flower Shoppe and had a dozen red roses sent to her, along with a note apologizing if he had hurt her feelings the night before. Then later he called her.

HOWARD (dialing phone)(to himself-"I hope she's in a good mood.") — "Hello, Louisa? This is Howard."

There was a pause while he listened.

HOWARD — "I'm O.K. Did you get the roses? You did? (pause) I'm glad you like them; (pause) your favorite? Mine, too. (pause) Listen, Louisa. I apologize about last night. Nothing personal, you know. (pause) I'm glad you didn't take offense. I didn't think you would. You're a good sport, Louisa. (pause) Thank you. Louisa, the main reason I'm calling: I have four tickets to the Chitauqua musical concert tomorrow night at the High School auditorium. How about you going with me? And Tony and his girlfriend, too, if they'd like? (pause) Good, The concert is at 8 o'clock. I'll pick you up at 7:30. O.K.? Fine (pause) What? You have company? I'm sorry! Who is it? (pause) Sam? Sam who? (pause) Oh, that guy! (pause) I see. Well, I'll see you at 7:30 tomorrow night. Bye!" (a click as the phone disconnected)

HOWARD (aloud, to himself) — "I've never met this guy Sam. I wish he would stay in New York City with the rest of those speakeasy bums!"

He went out and had a beer, to calm his frustration. Louisa had planned to attend the concert anyway. She really wasn't angry about what he had said at the speaker's event, since she had said some pretty cutting things herself.

Scene 27

So the next night as they sat looking over the crowd in the High School auditorium, and while the band members were tuning their instruments:

LOUISA — "It's nice to relax for an evening after the hectic week of the election. I'm glad it's over. Now I can think of other things."

HOWARD — "Thinking of other things? Louisa, look down there, third row front, at the lady in the little green hat. That's Carol, but who is the man with her?" (He points)

LOUISA (looking) — "Why, it's Phil Green. I can't believe it! I wonder how that came about?"

HOWARD — "I told you she wasn't my girlfriend. I'm happy to see her with him."

LOUISA — "Phil is just a friend, like I told you."

HOWARD — "O.K. Now that's resolved. I've got a question for you. Louisa, will you marry me?"

LOUISA — "Oh, Howard!! I can't answer you on that tonight. I'll have to think about it."

HOWARD — "I realize it's a very serious question. That's what I want you to do. Think about it and we'll talk about it again later. O.K?"

LOUISA — "Alright, Howard."

HOWARD — "I've got another question I've wanted to ask you. Louisa, do you remember when we were separating after coming through Ellis Island; I looked back and you flashed a sign "L" to me. What did you mean by it? Were you calling me a 'louse'?"

LOUISA (laughing) — "I remember that! I wasn't calling you a 'louse'. I was afraid that I had left a bad impression and I was hoping that we would meet again. I meant the sign to be 'like'. It was just a spontaneous thing."

HOWARD — "Fantastic! Well, here I am, Louisa!"

LOUISA — "Howard, that was five years ago!!"

Chapter Three

After coming home from the concert with Howard, Louisa was sitting in the living room with Aunt Mary.

LOUISA — "Aunt Mary, I'm so confused! Howard, Sam and Phil, not to mention Luigi, have all proposed marriage to me. All my life I've been able to make decisions clearly and without doubt. This has me stumped. I love all of them, or do I?"

AUNT MARY (really concerned) — "Louisa, you're just worn out. The election was enough, besides all the other activities. I think you need a rest.

LOUISA — "I don't want to make the wrong choice. I'd feel badly for disappointing any of them. I need some time to myself. I'm under so much pressure right now, it's about to drive me crazy."

AUNT MARY (putting her arm around Louisa's shoulders.) — "Why don't you go spend a week with Nora. She's more your age. She invited you, remember? It'll help clear your mind."

LOUISA — "That's a good suggestion. I think I'll do it!"

So the next day she called Nora and arranged to come down to Scranton the following week, after getting the week off from work at the *Times*. She also called Phil to cancel a tennis date.

LOUISA — "Phil, I can't play tennis next week. I'm going to Scranton to spend a week with Nora. You remember her, don't you?"

PHIL — "Yes, I remember her. I was going to call you today, too. I've got to leave Monday for New York City. I'll be gone about four weeks. Anything I can do for you in the City while I'm there?"

LOUISA — "Oh, that will be a nice trip. Let me see. How about calling my cousin, Luigi Castovo. He plays in a band at the Rose Room Restaurant. I'll give you his phone number (She did.). He's a sweet guy and I'm sure he's lonesome. You two will like each other. He loves to play tennis.

PHIL — "I'll do that, Louisa. How many 'sweet guys' do you know, Louisa?"

LOUISA — "You mean besides you, Phil? Not too many.."

PHIL — "That's encouraging. Tell Nora 'Hello' for me. I'll see you when I get back."

LOUISA — "O.K., Phil. Have a good trip."

PHIL — "Same. Bye."

SCENE 29

So after work on Friday, Louisa got in her car and headed for Nora's apartment in Scranton. It was only about 80 miles away and Louisa expected to be there by dark. Traffic was heavy. She decided to stop at a roadside store for a candy bar and a pop. She also got gas. After she got back into her car and just as she started the motor, a husky, whiskered man jerked open her car door. He pointed a pistol at her.

MAN — "Move over, lady!"

He shoved her over, hopped in, gunned the motor and was quickly out on the road. Louisa had no time to get out. He put the pistol in a holster under his left arm.

LOUISA — "Why did you pick my car?"

MAN — "I noticed you filled up your gas tank, and you were alone. It was an easy choice."

LOUISA — "Where are you going?"

MAN — "I'm not talking anymore. You just be quiet. I'll put you out down the road somewhere. I just want your car."

He turned off on a smaller two-way road. It was dark now. After about 30 minutes more he suddenly stopped the car.

MAN — "Get out!"

He opened the passenger door and gave her a shove as he slammed the door and sped off.

Scene 30

Louisa wasn't hurt badly, just a skinned knee. She had no idea where she was. In the dark, it appeared to be desolate wooded country. Luckily there was a moon, but clouds occasionally obscured it. She decided to walk along in the direction that the carjacker had been going. Walking to find a house somewhere was her best option. After about twenty minutes she saw a light. Getting closer, it turned out to be a house a good distance from the road. There was a gate and a lane that ran up to it. She decided to try it. Maybe they had a phone or someone could take her to town, where she could report her loss to the police. It was an old house, surrounded by trees and brush, and in need of paint and repair, as best she could see in the dark. She approached and knocked on the door. A rough looking older lady answered.

OLD LADY — "Yes? What do you want ?"

LOUISA — "I'm lost. Do you have a phone?"

OLD LADY — "Come on in so I can see you."

It was then that she saw two men playing cards at a table. Stacks of money were on the table in full view. The men were rough looking. There was a very peculiar smell that pervaded everywhere.

OLD LADY — "We don't have a phone here. How did you find the place?"

LOUISA — "A man stole my car and pushed me out down the road. Is there a town close? I need to report my car stolen to the police."

OLD LADY (addressing the men at table) — "What do I tell the lady, Bruce?"

BRUCE — "I'll take care of it, Gertie."

He got up, went over and turned the key in the door and put the key in his pocket.

BRUCE — "Lady, we can't afford to let you go to the police. At least not yet. You see, we've got a big batch of mash cookin' and it will be a few more days before it will be ready. We'll take good care of you; treat you right if you'll cooperate. We'll cut you in on a bit of the profit, but we'll have to keep you from leavin'."

LOUISA — "I'm a law abiding citizen. You have no right to prevent me from leaving."

BRUCE — "Tie her up, Lem. She's not goin' anywhere for the next four days."

They grabbed her and secured her with a chain around her leg, and to the leg of a table in the far corner of the room. She was provided with a chair and a cot to sleep on. They spoke in both English and a foreign language. But Louisa learned from listening that they were bootleggers and had a big still in a shack in the rear.

She also learned that the mash cooking was to be processed into alcohol in four more days. And she learned that they had lied about the phone.

They had illegally tied on to a line that ran to a boathouse on a lake nearby.

Scene 31

Meanwhile, the next morning Nora called Aunt Mary and told her that Louisa had not arrived. Aunt Mary called the *Times*, and then the police, who found Louisa's car in Kingston. *The Times* and *The News* both ran the story of the disappearance. Howard, very upset, decided to take on the "story" and attempt to find Louisa. Sam, who read the story in the *Times* (he now subscribed to it) - took time off from his job and came to Middleton, determined to find her. He was very fearful that something bad had happened to her. He kept in close touch with Aunt Mary and decided the best place to wait for breaking news was at the Middleton Police Department. Phil was in New York City on business for a month and was unaware of what was happening in Middleton.

Scene 32

It was raining outside and we find Sam pacing the waiting room of the Middleton Police Dept. Suddenly the door is opened and a man rushes in, shedding his raincoat and shaking the rain off his hat. He approached the inquiry desk.

MAN — "Anything new on the Delano disappearance? I'm Google from *The News*. I'm also a personal friend of Miss Delano." He flashed his *News* badge.

POLICEMAN — "Yes. They found her car abandoned in a parking lot in Kingston, but no trace of Miss Delano."

Sam perked up his ears as he heard the words "I'm a personal friend of Miss Delano." He eyed Howard carefully. Is this the "friend" who had called Louisa the night after the election while he was at her house? Louisa had mentioned only that it was a "friend". Realizing that more news may come at any time, Howard decided to wait. He sat down and looked around. An older man was evidently paying a traffic ticket. A middle-aged lady with two small children sat waiting. A smartly dressed young man was pacing back and forth on the other side of the room.

Howard, not having had lunch, decided to buy a candy bar from the blind vendor by the door. As he pulled a handful of coins out of his pocket, several fell to the floor. Immediately the two kids pounced on several. A nickel rolled over to the feet of Sam. The kids quickly returned the coins. Then Sam brought the nickel over.

SAM (handing the nickel to Howard.) — "I heard you say you were a friend of Miss Delano. I'm Sam Brady. I'm also a friend of Miss Delano."

HOWARD — "You're Sam Brady? She's mentioned you. It's awful about this disappearance. Do you think she did it on purpose?"

SAM — "No. Something unexpected has happened, otherwise Aunt Mary would know about it."

HOWARD — "Aunt Mary? That's Louisa's aunt. Are you a relative, or did you just happen to be in town?"

SAM — "No. I took a week off. I'm very worried about her. You live here, don't you?"

HOWARD — "Yes, I work for *The Middleton News*. You live in New York City, don't you?"

SAM — "Yes, but I can't get any news of Louisa up there. I came down here in case I can be of any help."

HOWARD (Realizing that Sam was a stiff competitor for Louisa's affection) — "Look, Mr. Brady, I'm an old friend of Louisa's. I'll make you a deal. You don't need to lose a week's work. I'm a reporter. Things like this are my job. My specialty. Give me your phone number and I'll call you just as soon as any news breaks. I'm sure your company needs you. I'll be here anyway. It's my job. What do you say?"

SAM (Seeing through Howard's ruse) — "Mr. Google, I can't do that. I'm too worried about Louisa. She means a lot to me."

HOWARD (Resigned, but not defeated) — "Well alright. She means a lot to me, too, and I have a responsibility to my newspaper. I think I know now what I'm up against. May the best man win, Mr. Brady!"

SAM — "Agreed!"

They shook hands. There was a change of shifts for the station policemen and a general commotion. About twenty minutes later a phone call came in to the station from Aunt Mary. Louisa had called. She had escaped from her captors and was being rescued by the police from Richland, N.Y.

SCENE 33

On the morning of the fourth day as the two men were busy processing the mash into alcohol, Louisa and Gertie, the little Old Lady, were alone in the big room.

GERTIE — "You look like you're not doin' too well. Are you pregnant?"

LOUISA — "No. I'm just about exhausted. I was on my way to a friend's for a week's vacation. This is not good for me. When do you think they will let me go?"

GERTIE — "Probably not until day after tomorrow. That's when they'll clear out."

LOUISA — "Are you one of them, Gertie?"

GERTIE — "No. My husband was. He's dead now. Shot in a police raid. I can't stand this racket no more. They still use my property. I can't seem to get loose from them."

LOUISA — "What about the still? Do you keep it here?"

GERTIE — "No. They'll take it with 'em somewhere else for a new batch. Then they'll be back later for a new crop here."

LOUISA — "You sound like you want to leave. Do you have any children?"

GERTIE — "Yes. I have a son in Kansas. I haven't seen him for awhile."

Bruce came in.

BRUCE — "Gertie, Frank went in to Richland for some supplies. Lem and I are busy with the still. You watch the girl. If she acts up, just holler. We'll be right with you."

He went back out.

LOUISA — "How far is it into Richland from here, Gertie?"

GERTIE — "Not far. It's about two miles."

LOUISA — "When you bought this house, why did you buy so far from town? It's all trees around here."

GERTIE — "We bought because of the lake. It's called Moon Lake. Jim, my husband, worked at the boathouse 'till it closed because of high costs. I still have a key to it hangin' on a nail in the kitchen."

LOUISA — "How far is it to the lake? Do you ever go there?"

GERTIE — "It's just up the road to the right. I don't go there. A few people use the boat ramp there."

Later — Louisa was leaning against the old table. It was a bit rickety. Gertie was busy in the kitchen. Louisa felt the bolts underneath that secured the table leg that was chained. They were loose. She discovered that she could unscrew both nuts and pull the leg loose from the table. The other three legs would keep the table up. But then, how could she get loose from the leg? Nevertheless, she unscrewed the nuts and hid them just in case. Bruce came back in.

BRUCE — "Gertie, how about some coffee for Lew and me?"

GERTIE — "Alright. I was just about to make some. I'll bring it out. It'll be about ten minutes."

BRUCE — "O.K."

Bruce went back to the shack in the back. Gertie put the coffee on.

Louisa began thinking real fast. Ten minutes later....

GERTIE — "I'll be right back." She disappeared out the back door with the steaming coffee pot and two large cups.

SCENE 34

As soon as Gertie was out the back door, Louisa yanked the table leg loose. She hurried into the kitchen, found the key to the boathouse on the nail, and holding the table leg to her body in front of her, she dashed out the front door, up the lane and turned right on the road. She was terrified that the men might catch her. She was near exhaustion when she came to the boathouse. She opened the door with the key and sank to the floor to catch her breath. She wondered how she could get loose from the table leg. But first she must find a phone. She found it in a small office. Luckily it was still "live". The only phone number that she could remember in her excited state was her home number. She quickly made a collect call there. Aunt Mary answered.

AUNT MARY (Answering the call) — "Hello—-Louisa? Oh, thank Goodness it's you! Where are you? Are you alright?"

LOUISA — "Aunt Mary, listen carefully. I've been kidnapped. But I've just escaped. I'm at an old boathouse that's on a lake; it's called Moon Lake, just outside of Richland, N.Y.. Please call the police department in Richland and have them come immediately. I'll be here or nearby. The police will know where this place is. The place that I was held in is near here.

I'm afraid they'll be searching for me even now. There were two men; Bruce and Lem, and an old lady named Gertie at the house."

LOUISA — (cont'd) "A third man, Frank went to Richland for supplies. It's an old house back off the road and has a shack in back where the men operate a still. Please hurry! I'll be hiding here or somewhere near unless Bruce and Lem find me first."

AUNT MARY — "I'll do it this minute. Please call me later if you can. Bye!"

Louisa sank to the floor again. The only thing she could do now was wait. Hopefully, the police would get there before Bruce and Lem could find her. In the meantime she would keep watching down the road for rescue or capture. As for the table leg; it was locked on tightly with two little locks. She gave up. The police would have to free her. She went to a window to watch.

Scene 35

As soon as Aunt Mary hung up the phone she called the Richland police department. They knew where the old boathouse was and promised to send a police rescue squad immediately. She also called the Middleton police department where she knew Sam and Howard were. When the call from Aunt Mary came in and they learned where Louisa was, both rushed out to rescue her. Howard left in a "press" car and Sam in a taxi. It was about eighty miles from Middleton to Richland. In the mad dash, Howard and Sam passed each other several times on the busy highway. About fifteen miles from Richland the taxi ran out of gas. Howard, who was behind at the time, rushed by waving and honking at the stranded taxi. Buster, the taxi driver, had a three gallon reserve can in the trunk. It only took him about four minutes to empty it into the tank and they were back in the chase. About five miles on down the road, they came upon a stalled car. The driver was out trying to thumb a ride. It was Howard. Buster started to pull around him and go on.

HOWARD — "Hey, stop! Stop! BUSTER!"

BUSTER — "That's the guy who almost ran us down back down the road. Should I stop Mr. Brady?"

SAM — "Yes, stop! We should see what his problem is."

So they stopped and backed up to where Howard was.

HOWARD — "Brady, I've got a busted tire. A big rock fell off a truck in front of me. Can you give me a lift into town?"

Howard started to climb into the taxi.

BUSTER — "Wait! I can't take you unless my fare agrees."

SAM — "It's O.K, Buster. We should help him if we can. Get in Mr. Google. But wait. You had better put out a flare. Your car is only about half off the road."

Howard didn't have a flare. Buster did. They put out a flare and resumed the trip.

SAM — "You hit a rock? I didn't see one."

HOWARD — "I threw it in the ditch. And I don't have a spare tire."

They dropped Howard off at a gas station about two miles up the road, Sam and Buster then started on toward Richland.

HOWARD — "Thanks, Mr. Brady. You're a good sport."

SAM — "That's O.K., Mr. Google. It's my good turn for the day."

Scene 36

Meanwhile...Gertie came back in and found Louisa missing. She searched the house without success and finally realized that Louisa escaped. Fearfully she went back out to the shack.

GERTIE — "Bruce, I can't find the girl."

BRUCE — "What do you mean you can't find her! Your eyes givin' out on you, Gertie?"

GERTIE — "No. She just disappeared while I was bringin' you the coffee."

LEM — "That better not be so! For her sake and for yours, too, Gertie."

Bruce and Lem rush back into the house, followed by Gertie.

BRUCE — "I can't believe it. Look, she took off the leg of the table."

LEM — "We can't afford to let her get to the police. We've got to find her!"

BRUCE — "She can't be far. Probably hidin' in some of those bushes outside. Come on, Lem, let's start lookin'. Time's a wastin'."

LEM — "When we find her, she's gonna wish she was dead. Gertie, if she comes back, yell."

Bruce and Lem quickly start searching the scrubby bushes and the trees around the area.

BRUCE — "I don't think she could be far. I wonder how she got the chain off her leg?"

LEM — "She's probably still got it on there. I put it on pretty tight."

After a thorough search around on all sides they went back into the house.

BRUCE — "Gertie, do you have any idea where she went?"

GERTIE — "No. I don't. She didn't talk much."

LEM — "Did you and she talk any this afternoon?"

GERTIE — "Just a little. We talked about the area around here. The lake and the old boathouse."

BRUCE — "Lake? Boathouse?"

He went to the kitchen and came back.

BRUCE — "The boathouse key is missing! Gertie, have you seen it?"

GERTIE — "No. It was there this morning."

BRUCE — "Then that's where she's gone. Come on, Lem. We don't have any time to lose."

They started at a brisk pace for the old boathouse.

Scene 37

Louisa, waiting and watching the road to the old boathouse, was getting increasingly worried. The police should be getting there by now, if Aunt Mary had been able to contact them. Also Bruce and Lem were sure to check the boathouse after searching around the house. She prayed that the police would get there first. She had been watching about thirty minutes when she saw two men coming hurriedly toward the boathouse. It was Bruce and Lem. She was terrorized! What could she do? Hide? They would surely find her. She quickly looked toward the lake. She was a good swimmer. Then she noticed an old boat that was pulled up on the shore. If it didn't leak, it was a "Godsend". She quickly ran over, still carrying the table leg, and dragged the boat into the water. Luckily there were two paddles and it didn't leak. She shoved off and began furiously paddling toward the middle of the lake, just as Bruce and Lem ran up. They yelled at her to come back. Promised not to hurt her. But Louisa paddled even harder.

Suddenly there were gunshots and bullets began splashing around the boat. Evidently, they were trying to kill her. Another shot hit the boat. This one was close. Louisa quickly got out of the boat and swam away from it. She began treading water, laying as low in the water as she could. Several more shots hit the now empty boat, knocking a big hole in the side at the water line allowing water to rush in. Louisa knew that the boat would sink in a few minutes. Although she was an excellent swimmer, there was a limit to how long she could continue treading water. The table leg tended to float, but the chain was heavy on her. She was getting very tired. The boat sank. Louisa now realized she was on her own. She didn't dare swim back to the shore while Bruce and Lem were there. The other side of the lake was too far for her condition. A water moccasin swam near and checked her out. Horrors! She was deathly afraid of snakes. He disappeared. *Where did he go?* When the boat sank, the shooting from the boathouse shore stopped. Maybe they thought that she went down with the boat. But the noise of shooting started again, even more. What she saw was a great relief. The police had arrived in three cars and were in a gun battle with Bruce and Lem, who quickly surrendered. They had wasted too many bullets over the water at her. The police swept the lake with a powerful spotlight mounted on one of the cars, spotted her and motioned for Louisa to come back; she did. She told them of the illegal still. One group of police went and smashed the still operation and arrested Gertie. The other took Bruce and Lem to jail. The police cut the table leg chain and freed Louisa. An ambulance they had called took Louisa to the Richland Hospital.

Scene 38

Howard arrived at the Richland Police Department. about thirty minutes after Sam. When news came that Louisa was at the local hospital, they both rushed over there to see her.

NURSE (to Louisa, who was now resting in bed) — "There are two gentlemen outside who want to see you, Miss."

LOUISA — "Is one of them Sam Brady?"

NURSE — "One is, yes."

LOUISA — "I'd like to see him."

SAM (very worried as he quickly came in. He took her hand and gave her a warm kiss.) — "Louisa, I've been so worried about you! They say you're OK. Thank God!" He was still holding her hand.

SAM — "Is there anything you want, or anything I can do for you?"

LOUISA — "Yes! Yes! I want my ring! I want to be Mrs. Sam Brady! That's all I want."

SAM (kissing her again) — "That's all I've been praying for, Sweetheart! Here is your ring."

He pulled the ring out of his pocket and put it on her finger.

LOUISA (when the excitement had died down a bit) — "Nurse, will you tell Howard Google I'll see him now?"

NURSE — "He left, saying he had to get a hot story to his newspaper. He said to tell you and Mr. Brady 'CONGRATULATIONS'!"

END OF STORY.

POSTLOGUE:

Louisa and Sam's wedding was in Middleton. Present were: Aunt Mary, of course (She was much involved in the planning), Mrs. Angelo and Mr. Moschetti (They were now married and lived in Mrs. Angelo's apartment), Luigi (He later went back to Naples to manage Grampy's South Shore restaurant. He fell in love with a girl there), Nora (After graduating from college, came back to Middleton to be a nurse at the Middleton Hospital), Phil (He became a Junior partner in a New York City law firm but wanted to attend the wedding), Edith (was thrilled that Louisa was going to live in Paterson where they could see each other often), Howard (Louisa just couldn't slight him.) -He soon restarted his courtship of Carol. He received an advancement at the *News* and eventually became the Managing Editor).

After the wedding, Sam and Louisa moved to Paterson, N.J, where Sam became Vice-President in charge of Sales at the new Royal Shirt Co., where they manufactured several kinds of ladies apparel including shirts and blouses. Sam, who had known Ambrose for several years, brought him to Paterson to be in charge of maintenance and upkeep at a much better salary than the railroad job. Tony "gave his sister away" at the wedding. He and Rita after graduating from High School, attended separate colleges, but kept in touch and likely would end up getting married.

RIVER ROAD

A Story With Music

List Of Characters

In the year 1852

Mr. John Robb - Plantation owner (Minnie Robb's Father)

Mrs. Martha Robb - John's wife (Minnie's step-mother)

Minnie Robb - John Robb's daughter by deceased former wife (18 yrs. old)

Jose Jackson - Plantation manager (Minnie's boyfriend)

John Snow - Owner of the "Southern Belle" Showboat (Minnie's uncle)

Marie Jones - Minnie's best friend (19)

David Jones - Marie's brother (16 yrs. old)

Dr. Pitts - A medical supply salesman (Father of Chrissy)

Louise Foley - Passenger on stagecoach

Aunt Sally Norton - Minnie's Aunt

Charles Norton - Aunt Sally's son (works in law office)

Mr. Taylor - Owner of the "Plush" Room in the Jefferson Hotel

Guard - At gangplank of "Southern Belle"

Hoss Lowery - Detective hired by Mr. Robb to intercept Jose/Minnie

Pig Barnes - Detective hired by Mr. Robb to intercept Jose/Minnie

Little Old Lady in stagecoach - (mystery woman)

Captain Nutter - Pilot of steamboat on Mississippi River

Mr. Berkley - Owner of log raft

Jim - Poler on raft

Bill - Poler on raft

Betsy - Cow mascot on raft

Jack Brunelle - Pilot of the "Southern Belle" Showboat

Engineer - Of the "Southern Belle" Showboat

Chrissy Pitts - Daughter of Dr. Pitts (a run-a-way)

Officer - New Orleans Street Patrol

Police Commissioner - Of New Orleans Police Dept

Asst, Police Commissioner - Of New Orleans Police Dept

Assignment Officer - Of the New Orleans Police Dept

Ray - Promoter from New York

Angie Ferguson - Girlfriend of Minnie's

CHAPTER ONE

Two horses are seen coming into view. As they rapidly approach, it is obvious that they are in a race; a young girl on a sleek bay horse, and a young man on a roan. Suddenly, they arrive at the gate of the corral in a cloud of dust, as they reined their horses to a stop. "I beat you!" exclaimed Jose, as he dismounted. "It was a tie," countered Minnie, dismounting as Jose fumbled with the gate latch. "You're right, Minnie. It was a tie. I'd feel bad if I beat you, I like you so much." "Thank you, Jose; I'd feel the same way....How do you get off so easy when your horse is still stopping?" "It's easy. I'll show you." Jose demonstrated how he did it. "I know you said you used to compete in trick riding contests. Show me a couple of them." "That was bareback riding. The Indians were the best at that, but I learned a few good tricks." "You'll have to teach me some of them sometime," said Minnie.

"I'll show you a couple of easy ones." He pulled the saddle off his horse and rode bareback back and forth to demonstrate the maneuvers. "Those are fascinating. You're still very good. Thank you, Jose. "They opened the gate and released the horses, who dashed through toward the water trough. Minnie and Jose walked toward the barn with the saddles. "How was your birthday party?" he asked, "you said that your Dad was planning one for you, since it was your 18th," "It was fun. Dad took me and two of my friends, Marie Jones and Angie Ferguson, to St. James for a fabulous dinner and a concert. We had a good time. We came back and Marie and Angie spent the weekend with me." "I spent my 18th birthday baling hay on our farm." "Eighteen seems awful old. I suppose I'll get used to it." "It'll pass before you know it," said Jose. "Everybody, including you, seems to think that I should get married, now that I'm 18," sighed Minnie. "That's the trend. When you get around to considering it, I'm first in line, remember." "You are, Jose. Dad keeps talking up one of his friends, John MacDonald, as a perfect husband for any girl. I think he'd like me to be the 'lucky' one." "Before you'd do anything like that, just remember you'll have to get my permission first," advised Jose. "Ha! Thank you, Judge Jackson," she responded. They parted after a peck-of-a-kiss.

TWO WEEKS LATER: It was a pleasant day. The Robb household was busily preparing for a large picnic with friends and relatives. It was to be on a beautiful outdoor area adjacent to the Robb's large two-story Colonial house. Several huge oak trees shaded the spot. By 11:00 o'clock, most of the crowd had arrived. The men stood around in groups, talking. The kids were chasing each other, climbing the trees, and otherwise working off their excess energy. Most of the ladies were busy tending the youngest kids, or helping assemble the dishes of delicious food, on two long, covered tables. Two young girls waved small branches to shoo away the flies. Minnie Robb, just turned 18, and her friend, Marie Jones, were busy bringing out food from the kitchen. At last, Millie, the cook, and Marie brought out a large container of ice and two large pitchers of tea, and set them on the tables. "Mr. Robb, it's all ready," said Millie. "Thank you, Millie," and then to the crowd, "Dinner's ready, folks. Before we eat, Bro. Lennon will lead us in an offering of thanks. Bro. Lennon..." He did and the meal began. When the meal was well under way, Mr. Robb stood up, clapped his hands for attention, and announced: "Ladies and gentlemen, boys and girls, most of you have met my dear friend, Miss Martha Strickland. She's from Atlanta, Georgia. She's presently a nurse in a hospital in St. Louis. What I want to tell you this afternoon is that on Saturday at three o'clock, three weeks from today, we are to be married."

There was a roar of clapping and approval. "We'll be married at our local Baptist church. You are all invited....Stand up, Martha, to show that you approve of what I say." She did, and there was another round of applause. After the dinner was over, they were both personally congratulated. Most of the adults then migrated to the house for a relaxing afternoon. In the yard, John MacDonald and a couple of other adults organized and supervised various games and competitions for all the young people. One of the games was a tow-sack race. Minnie won it in a close race, barely finishing ahead of David Jones and Angie Ferguson. The prize was a box of peppermint sticks presented by John MacDonald with a kiss on her cheek. "That was a great effort by you. I'm impressed. You're my kind of girl, Minnie," he said. "Thank you," said Minnie, blushing, as she moved closer to Marie, who was standing near. "Next game," announced John, "is for boys, 5 to 9 years old." He moved away to organize the race. And so, the afternoon went. Soon, as the sun sank low, the crowd began to trickle off to their homes. Minnie went home with Marie for a couple of days. John MacDonald made a point to bid Minnie a farewell, and a hope to see her at the wedding.

When all the visitors had left, Martha and John (Robb) were settled down in the large living room. John -firing up his pipe- "Well, it's done. You can't back out now, Martha." "I didn't want to. I was more worried about you." "This house has needed you, very much," said John. "I like it like this; just you and me," she said. "That's the way it'll be. I'm sure Minnie will soon be married, now that she is 18, and John MacDonald has taken an interest in her." "That would be ideal," said Martha.

Minnie got back home from her visit with Marie and was grooming 'Shadow' in the corral when Jose came by. "Hi, Minnie. Is it true Mr. Robb is getting married?" "Yes. A couple of weeks from next Saturday. They announced it at the picnic." "Have you ever met the lady?" asked Jose, "I don't think I have ever seen her." "Yes I have; she was at the picnic and Dad brought her down from St. Louis about a week before that, to show her the house and farm, and to meet me and the household help." "Is she from St. Louis?" "No, she is from Atlanta, Georgia. She is a nurse supervisor in a hospital in St. Louis. Dad met her when my mother was in the hospital there, before she died. About eight months ago he started going up to see her." "You seem sad, Minnie. Is anything wrong?" "I am worried, Jose. I'm anxious about where I'm to fit in here. Dad says everything will be fine. I can't shake it. I want them to be happy. I don't want to be a problem."

"Minnie, you know how I feel about you. Maybe you should go visit Marie for a few days again. Anyway, when you need somebody to talk about it, I'm here to listen, if that'll help. I love you. Just remember that," urged Jose. "Thank you, Jose." She gave him a kiss and he left. Minnie put Shadow in her stall and went up to the house.

THE WEDDING: The wedding of Mr. John Robb, well known land

owner of the St. James area, and socially prominent Martha Strickland, daughter of Capt. and Mrs. Horace Strickland of Atlanta, Ga. had just been completed. The new Mrs. Robb and Mr. Robb were being showered with rice as they ran down the steps of the church to the waiting escape vehicle. John MacDonald caught the bride's bouquet as the happy crowd cheered.

He quickly gave it to Miss Minnie Robb, who was standing nearby. "That's supposed to go to the girl who's to be the next to be married, or the prettiest. In either case, it's for you, Minnie. I wanted to be sure that you got it," said John. "Boys are not supposed to catch it, John. It doesn't fit me. I'm not the prettiest, and I'm not planning to get married any time soon," said Minnie. "Well, I think you're very pretty, Minnie. I have always thought so. Would you consider letting me take you to the dance at the school in two weeks? I'd be honored if you would." Minnie - a bit flustered - "Thank you, but I'll have to wait and see. I'm not sure I'll be able to go."

"I understand, Minnie. You think about it. We could have a lot of fun together. Later, there's the Military Officer's Ball in St. James next month. I know you're a good dancer, Minnie. I'd be proud to have you go as my partner. I think your dad would approve. He's a good friend of mine." "I've got to hurry back to the house. I may be needed. This is a big day there." "Alright. Think about it, Minnie. I'll see you later."

They both left. Minnie went home worried. She hadn't thought much about it before. Her father and Martha Strickland had had a short courtship, and now there was to be a new lady to take the place her dear mother occupied. She couldn't seem to get comfortable with Martha.

Being the only child, she had been real close to her mother. The last two years, since her mother's death, she had felt so lost. That's why she enjoyed spending time with Jose and with Marie, her friend, who lived about two miles away. So, what should she do? What could she do? She felt like a bird, old enough to fly. She didn't want the decision to be made for her. She wanted to make the decision for herself. Minnie's high school sweetheart, David Nash, had left with only a "See you later", for the gold fields in California. It was a shock to Minnie, but she and David were never serious. Still, it added to Minnie's uncertain feelings. She felt that time was slipping by and she was stranded.

Minnie did go to the dance in two weeks with John MacDonald, at the insistence of her dad and Martha. It would be awkward to refuse. He picked her up in his fancy new buggy and they drove to the schoolhouse. The dancing was already underway. There was a large crowd.

Jose Jackson was playing in the band. Minnie liked Jose. Since he had come to the farm they had spent a lot of time together at the corral, and riding horses at the Robb farm.

John and Minnie were warmly greeted. They joined in on the newest gossip of the social and political scene. Most people knew both Minnie's and John's families. John was active in local affairs. He was a major in the community Cavalry. John was building a new house. People wondered who he had in mind to occupy it with him. Minnie was one of those mentioned. He was considered to be the "catch" of the season, in fact, pretty 19 year old Angie Ferguson had said, when Minnie mentioned she didn't care for him: "Are you crazy? I wish he'd look at me!"

John monopolized most of Minnie's dances, but being a popular person, he had to dance some of them with others. That gave Jose the opportunity to dance a couple with Minnie. "Minnie, I'm surprised to see you with him. You said last week you didn't like him. What's goin'on? I hope we're still good friends." "Jose, I had to give him this date to satisfy Dad and Martha. He's an old friend of Dad's. I won't give him another. You're still my best friend, Jose." "That's good to hear, but I'm jealous," said Jose. "He's not the one for me, Jose." Jose had to get back to his position in the band.

It was late summer in 1852. Millard Fillmore was President. St. James, Missouri was a town of about 2000 people. It was the center of a prosperous farm and plantation area producing such crops as cotton, fruit, grain and melons, etc. One of the farms of about 800 acres, was that of Mr. John Robb and his new wife, Martha and his daughter Minnie. One family in four owned slaves. Mr. Robb, several years before, had freed his 11 slaves. All of them but one had elected to stay and work for him on salary plus quarters and other benefits, on one to three year contracts. On his farm were the usual buildings. A large two story main house, workers cottages, smokehouse, large barn, corral, blacksmith shop, wagon and buggy sheds. There were places for horses, cows, chickens and pigs, etc.

Two months after the dance at the schoolhouse, Martha Robb was in the parlor when Minnie came in from the yard. "Martha, Cleo said that you wanted to talk to me." "Yes, I did, Minnie." "What about? Some problem?" "Minnie, you've been seeing a lot of that cowboy, Jose, recently. I see you together a lot in the corral. Your father noticed it, too. He's concerned about you," said Martha. "He thinks you should consider being more friendly to John MacDonald." "John MacDonald? I don't like him. He's too stuck on himself. He's too pushy. I like someone like Jose, even if he is only half English. I'm 18 years old. I should have some say about who I marry. Some people say John is building that new house for me. It embarrasses me. Anyway, I'm not ready to get married yet!" "Well, as to that, most girls get married when about your age. What do you plan to do? Marry your Mexican cowboy? John MacDonald would be a good catch for you. He likes you and he is very prosperous. Remember that, Minnie!" countered Martha. "He's too old for me. He's almost thirty. I hate him!" "He's only about twenty-seven. Anyway, You need to make up your mind. I doubt you'll be happy staying here forever. John MacDonald is one of your father's friends, and you should not slight him. I think you should listen to your father," said Martha. "I will listen to him..." But Martha had left the room.

Later Minnie approached her father at the corral. She had just come back from a ride. "Daddy, may I talk to you a minute?" "Sure, Sweetie. What's on your mind?" "Daddy, I'm eighteen now and I'm so in the way here. You and Martha should have the house to yourselves. You've just been married two months. I'd like to get a job somewhere. I can do lots of things; teach music, dancing, singing.." "Sweetie, I know you're very talented. You could even teach riding to girls, but you don't have to work. You are too sweet and pretty. You're eighteen alright, but you should just think of settling down in this area," said Mr. Robb. "How do you mean, Daddy?" asked Minnie. "There are several local eligible men who are interested in you. Our friend John MacDonald is one. But you don't need to hurry. As for Martha and me and you, don't worry. We'll be fine. Things will work out. I love both of you." "I love you, too, Daddy," said Minnie. "I didn't want to cause a problem for you and Martha." "Then that's settled. I'll see you up at the house." Mr. Robb left.

Minnie didn't go up to the house right away. She saw her cowboy friend, Jose, coming on his horse up from the pasture. He had his guitar with him and was leisurely strumming on it. She waited for him, putting her horse, "Shadow", in it's stall. "Jose, wait. I want to talk to you." "What's on your mind, Minnie? You look worried," said Jose, as he slid off his pony. Jose, I'm at a crossroads. I'm afraid that Daddy and Martha just shouldn't have me around. I know that Martha is uncomfortable with me under her feet. I can't seem to give them much privacy." "Minnie, let's get married! I love you so much! We could live in the guest house for the two years that I'm still under contract to your dad, if he'd allow it," pleaded Jose. "I know you love me, Jose, and I love you, but ...." "We could just elope and get married. Then we could strike out on our own later. There's still government land west of here. Wouldn't that be wonderful?" he added. "Jose, that would cause a big commotion. Daddy would be very angry with me. He wants me to marry one of his friends."

"I really don't know how to help, Minnie. I don't want to rush you.

Maybe later the circumstances will be better. I know that you are under a lot of pressure, if that's the situation," said Jose. "Jose, I don't think I'm ready to settle down and be married yet. I'm so restless! I feel like I'm missing something. I've lived my whole life here on this farm." "Minnie, I think you need a vacation of a week or two. Go visit a relative or go to the fair with your friend, Marie." "I do have an Aunt Sally Norton who lives in St. Louis. We've visited her several times. I may go up and visit her for awhile. Maybe that will help me decide what to do," said Minnie. "That may be a good idea. If you do, I'll sure miss you." While he was talking, he kept plinking on the guitar that he often carried with him. "That's a pretty tune. Is it new?" "It's a song I've written. Just the chords. No words yet, but I'm going to call it 'Josefina.' It just sounds like that name would fit it. I'm working on the words." "Those are beautiful chords, and what a pretty name! I'll call myself Josefina, and when I hear you play it, I'll know you're thinking about me." "That's a great idea! I think about you all the time anyway. From now on, you're Josefina. Makes my song much prettier." "That's very flattering. It'll be our own little secret." "You're a Sweetheart, Josefina. You will always be my sweetheart," said Jose. "Thank you, Jose. You're my best, best friend. I've got to go up to the house. It's nearly supper time," said Minnie. "May I have a kiss, Josefina?" "Yes, you may." They modestly kissed and Minnie left.

Twenty-three year old Jose stood watching as she walked toward the house. He felt frustrated. He really loved Minnie. They had been kind of "secret" sweethearts for almost a year, and this was the second time she had hedged about getting married. He sensed that Mr. Robb was not pleased at Minnie's and his talks and pony rides together. He always found something for one of them to do whenever he found them together. Jose felt put down on those occasions. Jose was the product manager for Mr. Robb, in charge of managing the planting and harvesting of the various crops. He was a proud, sensitive, well educated person.

His grandfather had moved to Missouri in the 1790's, when Spain owned it. His father and his Spanish mother still lived and owned a farm in Northern Louisiana. Jose believed he understood Minnie's situation. He didn't want to rush her in her decision, but he wasn't going to give up either. He gave his horse a loving pat and led her into the barn.

Minnie had mixed emotions about her situation. She was 18 now, had graduated from the local school the year before (grade 9). John MacDonald had been paying attention to her whenever he had the opportunity, which she endured but didn't encourage. She found Jose to be a pleasure and a relief from other pressures, but now he was also seriously urging her to marry him. She felt that she was being forced to make a decision that would be for the rest of her life. She wasn't ready for that yet. That night, Minnie lay on her bed several hours trying to decide what she should do. She wasn't ready to spend the rest of her life there in St. James. Besides, her dad might fire Jose to end their relationship.

Her uncle, John Snow, owned a showboat on the Mississippi river. He had visited them once when she was about 13, and had said to her: "Minnie, when you get old enough, you will be a beauty. I might use you on my showboat, the 'Southern Belle.'" Minnie wondered if that could be possible now. She was eighteen. Why not? How exciting that would be! Minnie-in a whisper to herself- "Oh, I think I'll try it! If I don't do it now, I'll probably never get another chance. I'll have to run away. Daddy would never allow it, and Jose would oppose it too. I'll write them both letters when I get to Aunt Sally's in St. Louis. I'll go visit Marie Jones and leave from there." There was a knock on her bedroom door. It was Martha. "Minnie are you alright?" Minnie -staying in bed- "Yes, I'm well." "I heard someone talking." Oh, I was just talking to myself. I'm sorry to have bothered you. I forgot your bedroom is next to mine. I'll be quiet," promised Minnie. "That's alright, Dear. I just wanted to be sure you're OK. Goodnight." "Goodnight," said Minnie.

Minnie had made up her mind. She was so excited, but finally went to sleep. Next day she arranged to spend a week with Marie Jones, her best friend. Marie was 19 and she would share her plans with her. Charlie, one of the workers took her over to the Jones farmhouse. Marie was very happy to have her visit. The two girls had been close friends and often visited each other. Lots of fun "girl" talk, as the two friends lay in bed on Saturday night. "Marie, I want to share a secret with you." "Oh, what is it? Are you engaged?" asked Marie excitedly. "No. I'm running away," said Minnie. Marie-shocked-"You are? Why?" "Marie, I'm just in the way. Dad and Martha need their privacy, and I'm not ready to just settle down and get married to somebody I don't love." "Minnie, you're really brave. Where are you going?" "I'm going to St. Louis to visit my Aunt Sally and try to get on board my Uncle John's showboat when it plays in St. Louis. When I was 13 he visited us and said I might someday," said Minnie. "Oh, that's so exciting! How I envy you!" Minnie-a sudden thought- "Marie, why don't you go with me? You're nineteen. Your house is crowded. You're not tied down here. We could have such fun together." "Do you think I might get a job on the showboat, too?" "I'm sure you could. You're prettier and more talented than I am," said Minnie. "Oh, this is so sudden! How would we do it?" Minnie-after thinking a moment- "This is Saturday. We'll plan on going to church tomorrow. Monday, we go for a buckboard ride and end up in town-just in time to catch the stagecoach to St. Louis. We can check the buckboard and horse at the hotel corral there, or maybe we can bribe David to take us. When we get to St. Louis, we'll write our parents where we are. It'll work." Marie-more excited-"Oh, I want to do it! I'll think about it the rest of the night and tell you in the morning." "I understand. You think about it hard, Marie. I don't want to over influence you, but we can do it!" said Minnie. They finally went to sleep.

CHAPTER TWO

The girls were awake early Sunday morning. Sitting on the bed and trying to get their eyes open and focused, they looked at each other. "Well?" asked Minnie, anxiously. "Yes! Yes! Yes!," exclaimed Marie. They grab each other in a bear hug. "I'm so relieved, and doubly excited," said Minnie. "I can't wait. Let's start planning right now," said Marie. David -knocking and coming in- "What are you girls screaming about? You two kept me awake 'til 2 am with your mumblin." David was sixteen and slept in the next room. "It's a secret. You'll find out later. It's not about boys; just 'girl' talk," said Minnie. "Then it couldn't be important. Can I use your horse today, Marie?" "If you'll do us a favor, David." "Alright, if it doesn't cost me any money. What is it?" "Take Minnie and me to St. James in the morning." "OK! That's a deal." David left.

Sunday morning they all went to church and Marie and Minnie got their things ready for the trip to St. James the next day. Monday morning they were loading the buckboard with the bags for the trip. It was 7 am, just in time to catch the 9 am stage in St. James. "You girls takin' all this baggage just for a trip to St. James? How long you gonna stay?" ask David. "We'll need every bit of it. We may stay a week," said Marie. "Who're you stayin' with? We don't have any relatives there." "It's Minnie's aunt," said Marie. "Oh, I see." They arrive in St. James. "Where to?" asked David. "Take us to the general store," directed Marie. "I know where that is. The stage stops there,-after a pause- "You know, I think I know what you girls are up to. With all that baggage, and I heard St. Louis mentioned last night; I believe you two 'outlaws' are running away to St. Louis." Marie-laughing-"David, I always knew you were smart. You must have heard everything we said in bed last night." "Well, I do have two good ears. Now, are you two girls about ready to go back home?" "Alright smarty! Yes, we are going to St. Louis. We're going to visit Minnie's Aunt Sally," admitted Marie. "That's right, David," added Minnie. "OK. But it kinda puts me in a delicate situation," said David, in

294

a tone of voice that said 'I ought to get something out of this.' "All you have to say is you dropped us off at the general store. We will write Mom and Dad and Mr. Robb as soon as we get there....and here is a dollar for that belt buckle you saw and wanted to buy," said Marie. "Well, alright. I'll be doing the same in about a year," he said. "Thank you, David. You're a real sweetheart. Don't tell anybody until we've had time to get to St. Louis," she cautioned. "I won't. You girls be careful!"-He kissed Marie good-bye. "Aren't you going to kiss Minnie, too? She's leaving, too." "Aw, I guess so." He gave Minnie a peck on the cheek. "Now, that didn't hurt, did it, David?" chided Marie. "You girls are ridiculous!" he said.

The girls bought tickets in the general store. Soon the stagecoach came. Their bags were stored and the girls were seated inside. The driver and two other men sat on top, along with several bags of mail. Four horses pulled the stagecoach. It was about seventy miles to St. Louis and about a ten hour trip. Facing the girls in the other seat were two people. One looked to be a salesman about forty years old. He carried a black bag, similar to the ones doctors carried on house calls. He introduced himself as Dr. Pitts, a salesman of medical supplies. The other person was a young lady about thirty years old, who said she was a school teacher. Her husband, also a teacher, was riding on top with the driver. They would get off at Sullivan, about twenty-five miles up the road. When everyone was all set for the coach to leave, Mr. Snyder, the driver, mounted to the top of the coach, slacked the lines and cracked his whip. The horses lurched forward, and they were on their way.

A strange thrill came over Minnie. She was FREE! Her future was now in her own hands. It was scary, but so exciting. She grasped Marie's hand and leaned against her. "We did it!" she whispered. "Yes we did! Pinch me! Isn't this exciting?" responded Marie, as they hugged each other. The man across from them spoke. "I'm Dr. Pitts. Are you girls going all the way to St. Louis?" "Yes, we are," answered Marie. "Do you live there?" "No. We're going to visit her auntie," - (pointing to Minnie.) "They are meeting you there, I suppose?" "No. They don't know we're coming yet," said Minnie. "Are you girls, by chance, running away from home?" he asked. He appeared concerned about them. "Yes, but we plan to get jobs with her uncle there," said Marie. "I'm glad you two are together and that you have relatives there. I suspected that you might be doing that. I have a daughter about your age: Christine...Chrissy. She ran away last year and I haven't heard from her. She had just finished high. school. Her boyfriend moved away and didn't keep in touch. She felt jilted. Her mother is dead. She was depressed and I couldn't seem to help her. I worry all the time and hope that she's safe." Tears welled up in his eyes, as he took a picture from his purse and gave it to them. "Here's a picture of her. I give them to people who are traveling. St. Louis is a wicked town in some areas. It'll be dark when you get there. Do you know how to find your auntie?" "I have her address. We'll take a cab," Minnie assured him. "I live in St. Louis, but I'm getting off at St. Clair. I have a client who lives there," said the doctor.

The lady sitting by Dr. Pitts spoke up. "I'm Louise Foley. I'm a school teacher in Sullivan, up ahead. I have a brother in St. Louis. He's a policeman. If you have any trouble there, contact him. He's at the central station. His name is Frank Dixon." "Thank you. We'll remember that. I am Marie Jones, and this is Minnie Robb," -she indicated Minnie. "You girls are on a real adventure, I'll bet. I envy you, but you two please be careful," said Mrs. Foley. The Foley's got off at the Sullivan stop.

Shortly after leaving Sullivan, and as they slowed down to cross a dry creek, two men on horses suddenly came out from the roadside bushes. They rode behind the stagecoach, firing their pistols in the air and yelling.... "STOP! STOP!" The noise scared the horses and they bolted forward in a fast run, with the robbers racing behind. The guard, up with the driver, grabbed his rifle and began firing back. The driver urged the horses on. The girls and Dr. Pitts inside the coach were being bounced around roughly. The robbers had to stay in the road behind the stagecoach because the sides of the road were bushy and rocky. However, one bullet did crash through the coach, barely missing Dr. Pitts. "MAIL! Throw off the MAIL!" yelled the robbers. But the men on top wouldn't throw the mail off.

Finally, after a chase of about a mile, the robbers fired several more shots and broke off the chase. But the driver had been hit by a bullet in his shoulder. The guard grabbed the lines and urged the horses on until out of sight of the robbers. He stopped the stage and he and Dr. Pitts lowered the driver, Mr. Snyder, down and into the coach. Dr. Pitts, with the girls' help attempted to stop the blood flow in the driver's shoulder. Mr. Ewing, the guard, then drove on into St. Clair, where they took Mr. Snyder to the hospital. He then drove on to the general store, dropped off a bag of mail and picked one up. Dr. Pitts prepared to get off. "Girls, thank you for helping me with Mr. Snyder. He'll be alright there at the hospital. Some pain and a little loss of blood. You girls will make good nurses. Here's two dollars for your help." We don't want pay for what we did. It was scary, but very exciting," said Minnie. "No, do take it. You earned it. It will be part of my report and expenses. The stagecoach company pays for things like this." "Thank you, Dr. Pitts," said Marie. "I'm just a bit worried about you two, and if you ever see my Chrissy, tell her I love her and miss her and to please write me." "We'll keep our eyes open for her, Dr. Pitts," promised Minnie. "Here's my card, and do be careful. Good-bye," warned Dr. Pitts. "Good-bye and thank you," said the girls in unison. Dr. Pitts left.

The guard drove the stagecoach on into St. Louis, after taking on an old man who was going there. It was 10:00 pm when they arrived and the girls decided to go to Aunt Sally's the next morning. They put up at the hotel next door. "I hope Aunt Sally won't be too surprised to see us, since she doesn't know we're coming," said Minnie. "I hope she's at home," added Marie.

In the morning, after inquiring directions to #10 Sterling Street (Aunt Sally's address) a cab took them there. It was a large two-story house on a tree shaded lane. A wide, deep lawn enclosed by a white picket fence. Evidently, Aunt Sally was still living where Minnie had visited her several years ago. Her husband had died since that time. Minnie rang the bell. Mrs. Norton, after a couple minutes, opened the door. "Minnie, Hello! It's so good to see you. What a surprise! Please come in," exclaimed her aunt. "Aunt Sally, this is my friend, Marie Jones. She lives next to us in St. James. How are you? We came up on the stage last night. It was so late, we stayed at the Stagecoach Hotel." "I'm so glad to see both of you. Are you going to stay a few days with me? How are your dad and Martha?" By this time, they were settled in the living room. "They are both OK. Aunt Sally, we came up to try to get jobs. We want to see Uncle John Snow about working on his ship. Is he in port here yet?" asked Minnie.

"Well, how interesting. You are eighteen now, aren't you? John Snow was in St. Louis last week. He came by to see me. However, the 'Southern Belle' left for a four week trip up the Illinois River to Peoria and back. They'll be back through here then." "Oh, it's too bad we just missed him," said Marie, disappointed. "You're welcome to stay as long as you like. It's just Charles, my son and me here now. Charles, he's twenty-five, and works at a law office. Marie, I think I remember you when I visited Minnie's family about five years ago. You girls were about thirteen then." "Yes, I remember that. Minnie and I have been friends since I was about six years old," said Marie. "Aunt Sally, I want to tell you; Marie and I came up here without telling Dad and Martha or Mr. and Mrs. Jones. We will write them today to let them know where we are," said Minnie. "You naughty girls! I did the same thing when I was seventeen, only it was to get married," admitted Aunt Sally. "There wasn't any problem at home. Dad and Martha need their privacy. I was just in the way. Marie was in a similar situation. She's nineteen," explained Minnie. "Well, you write your parents today. I'll include a note to let them know you're safe and welcome here. Have you girls had breakfast? I was just going to brew some tea." "We had breakfast, but I'd love some tea," said Marie. So it went. Minnie and Marie wrote their parents, and Aunt Sally included her notes. That evening, Charles joined them for dinner. Minnie also wrote Jose a letter two days later.

"You girls should plan what you want to do until the 'Southern Belle' comes back. There are a lot of things to see in St. Louis," suggested Aunt Sally. "Aunt Sally, neither of us have much money. We can't afford much entertainment." explained Minnie. Charles -speaking up- "Our law office has a client who owns a very nice restaurant. Business is so good he needs to hire a couple more employees. If you liked, you might work there until you can get the other jobs. I can introduce you to Mr. Taylor, the owner." "I would love that! I love the atmosphere of a restaurant. I love to eat," said Marie enthusiastically. "Ha! They don't pay you for that. Can you cook?" "That's what I do best. When can we see Mr. Taylor?" asked Marie. "I'll take you there tomorrow, if you like." "I'd like to try it," added Minnie. "Fine. We'll go in the morning. Of course, I can't guarantee what he'll say," cautioned Charles. Aunt Sally agreed - "Since Charles and I have to work week days, that will save you girls from having to just sit here by yourselves most of the time."

The next morning Charles and the girls went to see Mr. Ronald Taylor, owner of the "Plush Room" in the Jefferson Hotel. Charles -in Mr. Taylor's office- "Mr. Taylor, may I introduce to you these two ladies; Miss Minnie Robb and Miss Marie Jones. They are interested in employment. Minnie is a cousin of mine."

"I'm glad to know you, ladies. I do have openings for a couple of girls. Do either of you cook?" asked Mr. Taylor. "I've done a lot of that. I come from a large family and did that along with my mother," said Marie. "And you, Miss Robb. What are your talents?" he asked. I can wait tables, among other things," said Minnie. "And just what are those 'other things', Miss Robb?" I love singing, acting, and I play the piano. I have taught dancing and horsemanship, but you don't have them here, I don't suppose." "You are a very talented young lady. But we do have singing and dancing in our 'Plush Room'. No horses. You see, we have a floor show and dancing after the dinner hour. What dances do you do, Miss Robb?" All the popular ones; the Cotillion, the Quadrille. I've taught a few people both of them, and I love to sing," said Minnie. "Well, this must be my lucky day. My singing and dancing lady just got married and is on a month or so honeymoon. Would you consider a temporary, maybe permanent job, as a singer and dance instructor? I'm sure we can use you, Miss Jones as a waitress, maybe a cook, if you'd prefer that." "Yes. I'd like to try it," said Minnie. "Yes. Same with me. When can we start?" asked Marie. "Well, this is Wednesday; you ladies report to me Friday morning," said Mr. Taylor in conclusion. "Thank you, Mr. Taylor," said Charles. They left.

Friday morning Minnie and Marie reported to Mr. Taylor. "Good morning, girls. You look sharp! Are you excited?" "We're on pins and needles," admitted Minnie. "I think both of you will fit in here, so you're both hired. You'll be waiting tables for the present. We have a large combination dining and ballroom with a stage, and many of our visitors eat dinner here before our show." He sent Minnie to see Art, who sang and also played the piano for the floor show. He took Marie to the dining area to meet Beth who was in charge of that area. In the ballroom, Art addressed Minnie - "Minnie, let me hear you sing this song." He started playing it on the piano. Minnie sang: "Just a Little Bit Crazy Over You." "That's very good. I don't think you'll have any problem. I enjoy accompanying a good singer. Where did you learn to sing?" "I've had some singing lessons, and my boyfriend plays the guitar. I sing along with him," said Minnie. So it went: Minnie was billed as the "Singing Waitress" and would go from waitressing to on the stage to sing. She would sing about four songs each night. Their pay would be one dollar per day plus tips, for 7 hours, 3 pm to 10.00 pm. Art could play anything that Minnie could sing. The first night went well, with generous applause. Things went well for the first month. Charles kept watch about the boats that came from up the river, in order that the girls not miss the "Southern Belle". Charles and Marie seemed to be increasingly attracted to each other.

MEANWHILE Back at the Robb farm: Mr. Robb received the letter from Minnie right away informing him that Minnie and Marie Jones were at Aunt Sally's, both had jobs and not to worry. He was surprised but relieved. Martha was, too, but for different reasons. When Mr. Robb showed Minnie's letter to Martha, she had mixed emotions. She was glad to now have the privacy of the house to themselves, but concerned that a young and inexperienced Minnie, might not be safe in a big city like St. Louis. She had hoped that Minnie would marry John MacDonald, the good friend of her husband. "I'm glad she's there with Sally. She'll be alright there, and Marie's with her. Marie is older and a very sensible girl. I hope that Minnie will realize the opportunity she has back here, with John preferring her over the other girls," said Mr. Robb. "She's only dated him once. Girls her age are more emotional than practical. John is a very good person. She'll learn to love him, if she gives him a chance," agreed

Martha. "I agree," said Mr. Robb, "but John wants me to persuade her to go regularly with him. He mentioned it to me again today when I saw him uptown." "It isn't right to force a girl to like somebody, especially to love them. I wouldn't stand for that either." "I think she'll be back down here when she gets her visit with Sally over in a couple of weeks or so," said Mr. Robb. But Jose got no letter. He waited patiently. He couldn't understand why she hadn't written.

Jose didn't want to inquire of Mr. Robb, knowing of his objection to him and Minnie seeing so much of each other. But he learned from an employee of the Jones farm that the St. James post office had lost two bags of mail in a stagecoach holdup a few days after Minnie left. He decided that maybe Minnie's letter to him had been in one of those sacks. He wanted to go and find her and ease his worries. After all, they were supposed to be in love with each other. He was under contract to Mr. Robb. Most of the crops had been harvested. The cotton would be done in about three weeks. Surely Minnie would be back by then, or he would hear from her. He remembered that Minnie had an Aunt Sally Norton in St. Louis and had mentioned a possible visit to see her. Maybe he could go to St. Louis to see her, and come right back.

IN ST. LOUIS: Days passed and it was almost at the end of the seventh week, and still no "Southern Belle" docked yet. Then one night as Minnie was singing "I'll Be Back Real Soon", a waitress brought her a message: "A Gentleman at table #9 wishes to speak with you." Minnie was excited. She wondered who it could be and went immediately to see him. "Hello, young lady! I want to commend you on your singing. It was very good. I seem to remember a little girl in St. James five years ago. Aren't you—?" "Oh! you're Uncle John!" Instant recognition by both.

They happily embraced. "I came up to meet you. We've been waiting, my girlfriend and I, for you to come back from Peoria." "You have really grown up, young lady. How are the folks in St. James?" asked Capt. Snow. "They're fine, Uncle John. I came up to see if you would let me work for you on your boat. I want to talk to you about that. Are you docked in the harbor?" "Yes. We came in today. How about coming aboard the boat tomorrow morning and we'll talk. It's the "Southern Belle" and we're docked at pier #2," said Capt. Snow. "I want you to meet my friend, Marie Jones," said Minnie. She came up with me." She called Marie over and introduced her. "I'm very glad to meet you, Marie. Minnie, bring her with you tomorrow." "We'll be there, Uncle John." Minnie and Marie went back to work and Capt. Snow left. The girls could hardly wait for closing time. They were so excited they slept little that night. Early the next morning Minnie and Marie took a cab to the boat harbor. It was crowded with watercraft. In 1852 there were hundreds of steamboats that plied the Mississippi river. They soon spotted the "Southern Belle". Looming up in view as they approached pier #2 was a beautiful white ship with wisps of smoke coming from the two tall white stacks. Two side wheels, one on each side, and two gleaming brass boilers between them, amidships.

The gangplank was down and a guard stood at the top. The girls approached him. "I'm Minnie Robb. My uncle, Capt. Snow, asked us to meet him on the ship this morning." "I know," said the guard. "I'll take you to his office. Come along." He turned and they followed him aboard. They were impressed by the clean shiny interior; crystal chandeliers, pretty lamps, paintings on the walls and other decorations here and there. They arrived at Capt. Snow's office. The guard went back to his station. "So you girls want a job on my boat?" asked Capt. Snow. "Yes, we do. It's time we strike out on our own," said Minnie. "I have three people leaving the ship when we leave St. Louis. Marie, do you have any acting experience?" "Only in high school, but I loved it," said Marie. "Minnie, I know that you are a good singer. How are you at dancing?" he asked. "I know all of the current dances; the Cotillion and the quadrille, mainly," said Minnie. "Of course, both of you will have other duties during the day." "I would expect that," said Minnie. "Fine, I'll have my program manager, Mr. Stead, talk to you. He'll answer any questions and settle you into your roles and duties. Then come back Friday morning. That'll give you a couple of days to settle your affairs." He sent them to Joe Stead. Joe assigned Minnie to sing on the program and to teach the customers the current dances. Marie was to take part in the plays that the group put on at each stop, which was 2 or 3 nights at each place. She would also sell tickets.

Later that afternoon Charles took the girls to square up with Mr. Taylor at the "Plush Room". Since it was the dinner hour, Mr. Taylor offered to treat the girls and Charles to dinner as a going away gift. They gladly accepted. The "Plush Room" was indeed plush. It had a beautiful polished hardwood floor, decorative lighting around the walls that could go dim or bright, and pretty candle lighting for the tables. The band was playing. There were many people dining at the tables. A few couples were dancing as Charles, Minnie and Marie were seated. The waiter took their orders. "I can't realize that you girls are leaving us," said Charles. "Your stay has been a real pickup for our house. I'm going to miss you an awful lot." "It's been great. You and your mother have been so good to us; we are real lucky to have had your help, Charles. I can't thank you enough," said Marie. "It was a pleasure. I look forward to a repeat when you come back through in the Spring." After they had enjoyed the delicious dinner the band appeared and started playing again. "Charles, you mentioned earlier that you were not very good at dancing. The band is playing an easy one, come be my partner. I'll help you get back in practice," said Minnie. She reached her hand out to him. "You're really brave to ask me, Minnie. I was just sitting here wishing that I was a better dancer, and had the courage to ask one of you." "You just need practice. That will give you confidence, come on!" Charles complied. "I get the next dance, Charles," said Marie. "Alright, Marie, if you want to risk it." "She's as good a dancer as I am, Charles," said Minnie. Minnie and Charles got out on the floor and danced. He was a bit rusty, but Minnie soon had him relaxed. With renewed confidence, he spent the rest of the evening alternately dancing with Minnie and Marie.

Friday, Charles took the girls to the dock to board the "Southern Belle". As they left him at the gang plank: "Good-bye ladies. Have fun and be careful. Marie, if you will, write me how things work out. When you come back through next Spring, I want to see you. I'll have something 'special' planned." "I'll do that, Charles and I will look forward to seeing you and your mother," promised Marie. "I appreciate what you have done for me." They parted. As the girls started to walk up the gangplank, there was a different guard. He stopped them. "Whoa! What's all that stuff you have there?" "Capt. Snow hired us; told us to come on board today," said Minnie. "Oh, so you're the new girls. Welcome aboard. I'm Ray. I'm to help you girls get settled. Come with me. I'll take you to your quarters." They followed him to a stateroom. "This one is yours." He walked in with them and hung around making small talk. "Ray, we need to put our things away and go check in with our boss," said Marie. "I'll help you, then I'll show you where he is." "We don't need any help and we know where he is. So, thank you, Ray," said Marie, as she coaxed him out the door. "I wonder what his job is on this ship?" mused Minnie. They quickly stowed their things and went to check in with Mr. Stead.

They were assigned their roles and duties. After three days the "Southern Belle" gave a long blast from it's horn, backed out into the middle of the wide Mississippi river and headed South toward New Orleans and towns between; a distance of 1278 miles. It was a bit traumatic for Minnie. She couldn't understand why she hadn't received an answer to her letter, from Jose. She had used Aunt Sally's return address and he should know where she was. She had received a reply from her Daddy. She wondered if Jose was angry because she had rejected his proposal to marry, or if he didn't care. Did he really love her? But the excitement of her adventure soon diverted her attention and she looked forward to the exciting days ahead.

BACK AT THE FARM in St. James: Jose could stand the uncertainty no longer. He decided to go to St. Louis, find Minnie, and assure himself that she was alright and not angry, or whatever else might be wrong. So very early on a day eight weeks after Minnie had left, Jose prepared to leave for St. Louis. He packed a bag for the trip and left a note for Mr. Robb, explaining his trip because of an urgent personal matter. Jose knew that Mr. Robb fed his prize goats early each day, so he decided to leave the note on the gate to the goat pen. Jose -to old Billy- Billy, you and Nanny be good while I'm gone. No monkey business! I'll be back soon. Good-bye!" Billy just shook his head; made no promises.

Jose left on his trip to St. Louis. He was sure that Minnie was still there or Aunt Sally Norton could tell him where she was. When Jose got to St. Louis, he found only two Robbs listed at the courthouse, both at the same address. So he caught a cab out to the area. Finding the house, he rang the bell. Aunt Sally answered the door; "Hello?" "I'm Jose Jackson. I'm a friend of Minnie Robb. Are you her Aunt Sally?" "Yes, I am. But she's not here now." "Can you tell me when she'll be back?" "She left St. Louis two days ago. She's with her uncle John Snow, who owns the 'Southern Belle' Showboat." "two days ago? Looks like I just missed her. I'm sorry that I bothered you. I wrote her a letter seven weeks ago and haven't heard from her. I've been very worried about her." "I'm sorry that you missed her. But I remember her mailing a letter to you right after she got here. When I hear from her, I'll let her know you called, Mr. Jackson." "Thank you, Mrs. Norton. I'm relieved to know that she's alright," he said. Jose wasn't completely relieved. He still didn't know how he stood with Minnie. He realized that he loved her more than ever. What should he do now???

Jose realized that he had a serious problem. He had promised Mr. Robb in the note that he'd be back in a few days, if possible. He thought that he would find Minnie in St. Louis. If he went back to the farm now, he might never see her again. Minnie meant more to him than, any job. It was an agonizing decision to make. He thought about it while standing out at the street. If he went back to St. James without seeing Minnie, it meant more weeks or months of worry and uncertainty. Finally, it became clear to him that he had to see Minnie at any cost. He didn't want to lose her. He would find the "Southern Belle", see Minnie, and still get back to his job as soon as possible. So he headed for the dock area to check on the "Southern Belle". At the dock area, he verified that the "Southern Belle" did leave, going south on the Mississippi river two days ago. He needed to find a way to overtake the "Southern Belle". He didn't have enough money for steamboat fare, but was able to find and sign on as a poler, to a raft of logs about to start for New Orleans the next day. He figured on overtaking the showboat since it stopped at many towns putting on their show. The raft shoved off the next morning. It was a well put together affair. Logs bound together, it was about 30 feet wide and 70 feet long. About half of it was floored with planks. It had a canvas tent for sleeping for the five polers, who with long poles kept the craft near the middle of the stream. There were many boxes of produce such as furs, household goods, etc. on deck. There was even a pen for a cow that would keep the men supplied with milk. The trip to New Orleans would take about two weeks. After the delivery of the products and the logs, and the cow sold, the enterprise would be disbanded.

MEANWHILE, back at the farm, Mr. Robb missed Jose. On learning that Jose had gone to St. Louis, he suspected that his leaving was connected to Minnie's leaving. This upset him very much. Martha was in the library reading, when Mr. Robb came in and sat down. She put her book aside. "You look worried, John. Is something the matter?" "I am worried. You remember when we got the letter from Minnie, saying that she and Marie were at Aunt Sally's and both had jobs?" "Yes. Have you heard from her again? Is she alright?" "No, I haven't heard from her again. But Joe, our assistant crop manager, just told me that Jose Jackson has gone to St. Louis. He left two days ago, saying that he'd be back, but wouldn't say when." "That's unusual. Have you had trouble with him before?" "No, he's been very dependable. The problem is, that he and Minnie have been spending too much time together. I'm afraid they may be in love secretly, and plan to get married." "Oh, what about her chances with John MacDonald? I think she would be making a big mistake, if it's true what you say. She's only 18, and needs mature guidance in things like that." said Martha.

"That's the way I feel, Martha. The fact that Jose left without telling me is suspicious. He has two years left on his contract." "What can you do about it?" she asked. "I think I should intercept them before they're married, if I can. I think she would be making a mistake. I want to talk to her first. I'm going to town and see what can be done." "I think you're right, John." she said.

Hoss Lowrey and Pig Barnes had an office in a building across the street from the sheriff's office in St. James. There was a hitching rail in front and a sign on the front door that said, "Lowery & Barnes, Detectives". Both men were in the office. "Pig, we need a pickup in business. It's too slow right now. Maybe we should move our office to

St. Louis." "We need to collect from some of the people who owe us. Seems that everybody that hires us, after we solve their problem, thinks it isn't worth as much as agreed," complained Pig. "I know," agreed Hoss. "Old Mrs. Sims refuses to pay us for findin' her cow and bringin' it back to her. All because it died the first week back," "We need a real big job if we're goin' to stay in business here the next few months," said Pig. "It would be nice to get a regular pay check, like the sheriff and his deputy across the street," mused Hoss. Later, a tall, well dressed man tied his horse to the rail and entered the office. Are you fellows in the business of tracking down runaways?" he asked, addressing them.

Hoss -recognizing him- "Mr. Robb, that's our business. We're very successful." "I have a special problem. My daughter, who's 18 years old, ran away recently to St. Louis." "We're very familiar with St. Louis. Give us the details about her and we'll have her back down here pronto," said Pig. "Well, she's just the half of it. She has been up there for several weeks visiting her Aunt. Then three days ago my farm hand, Jose Jackson, who has two years still on his contract, also left. He left without letting me know." "That's too bad, Mr. Robb," sympathized Hoss. Mr. Robb -firmly - "I suspect they plan to get married, which I oppose. I want you to stop them and bring them back. She's my only child, and I love her very much. I just want to talk to her before she makes a mistake. I have a better plan for her. No rough stuff, understand. They both have my respect and concern." "Mr. Robb, we'll do the job just like you say. We'll catch 'em before they can get married. We'll catch him first. That'll stop the marriage. You say he left three days ago? We'll get started tomorrow," said Hoss. "Alright, you're hired. I'll give you the information that you'll need and some cash to start. You must be very respectful to Minnie. She has a right to be her own boss. Just bring her back if she's willing. I want the marriage stopped." They concluded the details needed and Hoss and Pig prepared to leave the next morning for St. Louis.

The next morning, Hoss and Pig caught the 9 am stage to St. Louis. Seated opposite them was a wizened little old lady. For several miles, they just sat and stared at each other. Finally: "Are you two fellows brothers?" asked the little old lady. Hoss and Pig looked at each other. "Absolutely not! That's a insult, Lady!" protested Hoss. "Oh, Yeah!" cut in Pig. The "brothers" started shoving each other, rocking the coach. Driver-from the top of the coach- "Hey! What's goin' on down there?" "Stop it! You got a bad aura. I'll put a curse on you!" warned the little old lady. "You can't do that! Who are you?" demanded Hoss. "Never mind. You two are up to some devilment. I'm not speaking to you again." She turned to one side, hid her face and appeared to be asleep. They noticed the butt of a pistol visible in her big purse. Hoss and Pig were spooked. They only whispered and were relieved when she got off at St. Clair. Arriving in St. Louis, they headed for the harbor area. They found out that the "Southern Belle" had left going south six days before. They also found out that a young man with a guitar had left on a log raft three days before. They hired a Capt. Nutter and his small steamboat to carry them in pursuit of Jose and Minnie. It was a 40 footer with a paddle turned by steam from a boiler type engine. It used coal or wood as fuel.

After getting the necessary supplies on board and getting the steam up, they shoved off down the Mississippi river the next morning, with Capt. Nutter at the wheel. He steered the "Wombat" into the middle of the stream. With a big head of steam from the old iron boiler, they figured on catching the raft very soon. "This is great! We'll catch that bunch of logs in no time," enthused Hoss. "Yeah! If this old crate holds together. I don't like the way that boiler sounds. Sounds like it may blow up. I worked at a cotton gin once. They had one that blew. It wrecked the whole place," said Pig. "Pig, you're the dangdest pessimist I ever saw. Capt. Nutter said it's acted that way ever since he's had it." Pig's worry was not entirely unfounded. Boiler explosions on riverboats were fairly frequent in 1852. The "Salada" had such an explosion that killed about 100 people that year.

All day they drove down the river, but no sight of the "Southern Belle". Late in the afternoon, Capt. Nutter decided that he had better turn down the boiler a bit. "Hey, One of you guys hold this wheel steady while I tone that boiler down. We don't need all that much steam." He handed the wheel to Hoss, who had never operated a boat, except a rowboat. "Just hold her steady. I'll be right back." Nutter went to the boiler at the rear. Hoss held the wheel steady a couple of minutes. It seemed like the speed was too fast, so he pulled back like he was driving horses. The wheel came off in his hands.

"HELP! This thing's broke! "screamed Hoss. The boat started moving to the left, narrowly missing a cruise boat going up stream. Capt. Nutter came rushing back. "What's the matter? Gimme that wheel!" But Hoss had dropped it just as the near collision had turned the boat sharply to the right. Before Capt. Nutter could get the wheel back on, there was a loud and shattering "BOOM" as the boiler exploded, clearing everything off the back half of the boat. As the rest of the boat began to sink, luckily it rammed into the bank of the river, where it's prow stuck into the mud. "Damn! I was afraid of that boiler. The owner's goin' to be awful mad!" said Capt. Nutter. "You don't own it?" asked Hoss. "No, I just rent it. I hope they have insurance." "How come the wheel came off?" asked

Pig. "It's detachable to avoid theft. I must have failed to lock it on today when I reattached it." "A fine pickle we're in. We need to get on down the river in a hurry," said Hoss. "Well, we're just a few miles outside of Cape Girardeau. The stagecoach comes along that road over there,"— he pointed. "They'll stop if you flag 'em down. I need to stay here." "Let's get goin' Hoss. It's gettin' late," urged Pig. Hoss and Pig retrieved their suitcases and went over to the road, to await a stagecoach or some other lift.

A couple of "odd" offers came by; they refused. They were sitting on their suitcases when a stagecoach did arrive. "It's time we got some good luck after that disaster," said Hoss. When they were seated in the coach, to their horror, the person sitting opposite them, was none other than the little old lady that had been on the other one, and had threatened to put a curse on them. For a time they all sat and stared at each other again. Then.... "Mam," asked Hoss, "didn't we see you on a coach 'tother side of St. Louis?" She said nothing. "You got out at St. Clair" added Pig. "That's none of your business! You two are following me! You'll be punished. *Fie on you!*" She turned her head away and pretended to sleep. Pig -in a whisper to Hoss- "She's the same one. She's some kind of spy or witch." "I don't like it. She gives me the creeps," agreed Hoss. "Let's catch another boat. I don't wanna ride with her," said Pig. They got off the stage at the next stop, which was Cape Girardeau. Hoss and Pig went to the dock at Cape Girardeau and were lucky to find a Mail boat that was going downstream. However, because of storms on the river farther south, most river traffic was stopped until clear. It was a two day delay and then the Mail boat headed south. For the next two days the Mail boat cruised down the river, stopping frequently to put off and bring on mail and passengers. There was no sign of the raft or the "Southern Belle".

ON THE "SOUTHERN" BELLE: On the second day, the "Southern Belle" was cruising down the river. They had stopped at St. Genevieve the night before. The girls had become accustomed to their roles and routines. It was rest time and Minnie was in the lounge getting coffee and croissants to take back to their cabin for a snack. As she was waiting for the order, Ray appeared. "Hello, Miss Robb. Just the person I wanted to see. I heard you sing again last night. It was beautiful." "Thank you, Ray. I appreciate your comment. Where were you? I didn't see you." "I was operating the colored spot lights on you from the balcony as you sang. Made you look gorgeous." "I'm just an ordinary singer, Ray." "I think you're very good. In fact, I think you have a future big time if you'll continue to cultivate your voice. Chicago, maybe New York City."

"That would be exciting, but I think you may be too much influenced by the colored lights." "No, I'm not, Minnie. I've spent a lot of time in New York. You're good, and will get better as you get older, especially with the voice training that you can get in New York City." "How do you know that?" asked Minnie. "I normally live in New York City. I have good connections there. I'm just on the "Southern Belle" for this trip to New Orleans. The Engineer is my brother. I'm going back to New York from New Orleans. I've managed singers before. If you'll go to New York with me, when we get to New Orleans I'll get you a sponsor. I know you can be successful in New York City, maybe on Broadway. How does that strike you, Miss Robb?" asked Ray.

By this time, Minnie had the order in hand and was ready to go. "I've got to go, Ray. This coffee is getting cold and Marie's waiting." "I'll help you carry that. Give me the coffee." "No, Ray. Marie's taking a shower and is probably in her underwear," said Minnie. "I've seen girls in undies before." "Shame on you, Ray. Good-bye!" Ray -as they parted- "Remember what I said about New York, Miss Robb."

IN THE CABIN: "What took you so long?" asked Marie. "I met up with Ray, Marie. I don't know what to think about him. He's the Engineer's brother. He's also from New York City." "That's interesting. I thought he talked funny. Is that all you learned?" "No. He thinks my singing is good enough to be a hit in New York City. He wants me to go there after New Orleans and he'll get me a sponsor and try it. He's a promoter." "Do they need good cooks in New York City, too? What did you tell him?" "I was so dumbstruck, I didn't answer him. He wants me to think about it. It's exciting and tempting, but can I trust him?" "Think about it for a long time, Minnie. Is that what would make you happy? Also, I'd check with your uncle John."

Minnie was Leary of Ray's claims of promoting her singing career in New York, but she couldn't just ignore it, either. What singer wouldn't be excited at the thought of performing on Broadway to cheering crowds? She happened to catch her Uncle John alone in his office a few hours after her talk with Ray. "Uncle John, may I talk with you a minute?" "Sure, Minnie. Sit down. How is everything going?" "I'm just fine, but I want to get your advice on a problem." "I'll be glad to help, Minnie. What's the problem?" "Uncle John, Ray thinks I have a promising future as a singer in New York City. He wants to get me a sponsor, and he will promote my career there. I'm not sure how much to trust him. It's an exciting thought. I'm not sure if I should try it or not." "Minnie, I'm happy to help, if I can. To begin with, I'm in the entertainment business myself. You are, too, as a singer on my boat. It's a wonderful, satisfying business, if you succeed. Be sure, if you take that route, you're willing to make it you're top priority. If you're going to New York City, it's competitive there." "As for Ray, he's OK. He is a successful promoter. I've known him for several years. His brother is my engineer. I'd hate to lose you as my singer. What are your inclinations about it, Minnie?" "Uncle John, I hadn't given it a thought before. I love my spot here with the 'southern Belle'." "Most girls would love to have the chance. You have to think of the consequences. What would you have to give up? Are you willing to struggle a few years as you study and progress?" asked her uncle. "You've answered my questions, and given me a lot to think about," said Minnie. "You're only 18, Minnie. You don't have to make this decision now. Later, if you decide to try that route, I'll help you to find a good sponsor. In the meantime, I'm happy to have you on my ship." "Thank you, Uncle John."

LATER- Minnie and Marie were together. "Marie, I saw Uncle John this afternoon. He said that Ray was a successful promoter. He's known him for several years." "Are you going to let him sponsor you? I'd be happy for you, but I would sure miss you," said Marie. "It's too important a thing to decide so soon. I'll be thinking about it." "What about Jose?" asked Marie. "That's why I can't decide right now," said Minnie.

BACK ON THE RAFT- Jose figured that they were starting about three days behind the "Southern Belle", which went much faster than the drifting raft. Two polers on each watch for six hours. When he wasn't poling, Jose often played his guitar and sang. The others, including "Betsy", the cow, seemed to enjoy the music. He played "Josefina", his favorite. He had added the lyrics to it since Minnie left. The weather, so far, was good. But it was late in September and getting more cloudy, sometimes foggy. Traffic on the river was heavy. Jose loved playing in the evening under the stars.

After a week had passed, he had not seen any evidence of the "Southern Belle". He didn't know whether he was still behind it or ahead. They could have passed it in the night when the ship was on one of it's "show" stops, or the occasional fog could have obscured it. It was on one of those foggy nights, when the raft was anchored next to the bank, that the "Southern Belle" did pass by. The fog seemed to be thicker than usual near the river bank. Jose and Frank were sitting on the deck talking. It was early in the evening. Both were depressed by the dense fog.

"Jose, you look like you're sad about something. I feel kinda 'down' myself," said Frank. "How about singing your song *Josefina*. It fits this foggy atmosphere." "Alright. I just finished new words for it." He got his guitar. "Who is Josefina? Is that your girlfriend?" asked Frank. "I don't know, Frank. She *was* my girlfriend. That's my problem. I'm not sure about her anymore. She left without telling me, and I don't know where she is." "I sympathize with you, Jose. It happened to me once," said Frank. Jose played and sang "Josefina" and other songs.

On the "Southern Belle", Minnie and Marie were standing out on the deck talking. Suddenly, they heard a guitar playing and a man's voice singing. Minnie -holding up her hand for quiet- "Marie, listen! That sounds like 'Josefina'. It IS 'Josefina'! I heard the word Josefina. That's Jose's song. He wrote it for me. That's his voice! How can I hear it here, Marie? Oh, I wish I could see him!" By now, the distance had faded out the music. "Minnie, maybe it was just a similar song. Cheer up. You're upset." "Maybe I'm losing my mind. Dear Jose, I should have written him again. I miss him so! Marie, I think I'm really in love with him. But I don't understand how I could have just heard him singing his song. Did you hear it like this?" She hummed a bit of the melody. Marie -also now puzzled- "Yes. That is what I heard, too, and I heard the word Josefina," said Marie.

"Sometimes I'm angry because he didn't answer my letter. Maybe he didn't get it. Oh, Marie, I'm so mixed up," said Minnie. "Minnie, Dear, things play out for the best. When we get to New Orleans, you'll see. Let's go in and get some sleep." They went in, but Minnie didn't sleep much that night.

MEANWHILE —the "Southern Belle" steamed on down the Mississippi. It's next stop was Cairo, Illinois for two nights, then on to Memphis, Tennessee for two nights. The second day after arriving in Cairo, Minnie and Marie were planning their day. "Since we have duties this morning, why don't we go into town this afternoon. I need to do some shopping," suggested Minnie. "Sure, I'd like that, as long as we get back in time for the ship's departure at five o'clock," said Marie.

"I can see the top of a Ferris wheel from here, so there must be a carnival or fair going on. I'd like to take a look if we have time." "Sounds interesting. It's been a long time since I've been on a merry-go-round," mused Marie.

So that's what they did. They left the ship about one o'clock. After shopping for personal items they needed, they decided they were hungry. They entered a nice appearing restaurant and were seated at a table. The waitress who came to take their order looked very familiar. After giving their order Marie asked: "Didn't you used to teach school at the Oak Grove school on the road south of St. James?" Marie asked. "Yes, I did, and you look familiar. That was about seven years ago. I was Mozelle Lewis then. I taught 5th and 6th grades; I'm Mozelle Lamb now.

You are... ?" "I'm Marie Jones and this is Minnie Robb -(she indicated Minnie) - I was in the 4th grade then." "I only taught there one year. I got married and we moved to Cairo. My husband raises mules for sale to farmers."

After eating, they again talked to Mozelle, who wanted to know how Oak Grove School and many of the people of the area were, and also about the girls and the "Southern Belle". "Oh, you girls are so lucky! That used to be my ambition," she exclaimed. After talking with Mozelle a while longer, they paid for their food and left. "It's almost three o'clock. Do we have time to see any of the carnival?" asked Marie. "It looks like it's only a couple blocks away. Let's take a quick look, then go to the ship," said Minnie. "Alright. It would be a shame to miss it."

They walked the two blocks to the carnival. There was a big crowd at the carnival. The girls began strolling the fairway. Music from the merry-go-round was loud and merry. The hawkers of the many concession stands kept up a continuous cry to the constantly moving crowd. "Come see the 30-foot boa constrictor"; "Watch them dance, these beautiful Chorus Girls"; "Win a cupie doll. How about you two ladies? Want a cupie doll?" —etc.-etc.-etc.

The girls took a ride on the merry-go-round, bought a couple of trinkets for souvenirs, and then an ice cream cone. Finally, Minnie whispered in Marie's ear. "Don't look now, but I think there's two boys following us. The ones with the funny hats." They walked on and Marie sneaked a look back. "I think you're right. I don't like their looks. What should we do?" asked Marie. "Let's walk on around to the Ferris wheel, and if they're still following, we can get on that," suggested Minnie. "That should get rid of them." agreed Marie.

As they continued on around, the boys got closer, and began making comments directed at the girls. The girls quickly bought tickets and were seated on the Ferris wheel. The boys stared at them. The Ferris wheel started and by the time the girls had made two loops, the boys had disappeared. A couple more loops and the wheel stopped to let a couple off. That put the girls at the very top. "Marie, look at the view! There's the 'Southern Belle' in the harbor, exclaimed Minnie. "It's fabulous! From up here you can see just how pretty the 'Southern Belle' is," responded Marie. The wheel resumed turning. After three more rotations, there was a sudden jolt that rocked their seat. The wheel stopped again with the girls at the top. They had that beautiful view again. The wheel stayed stopped. It was then that they saw a little puff of steam from the horn of the ship and heard a blast. It was the warning signal ahead of the ship's departure. "Let us off!" screamed both girls.

The operators were able to rescue those in the lower seats, but the higher ones, including the girls, would have to wait until a crew that had a winch could arrive to aid in the repair of the problem. "Oh, Marie, We're going to miss it. Uncle John will be angry. This is terrible!" "I think he'll understand when he hears what happened." While they were worrying about their predicament, and as they watched, the beautiful "Southern, Belle" gave out a blast of it's horn, backed out into the Mississippi and disappeared down stream. The girls were let off about 40 minutes later when the crew arrived with the winch to steady the wheel while the operators lowered each seat. "We are really in a pickle, Marie. What can we do?" "We'll be in a worse fix if we can't catch the ship. It will be in Memphis for two days. We should try to catch it there. Let's go to the stagecoach station and see. It's getting late, but maybe there's one still going to Memphis today," said Marie. "Let's hurry, I don't want to spend the night here."

The stagecoach station was near the harbor so they hurried there. As they approached the station, they were elated to see a stagecoach standing in front headed toward Memphis. But the driver was in his seat already. He cracked his whip, and the horses lurched forward. "Wait! Driver wait! Wait for us!" screamed the girls. Minnie and Marie ran as fast as they could toward the coach. A little old lady, who had just gotten off the stagecoach, luckily realized the girls' situation. "Ralph, stop! Ralph, wait!" she yelled. Ralph, the driver, quickly pulled on the reins and stopped the coach. "What the devil you want, Becky Rockhauser? You'll cause my horses to break a leg." "Here's two customers who want a ride. Isn't that what you're in business for?"

The girls were allowed to buy tickets to Memphis, which was about 140 miles and would arrive there late the next day. "Oh, thank you!" said Minnie," We really needed to catch this stagecoach." "I'm glad to help," said Becky, "I work for the company."

In a few minutes they were on their way. There were no other passengers, and the girls slept most of the night. They arrived in Memphis about five pm. The "Southern Belle" was in the harbor. Capt. Snow had been very worried about the girls, but believed that they would manage to join the ship in Memphis. He was prepared to hold the ship in Memphis if necessary. He didn't know that they had missed it until several hours after they had left Cairo. He was happy that the girls had managed to rejoin the ship, and after hearing their story, decided that they had learned a good lesson. So, the next morning the "Southern Belle" headed on down the Mississippi. They planned to spend two nights in Greenville, Miss. From there they would play only the larger towns, because it was getting late in the Autumn when fog and storms were likely to interfere.

It was the sixth day, and had begun to rain, after the "Southern Belle" had left Memphis. The river was normal, with a strong current out toward the middle, where the ship stayed. Later, in the afternoon, as the rain came down harder, the "Southern Belle" came to the place where the White River joins in from the West. The situation changed very quickly. A torrent of dark brown angry water from the White River poured into the Mississippi, including logs and all kinds of debris. The White was flooding from heavy rains, all the way back and beyond, where the Little River emptied into it. This made the Mississippi river a rough and dangerous one. Capt. Snow and the pilot decided to continue on down and drop anchor at Greenville until the storm was past. However, the thunder and lightning increased. It was getting darker and a strong wind came in erratic puffs, strong enough to blow one overboard if they were not careful. Strong dark and threatening clouds now raced over the ship. The river surface had waves now big enough to cause the "Southern Belle" to shudder. Capt. Snow feared that they might be in the path of a tornado. They needed to make it to safety in the harbor at Greenville.

Minnie and Marie, who had experienced many storms on their farms near St. James, were in the lounge with others. On their farms, they had storm cellars when in danger like this. They watched the storm out of the portholes. "Marie, I'm scared. I've never been in a storm like this. We had a storm cellar back home. Could this ship sink in this river? That would be terrible!" "You're talking to somebody who has no experience like this", admitted Marie. "I'm sure Capt. Snow knows what to do to keep his ship safe." "I don't think I'd want to live my life on a ship. It has it's drawbacks, I can see," said Minnie.

"Storms only last so long. They pass on through. This shouldn't be bad much longer." "Marie, I don't know what I'd do without you. You are always so reassuring. Just like Jose. I think we'll make it as you say."

But instead of getting better, it suddenly got worse. It got darker. The swiftly flowing Mississippi came to the confluence of the Arkansas River, where it also pours into the Mississippi. The river now became rougher, faster and wider. Water in every direction, it was hard to keep track of the stream's center. Everywhere there were logs, planks, out houses, snakes, and even small houses floating in the turbulent waters. Suddenly, there was a jarring jolt. The "southern Belle" came to a grinding stop. Furniture, dishes, etc. were flung to the deck. The "Southern Belle" was stuck on a sandbar. Capt. Snow, who was in the lounge, rushed up to the pilothouse where Mr. Brunelle, the pilot, was trying to see what they had struck. "What did we hit, Jack? That was quite a jolt!" "I'm not sure, it's so dark, but I think it's a sandbar just below the surface. It felt like a sandbar the way it stuck. If so, there may not be much damage," answered Brunelle. "I just checked down below. It's fine; no water," said the engineer, coming up from below. "Well, it's so dark," said Capt. Snow. "We're stuck. It's best to wait until daylight. Jack, do you think you can back 'er off in the morning?" "We'll try. The water may be less rough by then." "Then we'll just wait 'til morning. We're safely stuck here now," said the Captain.

When the ship hit the sandbar, all was confusion. Minnie and Marie were in their cabin. They were thrown to the floor. They immediately left their cabin to see what had happened. Others did the same. Suddenly someone screamed: "Man overboard! Man overboard!" The girls ran to the starboard side, where they saw a man struggling in the stormy water. "Help! Help!" he cried. Nobody appeared to know what to do....Then Minnie shucked her shoes and dove in to try to help him. Marie dove in right after her. The man was thrashing around, trying to stay afloat. He was evidently losing the battle.

The girls got on each side of him and kept his head above water. It was then that they recognized him as Ray. He was beyond talking. A recovery boat lowered and they were all pulled aboard, just as Capt. Snow and the engineer came from the pilot house and saw the rescue. Capt. Snow and the engineer warmly thanked Minnie and Marie for the prompt rescue of Ray. Ray was put in the ship's hospital. Later Minnie and Marie went to the hospital to see him. "Thank you, girls, for saving my life." said Ray. "I can't swim. It's a miracle you two were near and could swim." "In Missouri, we learn to swim in the creeks. It's one of our favorite recreations," said Minnie.

THE NEXT MORNING- pilot Brunelle reversed the two paddle-wheels to try to pull the ship off the sandbar. It worked just a little, then stuck again. There was danger in building up the boilers too high. "Capt. Snow, I'm afraid to build up those boilers any higher," said the Engineer. "Why don't we just have everybody get back on the stern. The weight there may lift the bow just enough to lift us off," said Brunelle. "It's worth a try," said the Captain. "Everybody except Mr. Brunelle and the Engineer, please go back onto the fantail. We're going to try to lift the bow enough that it can come off the sandbar. Be careful!", said Capt. Snow on the intercom.

It took about fifteen minutes for all to get to the boat's stern. Jack gave the signal, revved up the boilers, put the paddles in reverse, and hoped. The ship shuddered and suddenly lurched backward. It was free. There was a loud cheer from the passengers and crew. Capt. Snow, back on the intercom, "Everyone back to your stations, or off the rear deck. We can resume our trip." "We may have some damage, but she seems to steer OK." said Jack. "We'll put her in dry-dock in New Orleans to repair any damage. We're lucky. I think we'd better skip Natchez and also Vicksburg," said Capt. Snow. They headed again for New Orleans.

MEANWHILE —Jose, on the raft was wondering if he'd ever see Minnie again. The raft seemed to be playing hide-'n-seek with the "Southern Belle". He didn't know where the ship was. He was so lonely. He sang a new song that fit his mood! "Those Low-down Blues". Tears filled his eyes as he finished. Soon, however, his attention was changed. The huge storm that had buffeted the "Southern Belle" suddenly enveloped the raft. The polers had increasing trouble keeping the raft off the banks as the river curved right and left. Then when the current carried them past the spot where the White, then the Arkansas rivers poured into the Mississippi, things got desperate. The four polers, Jim, Frank, Bill and Jose, along with Mr. Barkley, the Captain, were all desperately trying to keep the raft together and on course. It was now dark.

"This is terrible!" exclaimed Mr. Barkley. "We've got to get anchored in a safe place somewhere. We're almost to Rosedale. If we can just make it there!" "I need some help on this side, quick! I can't hold it!" yelled Jim. He was straining on his pole to keep the front left corner of the raft off a projection of the bank that suddenly appeared in it's path. "Comin' over!" answered Bill. But the corner of the raft dug into the bank and swung the raft broadside to the raging current, just as a big wave lifted and pulled it apart. They were all thrown into the water, including "Betsy" the cow. Lucky for all, they were able to scramble to safety, as the water at that point was not very deep. "Betsy" was led out on her rope by Frank. The raft was quickly coming apart. They had no chance to save anything. Jose's guitar, too, was lost.

The five stunned men, wet and tired, stood watching as the broken raft further disintegrated and disappeared in the turbulent Mississippi. Mr. Barkley was the first to recover his voice. "Thank God we're all alive and unhurt. Let's walk into Rosedale and I'll see if we can get lodging for the night. I can see the lights in the distance. In the morning we can check to see if any of our things were washed ashore near here." "How about "Betsy"? asked Jose. "Oh, yes! She's a problem," admitted Mr. Barkley. Jose -pointing- "There's an old shed. Looks like it might be enough to keep out the rain. I'll stay with her and you'll know where to start the search. I'll start looking as soon as daylight. I'm sure we'll find some of our things." It was raining now, sporadically. "That's a good idea. I appreciate your offer," said Mr. Barkley. "Alright then, when you come in the morning, bring me some coffee and "Betsy" some oats and hay," said Jose. "Betsy" mooed, as if to say, "Thanks." "We'll bring both and we'll be early. I've got to salvage as much as I can."

Jose led "Betsy" over to the shed. After clearing out the trash, Jose was able to clear an area large enough for them to stay dry. "Betsy" seemed to take the terrifying events in stride. Other than blinking her big glossy eyes and flapping her ears and tail, she had nothing to say. Jose, on the other hand, was wet, tired, and trying to calm down. "What a day!" said Jose. "I'm thankful we're all safe, 'Betsy' old girl. All this trouble because I'm in love with a beautiful girl. Have you ever been in love 'Betsy'? Maybe you're lucky." Even though he'd lost his guitar, Jose sang "Lonely Road".

In the early daylight, Jose started searching the river bank for any of their possessions and cargo. He found his own water-logged pouch, but not his guitar. About 11:00 am Mr. Barkley and the others arrived with a horse and wagon. They brought coffee and biscuits for Jose and some hay and oats for "Betsy", who had been gorging herself on the lush green grass along the river bank. They searched and gathered many things from the nearby river bank, but the main body of the raft they found a half mile down the river, lodged against a fishing pier. Mr. Barkley decided to repair the raft using what was left of it, and take it on down to Vicksburg. This they did. The new raft was smaller but solid. The violent storm had abated. The water was still high and rough, but there was now only occasional rain.

At Vicksburg, Mr. Barkeley sold the raft of logs to a local logging company, and "Betsy" to a local farmer. Mr. Barkeley and the three polers decided to return to St. Louis. Jose was lucky to be hired on a

Mail boat headed for New Orleans, as a helper in the mail and baggage room. When Jose went aboard the Mail boat, he spotted Hoss and Pig immediately. It surprised him. What were they doing on this boat? Because of their size, Hoss and Pig were well known in St. James, but Jose didn't think they would recognize him. He had never had occasion to meet them. Nevertheless, he was leery. The reason for their presence there might be that Mr. Robb had hired them to bring him back because of the two years remaining on his contract. He decided to stay out of their sight as much as possible. He also found some black rope and fashioned a small mustache out of it.

Jose couldn't always avoid them because he had to help load and unload the mail and baggage at each stop. He knew that they had seen him, but passengers were not allowed in the mailroom, where Jose spent most of his time. "Pig, have you seen that guy who's sortin' mail in the mailroom?" asked Hoss. "Yeah! He looks familiar. Can't think where," said Pig.

"Well, he looks like the guy we're lookin' for. I've not been able to talk to him. We better keep our eyes on him, though."

"But he ain't got no guitar, an' he's got a mustache. I ain't heard no singin. Besides, he didn't supposed to work for no Mail boat," protested Pig. "Pig, you're a negative! I'm goin' to nail that guy if he's our man. Otherwise, we won't earn our bounty."

MEANWHILE - John MacDonald had heard that Minnie had gone to St. Louis and was working there. He was at the General Store one day when Angie Ferguson came in. He approached her and asked, "Aren't you a friend of Minnie Robb? I'm John MacDonald." "Yes, I am. I'm Angie Ferguson. I'm glad to know you."

"I'm a friend of the Robb family. I hear that Minnie is working in St. Louis now. Is that true, or just a rumor? I haven't seen her around here recently," said John. "I got a letter from her. She did work for a restaurant, but now she's working on her uncle's showboat on the Mississippi River." "She is? I'm surprised. I thought she was pretty well settled here. What does she do on the ship, or is she just a passenger?" he asked. "She sings and teaches dancing," said Angie. "Hmm. She could have done better. I thought she just went to St. Louis to visit her aunt....Are you working in town now, Miss Ferguson?" he asked.

"Yes. I've just started working at the bank." "Oh, you have? I'm in the bank a lot. I'll probably see you there. What's your job there Miss...can I just call you Angie? I hate so much formality." "Of course, you may. I'm training to be a cashier. I agree about the formality," said Angie. "Well,

I've got to go now," said John. "I'll see you at the bank, Angie. It was nice talking with you." "Yes. Goodbye," said Angie, with a happy smile.

BACK AT THE FARM— Mr. Robb had heard nothing from Minnie since receiving a letter from her the day she went aboard the ship. He had received no news from Hoss and Pig since they left for St. Louis. He and Martha were worried. One afternoon, a handsome carriage pulled into their driveway, and a man came to the door and rang the bell. Mr. Robb answered it. "I'm Mr. Jackson," said the distinguished gentleman. "I think my son, Jose, works for you. Are you Mr. Robb?"

"Yes, I'm Mr. Robb. Jose does work for me, but he is not here at the present," answered Mr. Robb. "His mother and I have just concluded some business in St. Louis, and since we were in the area, we decided to stop by and see him." Martha, who was listening to the conversation, came to the door. "Is your wife in the carriage? Have her come in. I'm Martha Robb. It's a warm day. I'm sure she would appreciate a little rest." "Yes, by all means. Both of you come in," said Mr. Robb, "I'd like to talk to you about Jose. He's my crop manager, and a very good one."

Mr. Jackson helped his wife out of the carriage and they settled down in the large living room. Mr. Robb had one of his workers lead the carriage horse to a shady spot. Mrs. Jackson was a very pretty Spanish lady, dressed in a flowing white dress and a wide brimmed summer straw hat. After a few casual comments about the weather, etc. Martha took Miranda Jackson to her boudoir to freshen up and relax. Mr. Robb offered cigars and they fired up and settled down to talk. "You said that Jose wasn't here. Will he be back soon? I'd hate to miss him on this trip," said Mr. Jackson. "Mr. Jackson, I'll tell you all I know. Jose left here, without notice ten days ago. I'm not sure, but I believe he went to St. Louis.." "That's not like Jose to do a thing like that," Mr. Jackson responded. "I don't understand it. Do you know why he left?" "I don't know for sure, but my daughter, Minnie, also left here about six weeks ago and went to St. Louis. They've spent a lot of time together here and I'm afraid they are in love and may be planning to be married. She's just turned 18 and I worry about this, Mr. Jackson." "Had they said anything to you about marriage?" "No. That's one thing that disturbs me. I think Jose is a fine boy. I'm just afraid it's the excitement of her turning 18 years old."

"I sympathize with you, Mr. Robb. I don't like to see kids running away to get married, but they do it all the time now. I'd like to talk to Jose about it." Mr. Jackson, continuing, "I'm sure your daughter is a fine girl, but if you think she's a little young yet...I understand." "Jose has never told me much about himself. Did he go to college?" asked Mr. Robb. "Oh, yes," said Mr. Jackson. He attended the Tulane University of Louisiana in New Orleans for two years. "I can tell he's a very smart boy." said Mr. Robb. "He needs to be," said Mr. Jackson. "He's our only child, and will have our 1000 acre farm and other investments to manage when Miranda and I are gone." "Do you have any slaves on your farm?" asked Mr. Robb. "No, I've never had any. I have hired workers who live on the farm, or near by," he said.

Finally, as the sun was setting, Mr. Jackson arose. "Mr. Robb, it's getting late. We need to go. If I hear anything from Jose, I'll let you know. Maybe things will work out for the best for our children... Miranda! we'd better get going." Martha, coming in with Mrs. Jackson: "Miranda and I have decided that you should spend the night here with us. We have plenty of room, and you can get an early start in the morning." The men agreed and so they did. Mr. Jackson and Mr. Robb happened to be members of the same political party, so their evening was spent amiably. In the morning Mr. and Mrs. Jackson returned to St. Louis.

BACK ON THE MAILBOAT — As it was docked in Natchez, Jose was getting the mail and packages sorted that were due to be left there, when he heard the blast from a ship's horn. Looking up, he saw the "Southern Belle" sailing past down the river, apparently skipping Natchez. As it disappeared down the river, Jose stood transfixed. There on that ship was his sweetheart, Minnie. His heart sank as it disappeared and he realized that he had no way of getting aboard the "Southern Belle". But it lifted as he also realized that at last, he knew where she was. But his spirit sank as he realized that New Orleans was a big city. Then he wondered if she missed him, or if she even thought of him. The "Southern Belle" was a "good-time", "happy-time" ship. She might have a new boyfriend on the ship. If he found her, would she be glad to see him? Tears filled his eyes. His spirit was pretty low.

CHAPTER THREE

New Orleans in 1852 was a very wicked city. It was the main center of commerce for that area of the United States, especially for the huge Mississippi Valley. Smugglers, slave traders, gamblers, land speculators, slaves both owned and free, prostitutes, etc. conducted their operations there.

Capt. Snow arranged to have all his girls stay at a very respectable boarding house on St. Charles St. At the boarding house, on the morning on which the girls arrived, a young girl dressed as a cleaning lady is standing looking out the window at the setting sun. She leaned on her broom. Her pretty face looked very sad. She wiped a tear from her eyes. Her thoughts went far beyond the now fading sunset. She softly now began to sing "No One To Care For Me". She sighed and resumed her sweeping. As she finished, a new group of girls came in and were assigned rooms. They were from the "Southern Belle", just berthed in the harbor. The girl saw the well dressed group, and heard the name "Southern Belle" showboat. They seemed so happy and free. She had always wished that she could be an actress or a singer. But that was out of the question now.

As soon as the girls were settled into their room at the boarding house, they wrote their parents where they were, and that they were in good health. They were looking forward to seeing the sights in New Orleans and coming back up the Mississippi in the Spring. The following morning, Minnie and Marie were sitting in the lounge on the first floor. They were just observing the coming and going of the people. "Minnie, do you still have that picture that Dr. Pitts gave us of his daughter that ran away?" asked Marie. "I think so." -she dug in her handbag- "Here it is." "Take a look at that girl sweeping the floor," said Marie. Minnie -holding the picture and looking- "It's HER!" "I'm sure it's her, too. What's her name?" asked Marie. "Her name is Christine or Chrissy Pitts. What can we do?" "I don't know, but let's go over and see," said Marie.

They went over to where the girl was busily sweeping. Marie, addressing the girl, "Hello, Chrissy." "How'd you know my name? It's Dorothy, not Chrissy," said she. "We met your father, Dr. Pitts, on the stagecoach out of St. Louis. He was on a sales trip. He said you ran away. We ran away, too. We're working on the showboat "Southern Belle". We just came in yesterday," said Marie. "Oh! How's my father? What did he say?" "Chrissy, he's fine, except he's so worried and lonely for you," said Minnie. "He wants to hear from you. He gave us this picture of you." She showed Chrissy the picture.

Chrissy -tears now in her eyes- "Oh, I'm so glad you met him. I'm so lonesome! I thought things would be better down here, but they're not. Not for me." Marie, calmly, "Chrissy, we want to be your friends. When you get off work, will you come up to our room #202? We can talk. You can tell us what to expect here in New Orleans. And please, will you write your Dad tomorrow? We'll help you." "Yes. I'll send him a letter in the morning. I'm sick of this place! I'm off at 6 pm. I'll come up then. Room 202?" "That's right. We'll be expecting you," said Marie. Chrissy went back to work. Marie and Minnie went to their room.

When Chrissy came up to their room later, they had a long talk together. "Chrissy, where did you go when you left St. Louis?" asked Marie. "I went to Natchez from St. Louis, then came to New Orleans 6 months ago," said Chrissy. "I couldn't find a respectable job except this one. I attended church on Sundays, but I didn't find any real friends there either." "Chrissy, why don't you go with us to the "Southern Belle" as soon as it's out of dry-dock. I'd like you to meet Capt. Snow. We'll be putting on some of our plays. We may be able to help you get a job on the ship. It'll be going back to St. Louis in the Spring," said Minnie. "I'd love to. That would be wonderful," said Chrissy. The three girls became good friends during the next few weeks.

ON THE MAILBOAT — Hoss and Pig decided that the Mailroom helper was indeed Jose Jackson. They planned to arrest him when they all got off the boat. Because Jose stayed on the boat a stop beyond the passengers, it ruined their plans. They quickly found out where the final stop was and grabbed a cab. Traffic was bad, and they soon found out why. It was a funeral procession, jazz band and all, passing across the street on the way to the cemetery. When the street was finally free, they rushed on down to the mail depot. Jose had already left. No one knew where he had gone. Hoss and Pig decided to check the "Southern Belle". He'd been there earlier, but had left, they didn't know where. The ship's personnel had been sent to quarters out in the city. The guard didn't know where. So Hoss and Pig decided to rent a room and stay around the downtown district. Sooner or later they would spot him and arrest him. They rented a room near Canal Street and began their vigil.

Jose, too, had rented a room. He considered that he'd never be able to find where Minnie was staying, but she was certain to come into the downtown area to shop or just see the sights. He needed a guitar, and he would play and sing on the street corners. That seemed to be a good idea. He would play "Josefina" and "You Will Always Be My Sweetheart" alternately. Minnie loved both. He found a pawnshop and bought a cheap guitar, sat down on a corner of Canal Street and started playing.

About a week later Minnie, Marie and Chrissy were in a horse drawn cab on Canal Street when Minnie heard again someone playing "Josefina". "Marie, listen! Can you hear that guitar?. He's singing and playing 'Josefina.'" Traffic was noisy and they were in a traffic jam. "I hear it, Minnie. It's the same song we heard that night on the river. It's creepy!" "Driver, please go around the block. And hurry!" urged Minnie. Because of the traffic congestion slowed down by a street repair crew, by the time they got back around, the music had stopped.

Then they saw Jose and two others being loaded into a police wagon. Quickly they ran over to protest, Chrissy included. The reason that the music had stopped at that time was that Hoss and Pig had suddenly come upon Jose sitting upon a box playing his guitar. "Hey, feller! Just a minute. Aren't you from up in Missouri?" asked Hoss. Jose -recognizing the two- "Yes, I am. I'm from St. James." "We know you. You were on the Mail boat. Same as us," said Pig. "Yes I was. What do you fellows want?" "You're Jose Jackson," said Hoss. "We are detectives. You are under arrest. We have orders to take you back to St. Louis. You are still under contract to your employer, Mr. Robb." They handcuff Jose.

"I don't think you can arrest me here in Louisiana. Hey, Officer!" He called to an officer nearby, who came to check. "What seems to be the trouble?" asked the officer. "These men from Missouri are trying to arrest me. I am a free citizen," said Jose.

Officer, to Hoss and Pig, "Let me see your credentials, please." Hoss and Pig gave up their detective licenses from Missouri. Officer, looking at the licenses, "I can't tell whether these are legitimate or not. I'll have to take all of you down to headquarters and let the Commissioner check them out." He gave a couple of toots on his police whistle and a police wagon arrived. He started loading them all into the wagon just as Minnie, Marie and Chrissy came running up.

"What are you doing? Stop Officer! Jose, how did you get down here? OH, I'M SO GLAD TO SEE YOU!" exclaimed Minnie. They grab and hug each other. "I've been following your ship. I knew you were somewhere in New Orleans. How did you happen to be here? These men were trying to arrest me," said Jose. "Knock it off, Lady. These men are being arrested. It's none of your business," said the officer.

"You can't arrest him if he didn't do anything. I need to talk to him!" screamed Minnie. "Alright, you can talk to him down at Headquarters. Get in!" "You can't arrest her! That's ridiculous," exclaimed Marie. "She's arrested already. You, too. Get in!" "Can I go, too? I'm with them," pleaded Chrissy. "You people are what's ridiculous. Get in!" ordered the exasperated officer, wiping the sweat from his face. While this was going on, a member of the crew of the "Southern Belle" had seen the arrest, and had decided that he had better tell Capt. Snow. So, he hurried over to the ship and told him.

MEANWHILE —Mr. Robb and Martha had arrived in New Orleans and found the "Southern Belle". Aunt Sally had written them that the girls were on the ship. They had decided to visit them in New Orleans, and then go on to Atlanta to visit Martha's parents.

MEANWHILE — Dr. Pitts arrived, too. Chrissy having told him in the letter that she was with friends from the "Southern Belle" in New Orleans. When the messenger arrived at the "Southern Belle" and told them that their daughters and Jose had been arrested, they all immediately rushed out, grabbed cabs and hurried to rescue the girls.

AT POLICE HEADQUARTERS — Present were the Police Commissioner, Asst. Police Commissioner, and Secretary. The patrol wagon arrived and all were seated in front of the Commissioner, who had a bandage on his jaw, the result of a severe toothache. "Will the arresting officer please explain the charges against these people?" asked the Commissioner. Arresting officer, standing up and clearing his throat, "Sir, all these people were creating a disturbance at the corner of Canal and Harbor Street. Traffic was heavy and they were having some sort of disagreement. I can't hold court there on a corner, so I brought them ..." He sat back down as the Commissioner interrupted. "Officer, make it brief. We don't want a riot scene here, either. I'm due in the dentist office in thirty minutes. What's the problem?" Arresting officer, standing up and clearing his throat, "Sir, I was directing heavy traffic at the corner of Canal and Harbor Street, when ..."

At this instant Mr. and Mrs. Robb rushed in demanding to see their daughter. The arresting officer sat back down as he was interrupted. There was a happy reunion of Minnie and Mr. and Mrs. Robb, and a surprise, pleasant greeting to Jose, who was still handcuffed. The Commissioner was furiously beating on his desk for quiet. "Everybody quiet!" exclaimed the Commissioner, - "Officer Struthers, continue your report."

Arresting officer Struthers stood up again and cleared his throat, - "Sir, as I was saying, I was directing heavy traffic at the corner of Canal and Harbor Street when ..."

At this instant Dr. Pitts rushed in through the door. He and Chrissy spied each other at the same time and rushed into each other's arms, upsetting chairs, etc, creating bedlam again. Commissioner —banging his desk — "Quiet! Quiet! or you're all going to be fined!" It became almost quiet again. Commissioner —about to explode — "Alright, Officer Struthers, your report!" He emphasized each word, as he banged his desk.

Officer Struthers - angrily, as he stood up — "Sir, as I said, I was directing heavy traffic at Canal and Harbor Street when...." Commissioner, trying to control his frustration, "For cryin' out loud, Officer Struthers, are you goin' to stay down there on Canal and Harbor Streets all day? Tell us what happened. Please!" There was beginning to be a chorus of mumblin' from the crowd.

Officer Struthers —in a loud voice— "Well, I was down there directing ...."

All of a sudden, Capt. Snow and several others from the 'Southern Belle' rushed in yelling..."Wait! wait! I can explain it all. It's a mistake!" He rushed over to Minnie, Marie and the Robbs. It was another loud commotion. The Police Commissioner threw up his hands, grabbed a rope beside his desk and pulled it. Immediately a loud siren sounded and a half dozen policemen rushed in. The Commissioner grabbed his jaw with one hand, put his hat on with the other, and headed for the door. "I've got to go to the dentist," he moaned. "You people are giving me a bad headache, too! Asst. Commissioner, will you take over here?" He rushed out the door.

It took several minutes for everyone to quiet down. "Now Officer Struthers, tell us your story," the Assistant Commissioner requested. Officer Struthers gave the details of the arrests. "Thank you, Officer Struthers. Capt. Snow, I believe you said that you could explain it. Will you please?" Capt. Snow - standing - "Minnie Robb and Marie Jones are from my ship. Chrissy Pitts is their friend. Jose Jackson is Minnie's boyfriend. Mr. Barnes and Mr. Lowrey, I'm not acquainted with. Mr. and Mrs. Robb are Minnie's parents. Dr. Pitts is Chrissy's father."

"I think it was all a misunderstanding," said the Asst. Commissioner. "All of you are free to go except Mr. Barnes and Mr. Lowrey. I'd like them to stay here until we can verify their licenses. That should take only a couple of hours." Capt. Snow - standing again - "I want to thank you, Commissioner on behalf of all of us from the 'Southern Belle'. We are having a dinner and program on board the ship tomorrow night to celebrate our just completed trip up the river and back. I would like to invite you, Sir, and the Commissioner to that dinner. It will be at 7 pm. I hope that you can be there." "Thank you Capt. Snow. I'll convey your invitation to the Commissioner. We'll be there if we can," said the Asst. Comm. Everyone left for the ship, except Hoss and Pig and the police officers.

TWO HOURS LATER: Commissioner - who had returned from the dentist office. - "Mr. Lowrey and Mr. Barnes, congratulations. Your licenses are valid. You're free to go. But I have a proposition for you to consider." "Thank you. What's the proposition?" asked Hoss. "You two fellows are strong and dependable. Just the kind of men we need here in New Orleans. I'm offering you a job as policemen in my department. Good salary. Twice what you'd get in Missouri. Paid uniforms, etc. How about it?" " That sounds great! I'd like that!" said Hoss. "Me, too. When can we start?" echoed Pig. "Right today. We're short handed here right now."

Hoss and Pig both accepted, signed up, outfitted with uniforms, billy clubs, badges, etc. and were sent to the Assignment Officer. "Welcome men," said the Assignment Officer. "There's nothing today" - checked a list—— "Tomorrow there's a dinner aboard a ship at the dock, starting at 7 pm. We usually provide a couple of officers for security at such events. I'll assign the job to you. You be at the job at 7 pm. It's the "Southern Belle" at pier #2." You can imagine the surprise of Hoss and Pig. "Yes Sir!" said Hoss and Pig in unison.

Just at that moment, the Little Old Lady who had "spooked" Hoss and Pig on the stagecoach, walked gingerly through the room. The Assignment Officer gave her a friendly wave. "Officer!" exclaimed Hoss. "Do you know her?" "Sure. She's old Becky Rockhauser. She's eccentric but harmless. She's a stockholder of the stagecoach company and takes it upon herself to check out it's operations each year. She's smart and helps us to avoid robberies with her tips at times." "We met her on the coach out of St. Louis," said Pig, relieved.

When Mr. and Mrs. Robb got back to the ship, Mr. Robb asked Jose and Minnie to have tea with them. Jose was still apprehensive that Mr. Robb was angry with him. "First, I want to say that I am not angry with either of you," said Mr. Robb. "I've had more time to think things over since you left. Martha and I have talked it over and we are happy to approve of you're wanting to be together, and to marry, if you want to do that. Our primary concern is that you, Minnie, would be happy."

"Thank you Daddy and Martha. I do love Jose, but he hasn't asked me to marry him, *recently*," said Minnie, as she shifted her gaze to him. "You know I want you to, Minnie. Will you?" "Yes! Yes! I will! Let's do it while Daddy and Martha are here. Capt. Snow can marry us. He's the captain of the ship," urged the excited Minnie.

"We didn't intend to rush anything," said Mr. Robb. But if you are going to, now is a good time, since we are all here together." "It would be wonderful, and on this beautiful ship," agreed Martha. And so it was agreed. Jose and Mr. Robb talked with Capt. Snow and the arrangements were made.

LATER — "Jose, I don't want to be critical at this point, but why didn't you let me know that you were going to leave?" "Mr. Robb, I felt like you would disapprove of my leaving. I intended to come back as soon as I found Minnie. I left you a note where I was sure you would find it." "Where did you put it? I didn't find any note," said Mr. Robb. "I tacked it to the gate of the goat pen. I knew that you fed them every morning," said Jose. "Then old Billy ate it!" said Mr. Robb. "He eats anything he can reach." "Oh, I'm sorry. I didn't think he would do that." "Well, that's past now. What will your and Minnie's plans be after the wedding?" "I'll talk to Minnie, and if she agrees, we can go back to take care of the farm right away. We could leave right after the ceremony." "That would be fine. Also, Jose, since you two are getting married, Martha and I would like you and Minnie to settle near us. We will give you 300 acres and help you build a house in the Spring. That will be our wedding present to you and Minnie from Martha and me. Martha's making the offer to Minnie." "Thank you! That's wonderful. Minnie will be so excited and thankful," said Jose.

ALSO LATER - Minnie sought out Ray: "Ray, I don't want to put off an answer to you any longer. I'm going back to Missouri, to be the wife of the one I love. We'll be married on the ship Saturday night. I appreciate the opportunity you offered me. If I was successful in New York, I wouldn't be happy without Jose, and he wouldn't be happy there. So we'll go back to the place where we both love to be." "My best wishes to you, Minnie," said Ray. "I sensed your answer earlier. I'm disappointed, but not surprised. Whatever you do, don't stop your singing. Sing to the cows, in church, other places. Keep your voice in shape. I have a friend in St. Louis. He owns the 'Plush' room in the Jefferson hotel. I'll write him. I know he'd like to have you as 'guest' singer at times," said Ray. "Thank you, Ray," said Minnie.

AT THE SATURDAY DINNER: most had finished eating. Capt. Snow -to the crowd- "Thank you for being here tonight. We've been celebrating our just completed trip up the Mississippi river and back. I want to introduce some of our people who made it a success, despite a few problems." "He introduced Pilot Brunelle, the engineer and others. "I also want to introduce the New Orleans Police Commissioner and his Assistant." They stood up. (Applause.) "Let me introduce also, two fine gentlemen who are protecting us tonight: New Orleans Police Officers Hoss Lowrey and Pig Barnes." There was generous applause. Hoss and Pig beamed with pride.

"And now folks," continued Capt. Snow, "We have the highlight of the evening, a real wedding right here on the ship, and I'll be the Parson who'll tie them together for life. Let me introduce..." A curtain was pulled behind him revealing a setting of an arch of flowers. Standing in front were Minnie and Jose, holding hands, both dressed in the finest available. ..."Miss Minnie Robb, daughter of Mr. and Mrs. Robb in the audience there. They're from St. James, Missouri. Miss Robb is our star singer on the 'Southern Belle'. She's the bride. And -Mr. Jose Jackson, son of Mr. and Mrs. Jackson, also in the audience. Jose is the groom. His parents live in Shreveport, Louisiana. Before we have the ceremony, I want you to hear Miss Robb sing. Will you, Miss Robb?" "Before I sing," said Minnie, "I want Jose to sing the song that he wrote for me. It's such a big part of our love story." The crowd applauded. "Yes, of course. You're on, Mr. Jackson." Jose sang "Josefina" (Applause.) Minnie then sang "You Will Always Be My Sweetheart", accompanied by Jose on the guitar. (Applause.)

THEN CAPT. SNOW PERFORMED THE WEDDING CEREMONY.

END OF STORY.

Tom Robb

POSTLOGUE :

Chrissy decided to go home with her Dad. Paul had returned and was very anxious to see her. She decided to return to school in St. Louis, maybe at the same school Paul was attending. Marie decided to stay and go back to St. Louis with the ship in the Spring, and maybe renew acquaintance with Charles.

After a few days, Mr. and Mrs. Robb went on to Atlanta to visit Martha's parents. Hoss and Pig, stayed in New Orleans and were very successful in the New Orleans Police Department. Ray went on to New York City where he was well known in the entertainment field.

Minnie and Jose elected to go back immediately to St. James to take care of the farm, and in the Spring, to build a house on the 300 acres given to them by Mr. and Mrs. Robb.

Mr. and Mrs. Jackson had arrived just in time for the wedding. Martha had written them as soon as the wedding was set. And what about "Betsy"? She had a darling calf in the Spring.

When Minnie and Jose arrived back at the farm: "The place looks wonderful! said Minnie. I'm so happy to be home, with you, Sweetheart!" "I second that," chimed Jose...."Hey! Look at that! There's Old Billy on top of the house, and Nanny is into Martha's cabbages!"